OATH OF FEALTY

OATH OF FEALTY

ELIZABETH MOON

DEL REY

BALLANTINE BOOKS • NEW YORK

Copyright © 2010 by Elizabeth Moon

Published in the United States by Del Rey, an imprint of The Random House Publishing Group, a division of Random House, Inc., New York.

DEL REY is a registered trademark and the Del Rey colophon is a trademark of Random House, Inc.

ISBN 978-0-345-50874-4

Printed in the United States of America on acid-free paper

www.delreybooks.com

2 4 6 8 9 7 5 3 1

First Edition

Book design by Rebecca Aidlin

For those there from the start and still here for the new beginning: Ellen and John McLean and Richard Moon, for encouraging me to finish the first Paks book, Joshua Bilmes for accepting me as a client, the late Jim Baen for publishing *The Deed of Paksenarrion*, and Betsy Mitchell for editing it.

Dramatis Personae

Kieri Phelan's mercenary company

Jandelir Arcolin, senior captain of first cohort (short sword)
  Stammel, senior sergeant of Arcolin's cohort
  Devlin, junior sergeant of Arcolin's cohort
  Arñe, corporal in Arcolin's cohort
Dorrin Verrakai, senior captain of second cohort (short sword)
Selfer, junior captain of second cohort
Cracolnya, senior captain of third cohort (mixed: sword/crossbow)
Valichi, captain of recruit cohort

Tsaian Court: senior noble families

Mikeli Vostan Keriel Mahieran, crown prince of Tsaia
  Camwyn, his younger brother
Beclan Mahieran, Knight-Commander of the Bells (order of Girdish knights)
Sonder Mahieran, Duke Mahieran
  Rothlin, his heir and the prince's friend
Selis Marrakai, Duke Marrakai
  Juris, his heir and the prince's friend
Galyan Serrostin, Duke Serrostin
  Rolyan, the prince's friend
Haron Verrakai, Duke Verrakai, Dorrin Verrakai's uncle
Konhalt (loyal to Verrakai)
Kostvan (loyal to Crown)

Donag Veragsson, Marshal-Judicar of Tsaia (interprets Code of Gird in Tsaia)
Arianya, Marshal-General (commands entire Company of Gird)

Lyonya

Sier Halveric, Aliam's older brother, inherited the title, vocal member of Council
Sier Belvarin, vocal member of Council, often disagreeing with Sier Halveric
Sier Galvary, vocal member of Council, in charge of treasury
Aliam Halveric, commands Halveric Company, Kieri Phelan's mentor and friend
Estil Halveric, his wife

Orlith, elf instructing Kieri Phelan in taig-magic
Flessinathlin, the Lady of the Ladysforest, elven ruler of that elvenhome kingdom
Amrothlin, Kieri Phelan's maternal uncle, elf

Carlion, armsmaster at King's Salle

Aarenis

Aesil M'dierra, commander of Golden Company (mercenaries)
Jeddrin, Count of Andressat
Alured the Black, former pirate, self-styled Duke of Immer
Arneson, one-eyed captain hired by Arcolin as recruit captain
Versin, captain hired by Arcolin as junior to Cracolnya
Burek, captain hired by Arcolin as his own junior captain
Fenin Kavarthin, Kieri's banker in Valdaire
Paltis, Kieri's factor in Valdaire

AUTHOR'S NOTE

What Has Gone Before

When Paksenarrion rode off into the fictional sunset twenty-odd years ago at the close of *Oath of Gold*, I knew I would want to return to her world someday and write more about the other characters there: Kieri Phelan, his captains Arcolin and Dorrin, Sergeant Stammel, and the rest. They had stories of their own waiting to be told. I never thought it would take this long to return . . . but finally I was able to find the door and here we are, this time seeing the world through other eyes than Paks's.

The Eight Kingdoms north of the Dwarfmounts, and the land of Aarenis, south of those mountains, have had a seemingly stable relationship for generations. Northern mercenaries fought southern wars; southern merchants kept trade flowing over the mountains along the Merchants' Guild routes and controlled most of the southern cities. The Elder Races—elves, dwarves, gnomes—kept their distance from humans for the most part, except that elves and humans mingled in Lyonya, the oddest of the Eight Kingdoms.

But change is upon them, brought by hidden forces and their instrument, the paladin Paksenarrion, whose story is detailed in *The Deed of Paksenarrion*.

Briefly, Paks ran away from her family's sheep farm to become a soldier, joining Duke Kieri Phelan's mercenary company in Tsaia. After three years of service in Tsaia and Aarenis, during which she matured from raw recruit to skilled veteran, she left to adventure on her own. Through many trials, she became a paladin of Gird, a holy warrior, and felt a call to return to the Duke's Company. There, the powers granted paladins led her to the discovery that her former commander was not a bastard duke, as most thought, but half-elven, and the true heir of the throne of Lyonya, next kingdom to the east.

Immediately, forces of evil tried to prevent Kieri Phelan's travel to Lyonya, capturing him and his companions. Paks pledged to exchange herself and endure five days and nights of torment for his freedom. She endured and survived, to be healed by the gods she served. She followed Kieri east, knowing he would be attacked again, and arrived with additional troops in time to save him.

Thanks to Paks, Kieri Phelan becomes king in Lyonya, a role he could not have expected. He must leave behind those he ruled, led in battle, and cared for so long, and that parting is wrenching. In a widening ripple, everyone Paksenarrion met or came near is thrust into change, from the powerful—the crown prince of Tsaia, the Marshal-General of Gird—to the powerless, including a ragged, starving, one-eyed former mercenary in Aarenis.

As this is a new group of stories, *Oath of Fealty* is an alternate entry point to the story-universe. No one needs to read the earlier books before reading this one. However, if you're so inclined, all the earlier books are in print, and the Paksworld website, www.paksworld.com, has a complete list.

OATH OF FEALTY

CHAPTER ONE

Vérella

A small boy clambered from a cellar wall into an alley. He picked his way through the trash along the wall to a nearby street, walked quickly to the next turning, went left, then right. The street widened a little; the people he passed wore warmer clothes. He ducked into an alcove and pulled off the ragged jacket that had concealed his own unpatched shirt and tunic, folded the ragged one into a tidy bundle, and tucked it under his arm. Now he moved at a steady jog into the wealthier part of the city, nearer the palace. Finally he turned in to a gap between buildings, found the trapdoor he sought, and went belowground again.

In the cellar of a tall house within a few minutes of the palace gates, he gave a coded knock. A hard-faced man with a spiked billet opened the door. "What d'you want, rat?" the man asked.

"For Duke Verrakai's hand only," the boy said. "From the Horned Chain."

"I'll take him," another man said, stepping out of looming shadows. He wore the red and black of Liart, and the horned chain was about his neck. "Come, boy."

Shaking with fear, the boy followed, up stairs and along a corridor, to a room where another man, in Verrakai blue and silver, sat writing at a table by a fire.

"I am Duke Verrakai. You have a message for me: give it."

The boy seemed to choke, and then, in a deep voice not his own, spoke the words Liart's priest had bade him say. "The man is free, and his companions; the paladin is ours. Without her aid, he can be taken. He must not reach Lyonya alive."

"He will not," Duke Verrakai said. "Is there more?"

The boy dug into his tunic and pulled out a folded paper; Verrakai took it and read it. "Well," he said, with a glance at the man in red and black. "It seems we must return this boy with our answer." He wrote on the reverse of the message, folded it, and handed it to the boy. "Go the way you came, swiftly."

Less than a half-glass later, a man in Verrakai blue rode out the south gates of Vérella and turned east on the river road. Later, after the turn of night, Kieri Phelan, newly revealed king of Lyonya, also rode through the gates, with an escort of the Royal Guard.

Duke's Stronghold, North Marches, seven days later

Jandelir Arcolin, senior captain of Duke Phelan's Company, rested his forearms on the top of the stronghold walls, where he had the best view to the south. On one side of the road to Duke's East, Stammel was putting his own cohort through an intricate marching drill. On the other, the junior sergeant of the recruit cohort supervised a sword drill with wooden blades. Beyond, the trees along the stream showed the first soft golds and oranges of ripening buds, though it would be hands of days yet before the fruit trees bloomed. Old snow still lay knee-deep against the north wall.

He heard steps behind him, and turned. Cracolnya, captain of the mixed cohort, came up onto the walkway with him.

"Are you putting down roots up here?" he asked.

Arcolin shook his head. "Hoping for a courier. We should have heard something by now. At least the weather's lifted. Though not for long." He tipped his head to the northwest, where a line of dark clouds just showed over the hills.

"Your worry won't bring the Duke faster," Cracolnya said. He turned his back on the view south and leaned against the parapet. "I wonder what we'll do this year."

"I don't know." Arcolin glanced down at the courtyard below, to be sure their inquisitive visitors, merchant-agents from Vonja, weren't in earshot. "He said not to take any contracts until he got back; I suggested they go to Vérella and talk to him, but they were afraid of missing him on the way."

"What are they offering?"

"A one-cohort contract to protect farmlands and roads from brigands. I told them we'd need two for that—"

"At least. Better the whole Company, or you're without reliable archery. Or were they planning to assign their militia to help?"

"No. From what they said, they disbanded half the militia. Trade's down. But what do you think the Council will say? With the trouble this past winter, the Duke can't say it's entirely safe here. Yet—we have to do something. This land won't support so many soldiers year-round."

Cracolnya leaned over the parapet, watching the recruit cohort. "We've got to do something with those recruits, too. They signed up to fight, and all we've done with them is train . . . and he's taken their final oaths: they'll be due regular pay soon."

"He'll think of something." Arcolin looked again at the line of clouds along the western horizon. Buds or no buds, another winter storm was coming. "He always does. But if he doesn't come soon, we won't get the good quarters in Valdaire." He looked south again, sighing, then stiffened. "Someone's coming!"

A single horseman, carrying the Company pennant, moving fast on the road from Duke's East. Not the Duke, who would have an escort.

"Should I announce it, sir?" the sentry asked.

"No. It's just a messenger." Unfortunately. They needed the Duke. Arcolin turned and made his way down to the courtyard with Cracolnya at his heels.

"I'll tell the stable," Cracolnya said, turning away. Arcolin moved to the gate, where he could watch the messenger approach.

Whatever the message might be, it was urgent enough for the rider to keep his mount at a steady canter, trotting only the last few yards to the gate and then halting his mount to salute the sentry before riding in. Arcolin recognized Sef, a private in Dorrin's cohort.

"Captain," Sef said, after he dismounted and handed the reins to one of the recruits on stable duty. "I have urgent news."

"Into the barracks," Arcolin said. Through the opening to the Duke's courtyard, he could see the two merchants hurrying toward them, but merchants were not allowed in the barracks. He led the way, and turned in to the little room where the sergeants kept the cohort records and brewed sib on their own hearth. "What is it? Is the Duke coming? How far behind you is he?"

"No sir, he's not coming, and you won't believe—but I should give you this first." Sef took a message tube from his tunic and handed it over.

Arcolin glanced at the hearth. "See if there's any sib left, or brew yourself some; you've had a long ride. And if I know Stammel, he's got a roll hidden away somewhere."

"Thank you, sir." Sef turned to the hearth, stirred the fire, and dipped a can of water from the barrel, setting it to heat.

Arcolin unrolled the message. A smaller wrapped packet fell out; he put it aside. There, in the Duke's hand—with a postscript by Dorrin, he saw at a glance—he found what he had never imagined. Kieri Phelan revealed as the rightful king of Lyonya—Paksenarrion had discovered it, come to Tsaia to find him—Tammarion's sword had been his sword all along, elf-made for him, and it had declared him. Arcolin glanced at Sef, who was stirring roots and herbs into the can. "Did you see this yourself? Were you in Vérella with the Duke?"

"No, Captain. I was with the reserve troop. Captain Selfer come up from Vérella, him and the horse both near knackered, and said the best rider must go fast as could be to the stronghold." Sef swallowed. "He thought it would be only two days, maybe, but that fog came in. I couldn't go more than a foot pace, mostly leading the horse. It's taken me twice as long as it should have, three days and this morning."

"I'm not surprised," Arcolin said. "We had thick fog for days, up here; you did well, Sef." He read on, while Sef stirred the can of sib, struggling to make sense of what had happened. His mind snagged on Paksenarrion—once in his cohort. *I must go, and leave her in torment,* Kieri had written. *Otherwise her torment is meaningless. Yet it is a stain on my honor. You will rule in my stead until the Regency Council confirms a new lord. I recommended you, but do not know what they will do. This letter and my signet ring will prove your identity and authority.*

Arcolin unwrapped the smaller packet and found the Duke's ring. Not one of the copies he lent to his captains on occasion to do business for him, but the original, the one he himself wore.

Dorrin's postscript was brief. She was going with Kieri, on his or-

ders; her cohort would follow. She feared more attacks on the Duke—
scratched out to read *King*—on the road east. She did not know when
she might return; it would depend upon his need.

Arcolin rolled the pages and slid them back into the tube. "Well.
You will have traveled ahead of any word of his passage to the
east—" He tried to estimate where Kieri might be, where Dorrin might
be, seven days on a road he himself had never traveled. Impossible.

"Right, Captain." Sef stirred the can again, sniffed it. "Want some
sib, sir?"

"No thanks. Go ahead."

Sef took a mug down from the rack and poured one for himself as
he talked. "Captain Selfer said Captain Dorrin expected his cohort to
catch up with the Duke before the Lyonya border. Wish I was with
them—" He took a swallow of hot sib.

"I'm—I must admit I'm shocked . . . amazed . . . I don't know what
to think," Arcolin said. "Our Duke a king—all the rest—" Remembering Paks as a recruit, a novice . . . the steady, reliable soldier she'd
become . . . why she left, and when . . . the rumors . . . and then her
return. He squeezed his eyes hard against tears, at the thought of her
in Liart's hands, shook his head, and looked again at Sef. "You've
done very well, Sef. Go tell the cooks to give you a hot meal, and I'll
get Stammel to find you a place to sleep undisturbed."

Sef saluted, then carefully rinsed the can and set it to dry before
going out. Arcolin followed him, wondering if he'd have to explain to
the Vonja agents before he found Stammel. Instead, Stammel met him
at the gate. Arcolin smiled.

"Your good instincts again, Sergeant."

"My insatiable curiosity, Captain. News from the Duke could
always be marching orders."

"It's strange news indeed, and I'm not sure what will happen
now," Arcolin said. "The courier was Sef of Dorrin's cohort—he needs
a quiet bed to sleep; he was three days in thick fog between here and
the south border. I sent him to the mess hall."

"I'll see to it, Captain."

"I need to talk to the other captains before I spread the news,"
Arcolin said. "I can tell you this—nothing will be the same."

"It never is," Stammel said. "That's why we like it. Your leave, Captain."

"Go ahead," Arcolin said, thinking again how lucky he was to have Stammel as senior sergeant.

He found Cracolnya in the stables, talking fodder with the quartermaster.

"And I don't know where more hay's coming from, this time of year," the quartermaster said. "Nobody's got enough stored; it's not to be bought, not at any price, and I know the Duke wouldn't want us to take from the farmers' stock."

Arcolin made a motion with his head, and Cracolnya nodded. To the quartermaster he said, "A messenger's come from the Duke; maybe an order to move out—that would help."

"I hope so," the quartermaster said gloomily. He spat into a corner. "I can't be sure . . ."

Arcolin led the way down the aisle between rows of tie stalls to the box stalls at the end, empty now but for his and Cracolnya's mounts.

"What is it? You look—strange."

"I should. You must read it yourself." He handed over the message tube; Cracolnya opened it, unrolled the message, and started to read. Arcolin's roan ambler moved up to the front of the stall and nudged him; he rubbed the velvety muzzle absently while watching Cracolnya's face.

"I—I don't know what to think," Cracolnya said, when he'd finished. "He's a king? In Lyonya? How did that happen?"

"I don't know more than this."

"They have a king already," Cracolnya said. "What's *he* think about it?"

"You missed a bit," Arcolin said. "He stuck it in between lines. Their king died without an heir. Paks was there—that's where she went when she left here. She felt called to find the heir." He ran a hand over his head. "But—what do we do now? He wants troops out guarding the Pargunese border; he thinks they might use this as an excuse to attack."

"Scouts haven't said anything."

"No. And this about a contract. You know what he said before he went south; he expected to take the Company south. But only one cohort?" He shook his head. "You know the Vonjans. They'll want twice the work for half the pay."

"One cohort out, with pack mules, would ease the fodder situation," Cracolnya said. "Two would be better, if you can talk them into it."

"What about protection here, though?" Arcolin said. "He's worried about the Pargunese, and the south border. A cohort each way, plus mine in the south, will nearly empty the stronghold. And we'll have to use the recruits, until Dorrin comes back." However long that might be.

Cracolnya shrugged. "This recruit cohort's the best-trained we've ever had. They can garrison this; I can split mine between east and south. Or, the recruits can do their first real route march and take the southern end—we haven't had trouble with either of the neighboring domains, barring the odd thief, since Count Halar's father died."

"That's a good idea, about using the recruits to garrison down there if needed," Arcolin said. "But first, I need to tell the Company about the Duke."

"Maybe we should wait until we hear from Chaya," Cracolnya said. "Just in case."

"In case—"

"He was attacked once. Suppose Verrakai raised a large force against him?"

"He's got Dorrin's cohort."

"He's got Dorrin's cohort on the way, but what if they don't get there in time? He could be killed. Something could go wrong in Lyonya."

"I don't—" Arcolin took two steps forward, turned, then took two steps back, avoiding the thought of Kieri Phelan dead. Instead, he said, "We have to tell the troops something—they have to know he's not coming back."

"He left it to you," Cracolnya said. "But if you want my advice—" Arcolin nodded. "Then," Cracolnya went on, "make us a contract, and tell the Company that, and then tell them what you've heard, that it's all we know."

"Ask the quartermaster how many beasts he can feed until spring grass," Arcolin said.

Cracolnya looked smug. "I already know. Twelve."

Arcolin looked down the rows of tie stalls, mostly full. "Better get moving, then." He left Cracolnya in the stable and headed back to the officers' quarters and offices.

The Vonja agents had retreated to the inner court, but came to meet him as he entered. "Have you heard from the Duke?" one began. Arcolin held up his hand.

"I have word from the Duke that I'm to make a one-cohort contract, subject to approval by the Council in Tsaia; he's reasonably sure they'll give it."

"But the Duke—is he coming?"

"He's . . . detained," Arcolin said. "But the messenger who arrived brought his word and seal."

"How soon can you leave? Today? Tomorrow?"

"Certainly not today. As the Duke himself is detained, I must visit the councils here, send couriers—" All at once the enormity of the changes ahead hit him, stunning him. Kieri Phelan had been the one constant in his life for years; he never thought that would end. He saw the concern on their faces, the uncertainty, and with his own uncertainty churning inside, it was too much. He bowed slightly. "Sirs, with this word from Duke Phelan, I have orders I must give; you must excuse me."

"Of course," the senior said. "I only meant, should we ourselves pack to ride today or tomorrow?"

"Not sooner than tomorrow, and probably the next day," Arcolin said. To his relief, he saw one of the house servants hovering in the doorway. To him, he called, "One less for meals; I'm riding to Duke's East and Duke's West; I'll eat there."

He felt like a fraud. As Kieri's senior captain, trusted and experienced, he knew how to do what he must do, but—he was not Kieri. He could not be Kieri. And to have this handed him, without being able to see Kieri, talk to him, ask questions, be sure . . . it was too much.

But Kieri trusted him. He had to do it.

Cracolnya was just coming from the stable as he neared it. "Well?"

"We'll split the recruit cohort tonight; I'm taking enough to fill out mine for a contract. I'll still have to get Regency Council approval, in Vérella. You'll command the remainder of the recruits and as many of your cohort as it takes to fill them out. You go east; Valichi will have to take the southern group until I can find him a junior captain—and you, too, for that matter."

"Val's not going to like campaign living," Cracolnya said, grinning. The recruit captain, oldest of them all, had talked of retirement all winter, and used the excuse of crowding in the stronghold to move into Duke's East after Midwinter Feast.

"He can have Kieri's tent," Arcolin said. "I'll take mine."

"Better take Kieri's yourself; you need to impress the Vonjans. All those southerners think bigger is better." Cracolnya, proponent of traveling light, had the smallest tent of any of the captains. "About supplies—"

"I can send back supplies from Vérella, after I've seen the bankers," Arcolin said. "You should have enough until then." He glanced at the sky, gauging the amount of daylight remaining. "I must go—I have to get to Duke's East—"

"Shall I tell Stammel?"

"My head! I need to do that first, of course. Thank you. Tell them to saddle the chestnut, will you?"

"Of course."

The tail end of his cohort was just entering the mess hall; Stammel, by the door, raised his brows at Arcolin, and Arcolin nodded. Stammel came to him.

"Captain?" Unasked questions danced in his tone.

"The Duke's not coming; we're going south. Usual route. One-cohort contract. We fill out with recruits. Captain Cracolnya will command here; he and Captain Valichi will patrol the east and south boundaries. I know you have more questions, but I must ride to Duke's East. We'll have a captains' conference tonight; join us then. How soon can we march?"

"Day after tomorrow, sir, if we get right to it. Unless it's an emergency, I'd like an extra day for balancing loads and the like. Road firm enough for wagons, do you think?"

"Talk to Sef. I'll be sending supplies back from Vérella, so if the road's good, we'll use them."

"Right, sir."

"Eat lunch first, Stammel."

"I always do, sir," Stammel said. It was an old jest; Arcolin felt better when he felt himself smiling again.

CHAPTER TWO

O n the road to Duke's East, the chestnut pulled hard at first, but finally settled into a smooth canter that eased Arcolin's tension. It would be all right. He would do what the Duke wanted, even without the Duke there—he had done it before. He had the Duke's signet ring and the Duke's written permission to use his funds. Worry returned. What if the Crown didn't agree? What if they wanted to seize the Duke's property, land, and money?

What if the sky and land turned upside down and he fell off the road? He taunted himself, then slowed to an easy jog as he came into the town. Small children ran alongside, waving. He looked around, seeing Duke's East with a new eye.

Heribert Fontaine, the mayor, opened the door of his house as Arcolin rode up to it, and two boys stood ready to hold his horse. "News, I'll warrant—I saw the courier go by, not even stopping for a word."

"News indeed. I'll come in, if I may." Arcolin dismounted, tossing the reins to the boys. "Walk him around; don't let him just stand in this cold."

Fontaine held the door open and Arcolin came in. "There—left—the parlor."

It faced east; sun had left the windows, but the room still held a little of its warmth. A bowl of apples on the table scented the air. Arcolin pulled off his gloves and took a seat at the mayor's wave.

"You'd better read this," he said, handing over the Duke's message. "It's all I know."

Frowning, Fontaine read, his brow furrowed. Then he looked up. "The Duke . . . *our* Duke . . . is a king? Of . . . of Lyonya?"

"It would only surprise me more if it were Pargun," Arcolin said. "All I know is that he's taken Dorrin's cohort, and headed east on the river road."

"And the paladin? Paks?"

Arcolin shook his head. "I don't know any more than this. Nor did the courier. I would suppose she is dead; that must be what the Bloodlord priests intended."

"And he's told you to do whatever you think best. Gird's right arm! I know you're senior captain, but—does he mean take over the domain?"

"I don't know that, either. I've taken a one-cohort contract with the Vonjans. I know we're squeezing supplies up here."

"So you'll take . . . how many away?"

"One all the way to Aarenis, if the Crown approves; the other two in the domain but not here. One cohort, under Cracolnya, to patrol the Pargunese border; one south, under Valichi, in case any ambitious lordling tries to move in. And I'll be sending supplies from Vérella for the troops."

"That will ease things," Fontaine said. "And I don't think we'll have more trouble up here for a while. Have you told Valichi? And will you be sending out recruit teams this year? When are you leaving?"

Arcolin held up his hands. "No, I haven't told Val—he's here in town somewhere. I'd like you to send someone to him, tell him to come up to the stronghold today—we must have a captains' conference. As for recruiting—not until the domain itself is settled. As for leaving—as soon as we can. I hope as soon as day after tomorrow. And now I must leave; I need to get to Duke's West today as well."

"And you're in a hurry. Let me have m'wife fix you a stuffed roll for the ride, if you won't sit down to eat."

"I can't stay, but I'd thank you for a roll . . . anything . . ."

In a few minutes, Arcolin was mounted again; he set his horse's nose to the west breeze and eyed the rising dark cloud there with apprehension. His horse was willing now to canter quietly; Arcolin unwrapped the stuffed roll—hot fried ham, onions, and chopped winter greens—and took a bite. Lucky mayor, he thought as he finished, to have such a cook in the household. A second roll nestled in his tunic, in case of need.

The ride to Duke's West took most of the afternoon as the cold breeze stiffened and the cloud rose higher, soaking up all the light. Before he arrived, he saw the glow of light through windows brighter than the day outside. A sentry called challenge; Arcolin halted his horse.

"Captain Arcolin of the stronghold to speak to the mayor," he said. He dismounted, stiffer from the cold than he'd expected. "It's gone dark early this evening."

"Storm coming, Captain. Sorry to question you—"

"No, that's right, after the mess we had before. But I need to speak to the mayor; we've had word from the Duke."

"I can take your horse, Captain. We'll find a place out of this wind. You're staying the night—"

"No, I mustn't." Now others had come out in the cold, windy neardark, some with torches, and Duke's West's mayor, Alwyn Foretson, hurried over. Younger than Mayor Fontaine, he'd lost a hand on campaign.

"What's wrong, Captain? Attack?"

"No, not that. Word from the Duke. If we could go to your house—"

"Of course." Foretson led the way. Duke's West, newer than Duke's East, was a little smaller, but the mayor's house was just as comfortable. Rich cooking smells permeated the front rooms. "You'll eat with us," Foretson said, as if there were no doubt.

"Gladly," Arcolin said. "Do we have time to get the business over with?"

"Yes. I told Melyin to hold the dumplings when I left the house and that's another half-glass."

"Good. You should read this—it came from the Duke by courier this morning and I know nothing more."

Foretson raised an eyebrow, took the message, and went into the passage, coming back with a four-stick candleholder. "She put the dumplings in and she's keeping the children in the kitchen. Let's see now—" His brows went up his forehead as he read. Arcolin walked about, stretching after the ride. The room had a fireplace, but no fire had been laid; a blanket covered the opening. He grimaced; the stronghold had asked the villages for more wood only the week before. Foretson looked up at last. "King?"

"So it says," Arcolin said.

"I served under the man fifteen years until I lost my hand. I didn't know he was royal bred." Foretson sounded as if that were a personal insult.

"Nor I," said Arcolin, who had been with the Duke longer, as they both knew.

"Well-bred, certainly," Foretson went on. "But a king?"

Arcolin said nothing. The mayor's wife came to the door, looked in, shrugged, and went back to the kitchen.

"This is going to cause . . . problems."

"I think so," Arcolin said. "But I have no answers. I do have a one-cohort contract with Vonja, and as the Duke requested, I'm moving Cracolnya's cohort and the recruits to the east and south."

"Think the Crown will accept that?"

"I'll find out," Arcolin said, trying to sound cheerful. "I don't know who the Crown will transfer the domain to—"

"Oh, gods! I didn't think of that one. We could end up belonging to Verrakai or someone like that—" He gave Arcolin a searching glance. "They should give it to you."

"They won't," Arcolin said. "I'm not a native; I have no family behind me—"

Foretson cocked his head. "Do you want it?"

Did he? Arcolin thought for a long moment; the mayor said nothing. "I don't know," he said finally. "I never considered it . . . I never thought beyond . . ."

"Well, you'd best think now. There's lords enough will want it, want it enough to squabble over it. Verrakai and Marrakai both, I shouldn't wonder, and woe to us if Verrakai gets it. Marrakai wouldn't be so bad, except his own land's so far west. No overlap. We'd do better with you, Captain, though without an heir—"

"Aye. And no one's offered it yet, and I have a cohort to take south. And I must eat and go, I'm afraid."

"Is this to be kept secret? And if so, until when?"

"It can't be," Arcolin said. "People must know; they deserve to know. But they need to know even more: what's coming next, and that I can't tell them. I should learn more in Vérella, and when I do I'll send word."

"I hope he's safe in Lyonya," Foretson said. Then, shaking his head: "Royal-bred and half-elf, and I never saw it . . . what a fool I must be."

"If you, then all of us," Arcolin said. "Including himself, for that matter. He had more chance to figure it out than any of us."

Foretson laughed. "I suppose . . . but I'm not calling the Fox a fool, even with him this far away and not coming back."

Not coming back. Arcolin shivered, but supper was hot and tasty, and he mounted again determined to do his best for Phelan's land and people, whatever that might turn out to be.

He refused the mayor's offer of an escort back to the stronghold, and rode away in an icy drizzle that stung his face. It would be sleet or snow by morning; he hoped it would blow over before they marched away in it.

Halfway back to the stronghold, he met a squad with torches; Cracolnya had sent them. Soon enough he was safely inside, cold and wet but in a seat by the fire, upstairs in the Duke's study. Valichi was there, with his personal pack; he had even brought his armor. Stammel, waiting for Arcolin by the inner gate, had followed him in and up the stairs. Arcolin waved him to a seat as well.

"Fontaine told me," Valichi said. "Though I find it hard to believe."

"So do we all," Arcolin said, pulling off his wet boots. Servants had put dry clothes to warm by the fire; he stripped off his wet ones and dressed as they talked.

"How'd the village mayors take it?" Cracolnya asked.

"Stunned. Confused. Glad we're taking hungry mouths away, but worried about the future. Who the Crown will give the land to."

"It could be you," Valichi said. "You were here from the beginning."

"I don't think so." But he could not help imagining it, seeing familiar things, familiar people, in a new way. He pushed that aside. "And anyway, I've got that contract to fulfill. I can't start off by breaking one."

"You need the Crown's consent, remember—if you don't get it, the merchants will understand."

"That doesn't produce gold or grain," Arcolin said. He yawned. "Believe me, I will argue hard if they refuse; I will not toss away what Kieri worked so many years to build. How's the preparation going, Sergeant?"

"On target, sir. All the farriery finished today. The smiths say they'll have the last of the weapons and repairs done by supper tomorrow. We'll be ready to march day after tomorrow, as far as the fighting troop's concerned. And Sef says the road's no worse than usual, this time of year."

"We split the recruits already," Cracolnya said. "Your cohort's up to the usual start-of-season strength. I didn't know what staff you'd want to take along for just one cohort—you'll want a smith, I'm sure, but will you want a quartermaster? Clerk? Teamsters and wagons?"

"Teamsters and wagons, yes," Arcolin said. "Most will come back here with replacement supplies. Kolya's still in Vérella; she can supervise that. A smith for certain, and one of the surgeons. Stammel, who in the cohort might make a quartermaster?"

"Devlin, sir, if he weren't my junior sergeant. Don't see how he could do both."

"Agreed," Arcolin said. "Others?"

Stammel shook his head. "No, sir."

"We need someone," Arcolin said. "One of the quartermaster's assistants, then; we need him here. Stammel, talk to the quartermaster— I'm inclined to think Maia, but leave it to him." Arcolin yawned, then stretched. "It's time we went to bed, captains. Tomorrow will be a full day."

They rose; Arcolin gathered up his wet things and carried them to the kitchen, to be dried by the cooking hearth. Back upstairs, he went into Kieri's office and looked around.

Kieri had asked for nothing from this office, from the stronghold. Things he had bought in Aarenis or Vérella: the striped rug Tammarion had chosen, a carved box with a running fox on its lid, a favorite whetstone always placed on the left of the great desk, a candleholder of translucent pink stone that glowed with light when the candle was lit, the chest in which—as Arcolin knew—Kieri's dead wife's armor and the children's daggers were wrapped in Tammarion's troth dress. Kieri had asked for none of these.

Not ever to return. Arcolin forced himself to take a deep breath and consider what records he might need, for either a contract or . . . that which he did not want to consider.

Tired as he was, he sat up late, making notes, packing away those records he would not take in the chest where they belonged, packing the ones he would need into waterproof bags. The room seemed emptier than it should, emptier than it ever had.

"I'm trying," he muttered to himself, then shook his head and went to bed.

A rcolin woke to the memory of yesterday's surprises, and the realization that he needed to parade the whole Company. They had given their oaths to Kieri, who had now left them. They must now give their oaths to him. That ceremony could not be omitted.

Outside, the previous evening's storm continued, alternating brief snow flurries with rattling sleet and icy rain. Perhaps it would stop by noon; Arcolin went down to breakfast and found Valichi staring thoughtfully at the weapons on the dining room wall.

A kitchen servant arrived with steaming bowls of porridge and loaves of hot bread. Valichi sat down and started eating. Arcolin poured a little honey, thick with cold, into his porridge and tried a spoonful as Cracolnya came in from outside.

"Nasty," Cracolnya said.

"Think it will clear away at all today?" Arcolin asked. "I need to parade the Company and take their oaths."

The two captains stared at him, then at each other. "I had forgotten," Cracolnya said. "If he's not coming back—if he's the one to break it—then we all—" His voice trailed away.

"We all swore to him, personally," Arcolin said. "He's not our duke anymore, so whether the Crown confirms me or not, for the time being we need a single oath to bind us. And—" He shrugged. "That's to me." As he said it, he realized he would also have to travel to the villages again, taking their charters, getting the oaths of mayors and councils, making a copy for the Crown. That would take an entire day.

"I understand." Cracolnya dug into his porridge, eating fast for five or six mouthfuls. "I'll do it, of course. It's what he'd want." He paused for a moment, then shook his head. "No, my pardon. It's what *I* want."

"Val?" Arcolin asked.

"Yess . . ." Valichi's answer came slower; he was frowning. He was older than Arcolin, and had spent more time in the North, as Kieri's recruit captain. Perhaps he had hoped to be chosen, if Kieri ever left. "But I can't say as I'm willing to stay on as the only captain of a cohort, not longer than it takes to find another."

"We all need co-captains," Arcolin said. "I'll be hiring captains, either in Vérella or Valdaire; I'll send them north." He leaned on his elbows. "You two take your cohorts away tomorrow, if the weather mends at all. Cracolnya, you take the other surgeon and smith; Val will be near enough Burningmeed for a Marshal to help with healing and they have a smith. I can't leave for another day at least: I need to find the village charters and take them to Duke's East and West, for all to take oaths on and sign. Val, let the merchants travel with you, if they want an escort, or they can go ahead."

They looked startled, but nodded.

By midafternoon, the storm had passed, though furrowed clouds still covered the sky. Arcolin had the Company paraded in the main court, cohort by cohort, to take their oaths. He gave the same speech to the recruits the Duke had given to every year's recruit intake. The veterans, who had already been told as much as he knew, gave their oaths willingly, as near as he could tell.

The Vonja agents chose to ride with Val's cohort to Burningmeed and travel on to Vérella by themselves. Arcolin spent the evening with one of the Company clerks, collecting the documents he would need the next day, making copies of those he would need in Vérella, rechecking his lists.

Next morning, the storm had blown past, leaving a thin skim of high cloud. After breakfast, the other two cohorts left, Valichi's down the road to Duke's East, and Cracolnya's straight across country toward the rising sun.

Stammel had Arcolin's cohort busy at once, cleaning barracks Arcolin was sure the others had left spotless, but it kept the troops busy. Arcolin gathered the bundle of charters and other documents he needed, and rode for Duke's West first.

"Can you hold a Duke's Court before you go?" Foretson asked, as he signed the charter under Arcolin's name.

"I'm not a duke," Arcolin said. "Authorization for a Ducal Court would have to come from Vérella. All I can do is hold petty court, same as usual."

"That would help—if you can stay a glass, I'll have Donag and Arv come in—they're wanting a ruling on a field boundary."

Once court began, others came in with problems; it was after midday when he rode for Duke's East, to do it all over again. This time he set up in the Red Fox common room. Duke's East had fewer cases for petty court than Duke's West, and he made it back to the stronghold before dark. There he found everything ready for next morning's departure.

A nother clear morning. Arcolin looked around the inner court, imagining it as his—if the Crown permitted—and strode out the gate to the main court, where Stammel had the cohort ready, in marching order. Arbad held the roan ambler. Arcolin mounted and looked back at his cohort—the young faces still unblooded, the veterans with their weathered skin, their scars, their eyes full of experience. Stammel gave him a crisp nod.

Was he really doing this, really taking a mercenary cohort to Aarenis by himself? As commander? He put his hand in his tunic, feeling Kieri's signet ring. No more time to doubt. If he could not do it, after all those years of serving with the best commander he'd ever known, north or south, he was a fool—and Kieri would not have trusted him with the Company. He lifted the reins and nudged his horse into motion.

As always, the villagers in Duke's East came out to wave as the cohorts passed. Arcolin smiled at them, called out greetings to the mayor, to the innkeeper, to the village council members.

The world had changed. The sunlight, despite a clear sky, felt thinner, muted. The trees looked different, the little river beneath the bridge; the road he had ridden so many times, so many years, looked new, untrodden, unknown.

He scolded himself, told himself it was the same: the road, the trees, the sun, the world itself. One man could not make that much difference.

He knew he lied.

At the border of the Duke's territory, the post Valichi had set up saluted them as they marched past on the road to Vérella. The marches were no longer than usual, but they seemed both longer and shorter as his mood shifted again and again.

CHAPTER THREE

Vérella, the palace

Mikeli, crown prince of Tsaia, listened to his best friend, Juris Marrakai, joking with Mikeli's cousin Rothlin Mahieran about the behavior of their younger brothers. Dinner this evening felt almost normal again, with his friends around him and the worst of the peril—his advisers had said—over. Fourteen days had passed since Kieri Phelan left for Lyonya, and nine since the paladin's ordeal ended. For a full hand of days, the city had been in turmoil as city militia, nobles of the realm, and Marshals of Gird sought to find and destroy Liart's followers.

He and his friends had wanted to take part, prove their courage, in those raids on the city's underground lairs. Their elders had refused to risk them despite their protests. Instead, his friends had been kept at home to guard their families, while he and his younger brother had been confined to the palace, closely guarded. They'd all been told to stay close, be careful, be alert, report anything suspicious.

But finally the city quieted, and the High Marshals had declared it safe enough to relax some restrictions. Once more his friends were together, sharing a meal, as they had so often before. When the door opened, Mikeli expected servants to bring in the next course, but instead saw one of the palace guards escorting a man in Girdish blue and gray, a yeoman by his tunic, travel-stained and obviously near exhaustion.

"My lord prince," the yeoman said, his voice hoarse with cold. "I bear urgent news." He glanced around the table, as if uncertain which was the prince, then dug into a pouch and produced a crumpled scroll.

"Here," Mikeli said. The man handed him the scroll and he unrolled and began reading. The words *"well-armed troops . . . refused your order . . . Pargunese . . . magery . . . treason"* sprang out at him. "Treason!" The word escaped before he could stop it; he heard the surprise, the horror, in his own voice. He forced himself to silence, and looked up, scanning the room. The startled faces of his dinner companions, their mouths open, stared back at him. Juris Marrakai, Rothlin Mahieran, Rolyan Serrostin, all dukes' sons whose fathers sat on his Regency Council. Manthar Kostvan and Belin Destvaorn, counts' sons whose fathers were also on the Council. He glanced at the messenger, noting the air of suppressed alarm.

"Treason?" That was Juris Marrakai, quick-eared and quick-witted as always. "Whose? Not Phelan's, surely?"

"No." Mikeli caught his imagination by the scruff of the neck, mastered his tongue, and tried to think how to say it. If he could say it at all to these, the friends he'd asked in for a quiet supper. The guilty party was also on his Regency Council.

"Not Phelan's," he said, this time more calmly. "Someone else, against us and against him. He was ambushed, but survived. The paladin reached him in time." To the messenger: "Sir, your name, if you please?"

"Piter, my lord," the messenger said. "Yeoman-marshal of Blackhedge."

"Were you a witness to this?" Mikeli tapped the scroll.

"No, my lord. To make haste, it was passed hand to hand, like. But the Marshal, he had it from the other Marshal, who was there, and he told me some. It's Gird's grace—"

Mikeli held up his hand and the man fell silent. "Gentlemen," he said to his friends, "this is grave news, and I must meet with those senior in the realm, your fathers among them. I must go at once—"

Juris Marrakai pushed back from the table. "Sir—Your Highness— if it is treason, you must not go unguarded—"

Mikeli tried for an easy laugh; it came out more as a cough. "I am hardly unguarded. The palace guard—"

"We are your friends," Juris said. "You can't leave us out; you can trust us—"

But could he? If a councilor could turn traitor, anyone might. He looked again at the papers—for now he saw there were two. One from Ammerlin, commander of the Royal Guard unit he had sent with Phelan, and one from Phelan himself. He held up his hand, and his guests stayed where they were, silent.

The second note, in Phelan's clear, even script, said much the same, more briefly and pointedly.

And I beg you, sire, that you take all precautions. A man who will so disobey your express order at the margin of your realm will have designs on your reign. I have seen this too often in Aarenis to doubt it. Forgive my presumption; I speak now as one king to another: you must not fail to destroy this threat, at once. For the sake of both our realms.

As one king to another: treating him as fully adult, as an equal; that respect steadied his pulse. For the sake of both their realms. Long at peace, but for minor incursions along the northern border, Tsaia had trusted in the stability of its neighbors to east and west. If Lyonya fell, if *he himself* fell, both kingdoms would be in peril. Verrakai's troops had used magery, Ammerlin said. Used the power of evil priests of an evil deity, the same who had tormented a paladin day after day beneath the city. Despite himself, the prince shivered. For a moment, he allowed the thought *Why me? Why in my reign?* but then thrust it aside. This was what kings did—dealt with whatever came. Kieri Phelan, thirty years his senior, believed he could do it: he must.

"What did you say to the captain of the guard?" he asked the messenger.

"Nothing, Your Highness. Never saw him. Just told the guard at the gate I had to see you, it was urgent, I had dispatches under the seal of Gird."

Mikeli paused to order his thoughts. If he called out, someone would come, but in a bustle; time would be wasted. He had messengers here whom every palace guard knew.

"Manthar." Manthar Kostvan stepped forward. "Take this note—"

He scrawled rapidly, poured on hot wax, stamped it with his seal ring. "—to the officer of the guard. I want the palace gates closed to all— no one to enter or leave, no matter what rank. He must alert the palace guard inside, but quietly. We want no panic, no confusion in which someone might be missed. Then find your father and ask him to come to—" He paused. Meet where? Where was safe? Who else would he need? The Knights of the Bells, certainly. "In the Knight-Commander's chambers, near the Grange Hall. I'm going there now. Go swiftly, but do not raise an alarm." Manthar nodded and hurried out the door. "Belin." Mikeli scrawled another note, and sealed it, as Belin nodded. "Escort Piter here to the steward, make sure he gets a meal and that someone takes charge of him, lest the traitor strike him down, then go for your father with the same message." He handed Belin that note; Belin and the messenger left.

Mikeli looked at the three dukes' sons still standing at his table. They all looked back, brows bunched a little as they tried to puzzle out what was going on.

"Gentlemen—you deserve to know what is amiss. Let me read this to you." He read Ammerlin's message, glancing up from line to line to gauge their reactions. Shock, horror, disgust, anger. When he fin- ished, and let the scroll curl up, they burst into speech.

"I can't believe they would—"

"After the paladin proved Duke Phelan—the king—was the king—"

"Even a Verrakai—"

"But *what* can we do?" Rolyan Serrostin, practical as ever, said it first.

"Are all your fathers in the palace this night?" Mikeli asked.

His cousin and Juris Marrakai nodded; Rolyan shook his head.

"My father isn't far away," he said. "He only went to have dinner with my great-uncle, a few streets west. I could fetch him—"

"There isn't time," the prince said. "And I've already ordered the gates closed. Roly, you stick with me. You two, go find your fathers."

"You need more than one of us with you," Juris Marrakai said. "My father's dining with Duke Mahieran—Rothlin or I could find both—"

"I'll go," Rothlin said. "My father was going to take yours to the stable afterwards, to talk horses—you know how they are when they get started. I know which stall they'll be hanging on the door of, if they're not still at table."

"I'll stay, then," Juris said.

"Tell your fathers I must meet them urgently," the prince said. "If they are alone, tell them it's a matter of treason, and who, but otherwise, only that it's urgent. Go now, and quickly. If any of you come to the Knight-Commander's chambers before I do, let him know there's trouble and I'm on the way. Roly? Juris? Let's go."

"Not without arming," Juris said, nodding to the prince's private chambers.

In moments, Mikeli had belted on his sword and the young men had retrieved theirs from the racks. Roly and Juris each checked that their saveblades were in place. Roly's, Mikeli remembered, was an ancient stone-bladed knife, supposedly brought all the way from Old Aare when his ancestors came over the sea. His own—he checked it—had been his father's, given to him after his father's death.

As they went into the passage, Mikeli felt his skin tighten on his body as if he had gone out in midwinter in summer clothes. For the first time in his life, he thought he knew how the older men felt, who had faced death. His training, he realized, had been only a shadow of the real thing. Kieri Phelan had been in danger, and so had others, but he himself had always been protected.

In the Knight-Commander's chambers, they found Beclan Mahieran, Knight-Commander of the Bells, and Donag Veragsson, Marshal-Judicar of Tsaia, enjoying mulled wine and pipes and toasting their sock-clad feet before a crackling fire. Their damp boots stood propped on bootholds a careful distance from the hearth.

"You look grim, nephew," Beclan said. He didn't rise, but raised a hand in salute. "What's amiss to bring three of you young rascals here this time of night?"

"There's trouble," Mikeli said. The two older men didn't move, but for Beclan nodding at the other two chairs, an invitation to sit. "It's serious," Mikeli said. He didn't want to sit down; he had to move, and strode to the far end of the room, to the table where Beclan kept a copy of the Code of Gird, before whirling and striding back. "It's treason. We must raise the Order of the Bells, uncle, immediately."

"Treason!" Both the older men sat up straighter at that. "What do you mean?" The Knight-Commander got it out first.

"A messenger arrived just now, from the east. Kieri Phelan was attacked by a contingent of Verrakai troops, joined with some from Pargun, and they used magery and had a priest of Liart—"

"But you gave a warrant of safe passage—and the Royal Guard escort—"

"This is from Sir Ammerlin," Mikeli said, handing the larger scroll to the Knight-Commander. "And this from Phelan—" He handed that one to the Marshal-Judicar. As they read, he moved around the room, noting the sword rack with Beclan's weapons, Donag's belt and sword hung on a wall peg, the men's damp cloaks hanging on adjoining pegs. They must have been out in the city together, he realized, checking what progress the Marshals had made in uncovering Thieves' Guild hideouts and secret passages.

"Sit down, will you? My neck hurts having to follow you around." Beclan rolled his head; the prince could hear the crackle. "Striding around in here won't accomplish anything. What have you done so far?"

Mikeli threw himself into one of the chairs; his friends remained standing. "I was at dinner—" He told them what he had done. "And then I came here."

"Good beginning. Though as we've been finding out, this palace isn't as secure as it could be."

"I suppose someone could come in over the walls—"

The Knight-Commander shook his head. "Not that way. Underground: it's a warren, with some parts left from Gird's day, additions and demolitions, no rational plan. I asked the steward to look into it, because I know some of the lads in training have secret passages to get from the barracks to the training hall and it occurred to me that the Thieves' Guild would no doubt benefit by a way in. I never thought of one of the nobles—" He glanced at the other two. "Do *they* know who—?"

"Yes; I read them Ammerlin's message. I didn't tell Manthar and Belin."

"Verrakai never liked Phelan," Beclan said. "He always resented him, and I suppose it was just too much—but ignoring a royal pass—"

"I wonder if that family has held on to any of the old magery," the Marshal-Judicar said. "That could be . . . difficult."

"Illegal," Beclan said. "But no one's seen anything like that since the Girdish wars. Surely you don't think they've managed to conceal it all this time?"

"My father says they had it longer than anyone," Juris Marrakai said. "He said that's why our families have always been at odds. We lost the magery early, and they didn't—they scorned us for that. Said we'd intermarried with stupid peasants."

"Leaving that aside," the Marshal-Judicar said, "the question is what resources does Verrakai have here and now. Which of the family are in the palace now, tonight, and what Verrakai retainers—"

"Or agents," the Knight-Commander said.

"Or agents. Which are here now, an immediate threat, and where might they be? I know the Duke maintains a house in Vérella; gods grant he's there, and not here."

"And gods grant he doesn't yet know that we know, that the attack failed and we have a message from Ammerlin." The Knight-Commander pulled his feet off the footstool with a sigh and looked around at his boots. "Not dry yet, I'll wager . . . but the palace plans, such as they are, are up in the library—"

"I'll go," Serrostin said. "I know exactly where they are. Do you need anything else?"

The Knight-Commander sat back. "Yes, Rolyan, if you wouldn't mind. The chapter secretary may still be somewhere about; if he is, ask him to attend me here. I don't suppose another few minutes of warm feet will matter."

"And beware," the prince said. "We don't know what the situation is, Roly, so be careful."

"I will," Rolyan said with a grin, patting the hilt of his sword.

In the quiet after Rolyan left, the prince wanted to leap up again and do something, anything. When would the other men come, those he was sure—almost sure—he could trust? How long would it take—how long had it been already? Just as he was ready to spring to his feet again, Juris Marrakai sat, with a sigh, in the other chair.

"I never liked Verrakaien, you know that, but I still have trouble believing any peer of the realm would act like this. Thieves, surely, but—"

"Those who follow evil gods become evil themselves," the Marshal-Judicar said. He struggled out from under his lap robe, and padded sock-footed across to a cabinet. "We need sib, Knight-Commander; my mind at least is clouded by supper and wine; I'll brew some." He poured water from a jug into another warming can, and set that on the hearth, pushing it close to the fire with a poker, and poured in a packet of dried roots and herbs. He sat down, pulling the lap robe back over his legs. "You young men don't feel the cold as much as we do, and you don't get as fuzzled with a little mulled wine, either."

"We have how many Verrakaien to worry about?" Beclan said. "The Duke, obviously, and his brother, who called that challenge on Phelan."

"All of them," Donag said, closing his eyes for a moment. "Your Highness, until they've been examined, we do not know how many still have, and use, the ancient magery, and if they do use it, with what purpose. It's possible that more—even women and children—are as guilty as the Duke. You must issue an Order of Attainder."

"The Council will have to approve," the Knight-Commander pointed out. "The prince can't issue an order like that without Council approval until he's crowned."

"Attainder!" Mikeli said. "It's not the fault of the whole family if one person goes wrong—that's what the Code of Gird says." And the youngest Verrakai boy at court was a close friend of his own younger brother, Camwyn. Camwyn would be furious if Egan was imprisoned.

"The Code of Gird does not forbid attainder in cases of high treason, Your Highness," said the Marshal-Judicar. "Your safe conduct was a direct order: defying your authority is sufficient. So is using magery in defiance of your orders. Every member of the family must be seized and examined; someone you did not suspect might start a rebellion."

"Or assassinate you and your family," the Knight-Commander said. "Treason is always a conspiracy; it's too big a task for one man, and throughout history has been the work of groups."

Mikeli wanted to jump up again but made himself sit still. Kings did not fidget.

CHAPTER FOUR

Rolyan Serrostin passed through the Knight-Commander's outer office to the corridor and moved swiftly to the Grange Hall itself—empty, no light showing under the door to the armory or the records office—then back to the main part of the palace, up a flight to the royal library. No one challenged him, though he heard a subdued bustle in the distance, the faint echoes of hurrying feet.

In the library, once he had lit the lamps, he saw at once what he needed. One set of plans hung from its pole on the wall beside the librarian's desk, and another lay loosely rolled on the table nearby. He lifted down the heavy pole and rolled that set of plans carefully, setting it beside the other. The High Marshal would want both, no doubt; notations might have been made on the second set of plans—Rolyan unrolled it a little, and saw fresh markings. Stacks of wax tablets in their wooden frames, quills, sheets of parchment, and a stoppered ink bottle littered the tabletop. One of the wax tablets, open, had other notes, something to do with tunnels. He might as well take as much as he could at once. Rolyan rolled both sets of plans tightly on their poles, secured them with leather thongs, tucked the poles under his right arm, and gathered up a double handful of wax tablets. Quills and ink he was sure he could find in the Knight-Commander's outer office.

On his way back to the Knight-Commander's chambers, he caught a glimpse down a side passage of Dukes Marrakai and Mahieran, men

he knew well, hurrying in the other direction—to their own quarters to arm themselves, no doubt, before coming to the Knight-
Commander's. He wondered for a moment if the prince's cousin had
told them any details. *Treason*. He could not really imagine it. Nobles
intrigued against one another—everyone sought advantage—but
treason was—was something else, something beyond that.

Outside the Knight-Commander's door, the sentry looked alert but
very nervous. "Anyone else arrived?" Rolyan asked.

"Just m'lord Marrakai," the sentry said. "And—and I feel something's going to happen."

Rolyan felt his skin draw up in prickles. "Marrakai—but I just saw
him down there—" He jerked his head back down the passage. "Get
help," he said. "Something's wrong." With that he opened the door
of the outer office—hurried across it, but silently—and through the
open door of the inner rooms saw the back of a man—the wrong
height and shape for Marrakai—in Verrakai blue and silver. The
blood smell raised the hair on his arms before he quite realized what
he saw.

Across from him, by the fire, the Marshal-Judicar sprawled on the
floor and the Knight-Commander of the Bells slumped in his chair, a
look of horror on his face and blood soaking the front of his robe.
The prince and Juris Marrakai both sat still as if carved in stone. A
bloody sword hung in the air, moving slowly toward the prince, and
the room seemed full of some pressure other than air. Magery! It
must be Duke Verrakai . . .

He wanted to yell, but he could not find breath for that. He had no
time to draw his sword; he dropped the tablets and swung the poles
as hard as he could, taking Verrakai in the neck even as the tablets
clattered to the floor. Verrakai staggered, his hand already grabbing
for his sword; Rolyan stepped sideways to brace for a thrust with the
poles, slipped on the dropped tablets, stumbled into the wall, and
missed. He saw the sword in the air fall; saw Marrakai dive to retrieve
it; saw the prince snatch at his own sword and draw it, saw Verrakai,
his own sword now in his hand, make some movement with the other
that once more stilled them.

"You!" Verrakai said, turning to Rolyan, where he sat sprawled
against the wall. Rolyan tried to push himself up, but could not. "You
would attack a duke, would you?"

"You would attack a prince, would you?" Rolyan said. He saw the telltale shift of Verrakai's weight, and parried with the pole as Verrakai's sword came down. The blade hung momentarily in the linen roll; Roly threw himself forward, over the scattered tablets on the floor, drawing his dagger left-handed, and stabbed at Verrakai's knee, but the blade didn't bite. Armor? It didn't feel like hitting armor.

Before he could yank the pole free of Verrakai's blade, he heard a *thunnnk* as someone's sword—he couldn't see whose—hit Verrakai in the back. Verrakai whirled, stumbled over Roly's legs, staggered, and half fell on him. Roly stabbed frantically with his dagger, holding on to one of the man's legs as Verrakai kicked and struggled to his feet again, but the blade would not go in. More magery? Cold sweat slicked his hands. Magery was evil; he'd heard that all his life. He could hear more sword blows to Verrakai's body now, and yet the man did not cry out, did not stop fighting, did not bleed.

Someone's boot and a lot of weight landed on his ribs; he grunted, now blinded by masses of dark blue cloak—Verrakai's—and he couldn't get his breath. Pressure eased; blades clashed, he heard thuds and clatters as things fell. He tried to get out from under, swiping at the cloak, but it snugged tighter around him, as if it were alive. Someone kicked his head; something whacked his hand hard enough that he lost the dagger. More yells from outside somewhere, more people rushing in—and a hand slid in, under the cloak, lifting it with a dagger blade. He rolled forward and sank his teeth into the hand.

The cloak whirled away from him, lifting to Verrakai's shoulders, and he could see again, see that he had his teeth in Verrakai's heart hand, just as Verrakai dropped the dagger he held. In that moment, arms free at last, Rolyan pulled the saveblade, black as death, from his boot, and surged up, striking at anything he could reach. He had a momentary glimpse of Verrakai's sword . . . and then the old blade slid in, like a hot knife into butter.

Over his head, a blade clanged, then screeched, as Verrakai sagged, his weight coming onto the knife blade, hot blood spurting down, soaking Rolyan's arm.

CHAPTER FIVE

"Are you hurt, Roly?" Mikeli knocked Verrakai's blade aside before it fell. Was that a stain near the tip? Was it poison? He looked around the room, now crowded with the men he had asked his friends to summon. Sonder Mahieran, Duke Marrakai, Counts Destvaorn and Kostvan; his friends crowded behind them, near the door, eyes wide.

"N-no. I—I just—I killed him." Roly was still trembling. Mikeli felt his own hands shaking; he knew what Rolyan was feeling. Neither of them had ever killed a man before; neither of them had ever been so near violent death. He'd been told it was like hunting: it wasn't. The stench of blood and death in the room sickened him. He wanted to spew; he did not want to shame himself in front of the others; he hoped he did not look as green around the mouth as Rolyan. He swallowed, hardening his jaw against the rush of nausea.

"Gods be praised for that," Juris said. He, too, was pale. He glanced at his father and Duke Mahieran, now inside the room. "You saved us, Roly. He was going to kill all of us and blame me and my family."

"Gird's blood, what a mess!" That was Duke Mahieran, kneeling beside the Knight-Commander's body. "Beclan . . . oh, Beclan . . ." Tears ran down his face into his beard; he kissed his dead brother's hand. "And the Marshal-Judicar." He turned and closed Donag's eyes gently. "It's hard to believe anyone would kill a Marshal-Judicar, a Knight-Commander—"

"And using magery," Duke Marrakai said. He looked as dangerous as Verrakai had.

"Don't remind me," Mahieran said. "I remember your warnings."

"I'm sorry to have been proved right," Marrakai said. Under his beard, his jaw muscles worked. "A sad day for Tsaia."

"A dangerous night," Kostvan said. "Pardon, my lord dukes, but Verrakai may have a secret way into the palace, and he has a brother as dangerous as himself. We have no time for mourning now—we must act. Your younger brother, Your Highness—is he safe?"

Mikeli gathered his scattered wits. "You're right, my lord count. Terrible as this is, worse may be coming. Uncle, will you take command of the palace guard, and Duke Marrakai, will you take command of the Bells, and order them out? Camwyn should be in his chambers, but if he's not—"

After a piercing glance, his uncle nodded, stood, and shouldered his way out the door. Marrakai paused. "Juris?"

"I need him here," Mikeli said.

"Very well," Marrakai said, and went out, his cloak swirling behind him.

Kostvan bowed. "My lord, the messenger who came—where is he? He might have more to say—"

"I sent him with Belin Destvaorn to eat and rest."

"Verrakai would want him dead," Kostvan said. "Shall I check, and also alert the household staff?"

"Thank you, my lord," Mikeli said. Kostvan turned to go, just as a squad of palace guards arrived.

"What is happening?" asked one from outside.

"Treason," Kostvan said. "The first one's dead, but there are others. Guard your prince."

Count Destvaorn beckoned to the guards. "We need to lay out the High Marshal and Knight-Commander with all due respect. In the Knights' Hall, or the grange, do you think?"

"Knights' Hall," Mikeli said. He wanted to sit down; he must not sit down.

The sergeant gulped, then glanced at Verrakai's body. "And him?"

"He was the traitor. He killed them, and tried to kill the prince. Make sure he's dead, and search his body for . . . for anything that might give us a clue what else we might face."

"What about that one?" He pointed at Rolyan, still sprawled on the floor, looking sick.

"He saved us," Mikeli said. "If Roly hadn't come back from the library and hit Verrakai . . . we'd be dead." He moved closer, avoiding Verrakai's blood. "Roly—are you all right?"

"I—I will be." Rolyan blinked; tears tracked down his face. "I never—never killed anyone—before."

Mikeli could not think of anything to say.

"Come on," Juris said to Rolyan. "Let's get you up and out of that mess." He held out a hand, and Mikeli held out his. Rolyan took hold; and they pulled him up. He looked better standing up, though bloody to the shoulder on his right arm. "You'll want clean clothes," Juris said. "My lord prince, may I take him off to clean up?"

"Not yet," Mikeli said. His mind whirled, tossing out ideas, images, faster than he could grasp them. "We don't know if there's someone else—Verrakai's brother, his son, Kirgan Verrakai—we should stay together, not wander about." He focused on Rolyan's face, still paler than normal, his gray-green eyes wide and staring. "Roly—did his blade touch you anywhere?"

"I don't—don't think so. It's just—"

"Get him into the other room," Count Kostvan said. "His first kill—he needs to be out of this smell, out of this mess. You all do. I'll take care of it." He turned to the sergeant. "Here—find something clean and warm in the Knight-Commander's cupboard for Kirgan Serrostin to wear. Kirgan Marrakai, fetch a can of water if you please. Cold will do. You and the prince can help him clean up. He'll do better then."

The Knight-Commander's outer room, furnished as an office, was cooler and the stench of death much less. "I'm fine," Rolyan said. "I'm sorry, I—"

"Nothing to be sorry about. You saved us both," Juris said. "*I* couldn't even move." He sounded angry; he was usually the leader in their activities, a stronger fighter than Roly.

"Nor I," Mikeli said. "Sit down, Roly—" It was easier to be calm, he noted, when he was taking care of someone else; his hands weren't shaking now.

"I'll get blood on the chair," Rolyan said.

"No matter," Mikeli said. "Ah—here's the sergeant with some

clothes." The man laid a stack of clothes and towels on the scribe's table.

"We'll get this off you," Juris said. He rolled up his own sleeves; Mikeli followed his lead and in moments they'd removed Rolyan's dinner capelet, unlaced his doublet, then his shirt, while Juris rolled up the bloody sleeve, then the clean one, and pulled the shirt over his head. With the tail and back of the shirt wetted in the can of water Juris had brought along, they cleaned the blood from him.

"I can't wear his—" Rolyan began, as Juris handed him an under-shirt.

Mikeli took his hand. "You can't walk about the palace half-naked, Roly. We need you. And my uncle Beclan would want you to have them. Now get dressed. It's going to be a long night."

Rolyan managed a shaky parody of his usual grin. "At once, your royalness."

That sounded more like the real Roly. Mikeli turned to the sergeant. "We'll need those plans and things Roly brought. They're on the floor in there—"

"At once, my lord." The sergeant bowed and went back to the inner room. More palace guards arrived, with litters for the bodies, and a servant appeared with a jug of sib and a plate of pastries.

"My lord Marrakai said to bring this—" he said. Mikeli gestured to the table; the servant set it down.

"We can't just eat," Juris said.

"If your father meant us to," the prince said, "we had better. Come now—we were interrupted at dinner. I doubt we'll see a bed tonight; we need something."

Food and sib restored Rolyan's normal coloring even as a distant clamor rose, nearing as Knights of the Bells gathered in their hall.

CHAPTER SIX

Vérella, two days later

As they came in sight of Vérella, Arcolin saw what he had not seen for years—a Royal Guard blockade on the road. He trotted ahead of the cohort and then halted at the blockade. "What is it?"

"Who are you?" demanded a man with officer's knots on his shoulder.

"Arcolin, Duke Phelan's captain, with a cohort bound for Aarenis— surely you had word. Our employers preceded us."

"They're all in Phelan's colors, Captain," one of the troop said. "It's got to be him."

"Do you have proof of your identity?" the captain asked, a shade less truculent now.

"I have the Duke's ring and a letter," Arcolin said, fishing the ring out of his pocket and handing it over.

"It's the Fox's, all right," the captain said, handing it back. "I suppose you know about the trouble?"

"The Duke wrote that he had been proclaimed king of Lyonya," Arcolin said. "That he was on his way to Lyonya. Is that the trouble?" He did not want to ask about Paks, not from a stranger.

"Nay. Worse. Treason and rebellion. Two nights agone, Duke Verrakai tried to kill the crown prince—did kill his uncle, Knight-Commander of the Bells, and Marshal Donag, the Marshal-Judicar of Gird. All the Verrakaien are under attainder, but it's thought many will try to pretend they're someone else, and they have magery."

"Magery?" Arcolin stared. "If you mean the old lords' magery, that's all gone—been gone since Gird's day. It's all wizard-work now."

"So we thought, but it's not. Anyway, Captain Arcolin, now I know it's really you and not some Verrakai putting a glamour on me, you're wanted in the palace. You're to go there at once. Your cohort can stay in palace barracks, if you like—"

"We usually march through," Arcolin said.

"Aye, but things are different now. You'll be here at least a day and a night, I daresay. The gate guards will know where your soldiers should go."

A night in someone else's barracks would at least not lighten his purse. Behind him, he heard the marching feet come to a final stamped halt. He turned in the saddle.

"Change of plans, Sergeant Stammel. I'm wanted in the palace; we'll be staying in Vérella overnight; the cohort will be housed in royal barracks."

"Very good, sir," Stammel said. He eyed the Royal Guard and asked no questions.

"There's been some trouble. We don't want more."

"No, sir." Stammel would need no more hint than that to keep the cohort—especially the young ones—on a tight leash.

As they went on from the roadblock toward the city, Arcolin told Stammel what he'd been told. "I suspect there's a lot more to it, and the city either roiling or too quiet. I don't know what the prince wants with me; I don't know if our employers are still here, or have gone on. I will need to contact the Duke's bankers, and see about finances, too, so we might be here even two nights, if the prince's conferences last a long time."

"Verrakai attacked the prince and killed his uncle? Why? Surely he didn't hope to take over the kingdom? And why now, just when the Duke's gone to Lyonya?"

"My guess would be that Verrakai tried to attack the Duke first. He'd always hated him as baseborn, you know." Stammel snorted, a very Stammel snort, and Arcolin went on. "If he did that, and attacked the escort of Royal Guard the prince sent with him, then that's already treason. Then he might think his only chance would be to assassinate the prince and try to hide the facts until—I can't believe he thought he could pull it off, though. But that Royal Guard captain said he used magery."

"He used a Liart priest, I'll wager," Stammel said. "Not magery— that's all been lost for hundreds of years."

"That's what I told him, but he thinks not," Arcolin said. "He thinks the Verrakaien have it. That's why they're all under attainder."

"Good thing Dorrin's with the Duke in Lyonya, then," Stammel said. "It'll be hard for her to come back through."

Arcolin felt a jolt. He had forgotten that Dorrin was a Verrakai.

"They wouldn't include her; she's not even in the family book," he said.

"They know, I would bet on it," Stammel said. "Proper mess, it sounds like. So—we need to smarten up, before we come into the city?" Under the circumstances, he meant. Before they went into a royal barracks.

"Good idea," Arcolin said, and raised his hand. Stammel halted the cohort. He and Devlin and their new corporals went through, checking equipment, sharpening the troops up, and then they started off again. Arcolin took the opportunity to check his own gear, stuffing his winter hat into one saddlebag and the scarf around his throat into the other, putting on his helmet. Stammel came back to the front of the cohort, gave Arcolin a nod, and again they set off, now near enough to see the guard at the first gates.

The palace guards, more alert than Arcolin had ever seen them, insisted he disarm before he came into the palace itself.

"One of us will bring your arms, sir," the taller guard said. "Under the circumstances no one can carry arms save with the prince's express permission."

"That's quite all right," Arcolin said, unbelting his sword and dagger. "I have a small boot knife, as well."

"That also, if you please."

Arcolin removed it, and watched as the guard wrapped them all carefully then put the bundle under his arm.

"This way, Captain," the shorter guard said, and led the way; the taller followed with Arcolin's weapons.

He had been in the palace many times, carrying messages from the Duke to the Council and even to the crown prince as he grew older and more active in the government. He sensed at once the change in atmosphere, the tension showing in the way servants, guards, and nobles moved, the glances cast at him.

A young man in Marrakai red and green with the shoulder knot of the kirgan stopped him. "Sir—aren't you one of Phelan's captains? Is there news of him?"

"I'm Arcolin, his senior captain, yes—but I'm just in from the north and only now learning what has happened. I've had no news from the Duke—the king—since before he left here."

The kirgan gave a short nod. "Thank you. I believe my father has met you before. I wondered why you were here—"

"The prince asked for him," said Arcolin's escort. "And we had best be going there, by your leave, Kirgan."

"Certainly, certainly." The kirgan bowed. "I beg your pardon, sir."

Arcolin smiled, returned the bow, and went on, following his escort. The Marrakaien had always been Kieri's particular friends, and Arcolin had seen the young Marrakai before. He'd then appeared to be one of the prince's friends content to leave Council business to his elders. Now he, too, looked different.

The crown prince was in his office, with armed guards at the door and inside both. Though it had been almost two years since Arcolin had seen him, Arcolin had not expected to find him looking so much more a king. Arcolin bowed.

"My lord prince."

"Captain Arcolin! I'm glad to see you arrived safely. Did you have any trouble on the road?"

"No, my lord. But then, I traveled with a full cohort. When I left the Duke's stronghold, I knew only that he had been proclaimed king of Lyonya."

"You know about the assassinations?"

"Only what your Royal Guard told me."

"You will need to know all of it; please sit down." He looked at the guard carrying Arcolin's weapons. "Return Captain Arcolin's weapons to him; I know him personally and he is not a threat."

Arcolin sensed the guard's reluctance and ventured a suggestion. "Perhaps you would prefer that my sword, at least, be in custody?"

"No, no," the prince said. "If we had not been armed, we would have died. You are known to me, and I will be happier when I see that sword on your hip."

Arcolin belted it back on, rearranged his other weapons, and sat down where the prince indicated.

"My Council would agree to my coronation being advanced," the prince said. "But I have chosen to wait until Midsummer, as is traditional. However, I have taken over additional powers in this time of emergency. Let me brief you on what happened."

Arcolin listened, horrified but fascinated, as the prince explained everything from Duke Phelan's arrival at court, having been summoned by the Regency Council, to the present. And all while he, Arcolin, had been up at the stronghold, unaware.

"Did you, did anyone in his Company, have any idea of his parentage?" the prince asked, finally.

"No, my lord," Arcolin said. "I was with him twenty years and more; we all thought him remarkable, but as for this—born to a throne and half-elven—it's hardly believable."

"If I had not seen the sword come alight in his hands, I would not have believed it myself. I cannot—I cannot comprehend the years he was lost, or how he was found, and once found, not recognized."

"Nor I, my lord."

"Well. You know most of what has happened here. To complete the story, we discovered lairs of Liart's worshippers in the Thieves' Guild, and with the help of the city granges, these were exposed. Certain of the Thieves' Guild have cooperated with the Crown . . . not all were happy to have overlords of any kind. That appears to be mostly through Paksenarrion's influence with a thief—or Thieves' Guild enforcer—she met in Brewersbridge years back."

"That would've been after she left us," Arcolin said.

"Yes. He's the one who got her out after . . . well, after what happened."

"I don't understand how she survived." He wanted to hear that, not what had been done to her.

For the first time the prince's face relaxed into a smile. "Nor does anyone else except Gird and the High Lord's favor. Witnesses say her wounds healed, slowly enough to watch and fast enough that in minutes she was whole again, broken bones mended, bleeding wounds but scars—or in some cases, no scars at all. It terrified those watching; they fled. She had been branded on the brow: she now bears a silver circle, the High Lord's mark."

Arcolin felt hollow . . . he had known Paks from her first year in the Company, and though he had recognized her basic good character and her fighting ability, he'd never seen *that* potential in her. How had he missed so much—the Duke's real nature, Paks's real nature? What else had he missed?

"You are an experienced soldier," the prince said. "And you have known many realms. More than I have, who have visited only within Tsaia. You must recognize how unbalanced Tsaia is now, with two domains vacated . . . if this were the South, what would you say about it?"

"A dangerous situation, my lord prince. Your eastern border, from north of the Honnorgat halfway down to the mountains, and your northern border all at risk."

"What would you do?"

Arcolin stared. "My lord—that is for you and your Council to say."

"But you know Tsaia—you have lived here how long? And you have studied military history, our history, haven't you?"

Arcolin tried to calm himself. "You need strong, loyal lords in both places. Not the same for each—that's too much, too big, for one to rule well and it would unbalance the realm. Verrakai—I know nothing about its resources, its people, even its terrain, but I would expect it's more thickly settled, and thus potentially more difficult than the North Marches. Though at least, with Kieri Phelan ruling Lyonya you should have no problems from over the border."

"Pargunese soldiers were also in that attack. It's believed they crossed into either Verrakai's lands directly or through Lyonya."

"Lyonya had a weak king."

"A dead king by then, but yes. I'm sure Kieri Phelan won't let that happen again, though what resources he will have I don't yet know."

"The northeast and north is your most vulnerable," Arcolin said. "We fought off the orcs this last winter—destroyed their base and the Achryan priest supporting them. They should be little trouble for a while. The Pargunese, though, test the border off and on—we keep constant patrols out for that."

"Who's commanding there?"

"Cracolnya—he has been senior captain of the mixed cohort for years. Experienced, a good tactician, good manager, too. When Captain Dorrin comes back—" He paused at the look on the prince's face and felt his heart sink. "She didn't—in that attack—?"

"No, no. She survived; her arrival with the paladin just saved the day, I understand. I would like your assessment of her. You do know she's a Verrakai?"

"Of course," Arcolin said. "She's never made a secret of it, or of her estrangement from her family."

"Do you believe that estrangement complete? Have you known her to contact her family?"

"No, my lord, never. I know she asked the Duke—the king—not to assign her to duties here, where she might meet Duke Verrakai. She and the Verrakaien both considered her no longer part of the family." He hoped to convince the prince Dorrin was not a traitor.

"Birth matters, in spite of choice," the prince said, a bit grimly. "It made your duke a king; it will make Dorrin Verrakai a duke, if she accepts my offer."

Arcolin stared. "Dorrin? You can't mean— I beg pardon, but— you want her to take over as Duke Verrakai? Of Verrakai?" He imagined Dorrin's reaction to the thought; she had spoken of her family only with revulsion.

"She's the only adult Verrakai I can exempt from the Order of Attainder, precisely because she was estranged and was said to be blotted from their records. Not every Verrakai is evil—I know that—but at present I cannot take risks. The innocent will clear themselves at trial, in time, but I dare not leave Verrakaien loose on the land that long. We have evidence they've colluded with Liart's priests—it's a danger to both."

"But—" Arcolin could not imagine the Duke's Company without Dorrin any more than he could imagine it without the Duke. He shook his head to clear it. "We were expecting her to return—the Duke said her cohort had been sent for, as escort, but are they staying?"

"I don't know yet. They went with him into Lyonya; if she takes up my offer—which is contingent on her gaining control of Verrakai and sending those resident at Verrakai House to Vérella—she may well want to keep them with her and I'm assuming the king or his successor as duke will agree to a contract with her."

Arcolin considered the situation back north . . . were two cohorts enough to protect the dukedom and Tsaia's borders? Probably. It had worked that way for years, with even fewer at the stronghold during the fighting season.

"I'm pleased to hear your opinion of Dorrin Verrakai," the prince said. "It accords with everything Phelan ever said about her, and I see her as the best hope to make Verrakai a healthy, sound, and loyal steading. There's a young man in another branch—whom I personally believe is loyal and not involved—who, after his trial, should be a good possibility as her successor, as she has no children and is unlikely to breed."

"Likely not," Arcolin said, almost choking at the casual use of a term that, applied to Dorrin, made her nothing but a prize cow.

"And that leaves the problem of Phelan's domain," the prince said. "For my part, I would let it stay in his name awhile, and consult with him on a successor, but the Council is concerned. They do not wish so large a domain to be under the control of Lyonya's king, more especially as it adjoins Pargun."

"I understand," Arcolin said, when a pause seemed longer than necessary.

"Tell me," the prince said. "I know he sent word to you—what were his orders?"

"Before he came south, to prepare the troops for a contract; he was hoping to get your approval to take some of the Company south again. Then this—" Arcolin handed the prince Kieri's letter. "I have a one-cohort contract with Vonja, if the Council approves."

"I don't think you'll have a problem," the prince said, handing the letter back. "Phelan maintained more troops than other nobles—everyone knew it was because he was a mercenary—but some worried."

Arcolin privately thought they had simply wanted an excuse to control Phelan, but he said nothing about that.

"But they expect me to appoint someone—at least temporarily, though they'd prefer a permanent status. I thought of you, of course, and he suggested it." The prince cocked his head.

"Me? But—I'm not of noble birth—"

"No one thought Phelan was."

"But—"

"He taught me that what justifies an appointment—any appointment—is how the person carries out their duties, not their birth. He thought you'd be capable, Captain, and his judgment has proven itself over the years."

But I'm taking the cohort to Aarenis almost escaped Arcolin's lips; he held it back and instead said, "I'm honored by his trust, and yours, my lord. However, I would need to take contracts, as Phelan did. Otherwise, I could neither afford the soldiers' keep, nor would it be legal under Tsaian law."

"I have no objection, and for the reason you state—our laws—it is as well that you continue to take them south. Moreover, as Phelan himself went south every year with the Company, you should be permitted to do so as well. The Council will want to know, as they did with him, who is in charge in your absence every year." The prince shifted in his seat. "What I would like is this: to change as little as possible now, when great change is happening in the East. Dorrin Verrakai as Duke Verrakai is shock enough; the trials of the other Verrakai will occupy the lords in Council for the rest of the year, at least. If you can protect the borders and maintain the same routine as Phelan, that seems best to me. I can call a Council meeting for to-morrow; can you be ready to present such a plan?"

Arcolin had not felt ready for any of the things that happened since Paksenarrion returned to them, but life did not wait on readiness. "Yes," he said. "I can be ready." He felt every moment of the day's ride, but one thing he'd learned from Kieri was that tired was just a word. "I will need more paper than I brought—"

"Of course," the prince said. "In fact, we've assigned you my late uncle's suite, as I haven't yet appointed a new Knight-Commander of the Bells. And I've assigned you a clerk, in case you need anything from the library, any research."

"My lord prince," Arcolin said, very carefully, "you are more concerned than you've said, are you not?"

"I have a—a strange feeling. It's not over, with Verrakai's death. I don't know what . . . but . . . I feel a menace." The prince swallowed.

"Not just danger to me, but to the whole realm. And yet—it's only a feeling, and when there *was* danger, before Verrakai's attack, I felt nothing."

"Nothing? After what you told me of the attack on Kieri—on the king?"

"Not that night. Beclan—my uncle—had told me they thought they'd found all the Liartian priests. At dinner with my friends, it felt normal—I missed it somehow—and now I don't know if my feelings are trustworthy—"

"If you are asking me whether to be concerned, my lord, the answer must be yes. Of course you must be. Gird may be giving you warning, as well as your own senses. From my experience I would say that such actions as Duke Verrakai took are not taken lightly, or without deep planning; I doubt that his death and that of his brother end it. Your Order of Attainder is certainly necessary."

"He held me motionless, Captain," the prince said. "I cannot get over that. I thought Gird's power was stronger than evil; I thought my faith was enough. This was not wizardry—this was the old magery that Gird once defeated, back again in today's world."

The prince looked angry; Arcolin knew that look. All the young squires looked that way the first time they were truly frightened.

"My lord prince," he said, "I believe the gods are stronger than evil, but faith must marry with deeds. Gird had his cudgel, after all. Yeomen of the granges do not merely pray for faith, but train for deeds as well."

The prince looked at him, almost indignant at first and then, his expression easing, rueful. "You are right, Captain. This was my first experience of violent death. I saw my uncle, whom I loved, killed before my face and could do nothing. And the Marshal-Judicar, as well."

"Yet you lived, and killed the killer, did you not?"

"That was mostly Roly," the prince said. "If he hadn't come in and bashed Verrakai with a map rod and then stabbed him with a stone knife, I'd be dead. Neither my sword not Juris's would bite, for Verrakai's magery, until Roly's old stone saveblade got him. Then the magery failed."

Arcolin could imagine the three noble youths, trained in weaponry but inexperienced, against a man like Verrakai, whose own sword skill was well-known at court. And with magery as well—even if it proved wizard-work at the last—

"You did well," he said, as he would have to a squire. "And I rejoice at your survival. Let me go to work now on a plan to present to your Council tomorrow." He put aside any thought of visiting Kieri's—and now his—banker that day.

"I nearly forgot," the prince said. "There's another of Phelan's people—a councilor for one of his villages—who came south with him. A one-armed woman."

"Kolya Ministiera, yes," Arcolin said.

"She was staying in an inn, but for her safety I had her come to the palace—I'll see she knows you're here."

By morning, Arcolin had a plan that—according to the palace clerks who had helped him—would fulfill the requirements of a grant-in-lieu-of-heir. They praised his foresight in bringing fair copies of the newly signed village charters. Kolya Ministiera signed the new Duke's East charter and congratulated him on the grant, but they had little time to talk over what had happened. Though he'd had little sleep, Arcolin was awake when the seneschal asked if he would care to breakfast with the prince; they discussed his plan through breakfast and the prince nodded.

"This should do," he said. "They won't give you a title at this time, but they should confirm you as grant-holder until you come back after the campaign season. Once I'm crowned, I can insist on a title, though not a dukedom at first—it wasn't for Phelan, either."

"I remember, my lord prince."

"Well, then. The Council meeting, and the oath—you do know you must swear fealty? Good—and then you can go about your business. I know you did not anticipate all this, but before you return for the Autumn Court, we'll need to know your mark, your colors, and you'll need court costume."

"The same colors and mark, if that's permissible," Arcolin said. "I am not Phelan's heir of the body, it is true, but—"

"You will need his permission," the prince said. "If you like, you can send him word by royal courier."

Arcolin nodded. It still felt unreal, but coping with details, moment to moment, he had no time to ponder how unlikely it was that he, like Kieri, might rise to noble rank and own land . . . his own land, his own people.

His appearance before the Council took less than a glass: he laid out the papers, the charters, his intent to guard the North and East as Kieri had, his need to campaign in the South to support the land until it could support itself. He recognized most of the faces from previous visits.

The Councilors agreed that Jandelir Arcolin should become liege lord of the vacated domain. That he could raise a military force sufficient to guard the North and also campaign in Aarenis, that he could transport said force across Tsaia and through Vérella on the same roads Phelan had used twice each year.

He bent his knee to the prince and swore fealty; he signed the documents that made him a lord-vassal of the Crown and defined his responsibilities. The prince waived the usual security until autumn—Arcolin hoped Kieri's bankers somewhere had that much gold—and by the noon ringing of the Bells, Jandelir Arcolin, Captain, had become Lord Arcolin of the North Marches.

He spent the afternoon first with Kieri's banker and judicar, and then with Kolya and the merchants Kieri dealt with in Vérella, buying the supplies Cracolnya and Valichi wanted. That evening he wrote letters to the North, again aided by the castle clerks who made copies so he need not write duplicates to each village and each commander, and a letter to Kieri in Lyonya, asking permission to retain the fox-head mark and the same colors.

Although he had carried out similar tasks for Kieri, it felt strange to be doing it for himself—to sign the letters and orders as *Lord Arcolin* and not *Arcolin, Capt, for Duke Phelan*. He supposed he would get used to it.

CHAPTER SEVEN

Chaya

Kieri Phelan woke, aware moment by moment that he was in a bed he had never slept in before, in a room he did not know . . . textures, smells, sounds, all unfamiliar. He blinked, in the almost-dark: yesterday and the days before fell into his memory like tiny paintings, bright and clear.

The journey from Vérella, the Verrakai attack, the victory, the welcome here, last night's acclamation by the Lyonyan nobles and his elven relatives.

Outside, a cock crowed, persistently, and another answered. A dog barked, then quieted. He heard nothing from inside the palace; it might be near dawn, to the cock, but apparently a very early morning to the castle staff.

A cold current of air came from . . . from there, to his left as he lay in the bed. He stretched again, sniffing the scents that rode on that chill current: stone, the spice of evergreen trees from without, and in the room more subtle spices. From somewhere across the room came a vague sense of warmth, and the smell of woodsmoke, very faint.

He had seen a fireplace in the room the evening before, and a crackling wood fire . . . now it must be banked, but still giving warmth.

He slipped from under the covers and padded across a carpeted floor—he remembered it was patterned with flowers and vines—to the nearer window. Below all was dark, silent. Above, stars still glittered, but there—it must be sunwards—a dullness dimmed them. Dawn was coming.

When did the palace awake? They had had a sick king—perhaps they slept late here? His own stronghold woke earlier than this; kitchen fires would be burning; recruits would be roused, chivvied into the jacks and out, readying their barracks for inspection . . . even as he wondered, he smelled woodsmoke from outside as the wind eddied. Abruptly, from below, boot heels rang on stone paving, followed by the lighter patter of soft-shod feet.

No lights, though . . . did they need no light? A small light bloomed in the distance; he heard the rasp and snick of a latch, the creak of hinges, and then the whinny of horses and the stamping of hooves.

He moved to the fireplace, guided by memory and the gentle warmth, and felt around on the hearth. There—a pot or vase, filled with reeds. He poked at the fire; ashes fell away from a crimson coal, and in moments a flame trembled at the end of the reed. It hardly lit the room, but in its dim wavering light he could see a candlestick placed handily on the hearth, and lit the wax taper there.

From that, he could see the larger candles on the mantel, arranged in a holder, eight of them. He lit only one, then carried the single stick to the bedside, where he lit a bedside candlestick with it. A draft from the window blew the flickering flames sideways, glinting on the jewel in the hilt of his sword.

From outside the door of his own chamber, a soft murmur of voices. He saw no robe within reach, and slid under the covers.

The door opened. Silhouetted against the soft light in the corridor he saw a single figure.

"Sir King! You're awake!" Lieth. It was Lieth, the youngest of the King's Squires who had come to Tsaia and accompanied him here. "My pardon, I intended only to stir your fire and begin warming the bath . . ."

"I wake early," he said.

"Let me light your candles," she said. In moments the chamber was softly lit by candelabra on stands, and she had stirred the banked fire into life. "I will send word that you are awake—we expected, after your long journey, that you would sleep longer."

"It is no matter," Kieri said. He looked around. The clothes he had worn were nowhere in sight. "My clothes—?"

"I'll send someone," she said.

Moments later, an old man appeared, Kieri's trousers folded over one arm and a green robe over the other. "Sir King, I am Joriam. Your pardon—I did not know you were awake. Your bath chamber is there—and let me show you your wardrobe—" He touched one of the carved wall panels, and it slid aside, revealing clothes all in shades of green and gold. "We have already taken measure from the clothes you wore, and tailors will have your new garments ready in a day or so. Meanwhile, these are clothes the previous king wore rarely or never, made for him before his final illness."

Bathed and dressed, in a mix of his own clothes and shirt and doublet in Lyonya's royal colors, Kieri felt more than ready for breakfast, but had no idea where to go. Joriam had taken away his robe and nightshirt and had not yet returned. He opened the door; two unfamiliar King's Squires stood guard on either side. Across the passage, Paks sat on a bench, chatting with another. She looked up and smiled at him, the same open smile she'd always had but now—with his memories of what she had undergone for his sake—he felt embarrassed. The corner of her mouth quirked, as if she had read his mind.

"Sir King," she said, standing. "They tell me breakfast is ready downstairs, or someone will bring it—"

"I'll go down," he said. One of the King's Squires went ahead of him; Paks moved to his side as if he'd commanded her; the other King's Squires fell in behind. "You did sleep last night?" he said to Paks.

"Enough," she said. He eyed her. She was still much as she had been when he first saw her. Yet . . . not. She had been just another recruit, and now she was Gird's paladin. Not, as she had pointed out, his to command any longer. "Captain Dorrin's awake; she has a report on the cohort for you."

"I wonder if Sir Ammerlin made it safely back to Vérella." More than that, he wondered what the Tsaian Council would do, with one of its dukes now king of a neighboring domain and another proven traitor.

Paks did not quite shrug; he could sense her lack of interest in these things. Her quest had been to find Lyonya's king; she had done so; now she had a respite before, he assumed, Gird sent her somewhere else.

In the passage outside the dining hall, a group of Lyonyan nobles milled about as if waiting for something to happen. He saw Dorrin, looking faintly amused, standing to one side, and a smaller group of elves even farther away.

"The king," announced the lead King's Squire, and everyone stepped back, bowing, murmuring greetings.

"Good morning," Kieri said. He could think of nothing else to say. Apparently that was enough, because the doors to the dining hall opened and he led the way in. A man in the green castle livery bowed him to a seat at one end of a table large enough, he thought, to hold fencing matches on . . . far too large for breakfast . . . and by the time everyone was seated, it was only half full, if that.

Breakfast, in Lyonya, meant hot breads, butter and honey, soft cheeses, fruit. None of the porridge he was used to, no meats, no eggs. He made no requests, wanting to know first what was expected. The talk at table was general, casual—nobles asked after each other's children, or discussed the likelihood of a good crop of wheat this year. Nothing of substance, and nothing addressed specifically to him. When he felt almost full, another tray came in, this one holding rolls of flaky pastry tied with thin green ribbons. One was placed before him, and then before each of the others. Silence fell. Kieri regarded the pastry roll; the others looked at theirs, and then at him.

He picked it up, unwrapped the ribbon, and took a cautious bite. Pastry crumbs scattered, as the others did the same. One of the nobles—Sier Belvarin, he thought he recalled—turned to him.

"Sir King, we really should begin planning your coronation."

So . . . the pastry rolls were a signal that business could be discussed? That the king could be addressed? He nodded at Belvarin.

"You know that I am not familiar with all your customs and traditions—what do you suggest?"

Glances passed back and forth across the table. "Well . . ." Belvarin seemed reluctant to go on. Kieri waited. "The period of deep mourning for the late king has passed, but by custom—"

"Not that it matters," another noble spoke up. "Your coronation must supersede—"

"We must respect—" another began.

"Excuse me," Kieri said. Silence fell; they all looked at him. He felt a moment's amusement. The former king had been sick a long time and perhaps had never been a commanding presence. He would have to be careful not to startle these men with his parade-ground voice too often. "If there is a traditional period of mourning for the death of your king, or ceremonies to be performed, that must be respected."

The impatient one opened his mouth and shut it again. Sier Belvarin looked relieved. "It would be—it would be appreciated, Sir King, if it suits you . . ."

"How long is the official mourning?" If they would not follow hints, he would ask directly.

"Four hands of days in deep mourning, during which no official business can be done except for emergencies. Sending the paladin to search for the heir was deemed an emergency."

"And then?"

"Four more hands of days preparing for the transfer of kingship, but that does not start until the king is chosen. As you are here now, that period can begin. With the ceremony usually performed on the fifth or tenth day after that."

"Surely there is a ceremony of mourning, which the new king should attend—"

Glances again shifted around the table. "Well . . . yes . . ." Belvarin said reluctantly. "But as custom requires, he was interred on the fifth day . . ."

"I must do something," Kieri said. "He was my relative on my father's side, though I never knew him. I have had no chance to honor or grieve for any of them—my parents, my sister, the others—"

Paks, down the table, nodded at him; he could see for himself that the other nobles and even the elves were relaxing a shade more.

Belvarin's brow furrowed. "Sir King, you would wish to combine all these into one ceremony?"

"I do not know your traditions," Kieri said again. "I depend on you for guidance—but surely the late king's memory must be honored now, before I am crowned."

"It would be better," said one of the elves, "if the other ceremonies—at least for the elfborn and half-elven—were separate, since their deaths were long ago in your human terms. Each life deserves its own measure of respect; they are not kindling wood, to be bundled together."

A few shocked looks from the human nobles, but no disagreement.

"Thank you," Kieri said. "I mean no disrespect and will be guided by your counsel—all of you—in this matter. Now, Sier Belvarin, tell me what is appropriate in the matter of the former king."

"It is what we call laying the boughs," Belvarin said. "It can be public or private, with someone to guide you through the ritual, but it should be soon."

"I will be ready whenever you say," Kieri said.

"And then your coronation . . ." Belvarin said.

"I see no need to rush," Kieri said. "At the regular time, after the days of preparation. You are not like to change your minds, I hope?"

A quick murmur of negatives.

"You came on an auspicious day," Belvarin said. "Forty-five days after he died. And four hands more brings us five days from the Spring Evener. Your coronation could be on the Spring Evener or another day that hand." Then, seeing Kieri's expression, he went on. "Nine times a hand, Sir King—the elves consider nine auspicious for deeds of power."

Kieri nodded; he knew the elves cared far more about numbers for their own sake than any other race.

"This is, I presume, an unusual—perhaps a unique—situation in your history?"

"It is indeed," Sier Halveric said. Though he was Aliam Halveric's elder brother, he looked younger and sleeker—he had not spent his life leading an army in battle, Kieri thought. "For that reason, it is my belief your coronation must be more elaborate—"

"We must consider our resources—" Sier Galvary said.

Kieri had no idea what resources Lyonya commanded. What did a kingdom covered with forest and full of elves and a few humans produce? He had only the vaguest memory of seeing goods identified as coming from Lyonya in Tsaian markets. Where else could they trade? What did they trade? Aliam Halveric had taught him long ago that finance was the foundation of a successful mercenary company—or steading—or kingdom.

"Excuse me," he said. They all fell silent again. "I was last here as a youth, a young man—living with Aliam Halveric as his squire, and then in Falk's Hall preparing for knighthood. I apologize for knowing so little about your—our—land, but I have no idea what these resources are. You will need to instruct me . . . it is not my intent to ruin the land before I know it well, by undue extravagance, but on the other hand, your honor is due some ceremony."

This time, as the glances passed across the table, he was able to pick out patterns. Of the humans, Halveric and Belvarin seemed to lead opposition groups; others looked to them first, then at each other. Familiar as he was with the workings of Tsaia's court, here he felt adrift, uncertain. They did not need his uncertainty: they needed the best he could give them. He tried to remember what Aliam had said about his brother.

"We have time," he said. "Time for me to learn more of what I need to know, time to plan." One of the elves nodded, approving. But elves always had time, if a rock didn't land on one. "I will need to check on my escort, after breakfast, but let us say midmorning, for a meeting of those who keep the finances?"

This time a look of surprise from them all. "You don't wish to rest a day or so?" Belvarin asked. "Your long journey . . . the attack . . . surely you are still fatigued. We do not wish to exhaust you."

Kieri managed not to laugh out loud. He, a mercenary, fatigued by a journey that had been, except for the battle, no strain at all? "I am not fatigued," he said, pitching his voice to reassure Belvarin. "You had a sick king so long, I understand and appreciate your concern, but having taken on this task, I intend to do a good job. Which means going to work now, this morning. If you, Sier Belvarin, will begin organizing the memorial for my predecessor—" He did not even know the man's name, and no one had mentioned it. "I will speak to you later about that. For the finances—"

Brisk nods. Sier Galvary raised his hand; Kieri nodded. "Sir King, those keeping the treasure rolls of the kingdom report to me. Would it please you to come to the treasury yourself, or would you prefer to see the records here?" He paused, and before Kieri could answer said, "The light is better here, to be honest, and the tables are larger."

Kieri smiled. "Here, then. I need to know all you can tell me about the economy of Lyonya, internal and external, from what crops are grown in the fields and fruit in the orchard, to what goods are traded here and abroad. I know it will take more than a day to learn . . ." He pushed back his chair and they all stood; when he stood, they bowed, and he nodded gravely. Paks and Dorrin, catching his hand signal, stood aside as the Siers and elves left the dining hall and waited for him.

"Do you want me to parade the cohort here, my lord—Sir King?" Dorrin asked.

"I think not," Kieri said. "I need to begin learning my way around; I'll visit them where they're quartered. Paks, I doubt I'll have time to check on my mount today—would you see that he's exercised a little? Tell whoever's in charge of the stables that he should be walked in hand for perhaps a glass, but nothing fast. He's in a strange stable and he can be fretful."

"Of course, Sir King," Paks said. "I can lead him from mine, if you like; I was going out."

"He doesn't usually—" Kieri began, then chuckled. Any horse would follow Paks's paladin mount, he was sure. "Yes, if you have the time, that would be perfect. Let him get used to the place." He turned to Dorrin. "A few minutes for the jacks and we'll be off."

The King's Squires went before and behind as he and Dorrin walked briskly across the palace forecourt toward the great gates. The air was chill and damp, but not cold; he thought it felt like a light frost the night before, but nothing to harm the early spring that had followed him from the border.

Kieri looked around, trying to discern more of the layout than he had in the brief glimpses he'd had the afternoon and evening before. His childhood memories of the place did not help: then, all the walls had seemed the same height, and the child's interest had been on knee-high things. It looked smaller now—but he had been smaller. Was it as big as the palace in Tsaia? He thought not, but he hadn't seen all of it yet.

Outside the gates, they turned left. A broad cobbled street, a few muddy lumps of snow still piled along the margins, lay between them and a stretch of winter-tan grass just showing a little green between ranked trees far taller than the palace. It stretched away in the distance. "What's that?" he asked.

"The Royal Ride," one of the Squires answered. "It leads to the Royal Forest, if you like to hunt."

If he *liked* to hunt? Kieri felt a grin stretch his face. His steading had no real forest, being far north of the Honnorgat, only patches of woods his tenants needed for wood and nuts and rooting for their hogs. He had hunted a few times with Marrakai, who had extensive forests, and once with the crown prince in Tsaia's Royal Reserve. He looked at the long stretch of turf, imagined riding there, galloping flat-out . . . but he had work to do first.

"Most of the meat on the palace tables is game," another Squire said. "The Royal Huntsman provides it as needed. Venison, wild boar, and small game."

His mouth watered. He ignored it; he had just had breakfast. But the thought kept coming back. He had a forest . . . a palace *and* a forest. A forest full of game.

"I do not know your names," Kieri said. "I met only those who came to Tsaia with Paks. How many King's Squires are there?"

"In former days, as many as twenty, but with our king's illness, he needed fewer, and dismissed the rest. Six only stayed at the palace. We—my pardon, Sir King: I am Astil, and these others—" He paused; they spoke one by one, giving their names: Varñe, Berne, Panin. "We were called back to serve for a time."

"How are you chosen?" Kieri asked.

"The king chooses, from those with the skills, and who desire to serve. King's Squires must be Knights of Falk, sound in body, skilled in weaponcraft, hardy, and must speak elvish well enough to be understood and understand. Some Squires have been rangers, others come from the Royal Archers."

"Are any of you elves?"

"No, Sir King. Elves do not serve that way. More were half-elven in the old days, but not in the former king's reign."

Beyond the strip of trees that bordered the Royal Ride, stone and wood buildings bordered the road on both sides; the wall enclosing the palace grounds ended, he realized, with that strip of trees across from it. Now there were people, scurrying about on their errands; he recognized the same styles of clothes as he knew from Tsaia, plus some he did not know, odd shapes in hats, wider trousers tucked into shorter boots. When people saw the King's Squires, they stopped, turned to stare, and then bowed to him. Kieri smiled; he wondered if he should speak to them individually, but after that polite bow, they turned and went on the way they had been going.

"They won't bother you today," Astil said. "It is considered rude to approach the king unless it is a day declared for such a thing. No one expected you would be out today, so they are probably confused and certainly not ready to intrude."

"Thank you," Kieri said. The street they were on curved this way and that around the massive boles of tall trees; he noticed gaps in the rows of buildings, where other trees—singly and in groups—grew undisturbed. It made the city seem smaller, more like a market town; he had no way to gauge its real size when he could not see more of it at once.

"Down here," Dorrin said. Astil and Varñe turned left into a side street with a narrow walking lane cleared between melting snowbanks. It sloped gently downward; Kieri could see all the way over a low wall to open land beyond, not trees. He remembered coming out of the forest through which they'd ridden from the Tsaian border, to see across wide meadows and a stream the city sheltering under great trees. No city wall, he remembered; only the palace had a wall. How did they defend—?

"It's that inn—the Smoking Chimney," Dorrin said.

A wider space had been cleared of snow in front of the inn. A heavy door stood open, with a blanket hung to keep out a draft. From inside, Kieri heard familiar Tsaian accents.

"An' I don't doubt the captain and himself'll be here soon enough, so there'll be no wanderin' off nowhere to get into trouble. You'll stay here until we get orders otherwise—"

Varñe knocked on the door; they heard footsteps approaching. A man with a long apron tied around his waist poked his head out from around the blanket and said, "I'm sorry, we have no rooms—oh! Sir King—come in—" He held the blanket aside.

Before Kieri could adjust his sight, the drum of boots on the floor told him what was happening. Sure enough, the cohort stood in perfect order, tables and stools in the inn's common room shoved aside.

"Well," he said. Their faces struck him to the heart. How many years he had led these soldiers up and down from his steading to Aarenis and back. How many years they had followed his orders, fought his campaigns and won them. And now . . . now he must hand them over to someone else.

But not just yet. Now was the time to do what they expected, to reassure them—after a night alone in a strange city—that they were safe, that he still cared. He walked along the lines, as at any inspection. Boots polished, brass bright. He knew without asking they had all had breakfast, all made their beds—whatever their beds were, here.

The innkeeper looked calm; the servants—over there, watching—looked more curious than anything else.

The main thing, besides letting them see him, letting them absorb the differences—his gold and green clothes instead of maroon and white, the King's Squires—the main thing was to keep them busy, until he must send them away home.

"Are the horses here, Captain?" he asked Dorrin as he moved to the end of the front rank, with a little nod for the corporal.

"Yes, Sir King," she said. This time she did not stumble over it; he didn't expect she ever would again. "This inn had enough stable room; I chose it for that reason."

"Excellent," Kieri said. "After inspection—Jamis, you missed a spot on your left boot—" Jamis turned red. "You'll want to check your mounts and exercise them." He glanced at Astil. "Where could a troop ride, and not cause a problem? The Royal Ride?"

"Sir King, the Royal Ride certainly, but closer to this inn are the river meadows. I'm sure one of the stableboys could show you the way."

"It's up to you, Captain," Kieri said. "The horses will need light exercise today and some work every day the weather and ground conditions allow. We won't want to turn the river meadows into a quagmire. Innkeeper—" The man came forward, face alight. "You have met Captain Dorrin, I know, but let me be clear about your fees—"

"You don't need to worry, sir—sire," the man said, flushing. "It's an honor, it is, to have you in my inn—"

"I'm not worried," Kieri said with a smile. "But I know how much my soldiers eat. Be sure that you will be paid, and regularly, for their board, as long as they stay here. And if there should be any problems, do not hesitate to tell Captain Dorrin."

"I *was* scared at first, sire," the man said. "Them being foreign soldiers, and mercenaries at that. But they're less trouble than some merchants, I'd say. Why that'n—" He pointed at a man in the third rank; Kieri recognized Ulfin, a ten-year veteran. "—he already rehung a door on its hinges that a drunk had kicked out two nights agone and I'd had no time to fix. They can stay as long as you like, sire, so long as I can buy the food to feed them."

Dorrin stayed with the cohort to organize their exercise; Kieri and the King's Squires headed back to the palace. Kieri looked around;

from this direction, he could tell the city—town—stretched off to the east, though he could not tell where it ended. He would have to spend a day exploring, or find a map.

As they passed the trees bordering the Royal Ride, Berne stared off down the grassy stretch. "Someone's there!" he said. "Coming down the Ride."

Kieri looked. A red horse, its tall rider leading a gray he also recognized. "It's Paks," he said. "She's exercising my mount Banner . . ." He hardly recognized the feeling that tightened his chest. She was another he would lose, when she left—when Gird or the gods called her away on quest. He wished suddenly he could have met her family, her father. Did they even know what she had become? Would they ever?

She had spotted him now, and waved; he waved back. The red horse lifted into a trot; his gray surged forward, then slowed at a flick of the red's ear, keeping polite pace without crowding or rushing. As they neared, Paks smiled down at him. "I didn't think a short trot would hurt," she said.

"He looks good," Kieri said. Banner took a step forward, toward him, then stopped, eyeing the red horse.

"Here," Paks said, tossing him the lead rope. He caught it neatly, and Banner came to him, lowering a velvety muzzle to his hands. "He was no trouble—a bit stiff at first, as you suspected, but loosened up quickly."

"I'll take him back myself," Kieri said, "if you want to ride longer."

"You? Sir King, one of us can take—" But as Astil reached for the lead, the horse threw up his head and snorted.

"He's used to me," Kieri said. "And he's trained for war."

"A gray," murmured Panin, who had said least so far. "You know they're high-strung, Astil."

Kieri sensed some bias he needed to know. Stroking the horse's neck, he said, "Grays are high-strung?"

"Everyone knows that," Panin said. "They're air and water—unstable, changeable, capricious. Earth-fire horses, like that—" He nodded at Paks's horse, standing like a statue, ears forward and only little puffs of vapor coming from its nostrils in the cool air. "They're much steadier."

"Hmmm," Kieri said. Not the right time to question their prejudices, but he'd never seen grays as particularly flighty. Certainly not Banner. He had an impulse to show them how steady Banner could be, but even Banner might act up if he swung up bareback in this strange place. "Come along, Banner," he said instead, and walked on, the gray horse at his side.

"Do you need me, Sir King?" Paks asked.

"No," he said, hoping she meant only "for the present" but knowing he must say the same if she was leaving forever.

"Then I'll let this fellow stretch his legs," she said. Some signal passed from her to the red horse, or the horse took it on himself to disprove the Squires' beliefs, for he pranced in place, half reared, then wheeled, and bolted flat-out back up the Royal Ride, wet divots spraying up behind him.

"She rides like a horse nomad," Panin said.

"She rides like a paladin," Kieri said. "Horse nomads would worship her as the Windsteed's bride, if they saw her on that horse."

"Sir King—Sir King—!" A groom hurried from the opening of the mews, to the left as they entered the palace gate. "I can take him, Sir King—you need not—"

"Just show me where he's stabled," Kieri said. "His name's Banner— I don't think I told anyone when we arrived."

"Sir—down here, then, if you will." The row of stalls seemed to be mostly empty, but the stall the groom led him to was amply large, clean, freshly laid with deep straw. Kieri stopped the horse outside.

"He's been exercised in the Royal Ride, and it's wet—you'll want to check his hooves, make sure he's thrown all the mudballs out."

"Of course, Sir King. Jemi—come hold this horse—" A younger man, hardly more than a boy, came out of a stall down the row and hurried to take the lead.

Kieri gave the horse a last pat and turned away.

CHAPTER EIGHT

B ack in the dining room, he found Sier Galvary and a younger man with stacks of records, scrolls, and books.

"You'll want more than this, I'm sure, Sir King," said Sier Galvary. "I brought the year-roll for last year, the final accounting to the Council upon the former king's death, and a list of the lands held by human Siers—their extent and their principal products. Most of our trade is in craftwork of one kind or another, but we do export some raw materials." He turned to the younger man with him. "And this is Egil, who despite his youth has earned his place as senior auditor of accounts."

"Excellent," Kieri said. "Let's get to it, then."

"The royal treasury is supported by taxes, like most," Galvary said. "Our arrangement with the elves limits the lands humans can farm or clear; land rights do not come from the Crown, as they do in Tsaia, and elves must approve any transfer of land by purchase."

"What about inheritance?"

"Firstborn, male or female, inherits the land—the elves have not interfered save when a firstborn was obviously incompetent, and then only to approve the transfer to someone else in the same family. Near as we can tell, them being so long-lived, if not immortal, they make alliances with families and not individuals."

"And the other children? Or do most people have only one or two children?"

"Usually that, Sir King—well, not just one or two, but not many, because the land grants will not support a multitude and the elves demand that land be well managed. They removed one family for failure to do that . . . a long time back, that was."

"So . . . does the Crown take taxes on the basis of landownership or production? Or do the elves?"

"Elves take no land-rent; their restrictions on land use, they say, are sufficient impediment to short-lived human ambition."

Kieri glanced up; was Galvary being funny? Or was that serious dislike of elves? "And the Crown?"

"Landholders owe the Crown, in kind or in coin, a portion of their production. Crafters, as well. Our taxes are not high, compared to what I know of Tsaia's system, but neither do we have the expense of a large standing army. The forest rangers watch the borders and observe the taig." He opened the first of the rolls on the table. "Here— this is last year's accounting."

The script looked different from Tsaia's, though Kieri could read it after a moment. Wheat, oats, barley, straw, hay, tree-fruit and bush-fruit, staves and timber, each specified by the kind of tree . . . "We get all this in kind?"

"The Crown does, yes. It does not all come here. The Crown maintains granges—not like Girdish granges of course—stores of food and supplies in each *faran*, each district or shire I suppose you'd call it, for emergencies. Rangers draw supplies there, but also if there's a flood, fire, or other disaster, relief supplies are at hand. What comes here supplies the palace, of course, though the Crown also has a large orchard and fields nearby."

"That makes sense," Kieri said. "Could the palace needs be met from those resources?"

"Not entirely. There's a large staff, and their families; as well, the palace share serves as the reserve for Chaya. Eight years ago, we had a very bad winter, much harsher than usual, and the palace stores meant no one in the city went hungry."

"That's good," Kieri said. He stared at the figures, trying to absorb it all. Accounting for the Company, or his own land, he was used to; this must be somewhat the same, but he could not fit his mind around Lyonya yet. He had not seen a map of it since his days in Falk's Hall, training with the Knights of Falk. "Do you have a map of the land here?"

"Yes, sire, of course." Another roll opened.

Kieri stared at it. He had forgotten exactly where the border with Prealíth was . . . how far from Chaya to the mountains. Each human domain had been marked out carefully: Belvarin, Galvary, Hammarrin, Tolmaric, Carvarsin . . . Halveric. Aliam's place . . . he put his finger on it. "This is Aliam Halveric's?"

"It belongs to the Halveric family—the Sier prefers to live here, in Chaya, and has granted his brother leave to stay at Halveric Steading and manage it for him."

Kieri felt his brows rise. He'd thought Aliam owned that land, that house, where he himself had found refuge and where he had grown from a terrified, starveling boy into a man. He could not imagine any lady there but Estil.

He traced the border with Tsaia with his finger, then the trade roads marked along the river, along the foot of the Dwarfmounts. He saw no markings that looked like fortified holds. Aliam had a wall, but Chaya itself did not. "How much trouble has there been along the Tsaian border?"

"Not a great deal, except where it borders Verrakai's land," Galvary said. "The Duke has not attempted invasion, but people come from there and poach in the forest or raid farms for food. Konhalt, too—"

"Konhalt's under Verrakai control," Kieri said. "Not fond of me, either of them, though I think Verrakai will be busy enough explaining to the Council in Vérella why he ordered his people to attack the Tsaian Royal Guard to keep him from causing trouble here."

"We shall hope so," Galvary said, in a tone that suggested disbelief. "In Tsaia all you dukes had your own armies, didn't you?"

"Not exactly," Kieri said. "We all owed troops to the Crown, in case of need; some maintained them at home, and some contributed money to maintain an equivalent number under Crown control."

"But *you* had—"

"I had troops, yes. A condition of my grant of land: as a marcher lord, I had a duty to protect the northern and eastern borders from all enemies—mostly Pargun, but also any invasion of horse nomads from the north. They never bothered us; we had far more trouble with orcs under Achrya's guidance . . ."

"And you brought troops with you . . ." Egil spoke for the first time, sounding nervous.

"Only as an escort," Kieri said. "If I had not, I'd have died on the way."

"Ah. Then . . . they will go back to Tsaia? Or . . . were you going to keep them here, as your personal troops?" Galvary asked.

"I had not considered that; they will go back, I assume, to join the others, though . . . it has all been so fast . . . I do not know what will happen to that land, or those people . . ."

"Surely Tsaia will let you keep it—"

"I doubt that. And even if they do, how could I govern both there and here? And yet—"

"They are your people," Galvary said, nodding.

"Yes. As you are my people now, though I do not yet know you." Kieri smiled at Galvary. "I must make you first in my heart, I know that. But it is—it will be—difficult for a while. For me as well as for them. Some of them I have known for thirty years."

"Are you sorry?" said Egil.

"Sorry? To find out at last who I am, that I had a loving family, that I belong somewhere? Not at all. I pray that I become such a king as you will not be sorry to have."

A moment's silence; Kieri sensed that something had changed between them, but he was not sure what.

"I—I meant having to give up your friends, having to come to a strange place—and not having known all along." Egil darted a glance at Galvary, who was glaring at him.

Kieri looked at Egil, thinking how young he seemed. "I regret my own mistakes, but to regret the things that made me what I am . . . that would be ungrateful to those who did so much for me—and to those powers that perhaps knew when it was best for me to come back. Would you quarrel with the gods' will? I wouldn't." He turned back to the map. "Now—what are these lines here?"

"The approximate boundary of the Ladysforest in normal times," Galvary said briskly. "As you may know, it expands and contracts at the will of the Lady, but this is the boundary fixed on our maps, beyond which humans must ask permission to enter. No human dwelling or clearing may extend past it, though strayed livestock are not harmed and in times of dearth, the elves have granted permission to gather firewood and hunt."

Kieri estimated the extent as perhaps a third of the kingdom that might otherwise, as in Tsaia, have been populated, but also extending up the foothills of the Dwarfmounts.

After a break for lunch, they finally worked their way to the present financial status of Lyonya.

"I'm used to Tsaian crowns and Guild League nitis and natas," Kieri said. "What does this—" He pointed to the sums at the bottoms of three columns. "—mean in those terms?"

"About twice as much in Tsaian gold crowns," Egil said, a little smugly. "Our coins are marked with tree and leaf: those are trees."

Kieri felt his brows rising. He had heard Lyonya spoken of as a backward, secretive land, poor because "elves won't let humans get rich," but he knew the Tsaian treasury had no more than this, and often less.

"We are not bankrupt, at least," Galvary said. Again that hint of a smile.

"And has the balance changed much, year to year?"

"There has been a slow trend downward, over the past ten years," Egil said. "Not large, but troubling. The late king's illness made necessary some expenses here at the palace . . . unavoidable, of course. There have been crop failures, some difficulties with bands of robbers coming over the Tsaian border, requiring more patrols, more rangers. The Council has not been concerned." He glanced at Sier Galvary, a look almost rebellious.

"Ten years . . ." Kieri said. "That's a long time for a downward trend."

"But we have quite enough for a coronation celebration," Galvary said. "If it is not too extravagant."

Kieri let that stand, ridiculous as it was when he had just seen the figures. Still, more than the total mattered. "Let's look at the previous years," Kieri said. "Has the income fallen, or the expense grown?"

"A little of both. Crop yields have dropped a little, and prices for our usual exports are down, too."

"Hmm. You have a Merchants' Guild?"

"In Chaya, yes."

"And their representative to the Council would be—"

"Oh, they're not on the Council."

"Not at all?"

"Er . . . no. Did you . . . are they . . . in Tsaia?"

"The Merchants' Guild has a representative, not much power, but someone there to know what's going on. In Aarenis, the Merchants' Guild runs the Guild League cities."

"The elves don't think much of merchants . . ."

Kieri wondered if that was true. He'd already encountered beliefs about elves that didn't match his knowledge of them.

"Merchants bring change; they make people greedy," Egil added. "Elves prefer stability."

"Stagnation," muttered Galvary.

"I thought people were greedy enough by themselves," Kieri said. At Egil's shocked expression, he went on. "Do not your people commonly want more than they have?"

"What could they want that they do not have?" Egil asked.

"You've already mentioned that our human subjects wanted more land, more access to forest resources," Kieri said.

Brows furrowed; clearly they had not made this connection before.

"In my experience," Kieri said, "most want more than they have, even if they call themselves content. And some resources do not grow of themselves. When I got my grant of land in northern Tsaia and people applied for permission to live there, I soon learned that what had seemed abundant resources for a few were not so abundant when the population grew. I, like the elves, had to institute rules about how much wood could be cut, and so on."

"Perhaps it was your elven half . . ." Galvary's words slowed and stopped as Kieri looked at him.

"Come now," Kieri said. "You must know—your wives do, if you do not—that if you have only one barrel of meal in the pantry, you cannot feed a hundred with it. And how many teams of plough must you have for that barrel of meal?"

"Well, but . . . if there were more land . . ."

"Land does not grow wider because you wish it," Kieri said. "We have neighbors: would you have us invade them, to get more land? When Tsaia runs short, do you not watch our borders here?"

More furrowed brows. "Yes . . ."

"Have you never told a son or daughter to trim their desires to the purse you give them?"

"Of course . . ."

"Well, then. Lyonya is the size it is; our human share of it is the size it is; we must make the best of it. Having merchants on the Council will help—they know foreign markets better than anyone here, I daresay, and can advise us on the most advantageous types of trade—"

"But they make money off us—"

Kieri sighed, but silently. "We make money off of trade and they carry the goods—they must live, just as we do."

Yet again, the furrowed brows. Finally Egil said, "I have heard—from a wine importer—that one reason we are not exporting so much jewelry is that our craftsmen now live and work in Tsaia and even Aarenis."

"Exactly the sort of thing I meant," Kieri said. "If we cannot support them at home, they must move elsewhere, and if they move elsewhere, their work profits us less."

"Well . . ." Galvary scrubbed his hands over his face, as if trying to put on a new skin. "I will not oppose including a merchant or two on the Council. If it means restoring the treasury . . ."

Kieri wondered if they would accept the next step. Might as well try . . . "It is not so much the size of our treasury as what circulates among our people. Yes, the royal treasury must have reserves for emergencies, but the wealth of a kingdom lies in more than a heap of gold." At their doubtful expressions, he tried another tack. "The food in your pantry does you no good if you never eat it."

"The elves said something like that, the last time I spoke to one of them about it," Galvary said. "It didn't make sense to me, though."

"Well, first things first," Kieri said. "I want to see merchants represented on the Council by midsummer. I'd like a list of those you consider suitable in ten days. I will then meet them and interview them."

"So soon? I mean—yes, Sir King, but—there is still your coronation to plan."

"And plenty of help to plan it," Kieri said. "If you will give the Council a limit to spend, I believe Sier Halveric can take it from there—"

Galvary looked shocked, but nodded. Kieri stretched and glanced around. Outside the light was fading—near time for dinner, surely.

"Thank you, Sier Galvary, and Egil," he said. "We can go deeper into this tomorrow, but now—I would like to explore more of the palace grounds while there is still light."

"Of course, Sir King," they both said, looking relieved.

In the low slanting light of evening, Kieri asked Astil how to find the garden he remembered. "It had roses," he said.

"Yes, Sir King! I know the one. It's through here—"

Kieri came out into the evening sky, pale blue with high wisps of gold. In the silence, he could hear the sound of water trickling somewhere. Stone-flagged paths curved among thorny bushes, some pruned low and some as high as his head. A few tiny leaves showed purple-red; most of the leaf buds looked pinkish.

"By your coronation, the early flowers will have opened," Astil said. "It is not all roses here; you will see. It is said the elf queen planted it."

"My mother," Kieri said. He had a moment's clear memory: the smell of roses and the sound of her laugh.

After dinner that evening, Kieri asked Dorrin and Paks to look at the maps with him.

"What do you see?" he asked.

Dorrin ran her finger around the line of the border. "Where are the defenses? I see no indication of fortresses."

"Rangers," Paks said. "I served with them, as you know. They're effective on the Tsaian side, at least."

"Effective against brigands and poachers," Kieri said. "Paks, you've seen them—how would they do against a few cohorts of infantry—mine or Halveric's?"

"In pitched battle—their longbows have more range than you'd think. But they don't fight in formation at all, as far as I know. On open ground, the cohorts would win, but rangers would hide in the forest and it would be hard to keep a camp safe from them."

"And if an attacker cut down or burned the forest? How many are there, anyway?"

"I don't know," Paks said. "They work in small groups—even singly sometimes—moving every few days."

"Someone will know," Dorrin said. "Cutting down the forest—that would be a task. I wouldn't want to try it, not unless I had more than two or three cohorts. Would the elves intervene, do you think?"

"I'm not sure," Kieri said. "I saw what you saw—the kingdom's practically unguarded—there may be elven magery I don't know about, but as it is . . . with Verrakai and Konhalt on the west, and Pargun and Kostandan on the north, it's not safe. The palace walls are for privacy, not defense. The Council, though, acts as if having even one cohort of real soldiers here means I want war. And you, Paks, told me the elves feared me because I had been a soldier and might bring war upon them." He stared at the map. "I swear to you, to the gods themselves, though I have fought in one war after another, I do not want it. And yet the first duty of a king is to protect his realm. And this—" He laid his heart-hand on the map, thumb on the Tsaian border, small finger on Prealíth. "This is not safe. Not yet. But I will make it so."

Paks cocked her head. "Sir King, I understand you, but consider— these are as sheep who do not yet know you as their shepherd. If you push them too fast toward the sheepfold, they may break and run in panic, as sheep do. Go gently with them."

He glanced at Dorrin, who nodded. "With respect, I would say the same. You have commanded veteran soldiers before, used to both danger and taking orders; these are not, and will flinch away from roughness."

"I hear you," Kieri said. "And yet I worry."

That night, only his second in Chaya, Garris—oldest of the King's Squires—and Lieth stood beside his door when he came to his chambers.

"So you pulled night guard, Garris? Don't they respect your gray hairs?"

Garris grinned. "They think you're safe enough at night, Kier—Sir King. And Lieth's young; she stays awake half the night anyway, if I should doze off. What time will you wake? I hear you surprised them this morning . . . I slept until almost noon."

"Cock-crow," Kieri said. "And you slept late back at Aliam's; don't blame that on age."

Garris laughed. "So I did, and many's the morning you tumbled me out of my bunk in the squires' room and then shoved my head under a pump. I hope you won't do that now you're king."

Kieri clapped him on the shoulder and Garris opened the door for him. In his chamber, he found the bed already turned back, with the handle of a warming pan sticking out. He pulled it from between the sheets and shook the coals into the fireplace. Sleep came slowly; his mind raced with questions and ideas.

He woke in the dark again, but this time he knew exactly how to find the fire and light his own candles. He felt stiff; he needed the exercise that had always started his day. Surely they had a salle somewhere . . . or, if not, he could practice in the forecourt. He pulled on trousers he'd left on a chair, and fumbled at the paneling to find the touchlock that would open to reveal his clothes.

The chamber door opened and Garris looked in. "Aha! I thought I heard you stirring. What can I do for you?"

"I need a shirt," Kieri said. "Something I can get dirty, not one of these elegant kingly ones."

Garris touched a panel and it slid aside. "It's that ivy leaf," he said, pointing it out. "And what are you planning to do, dig in the garden?"

"Loosen my muscles," Kieri said. "Is there a salle?"

Garris grinned. "Is there a salle? You've never seen anything like it, Kier—Sir King."

"Quit that," Kieri said, pulling on one of his old shirts. "I know you have to be formal some of the time, but I told you in Vérella—call me Kieri, at least when we're alone—and where is Lieth, by the way?" He unrolled a pair of socks and put them on, then pulled on his boots.

"I sent her to the kitchen to fetch sib."

"So—where is this miraculous salle?"

"Kieri—can't you wait until the sib comes?"

"I could—but I'd rather not." He went to the bed and lifted down the great sword. As always, the jewel flashed as he touched it.

"Well, then. I'll take you."

As they came into the passage, they met Lieth, carrying a tray with a steaming pot and several mugs. "Where are you going?" she asked.

"To the salle," Garris said. "Our king is not only awake, he's ready to poke holes in us."

"Sir King—?"

"Lieth, it is my habit: swords before breakfast. I would like to do that here, as well. I understand this is a change for you—"

"It is no matter, Sir King," Lieth said. "Do you want sib before, or should I bring it—?"

"Let's each have a mug," Kieri said.

She set the tray on a table in the passage and poured; Kieri noticed she took only a half cup, but Garris drank a full one. Then they walked together down the passage, down stairs to the main level, back the length of the main passage there, right into a narrower passage that turned sharply twice, to an outside door that opened onto a small paved court. Facing them was another wall, with a taller door; Garris opened it wide and gestured Kieri in.

He sensed a large empty space—dark at first, but slowly brightening, the pale pearly glow he associated with elf-light. Nearest the door, a smooth wooden floor covered perhaps a quarter of the length. Beyond was stone—uneven, like an old paved street—and beyond that more stone, even rougher.

"Have you ever seen one like this?" Garris asked.

"No, but it's what I always wanted," Kieri said. "A salle for serious fighters." He looked around. To the heart-hand side of the door stood a weapons-rack, beautifully carved.

"The King's Stand," Garris said. "You're the only one can use that."

"Practice blades?" Kieri asked, hanging his sword on the stand.

"Here," Lieth said, opening a chest full of wooden blades. "And bandas." Kieri put on a banda and took one of the wooden blades.

"So—shall we go a round?" Kieri asked Garris.

"Lieth will stand guard," Garris said. "One of us always does, when the king practices." She took up a position in the doorway, sword drawn, while Garris took one of the wooden swords and faced Kieri.

They had scarcely exchanged five blows of a standard training sequence when a clatter of boots and an angry voice brought them to a hold.

"Who do you think you are, coming to the salle without an armsmaster present! It's not your time to spar, Squires! You'll wake the king with this racket!"

"No," Kieri said, coming to the door. "They will not wake the king, for the king was already awake." He smiled down at the wiry little man who now gaped up at him.

"Sir . . . King."

"Yes," Kieri said. "And you must be an armsmaster."

"Carlion, my lord king. Senior armsmaster of the Royal Salle.

I wasn't—I didn't expect—it's just, Sir King, the young ones come sometimes when they shouldn't, and there's been accidents—"

"I'm not angry," Kieri said. "And I should, in courtesy, have spoken to you first. But I am used to training early in the morning—before affairs of the day take over. I would like to continue that training, under your guidance."

"My guidance—" Carlion looked sharply at Kieri. "Sir King, you have been a soldier; you are not ignorant of arms, but I do not know what guidance you think I can give."

"Let us see," Kieri said. "How would you test anyone who first came into your salle?"

Carlion cocked his head. "Is that waster near the weight you're used to?"

"Close enough," Kieri said.

"Then you and Garris spar. Garris's skills I know. Garris, do you attack, and let the king respond."

Garris attacked; Kieri fended him off easily, making only parries to see what Carlion would say.

"Sir King, you are slacking and that is a bad habit. Make your attacks as you would—"

Kieri did, and quickly penetrated Garris's guard, once, twice, three times.

"Hold," Carlion said. "I see I must test you myself; you are beyond Garris."

"He always was," Garris said. "We were squires together at Aliam Halveric's."

"Ah," Carlion said. "And he has fought often, and you have not."

Carlion, Kieri found, was no easy opponent. Wiry and fast, his shorter stature made low attacks easy for him, but he had the ability to strike high as well. Kieri was soon drenched in sweat, despite the morning chill, as was Carlion. They paused for breath again, and Carlion nodded. "You, Sir King, are ready—and more, I would think—to practice in the middle range. I warn you, some stones there will tip. At the far end, in the roughs—well, come see, while you catch your breath."

Great blocks of stone, loose rocks here and there—Kieri wanted to try it then and there, but enough light showed in the windows to make it clear he must get to breakfast and the meeting he had called.

"Thank you, Armsmaster," he said. "I will come again."

"Come every morning, if you like," Carlion said. "I rise early my-self."

Back in his own chambers, Kieri found his bath waiting, and went down to breakfast with his mind full of what he needed to accomplish that day: the mourning ceremony for the old king—and he had to find out the man's name!—making sure Galvary had an estimate for Halveric, so Halveric could begin planning the coronation, finding out who could help him with Lyonyan laws and customs—and at some point he would have to broach the topic he knew they would not want: that of security, the need for a defensive force. Could he wait until his coronation? Would the Pargunese, or the Verrakai?

The Council meeting that morning raised new concerns. His nobles were not stupid or lazy, but under a weak king they had lacked effective guidance, and wasted their energy competing among themselves for power and influence. They had no long-range plan; they expected matters to go on as they had, without requiring any intervention from them.

Only a glass later, they fell to quarreling over something that happened before he arrived, when someone's cattle had encroached on someone else's pastureland and heifers had been tupped by the wrong bull.

"Siers!" he said. The room fell silent. "Your quarrel is ill-timed; that happened years ago, and we have immediate matters. I will hear no more of that quarrel, is that clear?"

Three of them reddened, but bowed from their seats, and the murmur of "Yes, Sir King" included their voices.

"Good. We have immediate concerns: first is the mourning ceremony. How soon can it be arranged, Sier Belvarin?"

"Five days, Sir King. All is in readiness except the ritual boughs; they should arrive day after tomorrow, and then a day to trim them."

"Then on that day, I will ask Council members to attend me, and the day before I will need advice on the ceremony itself, never having seen one."

"I am at your service," Sier Belvarin said. "That should take no more than two turns of the glass."

"Sier Galvary?" Kieri said. "The budget for the coronation?"

"I handed the total in to Sier Halveric this morning," Sier Galvary said.

"And I have begun," Sier Halveric said. "Beginning with the invitations to distant personages."

"What foreign guests should we expect?" Kieri asked.

"At the coronation of your predecessor Prealíth sent a representative; they should certainly be invited. The court of Tsaia sent a member of the royal family; they too should be invited. Kostandan sent a gift by their ambassador; I would expect the same. Pargun sent a member of the royal family; it . . . did not turn out well."

"Oh?" Kieri raised his brows.

"His speech at the feast . . . was belligerent. He pointed out how many troops Pargun maintained, and claimed it was only by his father's forbearance that we were suffered to exist a separate realm and that might not last. To put it plainly, he got drunk and made a fool of himself, and the Pargunese ambassador chose to believe it was our fault. Led the poor lad astray, he said, or poisoned him with elvish wine." Halveric grimaced. "It was perfectly good brandy from Aarenis, not elvish."

"That sounds right for the Pargunese," Kieri said. "But after they attacked me on the way here, I'd sooner invite a pack of wolves. Surely they won't expect an invitation."

"Who knows how they think?" Halveric said. "But no, we need not. I will have more details for you, Sir King, after the mourning service—if you do not object."

"No," Kieri said. "But I do have an assignment that will not take long, and will set us on the way of thinking into the future, the unknown, as elves do—though not quite that far." He allowed himself a chuckle; the two elves said nothing but looked pained. "Let us consider it in manageable numbers. A hand of years hence . . . then two hands, then four, then ten. As a start, you will each write three things you want to see accomplished for the realm within a hand of years. Only three—there will be more."

His own list, already prepared, lay before him. In a few minutes they had completed their task. "Now read them," Kieri said. One by one, they read their lists. All but one started with "The king marries and begets an heir" and none contained what was at the head of his own list, "Peace." When they had finished, he read his own list, continuing to ten hands of years. They looked stunned.

"Sier Halveric, you are the only one who did not list my marriage and getting an heir at the top of your list. Why?"

"You promised to marry and give us an heir, Sir King. I trust you." Halveric sounded smug.

"I can understand," Kieri said, looking at the others, "after what you have been through, your intense interest in this. Indeed, providing you with an heir *is* my duty, and it is important to the realm. Yet remember, when the king left you no heir, the gods provided. I don't intend to trouble them again, but you should not fear unduly. Your goals are worthy; what matters to you matters to me. But what matters to me must also matter to you . . . and assuring peace is more important even than assuring an heir."

"We *are* peaceful," Sier Belvarin said, looking puzzled. "I am glad you want to remain so, but—"

"It is the peace of a lamb who does not see the wolf crouched at the forest edge," Kieri said. Belvarin stiffened. "It is not the peace I want for this land, and it is not the peace you should want."

"Peace is peace," Sier Carvarsin said, glowering. "We have not had a war here for generations; we are no threat to our neighbors, so they have no reason to attack us."

"And no reason not to," Kieri said. Now all of them looked shocked. "Think you: If the Pargunese will come to Tsaia to attack me, as they did on my way here, why will they not attack here?"

"They never have," Sier Belvarin said. One of the elves stirred.

"Amrothlin?" Kieri said to him. "Is that your memory?"

"Long ago in human time," the elf said, "when first the Seafolk came up the river in their pointed ships, they would have settled on this side. We did not permit it, for we had seen how they dealt with the trees, as if trees existed only to make more ships. They were easily frightened, and kept to the north side of the river after that."

"How did you frighten them?" Kieri asked.

The other elf looked down his nose for a moment. "The taig, Sir King, has many powers of which you are as yet unaware, but as I am to be your tutor in such things—" Kieri stared; he had not expected that. "—I will show you when it is time. That is many lessons hence."

"Does that mean elves will defend the land against the Pargunese, if they attack?" Kieri asked.

"We defend the Ladysforest," Amrothlin said. "Since the Compact, that is all we are bound to do. It is up to the king to protect the people. Though, as you know, we may choose to aid the king."

"Let us hope the Pargunese do not know that," Kieri said.

CHAPTER NINE

In the days before the mourning ceremony, Kieri's daily schedule acquired some stability. Waking at dawn or before, a session in the salle with his Squires and Armsmaster Carlion, breakfast, a meeting with the Council, and then a longer session with one Council member after another. In the afternoon he visited his cohort and took exercise, then met again with his advisers. His elven relatives insisted they needed at least two hours a day for his schooling in matters elven, but the first session with Orlith consisted of sitting in silence as he tried—with little success he was sure—to open himself fully to the taig.

On the day before the mourning ceremony, Sier Belvarin came to instruct him in the rites, bringing with him two other Siers and the Seneschal.

"The ceremony's . . . different . . . than it is in Tsaia," Belvarin said.

Kieri waited out the glances, the shifting of hands on the table.

"You see," one of them said, with a quick glance at the others, "we bury them."

"Yes . . ." That didn't sound different.

"It's—you do know the Lady of Peace?"

"Of course," Kieri said. Did they think because he had been a soldier he would not know of Alyanya?

"It's the land." Another long pause, another set of looks exchanged. "Well, we're old in the land here, you see. Before the magelords came,

there were people here. Humans. In Tsaia, too, but the magelords conquered them. Here, we have the old ways."

The old ways. Kieri had read, with some scorn, the Girdish beliefs
about their origins before the magelords came. All peaceful farmers
and herders, but they had shed blood to thank Alyanya for the gift of
fertility . . . was that what this was about?

"You blood the blade before setting iron to the soil?"

A look of relief from all of them. "Exactly. You know this?" Belvarin asked.

"Well, yes. I thought everyone knew that. I know some of my—
my former—landholders did that before ploughing or digging. We
blooded our blades at the Spring Evener."

"So you see, then, that when someone dies, they go to the land, to
return to Alyanya the gifts of flesh she gave them in life. They feed
the land, so the land will feed others. That's the first ceremony, returning to Alyanya what she gave, fruit for fruit. And then, when the
time has passed, they rise again, clean bone—"

A distant memory pricked. Before Aliam raised him to squire, he
had been sent up in the attics to look for holes in the roof after a
windstorm—there'd been broken slates in the courtyard—and as he
looked around in the dim light he'd seen a gruesome face leering at
him. He'd managed not to scream, but he'd fled down the ladder,
shaking, only to have Estil tell him it was only a skull. Only.

"You dig them up?"

"Yes. And that's the greater ceremony, raising the bones and carrying them to the memory-hall."

Kieri felt the small hairs rising on the back of his neck, as if they
were tiny bones themselves. "Memory-hall?" he said, keeping his
voice as level as he could.

"Every village had one, once," Belvarin said. "It would be in the
appropriate place, and the elders' skulls were mounted to the center
posts—but we don't do that anymore. After the elves came north and
made a pact with our people and those of our people who came from
Tsaia when the magelords invaded—the old people, this is—the customs changed."

"I had forgotten the skulls," Kieri said. "In the attic at the
Halverics'—"

"A fine family. Very traditional. So you see, my lord king, when the time is come, your part in the ceremony of recovering King Sarnion's bones and placing them in the palace hall of memory will be longer than this one. It is a celebration: the Lady has accepted the gift, the land has been renewed."

"I see. And when will this be?" Kieri had no idea how long it took for flesh to peel from bone in the earth.

"Not this fall harvest or the next but the one after that: the Fall Evener."

Since the old king's body was already in the ground, the formal memorial in which Kieri took part consisted of a short procession in which Kieri carried boughs of the important trees, and laid them in a certain order on the grave. He did not recognize the boughs, leafless as they were, but trusted Belvarin would have made sure which was which. It did not seem enough, for a king's recognition of his predecessor, but it was what tradition required.

Afterward, the Seneschal led Kieri to the palace ossuary. "It's a bit different here, because it's the royal residence, you see. In a private home, there's just the skulls in the attic, and maybe a bone-house somewhere. But here, it's a kingdom's history. All except the skull of King Darien, the first king, of course, because that was mortared into the top tower."

The ossuary lay underground. Kieri had no idea what to expect, but did not expect to be impressed by mere bones. He'd seen enough of them on battlefields, especially that last year in Aarenis, when every field sprouted bones instead of grain.

The Seneschal unlocked a brass-bound wooden door. Above it Kieri saw fresh green branches laid across wooden pegs. "This one's the ancestors' home and that other one—" He jerked his head toward another similar door. "—is the treasury." The treasury door had no green branches over it. "Now, this line of green stone, my lord, this is for respect. We go barefoot here." He kicked off his palace slippers, revealing knobbly old man's feet, blue-veined, and looked at Kieri's boots. The look conveyed a command, but he said nothing. Beside the door was a bench; the Seneschal waited until Kieri sat on it, and then knelt to help him pull off his boots and socks. Kieri's bare feet looked incongruous to him, under the formal robes he wore, but the stone felt warm and smooth, almost comforting.

When the Seneschal pulled the door open, Kieri expected a musty smell, familiar from cellars and barrows, part earth and stone enclosed, part bone. Instead the air had the freshness of spring outside. He'd expected a dim chamber filled with dusty old bones, cream, white, yellow-brown, gray. Instead, the ossuary blazed with color against whitewashed walls. Kieri stared. Human bones didn't come in those colors—colors as bright as fresh-dyed yarn, as flowers, scarlet, green, blue, yellow. Here and there light glinted from other things— from curves of metal, copper and bronze and gold and silver. And on every skeleton, fresh green leaves, one between the teeth, one across each eyehole, one on either side, where ears might have been. They looked as if they'd been picked that very morning.

"What—?" Kieri choked back all he was tempted to say and instead said, "I've never seen anything like this."

"No, you wouldn't have," the Seneschal said, obviously pleased at the surprise he'd arranged. "This is the old way, you see. Remembrance is a form of honor, so nothing should be forgotten that is honorable to a king or queen. In the old days, before the magelords came, it was mostly simple things—this one was good with sheep, that one was a good cook. Simple dyes and a little knife-work made that clear. But kings, my lord, as you know, have more complicated lives, and so their bones must hold more . . . the first few kings, indeed, were scarce honored more than their people; their bones hold simpler stories and the old-fashioned decoration. You'll see that in a moment. It was two or three generations before a king thought to find a bone-artist while he still lived, and explain what he wanted. But here's your father, you'll want to see him."

Kieri did, and did not. The father he barely remembered, the bearded man who had picked him up and swung him about . . . that was a live man, however brief his memory. Bones meant death, meant he would never see his father in the flesh again. But it was tradition, and he followed the Seneschal farther into the ossuary.

"Here he is," the Seneschal said.

The bones were neither fresh nor ancient, each set neatly as near to its place in life as possible, and each painted in brilliant colors, scribbled with thin black lines that Kieri now realized were script.

His father. His father's bones. Kieri stared at the skeleton, wondering what he was supposed to feel. The colors made him uneasy: white bones, clean bones, were natural things, but these colors, this writing, seemed . . . alien.

"You may not be familiar with the script used," the Seneschal said. "It is very old. I can translate for you." Without waiting for Kieri's word, he bent over the pelvis. "This, right here, tells of your birth. See, the background color is that used for sons, and it gives your birthdate, your mother's name—"

Kieri shivered. He could read the script now, as he could not a few moments before; the words flowed through his mind in a voice he knew instantly was his father's.

For on this day my son Falkieri was born, and we rejoice in his strength and pray all the gods for his long life, health, and joy.

"I can read it," Kieri said, fighting the lump in his throat. He could read all of it, the writing voicing itself, the colors and script together making pictures as well as words, telling the story of his father's life. Not far from his own birth was the birth of his sister. Not far from that, the anguish his father felt when his wife—Kieri's mother—and Kieri disappeared, when word came back of her certain death, and his presumed. His father had grieved for years, pouring all his affection onto the sister . . . had died of grief, in the end.

Tears rolled down Kieri's cheeks, through his beard. He could feel them, but he could not stop them; he did not try. His father . . . what would his father have thought of the man he'd become? He could be glad his father did not know what had happened to him, those bitter years of captivity; he wished his father could have known how his son was saved by a family he loved—his friends. He felt now, bone to bone, that human kinship; he knew his father's favorite flavors, colors, pursuits, as if they were his own.

More than the elven sword, more than the Council's acclamation, bound him here now. This was the human half of him, bone and blood, not song and immortality and the uncertain bounds of the elvenhome kingdom where his grandmother ruled. This was truly home, not just a childhood memory, but the place his bones knew, and where his bones would lie.

At last he turned from his father's skeleton. "My sister?"

"Over here, on the women's side."

Laid with her were the few fragile bones of her child born dead.

She had been taller than their father, as he was; her skull bore the shape of her elven blood, and her pelvis had not yet broadened as much as it might have, had she lived longer. The writing on her bones included the stories she'd been told about him, about the older brother who had disappeared, about her sense of duty, born of his loss. She had resented it sometimes; she had once or twice blamed him for their mother's death, since that journey had been for him, but she had transferred that blame to their grandmother, and that—no forcing by a nervous Council—was the real reason for her early marriage, her decision to bear a child when the Lady advised against it. It had not been her brother's fault, she had decided, but their grandmother's, for insisting that the boy must come to the elfane taig to have the sword pledged to him and his own powers wakened.

Yet she had been, within her understanding, a good queen: loving, diligent, worthy of all the honor heaped on her. He remembered her now, her voice coming to him and wakening all the old memories of her birth, her baby face, her first struggling steps. He had been told he must care for her, protect her, that his status as elder brother meant responsibility, not power . . . and she had died because he was not there.

He could not have been there. Tangled in that he felt all that had happened over again, including Aliam's decision not to tell anyone he might be the prince. He did not blame Aliam . . . but was that true? Had he not, for an instant, blamed Aliam? He had, just as his sister had blamed him . . . but fifty-odd years of experience refused to lay that guilt on the man. *We are not gods, to know all. We do the best we can.* Aliam had said that, when someone made a mistake and Kieri had laid blame. *He could not have known. You would not have known.* His sister had not known. She had been willing to die for her kingdom, but she need not have died, and the kingdom would have prospered more if she had not.

He would not blame her. He would not blame Aliam. He would not blame the Council that had pressured her, or their grandmother, who had told their mother to bring him.

When he was ready to leave that chamber, the Seneschal offered a green cloth, to wipe his tears, and then another. One was laid on his father's breastbone, and the other on his sister's. Kieri had no more tears to give.

With his boots back on, he came out into the spring sunlight, aching a little as one does after long sorrow's ease. The King's Squire he had left to wait for him stepped forward. Kieri turned to the Seneschal. "The leaves?"

"Connect the bones to the living earth, to Alyanya of the Flowers. So the bones remember their life, and the living remember those whose bones lie there." He said it as if Kieri should have understood that himself, and Kieri realized he would have, in a few minutes.

He felt the sunlight on his face, on his shoulders through his robes, striking warm and comforting as his parents' hands once had. Through the air came scents of spring, green things growing, flowers' sweetness. When he died, his bones would have that connection, would not forget that he had lived, had been nourished by the same soil, the same air and water, that fed the great trees. His growing taigsense felt the trees, steady, comforting.

"Thank you, Seneschal," he said. "Thank you for all you have done, and do, and for teaching me, who should not need teaching—"

The Seneschal bowed, a deeper bow than before. "My lord king, it is an honor to guide one who needs no teaching, but only the chance to learn. Your father is well pleased; you have taken away the fear and grief of his life and death."

"You felt that?"

"Oh, yes. No one may serve there who cannot sense the bones." The Seneschal looked past Kieri to the trees. "I know, my lord, that you are trying to heal the breach between human and elf, and this is a fine thing to do, and something that must be done. But here, in the house of bones, this is a human thing. It is not what elves do; it is, they have said, beyond their understanding. We keep very old ways here, my lord, and they have agreed it is right for us to do so."

"It is in my bones, too," Kieri said. "I have no wish to interfere, even if all your assistants are of pure human heritage. And yet you lay out the half-elven, such as my sister."

"It is hard to explain, my lord. You are right: only those of human blood—and old human at that—serve under me. The bones need those around them who understand, and elves do not."

"Yet I am part-elf and they spoke to me."

"They are your ancestors and relatives; it is a family thing with you. With others, not of the family, it is harder."

"I will not interfere," Kieri said again. "I do not fully understand, myself, and perhaps that is my elven heritage showing. I do understand that it is a good—no, a vital—task that you perform, and you have my goodwill in it."

"Thank you, my lord," the Seneschal said.

Kieri turned back to the palace, and went inside, flanked now by the King's Squire. His stomach growled suddenly and he realized he had spent half the morning in the ossuary. Lunch should be ready . . .

The small dining room's table was centered with flowers, and a nosegay of flowers and herbs lay beside every plate. Kieri looked at the steward, brows raised.

"The ceremony, my lord. Marks the end of the mourning period."

Around the table, those he'd asked to come in for the afternoon's work waited for him to begin, so he helped himself to cheese and bread and pickles. A jar of his favorite chutney sat beside his plate; none of his staff had yet acquired a taste for it, spiced as it was with southern peppers. When all had finished, the servants cleared the table.

"So now we have your coronation, my lord," said Sier Halveric. "I brought the plans . . ." He handed over a sheet of parchment with the order of ceremony, the list of participants and invited guests, and another with the supplies, and finally the total cost.

Kieri read both carefully, while the others waited, chatting quietly among themselves. His mother's mother, the elven Lady of the Ladysforest, from whom the humans of Lyonya held their rights to the land, and who ruled the elvenhome kingdom, would be a participant. Halveric had left spaces for the names of her attendants. The Captain-General of Falk, the members of the Council, all had roles in the ceremony. So did Paksenarrion, who had found and brought him. The main part of the ceremony would take place in the King's Grove, not in the palace or its grounds—that did not surprise him, not after the time he'd spent here. Nor did the presentation of the new king to the bones below, including another visit to the previous king's grave.

A procession through and around the city . . . a feast for all who came . . . that was the greatest cost to the Crown. Kieri had specified that no one else need wear new clothes, and the ceremonial banners of the previous king's reign—used so seldom—could be reused. The cost lay well within the amount he had given Halveric.

"This is excellently done," he said finally, looking up at Halveric. "I am surprised you managed the cost of so large a feast so well . . ."

Halveric flushed a little. "Your elven relatives, my lord, offered to share the cost and pledged half the feast."

"Even so," Kieri said. "It is excellently done and I appreciate your efforts. Now—have we heard from foreign guests?"

"I have heard from Tsaia—under the circumstances, they cannot risk the crown prince, but an envoy will come. Prealíth and Kostandan will send envoys as well. We have heard nothing from Pargun, as expected, since we did not invite them."

"If they come in peace," Kieri said, "we will be polite. If they sulk at home, so much the better."

"If it were up to me, I'd build river forts against invasion, but most on the Council don't agree." Halveric kept his voice low.

"So . . . is it the elves who set the people against defense? Is it their enchantment?"

Halveric shrugged and spread his hands. "Truth be told, we don't ask things like that. Aliam tells me war is brutal and he hopes there's never another war this side of the mountains . . . and he makes his living by it, as did you. He says those of us who want to arm against Pargun don't know what we're asking for." He looked at Kieri expectantly.

"He's right that war destroys . . . can destroy everything." The memory of that last campaign in Aarenis came to him again, barren fields sprouting bones, burning cities, once-prosperous villages sacked and their populations scattered, to beg along the roads. He wrenched his mind back to the present. "I profited by war, Sier Halveric, because it existed, not because I thought it good." All but that one year, when a rage for vengeance had driven him past all reason. "Like Aliam, I would not see here what I saw in Aarenis—or for that matter in my own lands in Tsaia, when the Pargunese or the orcs attacked and good people died. And yet, unlike the elves, I am more willing to recognize the reality of intractable conflict, and use force when nothing else will serve. I would appreciate your assessment of any strategic dangers. Or those of anyone else who has studied these things."

Halveric nodded sharply. "So I had hoped, my lord king. So I had hoped. I have no fear or hatred of the Sinyi, and indeed some Sinyi blood runs in our veins, but I worry about the security of the realm on several accounts. We cannot trust in elven powers alone—your mother's death and your captivity prove that, if incursions from Tsaia, through Verrakai lands, and threats from Pargun, were not enough."

"We will talk again in a few days," Kieri said. "For now, we have my cohort of trained troops, should anything happen before the coronation. I would appreciate your assessment of what other defensive measures we could take."

Halveric bowed, and took back his lists. The rest of that meeting, as the others discussed the coronation plans and which of their relatives were coming to Chaya, Kieri's thoughts wandered to Tsaia and his stronghold. Arcolin should have been to Vérella by now. Would the Regency Council have taken his advice and given Arcolin the North Marches? Would he have taken a contract? He might be on the road to Aarenis. And why had no courier come from Vérella, to let him know what was happening? Surely they realized he needed to know how things stood with the Verrakaien.

As if in answer to that thought, Garris stepped into the room, escorting a man in Tsaian colors. "Sir King—a courier with urgent messages from Tsaia."

Kieri's glance cleared the room. The courier handed over a dispatch case. Kieri opened it and unrolled a scroll tied with rose and white ribbons and sealed with the royal seal.

To my Brother Sovereign, Kieri Phelan of Lyonya, with all hopes for Your health and welfare, from Mikeli Mahieran, Crown Prince and Ruler-elect of Tsaia, greetings . . .

Kieri read with growing alarm of the attempted assassinations, the deaths of Duke Verrakai and his brother, the Order of Attainder on the Verrakaien as a whole and those in the immediate family of Konhalt, the unsettled state of the eastern half of the realm.

For this reason, the Regency Council acceded to your request that Jandelir Arcolin be made lord of the North Marches, despite his foreign birth. He has gone south with a single cohort, leaving behind

loyal troops on which We can call if it becomes necessary. We will
also need those troops you now have in Lyonya and their captain,
unless it is necessary for you to retain them. I am sending a courier
to their captain, as well.

Kieri frowned. A single cohort in Aarenis—that would be hard to
manage, unless Arcolin took along extra support staff. Had he
thought to do that? Then he shook his head. Arcolin was no longer
his concern. His concern was here and now: Lyonya's west border
and the Verrakai. They had recently lost a battle—how much had
that degraded their ability to attack? Dorrin's cohort was all he had—
if he gave that up and sent her back to Tsaia, he'd have no real troops
so far as he knew. He wondered if Aliam Halveric's company had left
for Aarenis yet. And how many forest rangers were there? Who commanded them?

He asked Garris to find Sier Halveric. Halveric came back into the
room looking worried.

"Here's the word from Tsaia," Kieri said, handing him the letter. "I
wanted to talk to you before telling the whole Council, since you
seem to have more grasp of our defensive situation. What forces do
we have, to oppose the kinds of trouble you think likely?"

Halveric ticked them off on his fingers. "Our forest rangers, to the
number of perhaps a thousand. Not many, to cover the entire realm,
but the greatest number are deployed along the western border. They
operate in small groups—mostly a hand or so, rarely more than three
hands unless one calls for help—"

"What are their arms?" Kieri said.

"Blackwood bows," Halveric said. "And swords, of course."

"Training?"

"Woodscraft, primarily, and archery and fencing." Halveric made
a face. "Aliam's pointed out to me before that they are not trained as
a regular fighting force, the kind he uses. Archers, he says, are an ad-
junct to soldiers in formation, soldiers armed with polearms or sword
and shield, like his company. Then he goes off into a spiel about
mixed-arms tactics and I get lost. But I do understand that we have
nothing that counts as an actual army, unless you count the Royal
Archers."

"And what are they?" Kieri asked.

"A longbow archery company, two hundred strong. You'll see them at the coronation. They march and drill just like other foot soldiers."

Kieri thought back to Aarenis. No one there used longbows; he'd had one of his cohorts trained in crossbows and had hired or allied with specialist crossbow units as well . . . but two hundred long-bows . . .

"I suppose longbows haven't the range of crossbows," he said. "Or do they? They must be more awkward to carry and handle." In his mind, he saw archers struggling through the woods, the longer bows catching on every vine and twig.

"Hardly," Halveric said with a smile. "Didn't Aliam talk about them? And doesn't your paladin have a blackwood bow she got from our rangers? Talk to her, and find out why we never export bow-length blackwood."

"But two hundred archers . . . against the Pargunese—" The Pargunese, he knew from paid spies and his own observations, could put two thousand troops in the field.

Halveric raised an eyebrow. "Do you know what happened during the Girdish wars?"

"No." And what could that matter, as long ago as those wars had been.

"Quite a few Tsaian magelords thought it would be a good idea to shift into Lyonya, and drive us out. They knew we had no standing army, and even though they had been held back when the magelords first came over the mountain, they thought they had the resources to succeed."

"But they were already fighting the Girdsmen," Kieri said. "Why would they start another war?"

"They didn't think they were starting another war," Halveric said. "They thought they were invading a helpless neighbor who didn't have the population or will to stand up to them. They knew that the humans in Lyonya were the same stock as those they'd conquered. And they knew somehow—how, I don't know—that the Ladysforest elves were away, involved in something else." He paused, and picked up a pastry from the tray. "They expected us to break as easily as this—" He broke the pastry. "And to be as soft inside. But they failed."

"Because of blackwood bows?"

"Blackwood bows and those who know how to use them, to ad-vantage." Halveric spread his hands. "I know what Aliam does, what kinds of troops he has. He told me how you fought in Aarenis. Open ground, for the most part. Sieges of walled fortresses and citadels. Blackwood bows—if you could even get them—might not do as well there. But here . . . I think you will be pleasantly surprised."

"Who commands these forces?" Kieri asked.

"You do, Sir King, if you choose to act directly. In the past hand of years, the king has left such matters to the Council in whole, and the Council has not been much interested. I am seen as dangerously in-fluenced by my brother, but in fact Aliam's descriptions of war ter-rify me. Only, like Aliam and you, I see that intending no harm is no protection."

"But in the field—who decides where they go and what their or-ders are?"

"The forest rangers are divided into four groves, one for each bor-der, and each commanded by a grove-captain. These have their or-ders from here—from me, if it seems needed. It was my decision, for instance, to move a half-grove from the southeast to the southwest, to provide more protection from Tsaian problems. Most of our south-east quarter, after all, is within the Ladysforest."

"A wise move," Kieri said. "What protection for the riverside?"

"The northern grove of rangers, and the three river towns with forts," Halveric said. "The forts are manned by city militia . . . per-haps twenty or thirty in each."

Clearly inadequate to prevent a river crossing. Though, he sup-posed, archers shooting from the forest cover could make rowing across the river very difficult.

"And who commands the Royal Archers in the field?" he asked.

"In the field? I have never known them to be more than a half day's march from Chaya. They have a captain, of course. You should meet him, I suppose."

"Indeed I should," Kieri said. He sighed, thinking how far all this was from any real defensive force. Bowmen skulking in the woods could certainly delay an attacking force, but he wanted better. "How do you think others will react to this news?" He tapped the letter.

"They'll be frightened," Halveric said. "As I am. Worried. And the

Tsaians want that cohort back. I was half hoping you'd retain it permanently."

"It seems a time to press the Council about defenses," Kieri said. "I was going to wait until after the coronation, but this gives reason."

"They'll balk," Halveric said. "I would advise waiting—but then, they will balk any time."

"They must at least know what the news is," Kieri said.

He called the Council in, and read them the letter from the crown prince.

As he'd expected, they were frightened.

"They can't make you send your soldiers away," Galvary said. "Can they? They're yours—"

"Mine when I was a duke in Tsaia," Kieri said. "They're Tsaian. Besides, only days ago you were wanting me to send them back, remember?"

"Yes, but—but if the Tsaians are going to cause trouble we need something—"

"We do," Kieri said. "But until we know what Captain Dorrin's orders from the Crown are, we can defer this discussion." Down the room, the elves and Sier Halveric all gave short nods of approval.

CHAPTER TEN

Dorrin Verrakai had just returned from her morning visit with her cohort, and settled into one of the small reception rooms with pen and paper to write the necessary orders for the next hand of days, when one of the palace servants knocked on the door.

"Captain—there's a messenger from Tsaia."

"For the king, I presume . . . did the king ask my presence?"

"No, Captain. This messenger is for you. In the royal livery." The servant's demeanor was perfectly correct, but Dorrin could see intense curiosity in his glance. Did he wonder if she were being recalled to stand trial?

"I'll see the messenger here," Dorrin said.

The messenger, in Tsaia's rose and white, bowed to Dorrin as he came into the room. On one shoulder was the gold and silver knot that meant he was of noble birth, assigned to carry messages for the royal family only, and on his collar the silver bell signifying a knight in the Order of the Bells. Such would not usually bow to her, a mercenary, even though she wore the ruby of a Knight of Falk.

"Sir," she said courteously, with a bow in return.

"I bring an urgent message from the prince and Council of Tsaia," he said. "It concerns you and your family, and the welfare of the realm."

The welfare of the realm? Considering the behavior of her relatives, the only welfare of the realm she could imagine meant eradication of the entire family. But would the prince or Council really send her a message consisting of "present yourself for execution"? To cover her surprise, she tried courtesy. "You have traveled far," Dorrin said. "You will take refreshment, surely."

"Not until I've done my duty," he said. He pulled from beneath his messenger's mantle a red leather scroll case. "I am to hand this to you personally and remain at your service to answer any questions you may have."

Dorrin took the scroll case, untied the intricate knots, and slid out a scroll sealed with the royal mark as well as bound with a twist of rose and silver ribbons.

"He wrote it himself," the messenger said. "He wanted no scribe to have knowledge of it."

Dorrin slid her thumbnail under the seal and cracked it, then unrolled the scroll. It began as all royal documents did, flowery and formal . . . *Greetings from the Crown of Tsaia to Captain Dorrin Verrakai, formerly under command of Kieri Artfiel Phelan, Duke of Phelan, now rightful King of Lyonya* . . . but then the sense of the next section hit her. *It is Our wish that you accept the charge here laid upon you, to take the title of Duke Verrakai* . . .

"You . . . he . . . cannot be serious." Dorrin was sure her face had paled. It would not do to say that the prince was crazy, but he must have lost all reason to think elevating an exiled Verrakai mercenary to the dukedom would work. She had not been there—she had refused to think of it as home for over two decades now—since her last, successful flight.

"I assure you, Captain, that the prince is serious. Pray read the rest. No other member of the family is free from the taint of treason; you alone are known to be a loyal friend to Kieri Phelan. The prince charged me to tell you that he is convinced breaking up the duchy would create more problems. It needs a strong duke—duchess—and you have both command and combat experience."

She did, that was true. She read the rest, the formal phrases explaining why her uncles and aunts, her siblings, her cousins, were under order of attainder. *Haron Vasli, the Duke who was, and his brother Kalin, are dead, following a merciless attack on my person, resulting in the deaths of the Marshal-Judicar and the Knight-Commander of the Bells.* Dorrin shivered. *Other Verrakai have ignored a summons to court. We have reports that Haron's next brother fled south, to Konhalt.* That she could well believe. Konhalt, a minor family, had been allied to Verrakai since the Girdish wars, though with one branch that had moved north and away. *We need decisive, quick action to take control of Verrakai and prevent open rebellion.* Indeed they did need that. *You are authorized to use whatever force you must.* Did that mean—could it mean—using magery against magery? But even if he allowed it, hers was too weak.

Dorrin read on; the prince explained why he had decided against breaking up the Verrakai holdings and handing them over to others. Doing that before he was finally crowned would cause more chaos, possibly even civil war. He could not afford to wait until his Midsummer coronation. He must act quickly. If she accepted, he would send further instructions to meet her on return to Tsaia.

Her imagination flared, showing her the great steading as it had been, the old stone of the original keep still standing, the more modern mansion and outbuildings around it. She saw herself arriving there with loyal troops behind her, striding up those steps worn by the feet of centuries, into the great hall . . . her imagination stopped short before peopling that hall with any of the relatives and servants likely to be there. Not her uncle the late duke, or her uncle his brother or her father, dead a decade by rumor. Her mother? Perhaps. Her aunt? Cousins? She shivered. She could not go back there, not after all these years, not to face their malice, their magery.

And yet. If not Dorrin Duke Verrakai, who could possibly take over? Did the people Verrakai ruled deserve to be scattered, handed over to strangers who might not understand what they had endured? If Konhalt also fell, as the prince's letter suggested, who else—?

"It is not a royal command," the messenger said, when she looked up. "The prince realizes that you have been estranged from your family these many years. But it is a heartfelt request."

"He will need an answer quickly," Dorrin said. "It must be settled . . ."

"He is sorry to inconvenience you . . ." the messenger said.

Dorrin almost laughed. *Inconvenience?* If she accepted, governing Verrakai would be far more than an inconvenience. "My situation here must be settled before I give my answer," she said. "I must speak to the king, and arrange for someone to command the troops I brought with me."

"Then you accept?"

This weight she had never sought, never wanted, never dreamed of, settled on her shoulders. "I will give you my answer when I have spoken to the king, who is still my liege."

But he had read her real answer in her eyes, for now he was smiling. "Of course, my . . . Captain."

"And now," Dorrin said, ringing for servants, "you must take refreshment, and rest. Whatever my answer, you have a long, cold ride ahead of you."

The king was studying rows of figures and making notes as she came into the small dining hall.

"Sir King," Dorrin said. He looked up and smiled.

"What, Captain?" His expression sobered. "You're upset . . . the troops?"

"A messenger from Tsaia, from the prince—for me."

"He wants the cohort back," Kieri said. "He wrote me."

Dorrin shook her head. "Not that—he wants me to take over Verrakai. As the only—as he puts it—honorable Verrakai of my generation." She laid the scroll before him, and watched as he unrolled it.

"That's . . . interesting," he said as he read.

"No, Sir King, that's terrifying. And worse, I feel a pull . . ."

"You'd be good, Dorrin," he said, looking up. "You *are* the best Verrakai; you could change the family history."

"But you know my story, my lord. The family hates me, and I left . . ." He gestured to a chair and she sat, too tense to relax into it.

"Dorrin. Captain. Change comes. I must give up my land and my Company, abandon the home and life I made for myself, the people I swore to protect and care for, to assume the responsibility for these people, this place . . . to assume the responsibility of a king. Even the Company will not be the same—"

"I know." Tears stung her eyes. The Company without Kieri Phelan—she had already contemplated that, with misery. Jandelir Arcolin was a fine man, a good commander, but he was not Kieri Phelan.

"Then perhaps it is time for you, too, to take a bold leap."

"I understand that things will never be as they were. But this—this is different."

"And yet you feel a pull. At some level, Dorrin, you want it. You have always wanted to redeem your family."

She sighed. "Yes. But I cannot imagine how it can be successful. How to go about it."

He laughed, startling her. "Oh, Dorrin—do you not remember when we were building the stronghold in the north? No one thought that would be successful. An upstart no-name granted land and title? No family fortune? And yet you joined me, and now—barring the fact that I can no longer be there—it is a thriving land. You have more experience than I had then."

"If I can gain the support of the people, who have known only bad Verrakai." And if the magelords still there didn't kill her outright.

He cocked his head. "What you really doubt is yourself, not your people."

Your people. He said it as if he knew already that she would take it on.

"In a way, yes." She spoke slowly. "Back there, in that setting, away from the Company—from you—what if it comes back?" The fear, the immobility, against their power.

"What is it you fear, Dorrin?"

"I never told you what the Knight-Commander told me—"

"You wear the ruby. You would not have been knighted if there'd been much wrong."

"Yes, I wear the ruby. But I wanted more. Wanted to be what Paks is. He said I bore the same flaws, heart-deep, as those I fled. That no Verrakai could be free of them—"

"You wanted to be a paladin?" He sounded surprised, but less so than she'd feared.

"I wanted to go back and change them all. I thought that was the way. He said I was unfit for that."

"You were *then*, yes. Like me, you were a youngster with little experience and few skills. And I would agree that you are not a paladin. Nor am I. We were born with other talents, Dorrin. We are meant to govern. You have been doing that, superbly, since you joined my Company."

"Under your command. And not exactly governing."

He gave her that challenging grin she had known so long. "You know better. Each of you captains has had independent command, and you've all been involved in the dukedom. Come now, Captain: If I can go from running a mercenary company and a duchy to this—" He waved his arm at the room, encompassing the kingdom. "—and face my formidable elven relatives, then you can deal with mere humans and a duchy that desperately needs an honorable sane leader." He paused; she said nothing. "And there's this," he said. "I expect trouble with Pargun, as well as some internal upheavals. Having you on my flank, someone I know and trust, would help me. I would not expect miracles, Dorrin—I know there have been cross-border raids and there will be more. But you will not be trying to undermine my kingdom."

She nodded; it was both agreement and acceptance. "Not because *I* wish it though," he said. "It must be *your* consent to *your* prince— to Mahieran, to Tsaia, not to me. I cannot be your commander any longer." Regret softened his voice.

"I don't know the prince," Dorrin said. "I avoided court, as you know."

"Yes. And now you'll have to get to know Mikeli. He's going to be good, I judge. His father was. You may have some problems with the Council, until they know you—"

"They certainly know the Verrakai name," Dorrin said.

"We both face challenges. Do you think you'll have problems with Verrakai troops?"

"Probably," Dorrin said. "Even if they aren't disloyal to Tsaia, they've been told that I'm a traitor."

"Take your cohort," Kieri said. "They'll go with you willingly, and the prince has asked me to return them to Tsaia. Jandelir is headed south with a cohort—they are giving him the North Marches." Dorrin noticed that Kieri did not say "my domain."

"But they're not mine—"

"Essentially they are," he said. "Ask them, tell them I approved it. See what happens."

"I—" For an instant her vision blurred. She blinked back tears. "You really think I can do it."

"Don't you?" Answer and challenge both.

She stared past him, out the narrow window; snow fell again, fat flakes in twisting curtains. "Yes," she said. "I can. I will."

"Then let me be the first to congratulate Dorrin, Duke Verrakai," he said, holding out his hand. "And let us toast it."

Dorrin clasped his hand, tears stinging her eyes. For so long he had been to her the elder brother she never knew, the father she never had—just, honorable, kind. And now she must take the lessons she had learned and apply them . . . without him.

saia's messenger rode off the next morning before dawn; Dorrin marshaled her cohort in the inn's common room and marched them to their usual drill field, thinly covered with snow. Weak sun bloomed the clouds to pale gold; the snow was soft, already melting.

Instead of drill, she called them into close formation. "A messenger arrived from Tsaia late yesterday. A message to me from the prince."

They stared at her, some faces showing confusion and others calculation.

"Most of you know that I am a Verrakai. You all know we were attacked by Verrakai soldiers on the way here. That act of treason was compounded by an attack on the royal family in Vérella. The entire family is under an Order of Attainder—all except me, because I have been estranged from them for so long. The prince has asked me to take over as Verrakai. I have agreed to do so. Now I ask how many of you will come with me. King Kieri does not command, but says you may come if you like."

"To serve under you, or someone else?" Selfer asked.

"My command," Dorrin said. "And you would be going back to the Duke's—to the North Marches—eventually. Arcolin's been granted that domain; he's on his way to Aarenis."

They looked at each other, saying nothing. "I will walk," Dorrin said. "You will think."

"I don't need to think," Sergeant Bosk said. "Captain, I'll follow you anywhere. To Verrakai, to clean up that mess—of course! What better could we do, with our Duke—the king—gone?" Others nodded.

Dorrin felt a surge of elation. "All of you?"

"Well, you aren't like that other Verrakai. You're loyal to the Duke—to our king, aren't you?"

"I will be swearing allegiance to *Tsaia's* king."

"Of course, Captain, but he's Phelan's friend, right? And you'll need some loyal soldiers to start with. Couldn't trust those Verrakai soldiers." He spat into the snow.

"They probably outnumber us," Dorrin said.

"They outnumbered us on the way here," Bosk said. "They've had one lesson; we can give them another. They're not worth a worry, Captain."

"Well, then." The first lift of elation, of possibilities other than dire, filled her. "Let's get to work. The prince has sent troops to Verrakai; he should get my message that I'm accepting his offer. We can't wait for Kieri's—the king's—coronation; we should go on as soon as may be. Jens is still unable to travel, and we need to ensure that all our mounts are fit."

"Farrier came by yesterday, Captain," Selfer said. "All trimmed and all loose shoes reset. We're down three mounts, though, and seven pack animals . . . all but two could travel in another hand of days maybe, but not sooner. I'm thinking you'll want us to be fully supplied?"

"Yes." Dorrin thought. "I'll ask at the palace about buying spare animals. Make up a supply list—ten days on the road, if the weather worsens. I don't know what the road conditions are, once we're in Verrakai lands. I'll try to find out. I'll be back at the inn soon after midday, if not before. Do we need any additional weapons?"

"We can always use more," Selfer said. "The smithies are backed up, so if we could get twelve swords, fifteen shields new—if there's an armorer here—"

"If there is, I'm sure you can find him," Dorrin said. "I'll go check on mounts and pack animals, and the routes we might take."

By early afternoon the sky cleared from the west to a hard blue. Dorrin had found, as she expected, few available mounts outside the royal stables, but pack animals and even wagons were available. She found maps in the palace library, but only one trader who admitted any knowledge of the roads into and through Verrakai lands.

"Charge a ruinous toll, they do," he said. "Unless they order goods, they don't want trade comin' through 'less they get a profit. I was hired to bring in southern wine and silk two years agone. Road's a mess, once you get past Rockwater crossing; they leave it that way for protection, they say."

"Better with pack animals, then," Dorrin said.

"Better, yes. You'll find some brigand bands, like enough. Damned Duke starves his peasants; it's no wonder. But they'll steal if they can. You'll want to be careful."

"We're armed," Dorrin said.

"I hear the Duke's in trouble with the Council," the man said.

"His men did attack the king on the way here," Dorrin said. "What else did you hear?"

"You're one of his captains, right? I heard he brought his own army with him, and everybody knows he was a mercenary. We worry about war here."

"He doesn't want a war," Dorrin said.

"I suppose you would know," he said. "But a man who's lived by war all his life . . . what kind of king will he make, and what will that mean for us, the traders?"

"When you're in Vérella next," Dorrin said, "you should talk to the Merchants' Guild about trade to his dukedom. It's been profitable and he kept the roads in good repair. I expect he'll do the same here."

"I hope so. I've always traded on the east-west routes, not to the north, but if that's true . . . then good."

Should she mention that she knew Kieri wanted to include merchants in the Council here? No, that was for him to say.

By late afternoon, Dorrin had conferred again with the king and Selfer. On her way back to the palace, she stopped by the stables to check on her own mount, hoping to find Paksenarrion there. Paks, indeed, was in the stall with her paladin mount.

"Good evening, Captain," Paks said. "Did you ride out today?"

"No . . . Paks, I wanted to talk to you, if you've time."

"Certainly." Paks stood up, giving the red horse a caress as she left the stall. "What is it?"

"The prince of Tsaia has asked me to take on the Verrakai matter," Dorrin said. "I believe you know that I am Verrakai by birth . . . I left home and they erased my name, they said, but—"

"Why are you telling me?" Paks asked.

"It's complicated." Dorrin stopped in front of her own horse's stall. The sturdy bay put out his head and she stroked it absently. "I hated what they did; I ran to Lyonya and entered the Company of

Falk. At one time, as a girl, I had dreamed of coming back to them as a . . . a paladin, like you. Breaking the bonds of Liart's barbed chain, making them better . . . but I was not chosen for such training."

"They don't need a paladin," Paks said. "They need a good ruler. Paladins don't govern . . . I told the Council here that."

"Why?" Dorrin asked. "I always wondered about that. Why wouldn't paladins be good at it?"

"I'm not sure," Paks said. "Perhaps because good governance requires different gifts. Rulers must stay with their land, wherever it is, while our calls to quest may take us anywhere. It would not be good for a land if its ruler left suddenly."

"True. I had not thought of that."

"And most rulers have heirs of the body," Paks said. "Paladins are vulnerable in their loves . . . we are not encouraged to form families as rulers do."

"So it is not simply that we lack abilities that you—that paladins have?"

"No . . . I think not. We are not perfect, Captain, just different. A sword and a plough are both useful, but for different things."

"My family have done bad things, Paks. Very bad. I do not know how I will change their habits."

"Do you know why they follow Liart?"

"They say it is the only way to preserve and strengthen the mage-born abilities," Dorrin said. "They tried to initiate me, as a child. I was uncooperative. A spineless coward, as my father and uncle put it. But the others consented. I do not know how willingly." She swallowed. "Because the Code of Gird forbids magery, some magelords fled into exile—"

"Into Kolobia," Paks said. "Or so I suspect from the information in Luap's writings."

"My family would not give it up or go into exile. They hid it except in their own domain, using Liart's power and blood magery to preserve and strengthen it."

"This will come out now," Paks said. "Or will you try to hide it?"

"No. It must come out and it must end," Dorrin said. "But there is more."

"What?"

"This." Dorrin ducked into the shadows of an empty stall, almost dark in the late afternoon. Light flared from her hands. "I have a little magery. I do not use it, but I have it."

"The light of truth," Paks said.

"No. The light of fire. It will burn." The light died. In the darkness, Dorrin went on. "You saw my sword flare in Rotengre. It has its own magic, yes, but the light is its response to mine."

"You're certain it's the old magery?"

"What else could it be? I never trained as a wizard. I'm not a paladin. The Knight-Commander of Falk made that clear."

Paks led the way out of the dark stall into the stableyard. "Did you have any training in your magery? Anything useful?"

"No. What they wanted to teach me, I didn't want to learn. I can light candles or kindle a fire, but nothing like the light you produced for the battle."

Paks frowned. "I don't know what other magics the magelords were supposed to have . . . though the Marshal-General said the evidence out there in Kolobia suggested a variety of things, from lifting rocks to healing."

"The archives list a number of abilities, but they're all supposed to require training," Dorrin said. "Making light is the one they watch for in children, to see if they have the talent. Others are less likely to emerge without it, though it does happen."

"What does it feel like, when you make the light?" Paks asked. "Does it feel hot, there in your hand?"

"No. I don't feel anything. Do you?"

"Only inside," Paks said. "In my heart, there's a . . . a feeling of being . . . partly somewhere else." She shook her head and chuckled. "I can't describe it. Something feels open, and the light comes. Master Oakhallow told me that paladins' powers come from the gods. But we ask for light, or healing, and it may or may not be granted."

Dorrin looked at her, remembering the tall, yellow-haired peasant girl who'd impressed all the older veterans with her likeness to the Duke's dead wife. But every recruiting season brought peasant girls and boys, artisans' sons and daughters, into the Company, and Paks was not the only one who seemed special at first. She was not even the only one who had reminded them of Tammarion.

Now she bore the High Lord's silver circle on her brow, proof of the ordeal she had endured and the reward she had more than earned, and Dorrin was torn between resentment, admiration, and relief.

"I am not a paladin, but I would do what my people need," Dorrin said. "The king told me to take my cohort, if they were willing, and they have agreed. I'm not sure it will be enough."

Paks grinned. "Nothing's certain, is it? But what bothers you most?"

"I'm not sure I'll recognize everything that needs to be done," Dorrin said. "I'm not sure I can stand against the magery they have."

"The strength of their talent, or their training? Do you think your power is that much weaker, or is it that you don't know how to use it?"

"Training, I suppose. Like a novice picking up a good sword, but having no skills, no experience."

"You believe they could overpower you? Kill you?"

"I suspect so," Dorrin said. "It's not the danger to myself that I worry about—much, anyway. It's what will happen to the land and people should I fail. Not just Verrakai land, either, but the whole of Tsaia. I don't suppose you feel a call to come help me . . ."

"No," Paks said. "I feel no call at all right now, but I can think of a way to help you, if you are willing."

"And what is that?"

"If it is training you lack, then let us train your talents. Now. Perhaps it will not take as long as you think."

"You could do that? You would do that?"

"I can try. We can try." Paks grinned like a child about to try swinging from a vine over a river, all glee and eagerness. "What do you need most, do you think?"

Dorrin ticked them off on her fingers. "A shield against their magery, protecting not just myself but those I lead. A way to lock their magery, so they cannot use it. I saw one of my uncles do that once, to a half-breed, one of his bastards, who showed fight. Healing, if that's in me—by legend, it had become the rarest of the gifts, and I never saw any of my family use it."

"So first we find out what your gifts are, and waken them," Paks said. "We should start, then, with the one you believe most difficult, healing."

Dorrin felt her belly clench. Her family's stories of the healing magery all involved loss, despair, weakening . . . but Paks was right. If it could be put to good use, she might save some of the children that way, healing whatever hurts had been done them . . . and being able to heal might win supporters from those long damaged by her family.

"Let's go to my room," Paks said. "Quieter there."

Dorrin was expected at table with the king; she was sure Selfer or Bosk would come looking for her. "I must leave word that I'm busy—"

"I'll tell them I wanted to confer with you." Paks grinned. "For now, nobody interrupts me."

CHAPTER ELEVEN

P aks's room, at one end of the palace complex and a floor higher than her own, looked to have been a servant's once. Plain, a pair of narrow beds separated by a carved chest, a bare wood floor. A wardrobe stood against one wall; the opposite had pegs at various heights. Paks's cloak hung on one; her pack, neatly rolled, was at the foot of her bed.

"They could do no better for the paladin who saved their king?" Dorrin asked.

"They could, but I chose to move here," Paks said. "I needed solitude, not care, for a while." Her face had sobered, but now it lightened again. "Besides, this gives us the privacy I'm sure we need. Here—sit down on that bed."

Dorrin sat, bemused by the shift in authority, as if she herself were a recruit facing a captain for the first time.

"Give me your hand," Paks said next. Dorrin held out her hand; Paks's hand on hers felt warm and dry and oddly soothing. Dorrin waited; Paks said nothing, but looked past her, into something Dorrin could not see. Slowly, she felt something else, something that seemed to pass from Paks to her, a strange tingle that ran up her arm and from there into her head, and down her torso. She wanted to pull her hand back, but Paks had a firm grip. She glanced up. Paks's eyes were closed, her face unreadable, the slightest furrow of a frown between her brows, as if she were concentrating.

When Paks released Dorrin's hand, she sat down on the opposite bed. Dorrin waited.

"That was . . . interesting," Paks said. "Someone blocked your magery long ago, except for that light. Did you know that? Do you know who?"

"No," Dorrin said. "I suppose my uncle, or a cousin."

"I don't think so," Paks said. "From what you say, their contact would be evil, and leave a residue I should pick up. This was not an act of malice, but of protection. Who, that could do such a thing, might have chosen to do so?"

One name came immediately to mind. "The Knight-Commander of Falk," Dorrin said. "When I trained there, when he found out who I was, I told him about my small talent. He let me stay, but said I must not use any magery while there, having learned only its wrong uses. He might have blocked it."

"And not told you?"

"I can think of no one else," Dorrin said. "He is the only one outside my family who knew that I had it."

"Then we should ask him," Paks said.

"He died," Dorrin said. "Some years after I was knighted, I heard that he had died. The new Knight-Commander I have never met."

"Ah. I wonder if he has the same powers. At least he is here; we can ask."

"Do we need to involve him?"

Paks cocked her head. "I think so. I am not a Knight of Falk . . . I am not even a knight, for that matter, so I do not know what he did or how it was done. I do know we should not meddle in things like this without understanding them."

"I will go—"

"No. I will go, and while I am gone, if you have such rituals as the Girdish knights have, to pray and prepare for a trial of some kind, that is what I think you should do. You have great deeds before you, Captain, and whether your magery can be restored and trained or not, you need time alone to ready yourself." Paks leaned forward and patted Dorrin's hand. "Do not worry, Captain. I will not be long."

Dorrin sat on the bed, thinking. Worrying. Thinking how long it had been since she prayed to Falk in anything but a crisis. For the king's life, she had prayed. For Paks's safe return from torment, she had prayed. But though she wore the ruby, it had been years since she prayed for guidance, for Falk's Will to be clear to her. She had substituted, she realized, Phelan's orders, Phelan's well-being, for the will of the gods, though she held herself true to them as she understood them.

As she had understood them as a runaway, as a young woman.

Time to do more than that. Time to do better, to outgrow her role as Phelan's captain, as Paks had long outgrown hers as Phelan's soldier.

By the time Paks reappeared with the Knight-Commander of Falk—who looked decidedly grumpy at being dragged up flights of back stairs with little explanation—she had prayed for aid and guidance and felt, for the first time in years, connected once more to Falk's Company.

"Captain Dorrin!" the Knight-Commander said. "So it is you I have come to see—Paksenarrion here would not say."

Dorrin had risen; Paks, vanishing from behind him in the doorway, reappeared with a chair. "Here, sir—if you will take a seat—"

"Hmph." He sat, still staring at Dorrin, frowning.

Paks moved past him and sat cross-legged on the bed opposite Dorrin. "If I may, Captain, I'll explain—"

Dorrin nodded, and Paks began. "You have heard, sir, that Captain Dorrin has been appointed by the prince and Council in Tsaia to take over the dukedom of Verrakai?"

He glanced from one to the other. "No . . . I had not."

"Well, then, she has. And the difficulty is, as I'm sure your predecessor told you, that the Verrakai retain the old magery—the outlaw magery—and misuse it to maintain their rule. And she herself inherited that ability."

He nodded, now staring hard at Dorrin. "So my predecessor told me, when he was old and ill. She had it, but had refused to use it cruelly, and thus had left Verrakai for Lyonya and our Hall. I was surprised he accepted her—you."

"Did he tell you everything?" Dorrin asked. "That I came under a false name, that my family pursued and demanded my return, that he protected me from them?"

"Not that you came under a false name, no. I would not have let you stay, had you done that to me."

"I understand, sir," Dorrin said. "But it was his decision at the time."

"He was an interesting man," the Knight-Commander said. "And he felt strongly about you. He was glad to see you linked to Phelan—he felt you had an important role to play there."

"I did?" Dorrin felt only surprise. "He never told me."

"He wouldn't. But on the road from Tsaia, was it not your cohort who defended the king long enough to save him from attack—including by your relatives?"

"Yes, but—"

"So what, now, is your need? I'm assuming *your* need, since this paladin brought me here speaking of great need."

"Yes, sir." Dorrin put her thoughts in order. "As Paks said, and your predecessor probably told you, I inherited the family magery, but was never trained in its use—I refused to cooperate with the training they attempted and eventually escaped . . ."

"What was that training?"

"In cruelty." Dorrin felt the familiar tremor in her hands, and clenched them together. "It—it was their belief that our power was retained because of . . . of blood magery. When a child—when I—first showed any talent—such as making light, then we were taken into the—the inner keep. The old keep, with its dungeon. And there made to see what they believed maintained our powers."

"Describe it." The Knight-Commander's voice was hard and cold as winter stone.

Despite herself, Dorrin's voice trembled. "It was . . . it was an animal, that first time. A rabbit." She could still see it, in her mind, the terrified, trembling little creature, heart beating so fast and hard, nose twitching. She had felt its fear and her own had doubled. Other rabbits, in wicker cages stacked along one side of the chamber, all terrified. She tried to swallow; her mouth was nearly as dry as it had been then. "They showed me first . . . my uncle made light, as I had, and then . . . then he hurt the rabbit and it screamed and his light grew stronger."

"How did he hurt it?"

"I—I don't know for sure. I closed my eyes—" She had seen the aftermath, though. "He must have pulled off a leg . . . and then another . . . that's what it looked like after . . ."

"How old were you? Did you not know already what to expect?"

"No . . . I was very small. Still in shortlings—" She was not going to admit having wet herself, her uncle's disgust, her mother's slap that sent her reeling into the stacked cages. "I had never been in the old keep before, I know that. But then—" It had to be said; she had to say it. "Then they wanted me to do it, to prove to me it would make my light stronger." The next rabbit had been spotted, dark spots on fawn. Her uncle had put a knife in her hand; her mother had gripped her shoulders, forcing her to the block of wood on which the rabbit now crouched, shivering, held there—her uncle said—by his magery. He had pointed to where she was to stab, in the rabbit's hindquarters.

"Not to kill it, then?"

"Not to kill it," Dorrin said. Bile had risen in her mouth. "I didn't want to. I pushed back against my mother but I was too small. She picked me up—" She had kicked her mother; her uncle had done whatever he did to the rabbit to her legs; she could not kick again. Her uncle had told her "You must do it; you must try" with such menace in his voice that it scared her more than her dangling legs. "I dropped the knife," she said. That had earned another slap. Her uncle had put the knife in her hand again, gripped it with his, so she could not open her hand or pull away, and guided it down, slowly, onto the hapless rabbit. The sound it made as the knife entered its flesh . . . as her uncle forced her hand to twist, to drag the knife sideways, to cause greater pain . . . would never leave her memory.

"They marked my face with the blood," she said. "They forced my mouth open and put blood in—"

"My child—" Dorrin looked up again; the Knight-Commander was pale. "They did that to an infant! And this is what my predecessor knew?"

"Some of it." No one knew all, none but those who had done it, and she, their victim. "They told me that now I belonged to them, that now my magery would grow, and I would learn to maintain it with greater blood. That I belonged to the Bloodlord—who is the same as Liart, sir, though they insisted on calling him differently. And they punished me for resisting, so I would learn how useless it was . . ."

"Punished you how?"

"They left my legs useless for three days, by their magery, and put me on the floor. I could not walk, or reach the food and water they put on a table in the cell . . ."

"Did they punish you thus when you refused later?"

"Not the same way, no." Dorrin clenched her teeth on the horrors but it had to be said. "They tormented anything, anyone, that I cared for, as well as me. Animals. People. I tried to run away on my first pony. They killed the pony, slowly."

"Did you ever submit willingly—did you ever harm any you were told to harm?"

She felt the hot tears on her face again, as she had felt them long ago. "The last . . . the last before I got away . . . a friend—" A friend maintained in agony to secure her outward obedience. "I tried not to, but sometimes—sometimes I was too weak. I thought if I did it, did it quickly, they wouldn't. I learned better." So many years, so many suffering victims, so many times she had not been able to do anything for them. "The last . . . I killed him," she said quickly. "I killed him myself, to end his suffering, and then I ran, and that time I made it to the border."

Heavy silence filled the little room. The Knight-Commander's face might have been carved of stone. Then he sighed. "I understand now why my predecessor let you stay, and why he knighted you, Dorrin of Verrakai. If ever someone needed Falk's protection, and had earned it, you did, and you had. But how did you escape? Surely they were watching you."

"I thought there must be better gods, and I asked their help. Then I thought I should try to escape, and if I were killed, so much the better."

"And you were still very young," the Knight-Commander said.

"I was, yes," Dorrin said. Looking back now, her escape did appear miraculous. She shivered a little.

"I have a dilemma which I expect Lady Paksenarrion will understand better than you," the Knight-Commander said. "I now understand why my predecessor not only accepted you, but sponsored your knighthood. I concur with his judgment, which I did not before. But now . . . you say you still have those powers which in your family have been used only for evil."

Paks stirred, on the bed, and said, "Not by her, sir."

"Not by her, you say. And yet—she did kill once. By magery?"

"No," Dorrin said. "With a knife. As quick as might be."

"And he could not have lived, you say?"

"Not more than two days, and all of it in pain," she said.

The Knight-Commander pursed his lips. "So . . . it was an act of mercy, and not carried out with magery. But you have magery still, Paksenarrion said."

"Yes. Some. And I see no way to do what the prince and Council want me to do without using it. My family will certainly use theirs."

"Are you trained in its use?"

"No." Dorrin took a deep breath. "With your permission, this is what I can now do—" She paused; the Knight-Commander nodded, and she took up a candle and lit it with a touch. "This is child's magery, the first most children show. I did once manage to lift a fruit that had just fallen to the ground, but not again."

"I believe her magery was locked by your predecessor," Paks said. "And you could unlock it and teach her its proper use."

"Its proper use!" The Knight-Commander stared. "Its proper use is none. It is illegal in Tsaia—would you have her start her rule by breaking the law?"

"What we paladins do could be counted magery," Paks said. "And wizards and their magicks are not illegal."

"She is not a paladin nor a wizard."

"Nor is she an evil person," Paks said. Dorrin glanced at her; Paks gave her a brief smile before turning back to the Knight-Commander. "She has been given the task of dealing with her family; if they use their magery against her, she will not succeed unless she has the use of her own, to oppose them."

"And you trust her?"

"I have known her some years," Paks said. "And as a paladin, I sense no evil in her."

"You are *Gird's* paladin; Gird had no love for the magelords, as you must know."

"Gird loved justice, sir, more than any group. He would not condemn Dorrin."

The room brightened. Perhaps without her willing it, Paks had come softly alight, not as bright as in the battle, but enough to cast a soft glow through the room, drowning the light of the candle Dorrin had lit.

"You, I suppose, will take on the role of her supervisor?" he said.

Paks shook her head. "Not I, sir. She is a Knight of Falk; she is sworn to Falk. It is not my place, and I have no call to go with her. I do have a call to aid her here and now."

The Knight-Commander closed his eyes a moment, then shook his head. "Arguing with paladins is like arguing with wind and stone. Very well. I would say I hope you're right, but the light you cast is evidence of the origin of your words. Dorrin, give me your hands."

Dorrin moved from the bed, kneeling before him, and raised her hands. The Knight-Commander's hands enclosed both of hers. She felt nothing at first, then warmth flowing into her arms, like and unlike what she'd felt when Paks took her hand.

"Paksenarrion," the Knight-Commander said, "your hands on her shoulders, please."

Now Paks came behind her. Dorrin felt enclosed, sheltered, safer than she had felt in her entire life.

"Breathe slowly," the Knight-Commander said. She breathed . . . in . . . out . . . in . . . out . . . there came a pressure, building along her bones, as if from within them, as a weather change made pressure in her head. It grew; she concentrated on breathing slowly, steadily, as it pushed and squeezed inside her, as the warmth from his hands and the sensation of light from Paks's touch on her shoulders merged until finally with a sudden rush, a stream of cold fire raced through her body. She gasped at the intensity of it, and then it was gone, leaving behind a sense of great spaces burst open from within.

"Dear me," the Knight-Commander said.

"She has it," Paks said.

"She does indeed." The Knight-Commander's voice deepened. "What have I done? What have I loosed?"

Dorrin could scarcely hear him. In her mind, in her heart, the new spaces were both dark and sparkling with light, a clear winter's night, cold and clean. What was this?

This is magery, came the answer, a voice she had never heard. Sonorous. Joyous. *This is your heritage, Dorrin of Verrakai. Use it well.* Music rose in her mind, music dimly recalled from earliest childhood.

No human music, this, but the music she had imagined the gods might play.

She opened her eyes; the Knight-Commander, still holding her hands, was staring at her with an expression of wonder and horror mixed.

"What—?" she asked.

"Dorrin—you have it *all*."

"All?"

"The magery, all of it. As great as any I read of, in the archives, and more than I have ever known to exist in these days. What my predecessor locked down, and well he did so. I do not know yet if I did well to loose it."

"What did you hear?" Paks said from behind her.

"A voice," Dorrin said. Suddenly tears burned her eyes and ran down her face. "I—I can't believe it was—" But she did believe. "Falk," she said. "It was Falk."

"What did he say?" the Knight-Commander asked.

"He said *This is your magery. Use it well*. Only—I don't know how."

"You will," Paks said.

The Knight-Commander nodded, and dropped her hands. "Dorrin, if Falk approved the restoration of your powers, then it must be the gods trust you to use them well. I doubt any of your family have near as much, though they may have more knowledge how to use what they have. I suspect you will learn quickly . . . there are hints I can give you. What do you most want to learn?"

Dorrin repeated what she had told Paks.

"A shield for yourself and those you lead should be the simplest; as a soldier, you know how shields function, and you've seen Paksenarrion in action."

Dorrin tried to imagine such a shield; she felt a mental nudge, then another, and then felt a tingling in her head that ran down her body.

"I said you would learn quickly, but that—that is more than I expected," the Knight-Commander said. "I'm going to push again . . ."

This time Dorrin felt nothing but a faint pressure, as if someone laid a cloth on her skin.

"That was not an attack, of course. But your personal shield has already strengthened." He sat back. "I understand that you wish to leave soon, but my advice would be to spend another few days working with me and with Paksenarrion; it will be better for you and for those you lead if you have more understanding of your magery—both how to access it, and what temptations it presents."

Dorrin glanced at Paks. "The prince bade me come as soon as possible."

"You would not leave half-dressed, though that might be quicker," the Knight-Commander said. "Magery—even such magery as yours—is not learned in an hour. You might ask Falk." Implicit in that was his rank as Knight-Commander, second highest among Falkians.

Dorrin bowed. "Knight-Commander, I will do so, but I would not prolong the training beyond absolute need."

"Understood," he said. "With what I have seen this night, we are speaking of days, not hands of days."

CHAPTER TWELVE

Kieri missed Dorrin at dinner; word that she was closeted with Paks reassured him. Selfer arrived after dinner, anxious to know if they were leaving the next day or not.

"Paks wanted to talk with her," Kieri said. "I expect it was about the gods, or magery, or something like that."

"Kefer was talking about her and that sword she has. My lord—Sir King—do you think she has magery of her own?"

"She might," Kieri said. "From what the prince wrote me, the former Duke Verrakai and his brother did, but perhaps that was Liart's spells. But she's never shown it to me. I knew her long ago, you know, at Falk's Hall."

"It's against the Code of Gird," Selfer said. "If she uses it, and we are with her—"

"With the Verrakaien showing their ability, I believe the Crown will approve Dorrin using hers, if necessary."

"I would like to know," Selfer said.

Kieri nodded, then said, "Captain, I have known you since you were my squire—less long than I have known Dorrin. If the gods gifted you with the power to make light or heal, would you use it ill? I think not. And I think Dorrin, if she has such powers, will use hers well."

"Excuse me," said a voice from the door.

"Come in," Kieri said. Paks, Dorrin, and the Knight-Commander of Falk were there. "Well," Kieri said. "This looks serious."

"It is," Dorrin said. "And Selfer should hear it as well, for it bears on him as well as on me and you."

"Go on," Kieri said, waving at chairs.

Dorrin repeated what she had told Paks of her knowledge of magery. "Paks discovered I had more, but it had been blocked by a Knight-Commander."

"At Falk's Hall when she was there," the Knight-Commander said.

"And now the Knight-Commander and Paks have released it." Tears glittered in Dorrin's eyes. "They think I should take instruction for some days before leaving, so that I will be better prepared to deal with my relatives and protect my people." She glanced at Selfer, sitting bolt upright in his chair. "Selfer—I know you are Girdish and this may trouble you."

His brow furrowed. "Indeed, Captain. I was taught—and it's in the Code of Gird—that magery is evil in intent and practice." He looked down and then back up. "But I have known you these several years; I have seen you in war and peace, both in command and under command. You have been honorable, just, as kind as war allows. Paladins—" He looked at Paks. "They also have magery of a kind, though it comes from the gods. Wizards cast spells and mix potions; we do not consider them evil. The Elder Folk have powers we do not, and are not evil. I am trying—I want to—think differently about this."

Dorrin met his gaze. "Selfer, I do not want to press you to do wrong. You agreed to come with me not knowing about my magery—if it troubles you too much, then be free of that promise. It is my hope that I can protect you, and the others, from the evil intent of my relatives, nothing more."

Kieri watched closely; he could feel nothing like a glamour or charm from Dorrin, and yet he could feel those from his elven relatives when they used them. Selfer's acquiescence, when it came, seemed wholly free.

"Sir King," the Knight-Commander said, "I know you have been daily in conference with Dorrin, but it is my belief that she and I and this paladin should retire from the palace to some quiet place where we can speed her mastery of her powers. I suggest the local Field of Falk, as she is Falkian."

"Selfer, you can manage the cohort alone, can't you?" Kieri asked.

"Yes, Sir King. Would it be helpful if I were to start the cohort on the way, and Captain Dorrin could catch up with us? One alone rides faster than the cohort can travel with supplies."

"A good thought, Selfer," Kieri said. "How many days, do you think?" he asked the Knight-Commander.

"Four or five. If you left day after tomorrow, you would certainly not come to the border before she caught up with you." He turned to Dorrin. "Do you agree with our arrangements?"

"Yes, Knight-Commander," Dorrin said. Kieri thought she looked less tense than when she had arrived.

"Then I will go and make arrangements with the Captain to make use of the Field."

"And I," Paks said, "must needs get my pack. I'll take yours, too."

Kieri looked at Dorrin after they all left. "Well, Captain . . . Duke Dorrin. You've surprised me before but . . . the old magery? In one way it is a relief to know you have it, given what you will face, but it's still a shock."

"I'm sorry I never told you about the magery," Dorrin said.

Kieri shook his head. "You weren't using it; it wasn't important then."

"The Knight-Commander is most concerned that I not yield to a desire for vengeance—indeed he wishes me to use magery as little as I can, lest arrogance negate Falk's support and open a gap into which the blood magery could penetrate."

"This Knight-Commander has not seen war himself," Kieri said. "You and I both know the dangers of uncontrolled anger, but we also know what war requires. And this is war you face, Dorrin: treason, rebellion, a civil war, at worst. My advice to you is to use whatever force you need at the beginning. You are not like to use it for your own glory."

"I am of the same blood—I think he fears it will affect my judgment."

"He has not seen you in battle. I have. Here—let's talk of it as if it were a Company campaign. Tell me what you expect to find, what your plans are."

Dorrin laid out the situation as she understood it, concise and crisp as all her briefings were. "And then there are the surprises—the things

I can't know ahead of time. I can't know how many of the servants are complicit, for instance."

Kieri nodded. "Of course, but you know to expect the unexpected. I agree with your assessment and your plan is sound. Dorrin, the prince is right—though this will take all your will and all your skill, as well as that magery you now have, no one else could do it. I believe you can. Trust yourself. I do."

Kieri bade a final farewell to the cohort two days later, as Selfer led them out of Chaya, on the road to the river. No inspection this time—he was no longer their commander, and already their faces turned more naturally to Selfer than to him for orders. Selfer, his former squire, bowed instead of saluting.

"My lord king. It has been an honor to serve you these few years . . ."

"An honor you have well repaid," Kieri said. "Go with Gird, Selfer, and Gird's grace be with you."

"Thank you, Sir King," Selfer said, bowing again. Then he mounted and rode to the head of the column, and the familiar commands started them on their way. Away. *Forever.*

Kieri pushed that thought aside, and went back to work. The more he learned of the long breach between elves and humans, the more concerned he was that this might be a primary cause of Lyonya's economic decline.

Within the human community, those of part-elven blood most often sided with elves and accepted elven values. Here were the strongest opponents to his proposals for an effective military, the strongest proponents of isolation. They were, in general, content to see Lyonya stay as it was, or return to an imagined ideal past: a forest land of peaceful folk who had no quarrels, no wars, no "foreign luxuries." A land where, as one put it, "We used to sit around the fire and sing, and the trees sang with us."

Those of pure-human blood—and especially those with magelord strains in their families—were most impatient with elven strictures, most annoyed by elven "arrogance," and most interested in foreign trade. They wanted change, growth within and without. And yet,

Kieri saw quickly, these had little experience outside Lyonya, and their notions of how other realms thought and acted were as naive as those of the part-elven.

His elven relatives themselves were little help. They were, as Kieri judged them, just as impenetrably arrogant as many humans thought them. Convinced they were right, without being willing to explain why, quick to take offense if they thought they were not sufficiently honored, and at root pleased with the division between human and elven.

"But you marry humans sometimes," Kieri said to his uncle Amrothlin.

"Humans are . . . irresistible at some stages," his uncle said. "Some of them. It's the very insubstantiality, knowing that they will fade and die in a day or two—as it seems to us. To share that vibrant life for the short time of their spring—it is a great pleasure. But then they're gone and we are still here. It is as you with flowers. You plant them, cherish them for the few days they bloom, and then remember them fondly." He smiled as if remembering some liaison of his own, and then shook his head. "Though flowers are not as demanding. But you see—for us, bearing children is a rare and wonderful event. With a human, it is easier."

"Except when it's deadly," Kieri said, thinking of his sister, who had died too young of early childbearing.

"That angered us all," Amrothlin said. "Our Lady was so wroth the taig trembled and all the trees in the Ladysforest dropped their leaves in sorrow at the perfidy of humans."

"And did you never consider that if you had told Aliam Halveric more plainly what you already knew about me, if she had known she had a brother—however unfit to rule at that time—she might not have felt the need to bear children so young."

Amrothlin jerked back, as if Kieri had hit him. "It is not *our* fault!" he cried. "She would not listen to our Lady; she was warned. It was those humans—"

"Have you visited her bones, Uncle?"

Again Amrothlin flinched. "Bones—we do not do that, as you surely know. She should not be there, hidden in stone: she should be set free—"

"She was half-human, as I am," Kieri said. "I have visited her bones, and I say it is not human fault alone that led her to her death. She grieved for her mother, who had left her to take me to see the Lady, and she grieved for me, the older brother who should have protected her. She was angry with you—with elves—because you cost her both mother and brother."

"We did not!"

"No—but think. She was reft of more than half her family, for something that would have seemed—to a small child—no reason at all. All the work was left for her, all the care. She loved her father— he was all she had left—but you, I have no doubt, considered him as lightly as you do all humans."

Amrothlin shifted uneasily in his seat. "No—not quite—he was the king, after all."

"A king with no taig-sense, as you've said. For her, the only family she had left—"

"She had us—"

"Whom she did not know. Could not know, as she had known her mother and me." Kieri felt the grief he had sensed in his sister's bones. "She died of sorrow as much as childbirth, I believe. Determined to do her duty, but without much joy, if any. I blame myself, Uncle, for not escaping sooner, while you might still have considered me worthy—for not somehow finding a way to serve her, save her."

"I—never thought any of this," Amrothlin said. "Her husband . . . her Council . . ."

"They erred, and they suffered for it," Kieri said. "So did the taig, and so did the kingdom. But I hold you, Uncle—you and all the elves, including my grandmother—partly responsible. Not that you asked my mother to bring me to the Ladysforest—that was innocently done, I am convinced. But that my sister felt abandoned and bereft—desperate enough to think risking her own death without need was her best way to prove herself—for that, we are all in part responsible."

"Not you," Amrothlin said. "Not after what you endured."

"I was near enough healed by then, grown to manhood. I sensed secrets hovering around me, but did not press for answers—"

"You would not have had them," Amrothlin said.

"I could have tried," Kieri said. "And perhaps, if I had—perhaps that might have changed some minds. I didn't, and that was part defiance. If no one would explain, I scorned to beg; I would make my own way—as I did. But that pride had its cost to more than myself." He waited; Amrothlin said nothing. "What I've learned, Uncle, in a life you despise, is that everything we do has more than one consequence, and half those or more we never anticipate."

"That is elven thinking," Amrothlin said. "And one reason why we are wary of acting in haste. It takes time—sometimes time that seems long to humans—to foresee all consequences . . ."

"Delay also has consequences," Kieri said. "Haste brings one set of hazards; delay, another. But I am not speaking only to chastise, but to insist that the breach between the peoples harms the taig and risks the entire realm."

Amrothlin opened his mouth to speak, but Kieri went on.

"It must end, and both peoples must work to end it; healing this cannot be done by elves alone or humans alone. I am asking you, Uncle, to take the lead among elves."

Amrothlin might have been asked to swallow a bitter fruit, from his expression. Kieri waited, and finally Amrothlin said, "Who is the human to whom you have given the task of persuading humans?"

"I have not decided yet," Kieri said. "But as you are my uncle, my mother's own brother, it seemed honorable to ask your help."

"You remind me of her," Amrothlin said. "Of the ways in which she annoyed me." But humor softened his tone. "I suppose I must. But please, do not choose Sier Carvarsin: it is not merely that he is more hasty and more . . . annoying . . . than others, but I cannot get past his appearance—that great lump on his nose, and the one on his cheek with those black hairs."

Kieri managed not to laugh, with some difficulty. "Uncle—"

"It is shallow, you will say. But beauty is, to us, an outward sign of inward health and soundness. Carvarsin may be, for all I know, honorable and kind, but to me—to me he is a caricature of a human. Those lumps are like cankers on the trunk of a tree, signifying damage within."

"I will not choose Carvarsin," Kieri said. "It is not my intent to make the task more difficult for you."

"On my part, I must ask how your work with Orlith is coming," Amrothlin said. "I have what he tells me, but what does it feel like to you?"

An intrusion into work of more urgency, Kieri thought, but he could not say that, not now. "It feels slow," Kieri said. "I already feel the taig, so sitting still and trying to let it enter me, as Orlith says, does not—I mean, I cannot understand what it is to accomplish."

Amrothlin nodded. "I thought perhaps that was it," he said. "You have taig-sense, but you do not know what can be done with it. Well . . . do you feel it more now than you did at first?"

"I think so. I am not sure. I don't think I feel it the way Orlith means. He asks me to feel the taig of individual trees—that is their life-force, is it not?"

"Not exactly. Consider a tree—what do you think of? What do you see in your mind?"

"A tree—the trunk, the branches, the leaves."

"That is not a tree," Amrothlin said.

"Well, and roots," Kieri said.

"Roots, indeed, but—a tree is and is not an individual. And you as well, of course."

"I'm sorry—?"

"Orlith should have started with simpler explanations," Amrothlin said. "A tree is not a thing, like this dish or the fruit in it—" He pointed. "A tree is alive, and thus it is always more than you see. Roots to leaves, yes—those you can, in part, see. But it is more—it is the lichens and moss and ferns that grow on its bark, the life too small to see that lives among its roots, a community we know of, but do not think on. It is every fly and bee and beetle that uses it for shelter or food, every bird that nests in its branches. Every one an individual, and yet every one part of the tree, and the tree part of every one."

"You mean . . . it's all connected? I knew that . . ."

"More than connected—" Amrothlin frowned. "It is hard to say in your speech. Your old humans had more words for it, the weaving of life's fabric, they called it, but more specifically. You cannot rightly speak of a tree as an individual, apart from the earth in which it grows, the air it breathes, the sunlight that wakes it to life, the living things that surround it. And yet each tree is also an individual—we think of them as having personalities, you know. They have fathers and mothers, brothers and sisters, throughout the forest; they have a history going back to the first Singing."

"I . . . think I understand."

"You do not now," Amrothlin said. "But to grow to full king-ship, you must. Orlith wants you to feel that—not know it with the mind—" He touched his head. "But feel it, know it in blood and bone. When you do, then you can not only feel the taig—discern, as you do now, whether it is healthy or not—but heal it and use it."

"Use?"

"To raise the taig. When called by someone of power, the forest taig can act—can maze human senses, herd men almost as a shepherd herds sheep, even resist some evil forces: health against sickness, you might think of it."

"So . . . I go on spending a turn of the glass every day trying to feel more and more of the taig, is that it?"

"Not so much trying . . . more letting the taig come to you. The taig is easily frightened at times—it is like a shy child. If you are pa-tient, it will come. Orlith cannot teach you much more until you can touch smaller elements than trees."

"How long will that take?" Kieri thought of all the other tasks awaiting him . . . and the possible need to have the taig on his side if an invasion came. And how could the taig be both easily frightened and any help against an invading army?

Amrothlin laughed aloud. "Nephew-our-king . . . that is such a *human* question. It will take as long as it takes, and longer if you are impatient."

"I will do my best to be patient," Kieri said. "But it would be im-polite to teach patience to my Council by making them wait longer for our daily meeting."

"Neatly said," Amrothlin said, with a warmer smile than usual. "And as courtesy is never haste, let us show them courtesy and begin."

That Council meeting and those following concerned mainly the coronation, now barely more than two hands of days away. Kieri himself found it hard to concentrate on other matters when the palace staff bustled about preparing guest rooms, taking down the winter hangings and pulling out formal decorations. Day by day the tension grew. A tailor came to measure him for the new clothes the occasion required. In one room, green-draped tables held a rapidly increasing array of gifts.

Dorrin came for a last visit, early the morning she rode away, and eyed the changes with amusement. "Have you ever seen a coronation?" she asked.

"The prince's father's," Kieri said. "But in Tsaia the rituals are very different . . . as you will see, at Midsummer." He led her into the room he now used as his study, and shut the door.

"If I can," she said. "If I can hold things together."

"What was the training like?"

"It was . . . a delight," Dorrin said. "Much easier than I expected, as if I were remembering skills, not learning them. Paks thinks it is the years I spent as your captain; the Knight-Commander thinks it's my age and experience both, and Falk's blessing." She gave a quick precis of the tests she'd passed.

"I agree," Kieri said. "You learned to use power well; the form of power is not as important as your judgment and discipline."

"Thank you, my lord. I will do my best." Then her expression changed. "I can't help remembering how my family used it," she said, then after a pause went on. "Some things I could not say—that I can say now." She stopped.

"Do you need to tell me?" he asked gently. Dorrin had never confided much about her past, just that she was estranged from the family.

"Yes. If you have time—"

"For an old comrade? Always."

The tale she told matched his own in ways he had not imagined: the suffering she'd endured, as a child, the final determination to flee at any cost. He thought back to his first impressions of Dorrin at Falk's Hall—a difficult, moody girl, not much liked by the other women for what they called her sullenness, her refusal to enter into easy friendships, her distrust of others. Like the other older students, he had dismissed her as likely to fail, as having none of the graciousness Falk's followers were supposed to show. He had said as much to the Knight-Commander.

"When we older students complained of you," he said when she'd finished, "the Knight-Commander said we did not understand, and such hasty judgment meant we ourselves were unfit for the ruby. He told us nothing specific, only that our opinions were the opinions of—let me see if I can remember—'rash, callow youths lacking wisdom or mercy, who could be judged as harshly by those without discernment.' He bade us fast a night and a day for our ungraciousness. It did not, I'm afraid, change many opinions, though we did learn to keep them to ourselves."

"And yet you hired me."

"It was seeing you covered in mud, working away in that ditch to get the wagon out, and then the look in your eyes—you still expected me to refuse. There, I thought, is a true Knight of Falk, whatever she seemed before, and I must honor that. As you have honored me, these many years." Kieri felt tears on his own cheeks and did not brush them away. "You and I, Dorrin, had more in common than either of us knew. I sorrow for your suffering, and I am sorry for my early arrogance, that assumed no one else had also suffered."

"Thank you, my lord," Dorrin said. "I was—I was not an easy person to like, back then."

"No . . . but now you are, as you have been for years, a Knight of Falk, grave and courteous to all, and I do not think Mikeli could have chosen anyone better able to save what can be saved of Verrakai. Go with my blessing, and know you have always a friend at this court."

She nodded, and then bowed; when she had gone, Kieri was immediately immersed in the myriad details that now filled every day before his coronation.

CHAPTER THIRTEEN

People poured into Chaya for the coronation: Siers and their families, merchants and craftsmen, musicians and jugglers and dancers and mimes. The crown prince of Tsaia sent his regrets, owing to the unsettled times, nor could the Regency Council members attend, for the same reason. Kirgan Marrakai, he wrote, would represent him, and was on the way with a squad of his father's militia. Aliam and Estil Halveric had already arrived, to stay with Sier Halveric.

Every inn bulged with travelers, packed as many to a room as they could manage, and anyone with space on the floor to let could make a quarter's living from it.

"Some families are moving into their outbuildings and renting the house," Sier Belvarin said. "Not ours, of course."

"Of course not," Kieri said. He did not smile; Sier Belvarin had already demonstrated a very limited sense of humor.

"Are your relatives staying with you?" Sier Halveric asked Belvarin. "I've got Aliam and his wife and two of their children and gods know how many grandchildren." Belvarin nodded.

The Pargunese had been informed, with cool courtesy, but not actually invited; to Kieri's surprise, their king dared send a representative, an elderly woman who arrived in Riverton in a boat with white and gold ribbons fluttering from every possible attachment. She was, she told the alert and very nervous port militia, Hanlin Orenalt, the king's wife's oldest sister.

"Pargunese arrogance," Halveric said, when the report came that she was on her way from the port.

"She's not likely to get drunk and assault us all," Kieri said. "Pargunese women don't drink alcohol. And who else could he send? A boatload of women was the only possible envoy we wouldn't kill or turn back."

"I didn't know they had women who could handle a boat," Belvarin said.

"Fisherfolk, along the river," Kieri said. "I imagine every fishwife can row, at least a little. Well, if they mean to show courtesy, so must we. A guest is a guest—but the host is allowed to be wary, though not inhospitable." Given the lady's age, he insisted she must be housed in the palace. The Council protested.

"We can also watch her better here," Kieri said. "If the Pargunese have agents in Chaya, as they well may, she cannot meet them without one or the other coming through the gates."

The lady's carriage arrived under guard; Kieri watched from a window to the courtyard as she climbed down, with help from her two attendants, both middle-aged, sedate women in plain dark dresses with the Pargunese king's crest in brilliant embroidery. She herself was a hand taller than they, almost as tall as Kieri. White-haired, moving a little stiffly, dressed in sumptuous clothes of the Pargunese style, she had the regal carriage of someone who has never had to ask someone to step out of her way. Kieri watched as his steward gave her formal welcome and offered an arm, which she refused for that of one of her women.

Once settled in her room, Hanlin of Pargun seemed—compared to others—to be the perfect guest. She asked for little, praised what she was offered, and made her formal bow to Kieri along with the other foreign ambassadors at a reception that evening. Close up, she had remnants of beauty, her ice-blue eyes not at all dulled by age. The lines of her face suggested someone who laughed easily, and indeed she had a merry twinkle in her eye as she was introduced and the herald stumbled over her Pargunese title.

"It would be a delight to my old age," she said, in the brief seconds allowed each guest, "to see peace between our lands. I am only an old woman—" Patently false, Kieri knew. "—but I have seen faults on both sides, begging your pardon."

"War brings anger, and anger brings ill judgment," Kieri said. What a clever man the king of Pargun was, to send an old woman as his envoy of peace! He smiled at her. "I have no delight in war, though I am good at it." Offer and warning.

"Indeed you are," she said, smiling up at him. "May peace bless both our houses." Then she turned, and the long train of her Pargunese dress rustled along behind her.

Kirgan Marrakai scowled at her, being young and rash, Kieri noted, but most others remained coolly polite. Kieri's elven grandmother spoke to Hanlin of Pargun, but Kieri could not hear their brief conversation. He hoped his grandmother would tell him later.

The talk he could hear concerned the coming ceremony or—annoyingly—his marriage prospects. On the edge of his hearing, quickly hushed if he neared, were speculations about what he might like, which style of beauty, which accomplishments. He noticed that every Sier had brought along a daughter or granddaughter or niece, and he wondered about the young elven woman at his grandmother's side.

He sought out the Kirgan Marrakai, with whom he could talk horses at least, but that young man was all too obviously interested in the young women. They did talk horse breeding, and the kirgan had ideas about which strains of Lyonyan horses the Marrakai blood would nick with, but his eyes kept straying to one girl after another. "I'm boring you," Kieri said at last.

Kirgan Marrakai turned red. "No—no, my lord king, not at all. I'm sorry—I just haven't seen—"

Kieri laughed. "At your age, I was the same. Tomorrow there will be dancing, and you can meet them there—or I can introduce you."

The kirgan shook his head. "No, my lord, please! I am not here to—to prance about with foreign women—"

"That's what your father said, am I right?"

"Yes."

"Well, when else will you have the chance? You're a well-bred, mannerly young man; you won't do anything stupid. Have your fun—meet them, talk to them. They know as well as you that it's not serious."

"But I'm supposed to be Mikeli's envoy—"

"And you are, and I've accepted you as such. Now go enchant some of my younger subjects and keep them from making sheep's eyes at me."

The kirgan grinned. "As it is a royal order—"

"It is."

"I obey with pleasure." And he was gone, intercepting three who had been heading for their corner, no doubt to flirt with Kieri.

"What do you think of her?" Sier Halveric said, with a nod to the lady of Pargun.

"A good choice," Kieri said. "If she does nothing overt, we can't kill her. She's obviously intelligent, and as people trust an old woman with her personality, they will tell her everything we wish they would not. She will go home stuffed with information like a southern date with chopped nuts. We can do nothing about that but note who talks most."

"I'm still worried about your safety."

"True, old ladies don't fear death," Kieri said. "If she wanted me dead—and she might—she would not hesitate to strike though it meant her own end. But I think her plots are subtler than that. She wants to know me, and take word back to Pargun of my weaknesses. It will be an interesting few days."

"If she asks a private audience—"

"Alas, my time is already committed, since I did not know she was coming, and I cannot ask one of those already promised an audience to yield to her."

"Thank the gods for that much," Halveric murmured.

"You're really worried," Kieri said.

"Yes. Perhaps the Lady will know why."

The Kostandanyan envoy bustled up and Kieri greeted him; Sier Halveric slipped away. Count Arpad began the chat with a question about the two Kostandanyan mercenary commanders Kieri had known in Aarenis—such different personalities. Kieri agreed: Sofi Ganarrion, flamboyant and socially ambitious, had been nothing like Count Visan Vladiorhynsich, grim and controlled. Arpad went on: And the Ganarrion girl marrying a southern noble, was that true?

"Sofi was trying to arrange it, but I hadn't heard lately."

"Well. You know what he claims—"

Kieri nodded. Sofi had dropped hints many times of his royal connections. Arpad talked on, finally bringing the conversation around to Alured the Black, the pirate-turned-forest-brigand-turned-ally who now claimed to rule a third of Aarenis.

"He's a very ambitious man, Alured," Kieri said. His mind wandered to Arcolin, now in Alured's reach with only one cohort. Would he remember how dangerous Alured was?

"You've met him, then."

"Oh, yes. Much younger than I, with a gift for command but also for cruelty."

"No danger to us in the north, of course, but for alliances," the envoy said.

"I would not be too sure," Kieri said. "I deem Alured dangerous, wherever he may be."

"Then surely it is unwise for any blood close to ours to become involved down there." The envoy stopped and gave Kieri a meaningful glance.

Kieri stifled a chuckle. "What cause have you to interfere?" he asked instead, though he began to see what might be coming. "If her father approves—"

"We are supposed to give permission—"

Admission enough that Sofi's occasional boasts were probably true.

"But I'm sure if someone with a more illustrious title were to offer for her—" the envoy went on.

Kieri raised his brows. "More illustrious than the ancient title of Fall?"

"Well, there is *one*." The envoy gave him a meaningful look. Kieri almost laughed.

"I'm afraid Sofi and I have had words too often," he said instead. "And besides, isn't the girl already in the south? I could hardly leave Lyonya to go pluck her out of the Duke of Fall's castle before the wedding."

"We have others," the envoy said, a bit sulkily.

"It is too early for me to think of marriage," Kieri said.

"It is never too early to secure the succession," the envoy said.

Kieri remembered that the Kostandanyan princes were usually married off before they reached majority.

"I'm sorry," Kieri said, nodding across the room as if in answer to someone. "But I must see my seneschal—"

Out of the room, in the passage, it was quieter and cooler. Kieri went on, flanked by his Squires, to the small parlor he'd had readied in case he needed it. Here, where he expected solitude, he found the Lady of the Ladysforest, his elven grandmother. As at their first meeting, he was at first struck dumb by her beauty and power; she appeared no older than a maid of twenty but carried with her the silvery radiance of the elvenhome kingdom, a glow that expressed her power. She smiled.

"If you need solitude, Kieri, I will go, but I was hoping to talk to you about the Pargunese lady."

"As long as you do not talk to me about marriage, I am content," Kieri said. "I just escaped from the Kostandanyan envoy, who would like me to marry one of Sofi Ganarrion's daughters."

"Isn't he—"

"A mercenary commander in Aarenis who claims some connection to that throne, yes." Kieri sank into one of the chairs. "I know Sofi. I would not marry one of his get for all the gold in the mountains."

"Then let us speak of the lady of Pargun," his grandmother said. "A subtle woman, for a human; more layers than an onion. What did you think of her?"

"The same," Kieri said. "She spoke to me of peace between our realms, and laid fault on both sides for past conflicts."

"So also would we, if we were asked," the Lady said. "Though I suspect we would apportion it differently than she. Was it then an offer of truce or an end to war?"

"Not really," Kieri said. He glanced at the table where he had arranged refreshments; before he or a Squire could move, the Lady poured water into two goblets and brought them to hand—all without moving. Kieri repressed the shiver he felt. He had seen her use greater magicks, but this homely familiarity chilled him. "We agreed that war is unpleasant, that peace is preferable—but that is all. I find it hard to trust such statements from a Pargunese." He took a swallow of water.

"She may find it hard to trust them from you," the Lady said. "I think it is a good thing that the word was so much as mentioned between you. If this enmity could end—do you truly want it to end, Grandson?"

"I do," Kieri said.

"Then you must make the effort."

"Without risking the security of the realm." On that he would not yield even to the Lady.

"I do not ask you to do that," she said. "But security is not just a matter of armies and weapons. It is also a matter of friendships."

Kieri tried to imagine being friends with the king of Pargun and failed. "I understand that," he said. "Yet the Pargunese and Tsaians have been enemies for a very long time."

"And you are not Tsaian. This is a chance for a new relationship, Grandson. Do not waste it." She rose and was out of the room before he could say more, withdrawing her light.

Kieri looked at his Squires, both of whom looked alarmed. "I have been scolded," he said. "And perhaps she has the right of it."

"The elves always want peace, Sir King," Edrin said. "And peace is a good thing; nobody questions that. But sometimes . . . sometimes it just can't be."

"*They* can withdraw to the elvenhomes," Panin said. "It's easy for them to avoid conflict."

"They are as the gods made them," Kieri said. "After a lifetime of war, I am finding that I, too, yearn for peace. And I don't think it's entirely my elven blood."

"Yet every day you find time for sword practice," Edrin said.

"Of course," Kieri said. "Wanting peace does not bring it . . . and if trouble comes, a king or a realm must be prepared." He stretched, and stood. "Besides—I like swordwork. It's like riding, that way—it forces concentration, and thus opens up the world. But now, it's time to return, before someone thinks I've fallen asleep."

The reception was just as noisy as ever, but the room quieted as he entered. "My friends," Kieri said, "I am reminded that tomorrow is the coronation and I, at least, must have some rest and the palace must prepare a feast. I would not stint your pleasure, but perhaps—"

"Of course, Sir King," Sier Halveric said, picking up the cue neatly. "We also have duties tomorrow and it would be well to rest now." He collected his family, and the others, the nobles and the envoys, all found a place in the line that snaked past Kieri, bowing and speaking farewell. At last they were gone, and Kieri went upstairs to his own chamber.

Out the window, a clear night, heavy with stars. He stood there awhile, smelling the fresh air, the sweetness of the first flowers just coming into bloom, looking at the stars, memory and hope melding as he thought of the next morning. He had come home, but too late for his family; he had become what his father had once hoped, but by a path that might make him fail . . . no, he would not think of that. He went into the bathing room without lighting a candle, stripped, dipped some of the cold water waiting for morning and a fire to become his bath, and washed off the sweat and smell of the evening. He still found Lyonyan nightclothes strange; he pulled on his old nightshirt, hung the sword on its hook by the bed, and stretched only once before falling asleep.

CHAPTER FOURTEEN

D orrin Verrakai rode into Harway at the head of her cohort, still wearing Phelan's maroon and white. She had briefed Selfer on what she expected, and on what her new powers were. She told him what Paks and the Knight-Commander had said about the melding of her years of military experience with the magery, about Falk's blessing. Selfer nodded, though he said little; she thought he was less worried than before about the magery. She repeated what she'd told Kieri, that in their last session, she had held an entire Field of Falk motionless at once and stopped arrows in flight so they hung in the air.

In the market square, forty Royal Guard Light Cavalry awaited her, all muffled in fur-lined cloaks against the cold. The commander introduced himself as Sir Valthan Destvaorn.

"My lord—lady Duke," he said. "It is the prince's wish that I give you his messages; I have arranged lodging for you and your soldiers."

"Thank you," Dorrin said. She did not dismount; it had been a hard, cold ride that day and she longed for a hot drink and something soft to sit on.

"Are these the same as battled for Duke—the king—on the way to Lyonya?" he asked.

"They are indeed," Dorrin said.

He looked them over, his expression wary. "They are the former Duke's troops, are they not? Mercenaries?"

"Indeed. And my cohort these many years. And at the moment, tired and cold, so let us proceed to lodging, where I will be pleased to explain more, if you wish."

"Oh . . . certainly . . ." He wheeled his horse in line with hers and pointed with his crop. "That way, away from the river."

The inn he had chosen was the largest, with ample stabling for their mounts and pack animals. Selfer took charge of settling the animals and the troops; Dorrin followed Sir Valthan into the common room and through to a private parlor.

As she hung up her cloak and warmed herself at the fire, he ordered in a pitcher of sib and sweet cakes hot from the oven.

"Since the prince wrote you," he said, when he returned, "we have captured those Verrakaien in Vérella. You know the Duke and his brother who attended court there are dead. The kirgan and a younger boy are in custody, as well as those Verrakaien in the royal service, and a few others visiting in the homes of loyal lords. But we have not captured other Verrakaien we know of, and we do not have a complete list. We have blockaded the roads that enter Verrakai lands, but after the first attempt to enter and arrest those at Verrakai House resulted in loss of that patrol—"

"What happened?"

"We found bodies just inside Verrakai boundary stones," Valthan said, grimacing. "And were ordered to wait until the new Duke—you—arrived before trying again. We'd heard all of Liart's priests were killed in the battle you were in—"

"All of them there were killed," Dorrin said.

"Well, there must have been more," he said. "There's dangerous magicks—traps, confusions of trails. And that patrol—" He looked hard at her. "We are charged to give you escort into the Duke's . . . your . . . domain. To assist you in taking your place as the new Duke. Do you anticipate resistance once you show your insignia?"

"Yes," Dorrin said. She poured herself a mug of sib and let the hot liquid burn down her throat. "My relatives will not yield to me because the prince named me duke; far from it. Surely the prince has told you that I left the family and was stricken from the rolls when I won my ruby." She touched the Falkian ruby. "They wanted no part of me; I wanted no part of them."

"Yet you are here." Both tone and look challenged her.

"My prince asked me," Dorrin said. "For the sake of the realm, for those long tormented by the Verrakai, I am here."

"I was given this for you." He handed over a velvet pouch; inside were a scroll case and a flat leather box in Verrakai blue. Dorrin opened the box first and found her uncle's chain of office and ring. "The prince wishes you to come to Vérella when you can, to be formally invested, ideally at his coronation."

Dorrin unrolled the first scroll and read aloud.

An Order to attaint such of the Persons concerned in the late horrid Conspiracies, to wit: First, to assassinate His Majesty Kieri Artfiel Phelan, king of Lyonya, and to subvert the royal warrant for his protection during his progress through Tsaia, given by the Royal Council of Tsaia under seal of the Crown Prince, by attacking not only His Majesty's person but also the Royal Guard of Tsaia after presentation of the royal warrant. Second, to assassinate His Highness Mikeli Voston Kieriel Mahieran, Crown Prince of Tsaia and attempt seizure of the Crown. Third, to assassinate other members of the royal family and household in furtherance of treason. This Order attaints all who have fled from Justice, unless they render themselves to Justice, and for continuing other of the said Conspirators in Custody. This Order pertains to all Verrakai, male and female, above the age of ten winters, within and without the realm of Tsaia, save Dorrin of Phelan's Company.

The next scroll held an order for her, personally:

It is ordered by the Royal Council of Regents and the Crown Prince that Dorrin Verrakai, acting as Serjeant of Arms for the Crown of Tsaia in the domain of Verrakai, herself or through her deputies or other assigns, do forthwith attach the Bodies of said Conspirators found in the domain of Verrakai, and do hold them in safe Custody for transport to Vérella to appear before the Council for judgment. Dorrin Verrakai shall have no power to exonerate or raise the attaint from any over the age of thirteen winters by common reckoning, but may at her discretion raise it from those between ten and thirteen. Dorrin Verrakai shall have the power to attach any other persons she finds associated with the said Conspiracy. Dorrin Verrakai shall have the authority to command this squad of Royal Guard to assist in her duties, and such other persons as she chooses to appoint. Persons attached may be sent to Vérella under Royal Guard escort.

Finally, a very short note:

As the Verrakaien are magelords using forbidden magery against Our realm, Dorrin Duke Verrakai has my personal authorization to use what magery she may command in furtherance of Orders given her.

Dorrin looked over at the Royal Guard captain. "Sir Valthan . . . were you made aware of the contents of these messages?"

"The Order of Attainder, and your appointment as serjeant of arms to enforce it? Yes. I am to place the troop under your command and assist you in your duties. We will take custody of Verrakai under the Order and transport them to Vérella." He said nothing about the third note.

"Have you conveyed noble prisoners before?" she asked.

"Yes, but not often, of course. Treason such as this, I have never known before, and if it were not proven by so many witnesses, including men I know myself in the Guard, I would scarce believe it. One of the old families . . . a duke of the realm—"

"Believe it," Dorrin said. "I was there when the Verrakaien troops attacked the king and his escort. I saw it with my own eyes."

"And yet . . . you are also a Verrakai. It is strange to me, my lady, that the prince and Council would trust a Verrakai, even one estranged for years."

His brown eyes showed worry, confusion, and not a little suspicion of her. As well, she could feel the tension in him, as if it were in her own body. Dorrin sighed.

"I do not wonder at your surprise," she said. "I, too, was surprised. It is only, I believe, because the prince thinks no one else can locate and bring the conspirators to justice that I was chosen for the task. I do not expect it to be easy or safe."

"I had heard . . ." He turned his head away for a moment, then looked down at the mug of sib he held. "I had heard stories about you, my lady, from Verrakaien at Court."

"I've no doubt you did," Dorrin said. "They hated me for betraying the family, as they saw it, and for my part I avoided Court to avoid them. I was there, this time, only at my lord—the former Duke Phelan's—command, because he wanted his captain more senior than myself commanding at his stronghold. He did not anticipate a need to travel through Verrakai lands when he went to Vérella in answer to a Council summons, or he would not have had me with him."

"I see." He took a swallow of sib, then another, and looked at her directly again. "What kind of trouble do you anticipate?" Sight came on her as his eyes met hers; she could feel his mood, the tenor of his thoughts, much like the churning waters of a stirred pot. *How bad will it be, and can I trust her?* he was thinking.

Now she was at the crossroads: either way, no turning back. Could she contain the family magery herself, protect this man and his command, without revealing the worst of the family's treachery? She felt the flick of Falk's Oath, as if her ruby had burned for an instant. No . . . either way she would betray someone, but she must not betray the greater trust.

"Magery," she said.

"Verrakai has wizards?" he asked.

"Wizards do magicks," she said. "Some better, some worse, some more powerful than others, but that is not magery. This is the *old* magery, Valthan. Southern magery, that all the magelords once had. Surely you know what the prince told me—it was used against him, when Verrakai meant to kill him."

His hand rose to his own knightly insignia, the Bells. The Order of the Bells was rigorously Girdish, in origin and practice. His voice trembled. "I thought—it must have been—Liart's spells the Duke used. The old magery was all lost, if it was ever more than the powers granted by evil gods. Gird destroyed it—"

"No," Dorrin said. Once having started, it was easier. "It was not all lost, and Gird did not destroy it. Magery was failing even before Gird's rebellion destroyed the old system . . . some families had lost it completely, and in others only a few individuals had it. The Marrakaien, for instance, had no effective magery then. The only Mahieran left alive after the war had none; that's why he was made king; the other surviving families agreed, to make the peace with the Girdish. But some families . . . our family . . . still had the old magery, and held it close. They chose then not to fight openly—they lacked the numbers—but preserve it for some future time."

"Did the prince know? The Council?"

"The prince certainly does now, since he experienced it himself. Before, I don't know—I don't imagine so. To be honest, Sir Valthan, I do not know how much of Haron's magery was his own innate power and how much was—as you thought—granted to him as one of Liart's worshippers. Its existence was always a close-held secret, and they believed alliance with Liart was the means to retain and strengthen it."

His face expressed all the disgust and horror she herself felt. "Is that the—" He gulped, then went on. "Is that the only way to preserve the magery?"

"No," Dorrin said. "Some children are born with it, long before they could swear service to Liart."

"Do . . . do you have this magery?"

"Yes," Dorrin said, and watched his already pale face pale even more. "I do. I was born to it, but never trained in its use."

"Does the prince know that?"

"Yes," Dorrin said. She handed over the third note. "As you said."

He looked up from the note, eyes blazing. "It's against the Code! The practice of magery is expressly forbidden. He cannot permit this—"

"He believes, as I do, that it is the only way—"

"He should have called for a paladin," Valthan said. "A Girdish paladin." His glance at her ruby was eloquent of scorn. "You had one with you—did you not think to ask her help?"

"Indeed I did," Dorrin said. "And her response was that she would not come with me—she felt no call to come—but she did help me awaken my own magery."

"Awaken?"

"It had been blocked by the Knight-Commander of Falk when I was a student at Falk's Hall. See here, Sir Valthan, I am no more happy about this situation than you are. I have no love for my family; I never meant to see the place again. I did not regret the loss of the little magery I then had; I made a good life for myself without it. But this is what my—and *your*—prince wants, for the good of the realm. Otherwise, he thinks, Tsaia might face civil war and thousands could die, leaving the realm weak against foreign enemies like, for instance, Pargun."

She bit into a sweet cake and gave him time to think that over.

He watched her eat; his color had returned. "I have no experience fighting magery," he said. "Do all the Verrakaien have it?"

"Most do," Dorrin said. "I will not deny it is dangerous, but not to the soul of one of your faith . . . you are a Knight of the Bells; you are Girdish. Gird will aid you, I truly believe."

"And you are Falkian."

"Yes, and I hope Falk will aid me. You may not know that Falkians are not forbidden magery, if they have it—most don't, but some, being part-elven, have that form, which is different from mine. If I did not believe my magery, and my experience in war, could prevail, I would not lead my cohort or your people into Verrakai lands; I would have refused the prince's request."

"But you said you were not trained in that magic—magery," he said.

"Not as a child. The current Knight-Commander of Falk and the paladin Paksenarrion released it from the bonds that had held it, and trained me after I accepted the task."

"So short a time . . ."

"The Knight-Commander thought it enough," Dorrin said.

He looked at her a long moment, then nodded. "I'm thinking we could use more troops."

Dorrin chuckled; he looked startled. "We could always use more troops," she said. "But we must do with what we have—or you could contact the grange here, or Marshal Pelyan at the next—or both—and ask their assistance. There are granges in Verrakai lands, and though some are dispirited—Darkon Edge certainly was—they are not corrupted, so far as I know. They should be your allies."

"And yours," he said.

"So I hope," Dorrin said. "Though they may well not trust me at first simply because I am Verrakai. No wonder in that." She ate another sweet cake.

A knock came at the door; she said "Enter" and Selfer looked in.

"All settled, Captain. Animals being groomed and fed; the troops can eat in sections or we can take meals out to the barns where there's more room. There's a hay barn almost empty." Selfer looked fresh enough to travel another half day. "There are locals come in for supper—"

"The barns then, if the landlord has no objection." She started to remind him about fire precautions and the other minutiae of settling a cohort for the night in civilization, but stopped herself. He was past needing that; what he needed now was her trust.

"Right, Captain. I'll report back when they're done. The landlord's set them up for sleeping in the loft upstairs, sergeants and officers to have rooms. I thought we should leave a guard in the barn with the animals."

"Excellent, Selfer."

He withdrew, and Valthan cocked his head. "He's very young."

"He's lived a lot," Dorrin said. "Youngsters grow up fast in combat." She yawned. "Excuse me, but I am going to need real food shortly. After that, perhaps we could visit the local grange together?"

In the late-winter dusk, the grange was brightly lit from within, though the big doors at the road end were shut. At the barton entrance two young yeomen stood guard, faces stern as Dorrin and Sir Valthan approached.

"Welcome, visitors," said one. Then his eyes widened. "Sir—you are a Knight of the Bells—I'll get the Marshal." He whirled and darted into the barton.

Dorrin grinned at the other guard, much younger, who looked confused and uncertain. "This is Sir Valthan Destvaorn, of the Royal Guard," she said. "And I'm Dorrin, a Knight of Falk."

Valthan glanced at her, his eyes glinting in the torchlight. But then he nodded; evidently he understood and accepted her reason for not proclaiming her new status this night.

One of the Marshals Dorrin had seen after the battle came to the barton gate, wiping his hands on his tunic, sweat gleaming on his face. "Welcome, sir knight—lady—oh! I remember you, don't I? I'm Marshal Berris."

"That's right," Dorrin said. "I'm Dorrin, and as a Knight of Falk ask courtesy of the grange. This is Sir Valthan—"

"Knight of the Bells, that's what the lad said. Welcome, sir. And you, my lady. Knights of Falk are always welcome, and you in particular. Come in, both of you. I've had to add drill nights, since the grange has grown so in size."

"This is Harway Grange?" Valthan asked.

"It's the grange for Harway now," Berris said. "It was established before the border was set, as a village barton in the early days of the war, Thornhedge. So it's on the grange rolls at Fin Panir as Thornhedge Grange, but Harway's long grown out to swallow the old vill and travelers call us Harway Grange. I suppose I should write the Marshal-General and see to getting it changed, but I don't like to lose the old name."

"And no wonder," Valthan said. In the barton, steam rose from the sweaty yeomen who had been drilling furiously—formation drills, Dorrin noticed; some were rubbing bruises from the hauks. "When it pleases you, Marshal, I'm ready to take my turn."

Berris chuckled. "And they're ready for a breather, I daresay. So am I, though. I daresay this lady, Falkian though she be, will not mind a few touches with you—"

"She traveled all day, Marshal; I believe her fatigued, as I am not."

Berris glanced at Dorrin. "My apologies, then. Perhaps—"

"I've had food and a rest, Marshal," Dorrin said. "I would be pleased to cross blades with Sir Valthan, though not to his hurt. I understand that your rules do not require blood be drawn?"

"No, certainly not. And should you prefer another mode of combat, you have only to ask. We will be glad to observe two knights of different traditions—"

"And one non-knightly tradition," Dorrin said. "As you know, Marshal—and many of you may as well—" She looked around at the interested faces. "I was one of Duke Phelan's—now King Falkieri's— captains when he was a mercenary."

"Good," Berris said. "We shall move into the grange itself, where others are now studying Girdish lore, who tranferred from Falkian fields along the border."

Inside the grange, Dorrin and Valthan moved to the platform; those who had been outside crowded in, and those who had been studying moved to the sides. Dorrin had watched the ritual exchange of blows many times and had practiced so many times in front of troops that she had no concern at all except for wondering if Valthan would start with a standard opening or one of his own. She intended to follow his lead; she was sure she could take him in real combat, but she needed him as an ally.

"I'm wearing mail," she said to the Marshal. "I was traveling and haven't yet changed."

"I also," Valthan said. "It's fine with me, if it is with you."

"Perhaps you should go to the training swords," Marshal Berris said. "No sense risking a nick on a quality blade, just for the exchange."

Dorrin nodded and, seeing no stand, took off belt and sword together, hanging them on one of the hooks on the wall nearby. Valthan did the same. The Marshal handed them wooden training swords, which had only simple crossguards.

"Knucklebusters," Dorrin said, grinning. Valthan grimaced, but ended in a grin. She jumped lightly onto the platform and walked back and forth, imprinting its dimensions in her mind; Valthan did the same. Then, from opposite corners, they waited the Marshal's signal, and when it came, began a slow spiral toward each other.

Valthan held the training blade a little loosely, as he would have a dueling blade, where the play of fingers had more effect. Dorrin, equally skilled with duelers' weapons, battle swords, and short swords, wondered if it was a feint. The sword he'd been wearing had a scabbard as broad as hers. She feinted; his response was so quick, she grinned as she parried, the clack of the wooden blades loud in the breathless silence. He tried a second thrust, just off where it should have been, and she made a parry that trapped his blade long enough to drive a thrust to his shoulder. A touch, no more than necessary, but he dipped his head, acknowledging. An honest dueler, then. Not all were.

He switched hands suddenly, and with a diagonal pace attempted her unprotected side; Dorrin spun with his move, instinct taking over, and the strong inner third of her blade met the outer third of his—strong against weak—with enough force to take it from his hand and send it clattering across the platform to land in someone's hands a length away.

Valthan stared at her, empty-handed and wide-eyed, for a moment. She forced herself to stillness, backed a step, and bowed. "My pardon, Sir Valthan," she said. "Enemies have made that switch before, and I forgot this was a ritual exchange. I struck harder than I should have."

"How did you do that?" he asked, still staring as if she'd turned into a wildcat. Or a wicked mageborn.

"I would be glad to show you in slow practice," she said. "It's a very useful stroke, but only against that particular attack. If the Marshal permits?"

Marshal Berris seemed as awestruck as Valthan. "Please," he said. "I was taught how to face an other-handed fencer, but only quick retreat and regroup if someone switched hands."

"Let's have that blade," Dorrin said, as if the fellow holding Valthan's wooden blade were one of her own cohort, and he handed it back, hilt-first, very politely. She checked the tip. "I'm sorry, Marshal—I cracked this blade. You'll have to get another. I'll be glad to pay—"

"No, no . . . these are practice blades; they break; it's their nature. Here—Sir Valthan, do you wish to be the demonstration model, or shall I?"

"I," Valthan said, reaching for the replacement blade. "I've never had someone disarm me with that move; I want to see how it was done."

"Very slowly, so they can see," Dorrin said. "Do exactly what you did. Do you have a count for it? If so, call it out."

He complied. The feint before the switch, one and two; the change of hands, three and four, but his foot was already moving in the diagonal step.

"If I had stood still," Dorrin said, standing still, "he would have had an excellent draw cut here . . ." As he moved past her, she allowed the cut, fore and aft. "That's how it's supposed to work. Now, if you don't mind, at the same speed, repeat." He returned to his place and began the same moves.

This time, moving at his speed, she demonstrated the footwork that moved her out of danger, and gave her opening to strike. She held up her hand and they both halted at the moment of contact, showing how the leverage was all hers by correct placement.

"It's a viable parry even if you don't disarm your opponent," she said. "But at full speed, it will usually jar them enough to cost them their blade, if your own has some weight."

After that, the Marshal wanted to try it, and soon Dorrin was tiring. It had been a very long day. He recognized that, and agreed to meet her at the inn the next morning to talk.

"That trick," Valthan said, on their way back to the inn. "It's just a trick of fence?"

"Yes," Dorrin said. "What did you think? Magery?"

"It was so . . . unexpected."

"I learned it in Valdaire," Dorrin said. "My third campaign year with Phelan. I'd taken a gash from someone who did what you did, only with steel, and a man with a withered arm approached me after, and said he had a foolproof response for such attacks. I didn't believe him, but it turned out he was a fencing master famous there, and though it cost good gold, it has been worth it since. He had lost the use of one arm to a poisoned blade, and knew more about fencing one-handed against many attacks than even the Duke's armsmaster Siger. Practice it in your mind, and in a salle only in private; use it only at full speed, and no one will know what you did."

"But you taught it to an entire grange of Girdish yeomen," Valthan said.

"I showed it to them. Not one in a dozen will work enough to make it useful to them. And I taught it to Siger, in the Duke's Company."

"You puzzle me," Valthan said, as they neared the inn.

"I puzzle myself," Dorrin said, grinning. "I must get some rest. I'll see you in the morning."

CHAPTER FIFTEEN

Dorrin woke before dawn and fumbled for the candle at her bedside. A chill draft came from the window, through both the inner and outer shutters. Above her, she heard a faint creaking of floorboards; below, the steady slop-slop-slop of someone mopping a floor, probably the inn common room. Somewhere outside a horse whinnied and mules brayed, the sound growing louder as more animals joined in. In the candle's dim glow, she could see the leather case with its contents, her pack, yesterday's clothes hung on a stand before the fire, now a bed of warm ashes.

Someone tapped on the door. "Light your fire?"

A very superior inn. "Come in," Dorrin said, and reached for her belt with its pouch of coins. A serving girl, with a canister of kindling and a lighted taper.

"Breakfast soon," the girl said, kneeling to place the kindling. "Can bring it here, if you'd like."

"I'll come down," Dorrin said. She swung out of bed—a clean one, she'd noticed the night before—and as the fire caught, crackling, she handed the girl a copper. "Thank you," she said. "What's the weather outside? Clear or snow?"

"It's not clear but there's no snow," the girl said, picking up the canister of kindling. "Cold, though." She left, and Dorrin heard her tap on another door. Already the room felt warmer.

Dressed in cleaner clothes from her pack, Dorrin made her way downstairs and out to the jacks. On the way back inside she stopped at the barn and spoke to the two guards Selfer had posted. Selfer himself was coming out the inn's side door.

"Morning, Captain. Favors of the day to you. They've almost got breakfast service started." He looked wide awake, eyes bright, cheeks flushed with the cold.

Dorrin grinned. She had been that young once, and Selfer could have been a son. "And a fair morning to you, Selfer. I'll be meeting with the local Marshal and possibly other town officials sometime this morning; we'll stay here another day, let the animals rest up."

"I'll see the troops get some drill in, then," Selfer said. "Any other orders?"

"Ears and eyes open. No one to wander off alone, but if you let Tam and Amisi go shopping for something, they might hear . . ." Tam and Amisi, Dorrin knew, found information the way pigs found acorns.

"Oh, I think we need several things. One of the mules' halters is worn; I noticed that yesterday. I'll ask the landlord if there's a leatherworker in town. And two horses need a loose shoe reset . . . have to take them to the smithy. Can't say I like the look of a girth or so . . ."

Dorrin chuckled. "You're learning, Selfer, indeed you are. Take care of it, then. Don't forget to eat your own meals."

She went on into the inn, where the smell of frying ham permeated the common room. A few locals huddled at one table over mugs of steaming sib. By their clothes, they were workmen of some sort, young and probably still unmarried. Through the door to the kitchen, she saw a file of her cohort, moving slowly past two serving women who piled ham on half loaves of bread and handed each a bowl of porridge, and then out the kitchen door toward the barn.

Dorrin caught the landlord's eye and he jerked his head at a table to one side, closer to the fireplace than the windows. She took the small table, and in a few moments he appeared with a wooden platter of ham and eggs and a pottery bowl of hot porridge. He went back and fetched a pitcher of cream and small pot of honey as well as a small loaf of hot bread.

She was halfway through breakfast when Sir Valthan came down the stairs, yawning. He blinked when he saw her. "You're up early."

"Not really," Dorrin said. "Just habit."

"I hate mornings," he said. "May I?" She nodded, and he pulled out a chair and sat down. "My da believed in early rising and used to yank the covers off and slap my feet with a wet towel." He rubbed his eyes. "I can stay up all night easier than I can get up before daylight—broad daylight."

"Breakfast will help," Dorrin said. She pushed the remainder of her bread across the table, and stood. "I'm full—get started. I'll tell them to bring you the rest."

"Thank you," he said.

Dorrin went into the kitchen; the last of her cohort had a tray of mugs and a big pot of sib. She told the kitchen staff about Valthan and followed her cohort out. They had the barn's big doors open and enough light came in to let them eat, sprawled on the earthen floor. They started to rise, but she waved them back down.

"I'll let you know what I find out later today," she said. "Selfer's looking for a good drill field; the grange here—which isn't Harway Grange, but Thornhedge—may let us use their drill field, or a Field of Falk may have some space. Some of you will be given errands in town; the rest stay close, don't wander about."

"Think there'd be trouble, Captain?" one of the younger soldiers asked.

"No more than we ever have in towns, but some of you have just made it into the Company. Listen to your sergeants: If you get drunk, gamble, or swive, you can be punished by locals and I can't interfere."

"I thought—"

Kefer shook his head. "Don't argue, Selis." He grinned at Dorrin. "He'll learn soon enough, Captain. Selfer said you had assignments."

"I won't know until after I talk to the Marshal whether we're marching tomorrow. Selfer's probably already set it up, but be sure the farrier checks all the shoes, not just the ones we know are loose."

Back inside with Valthan, Dorrin told him what she expected. "They would have had word their attack on Phelan failed—quicker here than in Vérella. I am sure the Duke and his brother had plans for that contingency, known to those at Verrakai House. They would have followed those plans and awaited word from the Duke."

"And no word would have come—"

"We cannot know that," Dorrin said. "Haron could have assigned messengers not known to be his agents—ordinary merchants, they might seem, innocent travelers—who'd carry word from Vérella of his success or failure there."

"And you're sure failure would not lead them to capitulate?"

"Cooperate with an Order of Attainder? No. For one thing, at least some of them must be guilty, and thus would face certain execution. They've all practiced magery and as you reminded me, the practice of magery was outlawed. They will not want to give that up any more than a man with two legs will volunteer to hobble on one."

"So we may expect violent resistance?"

Dorrin frowned. "I do not know how violent . . . but some combination of magery—which may be quiet and cunning rather than open violence—and force. Some of the servants, at least, will be Liartians by belief, not out of fear alone. We should be provisioned so that we need eat no food prepared there until I'm sure of the kitchen staff for instance."

"I still wonder—how can we know you will be able to hold off their magery? What if Liart strengthens theirs against you? Or—or invades *you*?"

"Do you, as a Girdsman, think Liart is stronger than Gird and the High Lord?"

"No, but . . ." His voice trailed away; he looked around the common room. "With all due respect . . . who in this kingdom knows what your powers really are, or whence they come?"

Dorrin wished Paks would walk in the door—the sudden appearance of a paladin of Gird being likelier than that of the Knight-Commander, and undoubtedly more to Valthan's taste—but when the door opened, it was for someone who looked like a mason, down to the mortar splashes on his clogs. "What proof would convince you?" she asked.

"I—I don't suppose you could show—something—somehow?"

"Violate the Code to satisfy you?"

He flushed. "I didn't mean—"

"I know," Dorrin said. "But it's what you're asking. The only reason the prince granted me permission to use magery is to ward off that of my relatives." Then she had a thought. "What if we talk to Marshal Berris, and if he agrees, I will show you a little in the grange, where you can witness whether or not Gird approves? Will that do?"

He nodded. "Yes, indeed."

"Then, we'll do that. My plan is this: Since you will have to transport those under attainder to Vérella, I will bind their magery for your protection. Unless a priest of Liart intervenes, they should be unable to break those bindings themselves. Therefore I recommend you lodge them in a Girdish grange each night, and have the Marshal help watch over them."

He nodded, clearly happy with that idea. "With so many granges between here and Vérella that should be easy enough, and I can use a courier to warn the Marshals."

Dorrin went on. "Even without magery, and without weapons of their own, they will do everything they can to injure you and your troops and escape. Do not assume that because they are women of high family with fine manners they will be docile; you must be as wary as if they were a band of brigands. Travel with all speed."

"I understand. Will you send the Phelani cohort with us for extra guards?"

Dorrin shook her head. "My cohort must stay with me, to keep order in Verrakai lands until I am certain all members of the family have been found and turned over to the Crown. I have been gone so long, I do not even know how many there are."

"What order of march do you recommend when we go into Verrakai?"

"Half your troop in front, and half behind, mine; I will ride with you in front. We need the royal colors visible; I have had no chance to change mine from Phelan's."

"You could at least change saddlecloths to blue," Valthan said.

"My troops are but lent, from Phelan—or whoever comes after him. They have their own colors."

"They're mercenaries; they'll serve who pays."

Dorrin stared at him until he looked down. "Mercenaries, sir, have loyalties as well as greed. My troops have fought years with me, and are loyal to me, but through me to Phelan, to whom I was loyal." To whom she had hoped to stay loyal, to become a vassal in Lyonya, but now that was impossible. "Nonetheless, a change of saddlecloths might be a good idea. Excuse me." She pushed back her chair and went outside.

"Captain, what orders?" As always, one of her cohort stood sentry by the door.

Dorrin took a deep breath and tried to relax the tension in her shoulders. "Where's Selfer?" she asked.

"In the stable, Captain, checking the farrier's work. I can go—"

"No, I'll go," she said. Calm. She must stay calm. She must not react to such slight insults as Valthan's assumptions about mercenaries; her relatives would try that, too, hoping for a chink in her mental armor.

In the stables, the familiar smells of dung and hay and animals took the last knot out of her shoulders. In the aisle, one of the men held a horse's lead, while Selfer picked up one hoof after another. Dorrin paused to watch, and when he was done, he looked around and saw her.

"Captain—I was just checking—"

"All done, then?"

"Yes; everything's shod, all the straps mended, ready to pack up—do we march?"

"I want your opinion on something, you and the sergeants. Find Kefer and Vossik and meet me in the harness room."

"Yes, Captain." He jogged away; Dorrin walked to the end of the stables and turned in to the small room lined with pegs for harness, now mostly empty but ready for the traders and their wagons come summer.

The three entered a few moments later. "You know what I'm going to Verrakai for," Dorrin said. "I'm thinking about the effect of taking you there—I need you, and you've all agreed to come, but under normal conditions a new duke would be wearing House colors and carrying the family banner. Instead—" She gestured. "We're all in Phelan's colors, and all our insignia are his."

"You want us all to change uniforms?" Vossik asked.

"No. But I'm thinking it might be a good idea to indicate that though you're Phelani, you're temporarily operating as legitimate troops of the Verrakai Duke: me. We could replace the saddlecloths with blue ones, get a blue banner made up . . . I'm asking your reaction to that, and your opinion of the troops' reaction."

Selfer frowned. "Won't they think you hired mercenaries to enforce your rule?"

"That's exactly what I *am* doing," Dorrin said. "But if I change my colors and your saddlecloths are blue, then I'm hiring mercenaries as a Verrakai—not coming in as a Phelani captain. It gives you some legitimacy as Verrakai troops."

"I've marched under the fox-head since I joined," Kefer said slowly. "Never thought I'd be anything other than the Duke's man. But now he's king, and he says we can't stay with him there in Lyonya . . ."

"Captain—or should we even say that now?—are you hiring us permanently? Or just for a short campaign?" Vossik looked wary.

Dorrin ran her fingers through her hair. "I hadn't thought about hiring you permanently; you're still technically part of Phelan's Company—"

"Which doesn't exactly exist," Selfer said.

"Of course it does," Dorrin said. "The Crown isn't going to dissolve it; they need it to protect the north against Pargun. It'll be Arcolin's instead of Phelan's, I expect."

"Not the same," Vossik and Kefer muttered together.

"True," Dorrin said. "But it's still the Company. The Duke—damn, I've got to quit calling him that—the *king* left resources at the stronghold for Arcolin and I'm sure you'll have work there as long as you want it."

The two sergeants looked at each other. Selfer looked at his boots.

"Well, Captain," Kefer finally said. "It's like this. Been in the Company nearly as long as you, as you recall, and nearly all of it in your cohort—transferred after Etund died, as you recall—" Dorrin nodded for him to go on. "And it's not something we talk about, but let's just say Duke Phelan didn't hire bad captains. Been your sergeant now for over ten years, and a lot of fighting, and I trust you. And Arcolin, of course, but—he's not the Duke—the king—begging your pardon." He glanced at Vossik again, and Vossik took over.

"Speaking for me, Captain, I'd be glad to soldier with you, if I can't with . . . with the king. I'd say most of the rest would too. Can't speak for 'em all, of course. But as for me, if you're asking, I'm saying my oath to you."

Here was a new problem. She had not intended to settle any outsiders in Verrakai lands, certainly not nearly a hundred fighting men and women. Yet it would mean having trusted people at her back. She turned to Selfer.

"Well?"

He looked up. "I'm not sure." Kefer shifted; Dorrin shot him a glance and he went stone-still again. "It's not any doubt of you,

Captain, or your ability. But I've been thinking, anyway—of going for knight's training. I've saved my pay, and—and you're a Knight of Falk, and—I wouldn't leave you now, in an emergency, but later—"

"I'm not asking a lifelong commitment, Selfer," Dorrin said. He flushed but she went on. "You've got the talent; you're a born commander, and if things hadn't changed I've no doubt the king would've recommended that you take formal knight's training, either at Vérella or Fin Panir, even if you came back to him as a captain. If you're willing to spare me a year, it would be helpful—it might not even take that long."

He nodded. "Of course I can, Captain."

Dorrin turned to the sergeants. "I do not feel comfortable offering you and the cohort a permanent position without talking to the king and to Jandelir. The king offered me the loan of you, and without his consent I won't commit for longer than a year. But if he consents, and if it poses no threat to his former holding—which Jandelir can tell me—then that offer is on the table."

The sergeants nodded, eyes bright. "Thank you, Captain," Vossik said.

"Yes," Kefer said. "Thank you—and you, sir, too," he added, to Selfer. Then, with a brisk nod, Vossik led them both out of the harness room.

Dorrin waited a moment, her mind buzzing with a thousand new details that had just sprung up to encumber what had been a simple plan. Then she turned to Selfer.

"I know," he said, before she could speak. "Blue saddlecloths and some kind of banner. A pennon. Blue and silver. It may take more than a day; I'll be as quick as I can." He paused. "Blue surcoats?"

"No. Not yet. We're not trying to fool them; we're just making legitimacy clear." She thought of something else. "I have the ducal seal. The prince sent it to me, along with the chain of office. If you run into any reluctance to sell to us—"

"Good. I'll be off, then."

Dorrin went back inside. Valthan was talking to some of the other Royal Guard, but turned to her immediately.

"Blue saddlecloths," Dorrin said, before he could speak. "That was a good idea. I've sent Selfer to arrange blue saddlecloths and a blue pennant. It may delay us a day or two."

"I'm sorry I upset you—"

Dorrin waved her hand. "It's the common view of mercenaries. I should be used to it by now. Come, let's talk of other things. Why don't you introduce me to your comrades? Then we'll visit the Marshal."

"Introduce you . . . as the Duke?"

"It's what I am, by the prince's own command. Best begin here, in Harway, as we mean to go on."

He bowed, but did not turn to the others. "My . . . lady . . . there is one problem. In living memory, Tsaia has not had a woman duke. How do I style your name and title? Are you my lady duke, my lady duchess? Surely not my lord—?"

"In Phelan's company, we always used *sir*, to man or woman commander. And I am displacing a duke's widow, who is used to the term lady. Let it be 'my lord,' odd as it may seem to your ear. It is an odd situation."

Valthan nodded, and turned to the others. He had all the names, the order of precedence, and presented each with grave courtesy to "my lord, the Duke of Verrakai" and Dorrin acknowledged each bow with a slight one of her own.

Marshal Berris listened as Dorrin explained what she wanted to do to reassure Sir Valthan and gave Valthan a sharp look. "I saw her fight over near Darkon Edge," he said. "I have no doubt of her loyalty to the Crown. And if the paladin I met there believes she has sufficient magery—and his own note proves she has the prince's permission to use it—"

"I am responsible for my troop," Valthan said. He sounded stubborn.

"Dorrin?" Marshal Berris said, using her name as if he considered her a friend. Her heart warmed to him.

"I was reluctant to demonstrate my powers to Sir Valthan alone," Dorrin said. "I suggested coming here, precisely because it is Gird's Code that forbids the use of magery, and thus we can assume Gird will be watching to assure that I do not go beyond the barest need. Also I believe that you, Marshal, will be able to discern if I am using any evil source of power. I fully understand why Sir Valthan feels he must know something of what I can do."

Berris chewed his lip a moment. Finally he nodded. "Come into the grange," he said. "First we pray, then we see what happens." He led them inside, then shut and barred the outer door. His yeoman-marshal came out of the back offices, brows raised. "Sarn, I have business I may not speak of this morning. Go to the barton gate, and tell any yeomen who come that I will open the main door when I can. We should be through here by noon, should we not?" He looked at Dorrin.

"Yes," she said. "I doubt more than a turn of the glass."

"You don't know how long my prayers will take," he said, with a grim smile. "Tell them, Sarn, and do not interrupt or come nearer."

"Yes, Marshal," Sarn said, and went out, closing the side door behind him.

Dorrin looked around the big room with its platform at one end, the weapons racked along the walls. High windows let in diffused light.

"Come onto the platform," Berris said. He himself went to a niche at the end of the room, and withdrew something from it. "This is a relic," he said. It looked to Dorrin like a roughly hewn knobbly stick. "We believe Gird actually held it. Dorrin, it is a truth-test, and I will not demand you take it—you are a Knight of Falk and I know Falkians to be honorable—but it might reassure Sir Valthan."

Dorrin took the stick, worn smoother at one end by long handling by many. "I am willing," she said.

"Do not be surprised," Berris said, "if something happens. I will ask questions." Dorrin nodded. "Dorrin Verrakai," he began. "Do you serve Falk and the High Lord?"

"Yes," Dorrin said.

"Do you intend your magery to serve good?"

"Yes," Dorrin said.

"Have you ever, in any way, consented to Liart's evil?"

Dorrin hesitated; the wood in her hands grew warm, warmer than her grip should make it. "As a child," she said. "In pain and fear, when I could no longer resist, I did a few times as I was commanded."

"Have you ever used magery for your own profit, in any way whatsoever?"

"No."

"By the power of Gird and the High Lord, I ask if truth be proved," Berris said.

In her hands, the wood glowed as bright as any magic weapon; she could see the bones of her hands through illuminated flesh. Then it faded.

"Well," Berris said. "I believe we may trust whatever comes, Sir Valthan. And now let us all pray."

They knelt in silence for a time, Dorrin with them. When Berris rose, Dorrin and Valthan did also.

"What proofs would you have?" Berris asked. "We cannot produce a Verrakai lord—other than Dorrin, here—to test her powers on."

"She has said she wants to shield us from attack—if there is any way to show that—"

"I cannot both shield you and attack you," Dorrin said. "But I can shield myself and you, or myself and the Marshal, while the other one attacks physically. Will that serve?"

"If that's the best you can do—" Valthan began.

"Gird's arm!" Berris said. "I suggest three things. Make light. Hold one of us—or both of us—still so we cannot move. Then as you suggest, protect yourself and one of us against attack. That would convince me, if I were going with you."

"You'd be welcome to come," Dorrin said.

"Nay, I spent time enough away this winter. Let's get to it. Can you make light?"

In answer, Dorrin set her hands alight and—as she had learned—expanded that light, making it brighter until the men squinted against it.

"Well and good," Berris said briskly. "Now—Sir Valthan, do you and I draw blades, and starting at the main door, walk toward her, and see if she can stop us, and how far her power extends."

Dorrin, on the platform, let them get to the door and turn, then sent her power out—and they both stopped midway of their first step. Valthan's eyes widened; Berris scowled. She relaxed the power slightly; they struggled forward, like men walking in deep water. When she increased it again, once more they stopped short; when she released it, they both staggered before walking toward her at their usual pace.

"That must be what happened to the prince," Valthan said, frowning. "Horrible feeling; I strained every muscle to move and could not."

"What interests me," Berris said, "is that I have seen and felt no taint of evil in it at all." He looked at Valthan. "Do you want to go on with the third test?"

"I—yes. I believe she can do it, but—I would like to see it."

"Curiosity," Berris said.

"If the Duke doesn't mind."

"I don't," Dorrin said. "Come, Valthan: Let the Marshal attack us."

She was used to making the shield, having practiced that most in Lyonya, and Berris—though a Marshal of Gird in Gird's grange—could not touch either of them with a weapon.

"And so her powers are proved," Berris said, putting a pike back in the rack. "And proved in Gird's own grange—I hope you're satisfied, Sir Valthan, because I can think of no more tests to perform here."

"I am," Valthan said. He bowed to Dorrin. "I'm sorry, my lord, for my doubts."

Dorrin shook her head. "Sir, no apologies are due. You proved yourself a true Girdsman by your doubts, and honorable by your willingness to accept evidence. I do not consider your wish to protect your troops a discourtesy to me."

"Good," Berris said. "And since it was Valthan's desire to come here, you, sir, owe me an exchange and the grange a gift. Dorrin, you go open the doors and tell Sarn he can come in." Valthan looked startled, but complied, taking one of the wasters Berris handed him and stepping up on the platform.

B y nightfall, all the mounts had blue cloth covers over Phelani saddlepads, and the troops, still in Phelan's maroon, had blue armbands. Twists of blue yarn marked halters and headstalls. Dorrin's own saddle now sported a quilted blue suede cover held on with star-shaped silver brads, a large blue saddlecloth trimmed in pale gray, and a drape of silver-gray brocade behind it. More of the silver brads adorned the cheekpieces and browband of her bridle. Dorrin felt her eyebrows going up.

"Leatherworker had some fancy brads," Selfer said. "He said the former duke always had fancy saddlery, so I thought it's what they'd expect."

"I see you put new stirrup leathers—"

"Not taking any chances, Captain."

"You've done well, Selfer. Now—from now on, I'm 'my lord Duke' to everyone, and you are Captain."

"Yes, my lord Duke," Selfer said promptly, without even a hint of a grin.

"Thank you, Captain," Dorrin said. "Valthan has introduced me to his men, and swears they'll be ready to ride on the morn."

"So will ours, my lord," Selfer said. "Did you have time to find clothes for yourself?"

"No success," Dorrin said. "I did ask at one place, but someone had already bought all the blue cloth they had." When Selfer looked abashed, she grinned. "Don't apologize, Captain. I have my formal clothes, and Marshal Berris has lent me a blue cloak. It's Girdish blue, not Verrakai blue, but it will do well enough." It would also infuriate those of her relatives who still thought, and spoke, of Gird as "that peasant upstart."

Next morning Dorrin woke more rested than she'd expected. She dressed: undershift, mail shirt, pale gray silk shirt, with her black velvet dress doublet over it, riding leathers, boots. She hesitated over the ducal chain—wear it? Carry it in its case? What would Kieri Phelan have done? She knew; she had been there. She lifted the chain over her head, started to tuck it inside her doublet and then, half-defiantly, left it exposed, gold against the black velvet.

She bundled the rest of her clothes, all the familiar maroon of Phelan's Company, into a pack, snatched up the Marshal's long blue cloak, and was downstairs before the first light grayed the sky. The innkeeper's watch lamp gave only dim light in the common room, but a streak of light from the half-open kitchen door lay across the floor. She heard the rasping scrape of a broom there, the crack of sticks broken for kindling, and low voices.

When she pushed the door wider, a sleepy cook setting out bowls on a work table glared at her, and a boy paused in his sweeping.

"No breakfast yet! The fire's not even up."

Dorrin smiled. "I woke early and did not want to go out the main door, lest someone think I was off without paying."

The cook's face relaxed. "Ah . . . you think Bal's even awake at this hour? Nay—'tis the smell of breakfast cooking that wakes him. If you're going to the jacks, best take a lantern—it's blacker than pit out there, and wet; the cobbles might've been greased."

Dorrin walked outside, into a chill drizzle; the drops sparkled in the light of her lantern. Across the yard, she could see a gleam of light; it vanished and returned, vanished and returned. Her sentries, she hoped. At the jacks, she met Selfer coming out.

"My lord Duke," he said, formally, with a bow. "A wet day for travel, but at least not snowing."

"Good morning, Captain," Dorrin said. "I think the weather will shift by midmorning if not before—the wind's already changed."

"The kitchen's awake?"

"Yes, but a half-glass or more from breakfast; they had just woken the main fire when I came through."

"I'll tell the sergeants." He moved off, into the dark yard that now felt, to Dorrin, a little warmer than even a few minutes before.

By the time the cooks had a hot breakfast ready, Selfer had roused the cohort. "And we woke the Royal Guard's night watch, who were wrathy with us, until we pointed out this gave them an equal chance at breakfast."

Dorrin laughed. "It's just as it was in Vérella, leaving with Phelan . . . remember how we were packed and ready hours before they were?"

"But they're brave," Selfer said, more to himself than her.

"Oh, yes, they're brave, and skilled at their style of warfare," Dorrin said. "What they're not, is used to constant travel. Not their fault; they're not often used for this duty." She could hear her soldiers in the kitchen now, and yet Selfer was with her. She cocked her head. "So you're letting Kefer and Vossik run the cohort?"

"Only to check on you, my lord Duke, and to see if you have additional orders."

"No, Captain; no new orders. We march when ready; you've seen what charts I have, and you know as much of the potential defenses as I do."

"Very well, then." He bowed and left her in the common room, now lit with several lamps.

Almost at once, one of the serving wenches brought in her breakfast platter. She was spooning honey onto the hot bread when Sir Valthan came in, yawning.

"Do you ever sleep?"

"I confess to waking unusually early—it should prove an interesting day."

"I hope not too interesting," he said. "My men tell me the town's not unhappy to see a new duke in Verrakai."

"Undoubtedly," Dorrin said, through a mouthful of honey and bread. "Haron was as bad a lord as a land could have. I've no doubt he threatened merchants and traders here and on the roads near and through his territory. We know that granges on the south road were attacked—people missing or found dead after torture."

Dorrin returned to her breakfast; his arrived and he set to. When she finished, she pushed back her chair. "I'm going for a last word with Marshal Berris; if I'm not back when you're ready to leave, it's on the way out of town."

"You're sounding like a duke already," he said.

"I should," Dorrin said, grinning. "Since I am one now." She left through the side door; Selfer was talking to Vossik as the last supplies were loaded on the wagons. She caught his eye and he came over.

"Yes, my lord?"

"My pack upstairs, and armor?"

"Already loaded, my lord. The rest of your armor is slung on your saddle." He nodded to her mount, now wearing its newly decorated tack.

"I'm going to the grange, to speak to the Marshal. I'd as soon walk, and stretch my legs; we've a long ride. When Sir Valthan's got his troop ready to go, swing by there and pick me up."

"Yes, my lord." Selfer cocked his head. "Pardon, my lord, but perhaps an escort?"

"You think I need one here?" Dorrin asked. She laid a hand on the hilt of her sword.

"I think it is due a duke's dignity," Selfer said. "Two or three—"

"Two." She waited to see which ones he'd select. He beckoned and two—the two she would have chosen—came up. "You're the Duke's escort through town," he said. Then Selfer sketched a salute; Dorrin nodded and walked out the inn gate followed by her escort. Her first real appearance as Duke Verrakai . . . the first time she had considered herself a Verrakai since she left home. How would the townspeople react?

CHAPTER SIXTEEN

Halfway to the grange, she was chuckling at herself. Early morning, still nearly dark, cold, dank—hardly anyone was out and those who were hurried along, heads bowed, paying no attention to her. So much for the blue cloak, the fancy ducal chain. She strode on, noticing as she passed that the Royal Guard sergeant was only now chivvying his men to tack up the horses.

But at that end of town, things were busier. A woman carrying a washing basket stopped, gaped, and dropped a curtsy. A man leading seven cows along a side lane stopped and tried to hold back the lead cow. A group of Girdish youths, straggling along the way to the grange, all turned to look; two of them pointed.

Dorrin slowed. "Aren't you supposed to be at the grange already?"

"Er . . . grange?"

"You're all wearing blue—isn't this your morning drill day? And the yeoman-marshal expecting you?"

"Uh—yes—uh—"

"You're that lady came to the grange the other day," one of them said, suddenly excited. "You're the new duke, the marshal said. But you're a lady! Ladies aren't dukes. They're dukes' wives."

"They're called duchesses, Matti," one of the older boys said, elbowing the first.

Dorrin chuckled. "I'm not a duchess; I'm not a wife. I am the Duke, because the crown prince said so and so did your Marshal. Get along now; tell him I'm coming to see him."

They dashed away, racing to the barton gate; Dorrin remembered when she could run that fast. She walked on; by the time she reached the gate, Marshal Berris stood there waiting. He lifted an eyebrow at her change in garb.

"Well . . . Duke Verrakai. We're honored . . . are we?"

"Marshal," Dorrin said, with a slight bow. "It's your choice, whether to consider this an honor—"

"Oh, I do. What's snared my tongue is something the boys said, as they came pelting in. What is the proper form of address for a . . . a lady duke? I should have asked before."

"The same as for a man," Dorrin said. "My troops said yes, sir and no, sir to me as they would to the other captains; a duke is a duke, whatever the person in that office."

"So you're 'my lord' the way he was?"

"Yes," Dorrin said, feeling foolish. Either way she felt foolish, and that was no way to feel setting off on today's mission. "What I came to ask—I forgot before—is your estimate of Verrakai's resources after their defeat. What kind of border guards do you think we might meet?"

"The Royal Guard was for killing them all, as you know," Marshal Berris said. "Only a few got away, and none of the officers. I think they took the rest prisoner. If I was a treasonous dog like the Duke— the former duke—I'd have sent everything I had to that ambush, to ensure the plan worked and to spread the guilt abroad, so none would be tempted to betray the plan." He cocked his head. "Still, my lord Duke"—heavy emphasis on the "my lord"—"I'm glad to see you wearing mail under that fancy doublet and shirt. What men-at-arms *are* left will be afraid of judgment and frightened men do desperate things. As I'm sure you know."

"Indeed, yes, Marshal," Dorrin said. "But your report suggests we're more likely to see irregular attacks than an organized force offering battle. Until we get to the house, anyway."

"If a Girdish Marshal may say it, ward of Falk, my lord Duke." This time no sarcasm edged his voice. "I judge the prince chose well, and I wish you well, both in your body and your spirit, for the sake of those who have suffered under cruelty and deceit for so long." He rubbed his hands. "And now, my lord, will you chance an exchange with me?" He lifted his surcoat to show that he, too, was wearing mail. "It would be educational for the lads."

"It would be a disaster if you broke my bones," Dorrin said, but she actually felt like sparring. "But it would settle my nerves. There's more light out here."

"My lord," one of her escort said. "We have all day to ride, you said."

"True," Dorrin said, "but a few buffets won't hurt. Much."

Berris called, and the boys poured out of the grange, forming a square; two of them brought wooden training swords. "No head blows," he said. "And first touch only—I do not wish to injure the Duke."

As she'd hoped, the exchange of strokes, so familiar over so many years, settled her breakfast and her mind both. She'd always enjoyed single-sword practice most, and she and the Marshal were well matched. Parry, circle, parry . . . the wooden swords clacked together, faster as she and the Marshal both increased the tempo. The knot between her shoulders loosened as she warmed to the familiar dance. This and this, and that again, and finally her blade slid past the Marshal's guard, a fraction faster than his, and she managed the perfect training touch—enough to be heard, but not to hurt. In the next instant, before he could stop, his blade thumped her side. They both grounded their blades, and bowed.

"Gird's grace," Berris said. "And the High Lord's favor, be with you and yours."

"And with you as well," Dorrin said. She heard down the lane the sound of many hooves and the jingle of tack. "We have timed it well, I think." She handed the wooden sword to one of the boys, shook her arm and flexed her fingers, then clasped arms with Berris. "Thank you, Marshal, for your good wishes and your aid. Gods grant I can be the duke Verrakai needs."

"My lord Duke!" came Selfer's call from beyond the barton wall. Dorrin felt better than she had the half-glass before, and left the barton, grinning. Marshal Berris shooed the boys back inside, then followed.

When he saw her horse in its finery, he raised his eyebrow again, but offered Dorrin his hands. She mounted, and while her escort held the horse, she stretched out one leg and then the other to buckle on her leg armor and fasten her helmet. Then, when her two escorts had mounted, she nodded to Sir Valthan and the column moved on.

For the first half of the morning, they rode along a track that became steadily rougher and less used. Dorrin had never been on this road as a child; she could *feel* the location of the Verrakai home, but did not know every twist and turn of the road. She had scouts out, forward and flank, as usual; they had nothing to report. As the road worsened, and the last farmland came in view, she turned to Sir Valthan.

"It may be too rough ahead for your supply wagons."

"The story is, the Verrakai could make the road disappear and reappear. Do you have that power?"

"Not that I know of," Dorrin said. Ahead, as the last fields petered out, thick brushy growth clothed the land from ground level to the height of two men. One of the scouts rode over to meet them.

"The track ahead is just wide enough for a team; it's rough, muddy, potholed, and perfect for an ambush. And on flank, we'll be crashing through that brush, if we can even ride at all."

Far in the distance, behind them, cattle mooed and a cock crowed. Close at hand, the land was silent. Dorrin looked at the open land to either side of the track, rumpled and pocked with burrows. Natural? It didn't have the look of a rabbit warren—it looked like a trap for outriders who tried to outflank an attack on the road.

"If they intend ambushes from the flank, they will have ways to travel parallel to the road. We'll pull the forward scouts back a little— stay in sight—and the flankers find their trails. If it's a force smaller than ours, do nothing to alarm them; if you can get past, block the trail beyond them and be ready to take them in the rear or flank."

The brush thickened into unkempt forest. Suddenly, a group of men on horseback rushed out from the bushes to bar the road. They wore Verrakai-blue tunics and steel breastplates and helmets, and carried crossbows and swords. "You're trespassing," said their leader. "Turn back, or die . . ." His voice trailed away as the rest of the column came into view. "Who—who are you?"

Dorrin would have laughed at his expression, but this man—these men—were her people now. "I'm Duke Verrakai," she said.

"You're—? No! You're not the Duke . . . you have a look of his family, but—"

"By order of the crown prince and Council of Tsaia, I am now Duke Verrakai. You see my escort from the Royal Guard."

"But—but where is he? Duke—the *real* duke?"

"He's dead," Dorrin said. "High treason against the person of the crown prince. These—" She gestured at the Royal Guard. "—are my escort from the crown prince, evidence of the legitimacy of my claim."

"That can't be right," the man said. "Our duke a traitor? I don't believe it! And even if it were so, the prince wouldn't appoint a woman duke. Women aren't dukes. And the others—that's a troop of Phelan's, the Red Fox."

"They're in my hire," Dorrin said. "You see that by the blue armbands and saddlecloths I told them to put on. As for the other—I am Duke Verrakai, by his and the Council's order." She pulled the ducal chain out from under her cloak and swung the medallion so it caught the light. His jaw dropped and he stared. "Now—who are you and by what orders do you challenge travelers?"

"We're . . . we're Verrakai militia," the man said. "The Duke told us what he always does, when he went to Vérella just after Midwinter Feast. Guard the borders well, he said, keep the rabble out and the domain safe and unsullied until my return, he said. There was bad trouble over across the other side, maybe seven hands of days ago. But we'd been told to stay this side, so we did."

"Well, Verrakai militia," Dorrin said. "You have seen my ducal chain, and the Royal Guard of Tsaia to declare my claim. You have *my* orders now to let me and my escort pass without hindrance. Will you obey?" The temptation to put a glamour on him, now that she knew how, was strong, but she would not start her rule with falsehood.

He glanced from side to side at his companions, none of whom had taken up anything like a useful position. "I—I need to be sure," he said.

"What proofs would convince you?" Dorrin said. "If the ducal chain will not?"

The man's gaze wavered, then steadied as he nodded to Sir Valthan. "If that one's really commanding the Royal Guard, let him explain himself—let him confirm what you say."

Dorrin realized he might never have seen the Royal Guard or its standard in his life. Without taking her eyes off the man, she said, "Sir Valthan, if you please: Tell this man what you know."

Valthan introduced himself first; Dorrin could see that his name alone impressed the man. Then he went on. "Your former duke tried to assassinate the prince. For that high treason his life was forfeit. The entire family is now under Order of Attainder. The prince and Council discussed dissolving Verrakai as a domain, and wiping that name from the rolls of Tsaian nobles, but chose instead the one unsullied member of the family, this lady, as the new duke, in the hope that she can redeem the Verrakai name. If she cannot, the Crown will expunge it and divide the land among those lords deemed best able to rule it, and most loyal to the Crown. Is that clear?"

"Yes." The man looked down. His troop continued to stare, wide-eyed, as if spelled. "I—I'm afraid," he said finally. "If . . . if I do let you pass, the duchess . . . she has the . . . the power . . ."

"So do I," Dorrin said. "Make your choice. I am here, in front of you; she is not. She will soon be on her way to Vérella, on trial for high treason, along with the rest of the family and all who support her. Which would you? A chance at a life with me, or trial for treason and a traitor's death?"

"What must I do?" Surrender was in every line of his body, but Dorrin did not trust that. Not with someone who had been loyal to her uncle.

"Lay down your arms," Dorrin said. "Then you may ride with us."

"Don't do it!" One of the men behind the leader started to rein his horse away. "They'll kill us, you know they will."

"HALT!" Dorrin's command voice, capable of carrying to a cohort in combat, stopped the man; his horse tossed its head against a tight rein. "I do not kill my people but for treason. If you disarm yourself, swear fealty, and obey, you will be safe."

The leader did not turn, but said, "Do it, Sim. There's too many, we'll all die else." He fished the crossbow over his shoulder one-handed and dropped it to the ground, unbuckled his sword belt and held it out. Those behind him did the same. Dorrin half expected the panicky Sim to bolt, but after a last frantic look around, he gave in.

"Captain," Dorrin said to Selfer. "Collect the weapons, stow them. Sir Valthan, attend me." She rode forward a few steps; Selfer and ten of the Phelani approached the little troop cautiously, but the Verrakai militia offered no resistance as their bows and sword belts were collected. "Dismount," Dorrin said to the Verrakai militia, "and stand before me."

They did so, clearly afraid; two of the Phelani took the horses' reins and tied them together. Dorrin and Sir Valthan dismounted then.

"Sir Valthan will witness your oath of fealty," she said. "He is a Knight of Gird, a Knight of the Bells, a noble of Tsaia and known to the prince himself. I am a Knight of Falk as well as your Duke." She touched the ruby of her order. "Understand that these oaths are binding, and that the gods themselves will know and punish disloyalty."

The leader nodded; the others, whey-faced, stared like cattle.

"Here is the oath you will pledge," Dorrin said. "I—and then your name, all of it—do pledge fealty to Sir Dorrin, Duke of Verrakai, to protect, preserve, and obey, by day and night, in fear, famine, fire, and frost, to the end of my blood and life. To this I pledge my honor."

"That's not the same—" Sim began, from the back row; one of his comrades shoved him.

"Haron was a traitor, and he's dead," Dorrin said. "His oaths were false. Swear or not; it is your choice."

"I will," said the leader. He knelt in the mud before her and said the words in a steady voice, looking her in the eye.

"Rise, then, Mikel Vadrison. I accept your oath."

One after another they knelt and pledged, even Sim, who stammered his way through with prompting from Mikel and others.

"Now, Sir Valthan, as you have witnessed their oaths to me, I ask you to witness mine to them." He looked surprised, but nodded. "I pledge to you the protection of my name and my honor, so long as you are loyal—" She named them all, one by one. "You will not hunger, while I have food. You will not freeze, while I have fire. No evil will haunt your homes, while this blade has an edge and I have strength to wield it." She drew the blade, and it flashed in sudden sunlight. Their eyes widened; surprise, fear, and hope mingled in their expressions.

Dorrin grinned at them. "Now, because you did not know I was your Duke, your earlier rudeness is forgiven you—but so you do not forget, you will march today without your arms. Captain, take charge of these men, and ensure that, as they are unable to defend themselves, they are not put at risk."

The troop moved on, the Verrakai in the midst of the Phelani. That night they camped in the cold damp, but the Royal Guard had tents for their own comfort. "You can have mine," Sir Valthan said, "if you have none of your own."

"No," Dorrin said. "I made a pledge to those fellows in blue; they need to know I keep promises. I will share their conditions, though not their food." She sat at the same fire with them and her cohort of Phelani, sword across her knees, and slept well enough. It was no different from campaigning with Kieri.

The next morning, she called the militia group to her, took a report from Vossik and Selfer on their behavior the previous day and night, and the inspection of their weapons. Their behavior had been satisfactory, but their weapons— "I found rust on four blades," Vossik said, "and one is already cracked from a nick no one bothered to file out. Scabbards oiled, but not really clean. Two belts are old dry leather, ready to give way. The crossbows need to be taken down and reassembled by an arbalest; the bindings on five are rotting. Two, the prod's loose of the stock. I don't know who their armsmaster is, but he's not doing his job. If these were our people, they'd have their pay docked for the damage to weapons."

Dorrin looked at the militia; the leader had flushed. "I'm disappointed," she said. "I demand better of my people. Rusty, nicked swords are good for scaring unarmed peasants, but not for real fighting. Crossbows with bad bindings are out of alignment and don't shoot straight. We haven't time to test your skills and see if they're as rusty as your blades, but I can't depend on you for my protection as you are."

They all looked downcast. Good. Whatever Haron had done to

them—and she suspected he had ensured their weapons and training were inferior, using them mostly for show—they needed pride in their work and their tools. "Mikel, what do you think of the swords the mercenaries carry?"

"My lord Duke, they're—they're beautiful."

Dorrin felt her brows rising. They weren't beautiful; they were ordinary, workmanlike swords that had seen proper care.

"If you had such swords, would you be willing to learn to care for them and keep them . . . beautiful?"

"Yes, my lord!" The others nodded.

Dorrin looked over at Selfer. "Captain, I wish to purchase eight of your spare swords, with scabbards, for these men. And—how many belts were bad?"

"Two, my lord Duke."

"And two belts. You have no crossbows, I think?" She knew perfectly well they did not, but this was too much fun. She could see by the twinkle in Selfer's eye that he recognized the game.

"No. We carry them only for certain campaigns."

"Swords, then, and belts. If your people can find any use in their weaponry, fine; otherwise, retain it for the metal. See that these men receive instruction in the proper care of their weapons."

She saw amazement in the men's eyes and turned away before she had to laugh. Soon enough they had mounted again, this time with Phelani-designed swords, and they were holding themselves with more confidence. Dorrin continued a slow march; she did not want to miss any traps her relatives might have set.

Midmorning of the third day saw them close enough to Verrakai House that Dorrin could easily feel the magery employed to screen it. She remembered the maze of trails and tracks; the glamours that would have led them astray had no effect on her. When they came out of the trees, there before her was the same stretch of fields, snow striping the furrows of the ploughland. Near the little river thin green showed where magery warmed the soil to ensure an early start to the year's crops, just as magery kept the stream from freezing over. In blocks of orchard, the buds of fruit trees showed varying shades of red, rose, and gold with the coming of spring.

And there was Verrakai House, the old keep rising grim and dark from its center, the various additions in less weathered stone . . . out-buildings around it . . . no wall, because, she'd been told, they needed none. Magery alone would protect the house.

Magery had brought it down—the prince had been clear. If she could not rule Verrakai, the Crown would take over, razing the house, the old keep, everything, and divide it between lords the prince thought loyal.

Dorrin reached inside her doublet and pulled out the ducal chain and medallion again. Valthan nodded approval as she spread it on her shoulders, folding back her cloak so it showed clearly, but it was not for him—or for her family—that she did so. For an instant she had felt again the panic of the child she had been, and fought it down with a soldier's discipline. The former duke's ring, large enough to fit her bare thumb, fit snugly on the heart-hand heart-finger over her riding glove; she made sure it was secure, and touched the ducal medallion. She was not that terrified, miserable child, nor yet an errant daughter returning to beg forgiveness; she was the prince's vassal, the rightful Duke, come to take control of a rebellious province. When she was satisfied, she legged her mount on.

"Do you want the Royal Guard to precede you?" Valthan asked.

Dorrin shook her head. "No. They must see that I am in command, and unafraid."

"An archer could take you out—"

"Remember my protection," Dorrin said. "I doubt they'll try anything that simple, but if they do I have nothing to fear—nor do you. You may announce me when we get there."

No one rode out to meet the column as it marched nearer. No sentry challenged them; nothing stirred in the empty, snow-patched fields, no cattle or sheep or horses—some should have been grazing the Winterfield—no peasants. Dorrin knew better than to think no one had noticed their arrival.

"Do you want me to send out scouts?" Selfer asked.

Dorrin shook her head. "I know it's what we would do ordinarily, cut off anyone trying to escape, but I'm not sure how far my protection extends. I think it's better to stay close, even though some may win free."

Halfway from the trees to the house, she felt the first tingle of personal magery. It had a flavor she remembered, one of her cousins'. She blocked it without effort, and checked to see if it had touched her troop. No. It had been meant for her alone, and her cousin would recognize her block as readily as she would recognize her cousin's probe. If they had not known before who was coming, that touch would reveal her.

❦

They waited on the front steps of the entrance hall, all the women she remembered and the children she had never seen. Her aunt Jeruvin, the deposed Duke's widow. Her other aunt, the Duke's brother's wife. Her mother. Her male cousins' wives and her female cousins, all their faces stony with hatred . . . only the children showed anything but hostility. The older male cousins—who should have been there, unless they'd been fostered to other houses—were nowhere in sight. They might be preparing an attack, or they might have fled.

She halted her mount and waited; the Royal Guard unit fanned out around her, and Valthan rode up beside her.

"By proclamation of the Crown Prince and the Regency Council of Tsaia, I present your new Duke, Dorrin—"

"We know who that is!" That was the Duke's widow, Jeruvin. She glared straight at Dorrin. "Traitor! You are dead to us!"

"That is your Duke," Valthan said. His hand dropped to his sword hilt. "Show respect!"

"That is no duke. That is a runaway, nameless, a traitor to this family and cast out long ago. It is an insult that it is here."

Valthan started to speak, but Dorrin waved him to silence. "You, *widow* of Haron Vasli Verrakai, are under Order of Attainder, as are all here save the youngest children. You see this chain of office—you see this ring." She held up her clenched fist. They would understand that, oh yes they would. "I am the Duke now, by order of the prince and Council—"

"Attainder!" That was her own mother. "What have *I* done to be attainted? What have any of us done that the prince should so maltreat us? I have had naught to do with Haron—"

"You lived under his rule; you chose to stay under his roof. You outlawed me."

"You are no child of mine!" Her mother turned her back.

"True enough. I am your Duke, like it or not."

"Liar!" One of her cousins, Syrila, flicked her hand and a bolt of flame spurted from it. "You are talentless, witless—"

Dorrin put out her hand and the flame vanished, to her own brief surprise. So easy? "Whatever you think, I am your Duke, and you will find it in your own best interests to stop this nonsense."

Syrila fairly gaped, an expression Dorrin had long wanted to see on her face. "But you—you can't—you never could—"

"I'm not a child now, Syrila. Don't do that again." Dorrin could feel, as if they were touching her, the shivers of apprehension that ran through the Royal Guard, Girdsmen all. They had been told; they had heard Marshal Berris agree that Dorrin must use magery against the mageborn if necessary. But now they had seen for themselves what they were up against—and what was on their side. Not a mercenary—not *just* a mercenary—and certainly not a Girdish paladin, but a magelord.

"Where did you learn—?" "How much do you know—?" A torrent of questions, during which her mother turned again.

Dorrin held up her hand, and for a wonder they fell silent at the gesture alone. She wanted to use her magery as little as possible, not only to reassure the Girdish, but to convince her relatives that it did not take magery to defeat them. "That is not your concern," she said, deliberately copying her uncle's tone, but adding no power to it. "Your concern now is proving to the prince and Council that you are not as guilty of treason as Haron was. All adult members of the family will be transported to Vérella, there to stand trial—"

"Treason! *I* committed no treason!" Jeruvin stamped her foot.

"The court will determine that," Dorrin said. "You will be escorted by the Royal Guard—" Her aunt's expression shifted, showing exactly what she had in mind when alone with Girdsmen who had no magery. "—and," Dorrin added, "I will bind your magery, for their protection. I doubt you can break my bindings, but should you do so, I will kill you myself."

Jeruvin glared but said nothing more. Haron's brother's wife said, "When must we go? It is starting to thaw, and the roads are vile—"

"You will start tomorrow, at first light," Dorrin said. The sooner she got the elder women out of the place, the better. Without taking her eyes off them, she said, "Kefer—assign someone the care of my mount."

"At once, Capt—my lord Duke—" He said something she did not attend, being concentrated all on her relatives; she knew, and they knew, that a moment's inattention would give the women a chance to attack, and she had no doubt they would. One of the soldiers ran forward to hold her mount.

Dorrin threw a leg over its neck and vaulted down without looking away; that impressed them, she could tell. The younger children were round-eyed, all but one boy who blurted, "I can do that, on my pony. It's not hard."

"Mostly you fall down when you try it, Bori," said a girl, shoving him.

"I do it sometimes!" he said, shoving back.

One of the adults thumped both heads, and they fell silent, glaring at each other. Dorrin had to struggle not to laugh.

"Sir Valthan, attend me please," she said, and headed for the steps. She felt a slight pressure as she reached the bottom step, and threw her power against it; it popped like a soap bubble. Was that really their strongest defense? Still looking Haron's widow in the eye, Dorrin said, "Don't do that again, Aunt, or I will drop you where you stand."

"It wasn't Jeruvin, it was I," her mother said. "Would you dare flaunt your power against your own mother?"

"You said I was not your child," Dorrin said. "Stand there, then, if you doubt me." She was within arm's length now; she touched her mother with her heart-hand forefinger and let her power out. Her mother stood silent, held motionless with one hand half raised.

Jeruvin, hatred blazing from her dark eyes, made some signal behind her back, and two of the younger women rushed forward, hands raised.

They slammed into the invisible barrier Dorrin raised, yelping with pain. "You only make it harder on yourselves," Dorrin said. A wicked glee flickered in the back of her mind; she stamped it down. They already knew arrogance and bullying; they needed to see another kind of power, another kind of leadership. "Aunt, you have caused another injury to these young ladies. You must be still." The magery for holding someone motionless took almost no energy at all;

she extended it to all the adults in view, and then, without hurry, one by one, bound their magery. None had magery as strong as hers. Despite the Knight-Commander's prediction, she was surprised. Was her power really that strong, or had theirs weakened over the years?

But she had no time to study that conundrum. The family she saw here, and their magery, was not all that menaced her. Somewhere men and older boys hid, planning an attack, unless they had run away. Somewhere servants lurked, possibly only frightened but possibly Liartians eager to do harm. "Captain, secure the outbuildings." Dangerous work, but it had to be done.

"Yes, my lord," Selfer said. "Search them as well?"

"For now, simply secure them."

He bowed and turned away. She looked at the gaggle of relatives. "You will all be under guard in the great hall for now. If you give trouble, you will be shackled in the stables. When I release you, it is only for you to walk into the hall and sit down on the floor, where the Royal Guard directs. Children under ten will go to the safe nursery when I have found nurserymaids; suckling babes you may keep with you." She turned her head a little. "Sir Valthan—proceed."

They had discussed this; he knew what to do. Some inside the great hall, to watch the Verrakaien come in, tell them where to sit, and guard. Some to herd them in, as if they were sheep. Dangerous sheep.

CHAPTER SEVENTEEN

They hated her with every breath; she could feel that, and yet it did not hurt, not the way it had when she was young. She eased back the power she had exerted, and slowly . . . staggering a little, some of them . . . they moved into the doorway, past her, with Valthan's soldiers.

She reached out, then, and felt for the other magic she knew was built into the place. The tang of the Bloodlord's cruel power tingled along her senses, disgusting and frightening at once. A whisper eased into her mind: *Broken blades, jagged hooks, whimpers, moans, screams . . . I give you these.*

"Ward of Falk," Dorrin said, aloud. "Ward of Falk against all evil ones—"

Falk is not my master. I have no master.

Dorrin pushed it out of her mind. Disembodied voices could come from anywhere; Liart's power needed a physical focus. If they had priests of Liart there—well, she had already bound her relatives' magery. She now believed she could deal with them as well.

The question now was how to manage her relatives until they could be transported to Vérella. Would the Royal Guard be adequate security? Did her family have allies between here and Vérella? And where were the men and older boys? Unfortunately, she had no magical vision that let her see through walls, or find anyone not using magery against her.

At least here and now, the Guard should be enough. When all the prisoners were inside and under guard, she and her escort moved on into the house. The great hall, scene of so many humiliations, looked much the same. She still remembered which of the doorways led where, to kitchens and other offices, to dining rooms and up front stairs or back to the rooms above. She nodded to Valthan, who read again the prince's order and called all to come forth.

This time it was servants, shuffling warily out of various doorways and edging downstairs to gather in a disorganized mass at the other end of the great hall from the ladies. Verrakai's household livery on the upper servants, and drab on the others . . . it had been so long, Dorrin didn't recognize any of them.

She took a step forward. "I am your new Duke, by order of the crown prince and Council," she said. "From now on, all orders come from me. Is that clear?"

A murmur, not of resistance but uncertainty.

"If you obey me, no harm will come to you. If you do not, I will consider you conspirators in the treason which brought the Attaint to all in the family, and you will be transported to Vérella to stand trial. What say you?"

"By what right do you treat highborn ladies so?" This from a tall man in the house livery pushing his way forward; the others edged away from him and averted their gaze.

"Who are you?" Dorrin asked, without replying to his question.

"I am His Lordship's steward," he said. His expression and voice expressed confidence in his own authority. "Grull Lanatsson is my name, and I am in charge of the household, under His Lordship."

"Did you not hear?" Dorrin asked. "Haron the traitor is dead. All adult members of the family are under attainder and as they have already tried to attack their Duke—me—and members of the Royal Guard, traveling under royal warrant, they are prisoners, and treated as such. As for you, you may have been the former Duke's steward, but you are not yet mine. Do you acknowledge me?" Dorrin sensed more movement in the corridor behind the servants, a shifting in the group of them, and another man came to the front, in footman's livery.

Grull said nothing, scowling as he glanced around the hall, where armed soldiers were obviously on alert. The footman leaned to him and murmured something Dorrin could not hear. He shook his head; the footman stepped back. Then he said, "I would see this so-called order—"

"You have heard it read by an officer of the Royal Guard, a Knight of the Bells," Dorrin said. "You see the Royal Guard uniforms. Acknowledge me as the rightful Duke, or not, but no more delay." She could feel, from the far end of the hall, her relatives' bitter hatred.

He looked around at the other servants, and by his expression did not like what he saw.

"I acknowledge you," he said, finally.

"You can't!" said the footman who'd been near him. "You know what he—"

"Be silent, fool!" Grull said.

"Come here," Dorrin said. "Both you and that footman. What is his name?"

"Coben," Grull said. He strolled forward, every movement confident. Behind him, Coben followed.

When they were a bare spear-length away, Dorrin halted them with her mage power; they both paled. Grull did not struggle, but the footman's strained face showed that he was trying to break the spell. She walked closer to them; her personal guard came with her. "Grull, what gods do you serve?"

"Whatever gods my lord commands," he said, raising an eyebrow.

"And what god did your lord command?"

"He—" Grull trembled suddenly, as if with a chill, and the voice Dorrin had heard in her mind spoke with Grull's mouth. "What do you think, little rabbit? He is *my* faithful servant."

"Then he cannot be mine," Dorrin said. She looked at the footman. "And you? Speak, Coben."

"You're not the Duke," Coben said. "I heard about you; you're just a runaway, not really a Verrakai, and anyway you're just an old woman."

"Do you also follow the Bloodlord?" Dorrin asked.

Coben smiled, showing his teeth, and licked them. "The mightiest of gods is Liart, Lord of Torments. You will never prevail against him—"

"Bind them well," Dorrin said. "For they have spoken treason and thus fall under a sentence of death, unless the prince commutes it."

"You cannot kill us," Grull said, this time in his own voice. "We have done nothing. And you lack the will—you are weak—"

"You tell your Duke she is weak?" Dorrin had her sword in hand before she quite realized it. Beside her, her two escorts had drawn blades when she did. "You were not told, perhaps, that I have been a soldier more than three hands of years. I have killed more men— aye, and women—" That with a glance at the women down the hall. "—than you can count on both hands twice over." A dark rage rose higher in her mind, urging her to prove Grull wrong, to kill both him and the footman, and that slowly. Her ruby flashed, bright in her mind. She shook her head. "You are not worth the loss of honor," she said, shoving her sword back into its scabbard. "To trial you will go, and I doubt not the royal hangman will soil his hands with you."

By then four of the Royal Guards were behind the two, with thongs to bind them. When they had bound the men's wrists, then their arms to their bodies, Dorrin released her control so they could be led aside, but both lunged toward her, eyes wide and mouths open. Before she could draw her blade, her escort had stepped in front of her, and run them through.

A disturbance broke out somewhere outside—clashing blades, a horse's squeal, shouts—and three more men pushed through the huddle of servants, waving knives and pokers as they ran toward Dorrin, only to fall to Royal Guard soldiers. Like a terrified herd of sheep, the rest of the servants surged back and forth, unsure which way to run.

Dorrin saw all this with awareness honed by many a battle. Diversion—who would want a diversion?—her gaze fell on her prisoners; her aunt and mother were grinning in triumph. Dorrin strengthened her control of them, and all those prisoners slumped. Phelani uniforms appeared behind the mass of servants; Vossik called over their heads.

"My lord, a stableboy and a gardener's lad suddenly attacked us, but it's all under control now."

"Casualties?" Dorrin asked.

"Captain Selfer's spare mount, and one of the privates had a gash to the arm."

The three final attackers lay tumbled on the hall floor; they'd had no real skill and no plan, easy kills for the Royal Guard soldiers now cleaning their blades. So many dead already, when she had hoped to bring peace and security to her new realm's people. Had they all been Liartians? Dorrin went to Grull's body—and yes, he wore Liart's symbol on a chain around his neck. When the guards checked, so did the others.

Dorrin walked around the bodies and toward the huddle of servants. Before she could speak, they all knelt. Dorrin sighed. It must do for now, but she did not want this kind of submission, clearly more fear than anything else. She touched them lightly with magery, and found no more who harbored evil intent. For now, at least.

"Well, then," she said. "This room will be used for those going to Vérella in the morning. Which of you are the nurserymaids?"

Six women shuffled forward on their knees.

"Get up now—you will have charge of the youngest children. Give this man"—she pointed to one of the Royal Guard—"the names of those ten winters and younger, point them out, and then you will take them to the nursery and keep them there. Supper will be sent up later. Which of you are kitchen staff?"

Others came forward, headed by a stout woman who exclaimed when she saw the nearest dead body. "He's tooken my best carving knife, that wicked Votik, and him no more than a kennelman! If that's nicked, I'll—get me that back, lord Duke. And I don't doubt them's my pokers from the kitchen fires!" Her indignation almost made Dorrin laugh, but instead she sent the cook grumbling back to the kitchen, with orders to prepare a meal for the younger children.

Soon, the nurserymaids and younger children were upstairs, far from anything that might happen, Dorrin hoped. Now to disarm the Verrakaien prisoners—for she was sure they would all have weapons of some sort, most likely poisoned.

"The rest of you servants," Dorrin said, "will change clothes with the prisoners. This will be a brief inconvenience." The women servants looked at one another; a few grinned and one younger maid, in drab, even giggled, stifling it with her hands when an older woman cuffed her.

"Do any of you know if there are prisoners in the old keep tower?"

Most shook their heads; a few nodded. Dorrin beckoned those to the front: two women and a man.

"What do you know?"

"Us'n heard screams," one woman said.

"Them guards left," the man said. "Days agone, that was. But after they dragged in those poor folk from the vill."

They could give no clear account of when the prisoners had been brought, or how many, or when the guards had left. Dorrin let them go; she must deal with the Verrakaien prisoners first, or it would not be safe to investigate the keep.

She turned to the Verrakaien women and eased off on the control she had forced on them; they opened their eyes and sat up. The women still looked angry, but the children were frightened.

"Now—one at a time, at my direction, when I release your bonds, you will strip to the skin, unloosing your hair if it is bound, and change into the clothes those wear—" She gestured at the servants standing near the inner passage.

Her aunt Jeruvin spat. "You cannot make me change here, in front of them, and wear peasant clothes—"

"I could have you stripped naked and hung by your feet from the tower," Dorrin said. "I suggest you change, and be quick about it. You are supplicants; your lives are forfeit unless the Crown grants you mercy. You would do well to act humble, however you feel."

On some of the younger women's faces, she saw now the dawning realization that this was real—the Order of Attainder existed, and they were indeed in mortal danger. She felt a concerted nudge at her magery, their attempt to break free of the power that bound them. Dorrin said nothing; best if they did not know she even felt it. She knew Falk had lent power as well; Falk had been magelord himself; he knew more of magery than she ever would.

Than you do now, knight of my heart. Her heart skipped a beat, raced, steadied again. What was that? Not Falk himself, surely! A soft internal chuckle, very unlike the harsh laugh of the earlier attack. *It is your heritage, your birthright, and you have finally freed it.* Dorrin just managed not to shake her head visibly. One thing at a time . . . get these women into safe custody.

As they undressed, she noted the number of weapons both physical and magical: all of them had more than one dagger, all had amulets and rings, charms hung on necklaces and bracelets. She could feel the magery, as she could detect the poison on the blades.

"It's a wonder you didn't kill yourselves, just dressing and undressing," she said. Her troop gathered the daggers into one basket and left the rest for the time. The women, now in their undershifts, glared at her but said nothing. "Now take down your hair—completely. No braids, no pins."

She expected trouble, and was not surprised when Jeruvin, unpinning the top coil of braid, suddenly flung a pin at one of the soldiers—a hand long, the two spikes undoubtedly poisoned. Dorrin snatched it from the air by magery and tossed it back; it struck in Jeruvin's neck, and the woman gasped, staggered, tried to wrench it free, and fell to the floor, writhing.

"You were warned," Dorrin said. Hate flashed from Jeruvin's eyes before they glazed in death. Dorrin looked from woman to woman. "You were all warned. Anyone who tries to harm me, any of these troops, or the Royal Guard will die. Now take down your hair."

A shower of clips, combs, pins, and ornaments clattered to the floor. Most were probably harmless, but Dorrin was taking no chances.

"One at a time, starting with you—" Dorrin pointed to her mother. "Go there, with those soldiers." Women she had had Selfer choose, experienced enough to be wary and thorough. Two others held a blanket for a semblance of privacy. Behind it, one at a time, the women were stripped naked, then given peasant clothes already searched for hidden weapons.

Furious as they were, the women offered no more resistance. They came from behind the blanket in house livery or drab peasant dress and sat on the floor where they were bidden, watching as Dorrin's troops carried Jeruvin's body out of the house, as their clothes and ornaments were examined and separated into piles—dangerous, safe, uncertain.

Dorrin knew they had not been converted from resistance: merely, for the moment, outflanked. She wished again that she'd had a Captain of Falk, Marshal of Gird, or paladin along with her. Selfer came to report.

"Aris's arm will heal; that blade wasn't poisoned," Selfer said. "My horse—well, he's lame, and like to be lame forever, if he lives."

"I'm sorry," Dorrin said. The charger had been Selfer's first purchase when he became captain.

He shook his head, and went on with his report. "We found none but servants in the outbuildings, but stalls lately occupied are empty: those you seek must have had warning."

"Or been living in the forest, ready for this, since the battle was lost," Dorrin said. "My family may be evil, but they were never stupid, and what little mother's milk we had was flavored with tactics and strategy. Not that it matters, but for the possibility of attack. They may well have had an underground passage; check the outbuildings and stable carefully."

"Could be one in the house, too, my lord," Selfer said.

"I know of one, but it leads only to the keep," Dorrin said. "I'll show you when we have time. For now, I need to check the keep and release any prisoners."

"Bring them in here?"

"No—not with my relatives. They should be safe enough overnight in the upper floors; we can take over food and water."

"My lord," Valthan said, "you must not go yourself."

"I must," Dorrin said. "The danger's too great for anyone who does not know the traps."

"If you die," Valthan said, "will your control of the magelords continue? Or will I be left with prisoners I cannot control?"

"It should continue," Dorrin said. "When the Knight-Commander bound my magery—when I was a young woman—that binding lasted through his death until the new Knight-Commander released it."

"We cannot afford to lose you," Valthan said. "The realm cannot afford to lose you."

"I am needed only if I do what the prince commanded," Dorrin said. "Sir Valthan, I have been a soldier too long to risk my life needlessly— or withhold risk where it is needed."

He gave her a long, puzzled look, then nodded.

"Stay here with the prisoners," Dorrin said. "I will take an escort of Phelani into the keep; they are experienced with the sorts of dangers that might be found here. I want to do this before dark, and afternoon is waning."

Selfer had posted guards at the keep entrance; now he told off a hand to be her escort. "I'm coming, too," he said.

"You are not," Dorrin said. "If I fall, someone must get word to Valthan, and then to the prince—and someone must burn out the keep."

"My lord—you know what I saw in Vérella, before Paks redeemed us. I need to be part of this—"

Dorrin turned to him and put a hand on his shoulder; tears gleamed in his eyes; she felt hers burn. "Selfer, in this I must command you. The need is greater—and the task more difficult—where I place you. I know you have courage to face what lies below, but what I need is your determination not to let any evil free. Do you understand?" After a long pause, he nodded. "With Falk's grace and Gird's, I will return unharmed, but if I do not, you must do what is necessary. Whatever that may be."

Before Selfer could answer, she turned to the others. "Touch nothing without my word; this place has as many traps as some of those Rotengre houses. Vossik, you and one other will come with me to the bottom of the stairs. Two on the landing partway down. One halfway down the first flight of steps, to call messages up and down."

At the foot of the stairs, Dorrin turned right, and twenty strides later paused before opening the door to the blood chamber. She could feel her own pulse pounding. Ridiculous. She was an adult now, not a helpless child. Of course the memories would rise here, of all places, but she had the skills to subdue them. This door had no lock. It needed none. It reeked of blood magery; centuries of fear and anguish had permeated the wood. No one would go there who did not seek what it hid.

"Stay here until I call," Dorrin told her escort, then touched her ruby, murmured, "Ward of Falk and the High Lord's grace," and pushed it open, hanging her lantern on the familiar hook by the door. A soft scuffling sound met her ears. Along the left wall, as in her childhood, cages held small animals . . . rabbits, kittens that started mewing at once. Eyes gleamed in the lamplight. She ignored them all for the time being, taking a second lantern from a shelf of them, and lighting it. The room was centered with the tables and frames on which the Verrakai bound their victims to practice blood magery. At the far end, another door led to the cells, where human victims might or might not wait in darkness, terrified. To the right, the chambers where, in her childhood, a priest of Liart might be housed if one came to stay.

Those doors were open; those chambers were empty; she reported that to Vossik. Another, smaller, held the instruments, glinting in the light of the second lamp she lighted and set on a ledge. She closed that door, and went to the one at the end, opening it after a prayer for those who had been, and might still be, suffering.

A terrible stench rolled out to meet her, all too familiar from her years of warfare; Dorrin pinched her lips and set the lamp on a ledge. Facing her were three cell doors. Her stomach roiled. She had been locked in the left-hand one, as punishment: days and nights of terror.

She lifted the bar on the first door. Empty. The second . . . she gagged at the stench. Here someone had died, and recently. As she stepped into the cell, light revealed the carrion beetles scuttling for cover from a corpse too small to be an adult. Tears burned her eyes. Too late . . . would she always be too late?

In the third cell she heard harsh, uneven breaths. By the lamp's light, she saw a naked man, curled on the floor, streaked with his own filth. She bent lower; his face had been battered, one eye gouged out. His swollen tongue protruded from cracked lips.

"Falk's grace," she whispered. "Give him ease."

At her voice, the man groaned and stirred.

"Help is here," she said. She unplugged her water bottle and dripped a few drops on his tongue. "Soon you will be better. I promise." He shuddered. Backing out of the cell, she called Vossik, who came into the outer room at once. "I need a burial party and someone to carry a wounded man," she said.

She went back to the wounded man and poured a little more water on his tongue as she waited for the others to arrive. He roused a little, groaned, moved his tongue, and opened his one eye. "Wha—nooo . . . no more."

"No more," Dorrin said. "It's over." She dripped more water in his mouth; he swallowed.

"Who—"

"The Duke's dead," Dorrin said. The man's ruined mouth stretched in what might have been a smile. "The prince sent me, to be the new Duke." She gave him a little more water. He blinked, and she realized that with the lamp behind her, she was only a black shadow. "We'll get you out of this very soon . . ."

"Tam—?" Hardly a breath of sound at that.

Dorrin had already realized that the young person in the next cell was probably this man's brother or son. She dipped her head. "I'm sorry . . . Tam . . . died."

"Gird's grace," the man said; his one eye closed.

A squad arrived then, clattering down the stairs and into the dungeon. Dorrin went back out into the main room, explained in a low voice what she'd found.

"Only three cells?"

"In this part of the dungeon, yes. There are twenty on the other side, through the door to the left as you came down the stairs. But this is where Liart's priests lived, where the most dangerous magery is, so I had to check this myself. You'll be safe enough now. Clean up the boy's corpse and lay it on a table upstairs, under a cloth. If his father lives to morning, he'll want to see it."

By full dark all the prisoners were upstairs in the keep, munching bread and cheese, their cells left to the rats and beetles. The man from the torture cell clung to life with the help of the cohort's physician; his son's body, under an embroidered bed hanging from the main house, lay surrounded by candles with two of the cohort to give an honor watch. Dorrin sent for Sir Valthan to witness what she had found, then told Selfer to supervise their care and the external security while she returned to the house with Valthan, who still needed an accurate list of Verrakai family members.

"Have you eaten, my lord? I know you ate no lunch—"

"No—"

"We have hot rations—"

Of course he would have seen the troops fed—and no doubt from their own supplies. She did need to be alert for her next task, rifling her uncle's study to find the family rolls. Dorrin nodded, and wolfed down the familiar Company rations, then went back inside through the kitchen entrance, where the head cook was scolding her assistants as they cleaned pots and prepared for the morrow. She asked the head cook's name.

"Farintod, m'lord," the cook said. "But I'm called Farin, or just Cook." Once more, Dorrin probed with her magery but could find no malice, only a combination of annoyance and fear, among the kitchen staff. Perhaps she might eat food they prepared the next day, when their former rulers were gone . . . but not until then.

In the main hall, Valthan's lieutenant reported that the prisoners had first refused to eat the simple meal served them, but eventually hunger overcame pride. Now they lay on the floor under the blankets

Dorrin had allowed after ensuring that they had no hidden weapons. The glitter of eyes in the lamplight proved they were not asleep, but at least they were down and quiet.

She asked Valthan for the loan of a Royal Guard sergeant.

"I could—"

"No. I will not risk both of us in my uncle's study. Remember what I told you of it."

She had been in the Duke's study only a few times before fleeing Verrakai, but she remembered its location well enough. She felt the inherent magery pressing against her as she neared it, and paused after pushing open the heavy door with the hilt of her sword. Haron's father had been duke when she left; Haron had the same taste in decor, elaborate and luxurious. The desk, with its blue leather cover tooled and painted with the Verrakai crest and motto. The chair, also covered in heavily padded blue leather, the crest centered in its back.

"Why didn't you use your hand?" the Royal Guard sergeant said, then added a late "my lord."

"Here I expect to find more lethal traps and tricks than anywhere else," Dorrin said, looking the room over carefully. "When I was a child, my great-uncle, the late Haron's father, set a spell on the door whenever he left, to prevent anyone coming in. It would knock an intruder down. When Haron left for Vérella, he might have set a lethal one. And do you see that chair?"

"Yes, my lord."

"Looks comfortable, doesn't it? A poisoned spike, spring-loaded, is hidden in that fancy crest. If anyone sits there but the Duke, to whom the secret of disarming the chair has been handed down, it is death. The chair before the desk has traps as well. Touch nothing here—not the doorjamb, not a chair or table or so much as a book—without my direction."

"That's—that's horrible," the sergeant said.

"Sir Valthan wants to see certain records, but I do not want to risk his life in here," Dorrin said. Or her own, but she had to do that. "You must do nothing but stand here and witness, until I am sure the room is safe. If I fall, tell Sir Valthan to fire the room. He will not obtain the records the prince wants, but it is too dangerous to send anyone else in, and fire should cleanse it."

"Burn the—your—body?"

"Yes. Better that than risking more lives. He and I have discussed what to do with the family should that occur." Dorrin touched Falk's ruby. "Ward of Falk," she said, and stepped into the room.

Magery coiled about her, invisible but palpable to her awakened mage-sense. Woven into the blue and gray rug, its patterns picked out in silver threads that drew her eye, urged her to move here, then there, in patterns that would entrap her if she obeyed. She ignored the urging, instead looking around once more—to either side, behind, above, below, probing with her awakened abilities for every trap, every compulsion, every evil design.

The room seemed more silent than it should, the silence oozing out from shelves of books and scrolls, up from the rugs, down from a carved and painted ceiling. Stillness, timelessness—Dorrin shook herself; it was not peace, but yet another protection built into the room, intended to immobilize intruders, and she had forgotten its existence. She stamped on the floor and said, "Your Duke returns! Verrakai hoert'a basinya bakuerta bavanta da akkensaar!" In the ancient language of the password: "Verrakai: not elven, not stone-folk, not air-folk, but mage-man." A spell and counterspell she'd been told were older than Verrakai House, old as the magelords' retreat from Old Aare. The stillness receded.

She glanced back at the sergeant, pale-faced and sweating in the doorway. "Just an old spell, don't worry."

"It looked like the room was filling with dust."

"It wasn't exactly dust," Dorrin said. She stayed away from the ducal desk and went to the shelves to the right. "I may disappear," she said over her shoulder. "These shelves are images; they should recede to the real ones beyond, but I might walk through them. I wasn't taught all the counterspells." Under her gloved hand, the shelves felt real; she knew better than to grope among the books and scrolls for the touchlock and instead pressed the ducal ring on the most likely shelf. "Tangat Verrakai!" she said sharply.

The shelves vanished, revealing a much larger room with two tables, plain wooden chairs set near them, and more shelves. At the far end, the portrait she remembered hung above a small fireplace; it had terrified her as a small child, a larger-than-life-size image of Aekal Verrakai, the first duke, grim-faced. But she was not a child any longer and found him more repulsive than frightening.

You should fear. Straight into her mind the words came. *Without me, you are nothing. Because of me, you were born. Because of me, you will live or die. Fear me.*

"You are dead these thousand years," Dorrin said.

A cold laugh. *This power never dies.*

"Nor Falk's power, nor the High Lord's," Dorrin said. She drew her sword and laid the sword's tip on the image's chest. "It is time this image died, as well as its ghost." A little pressure, and the tip pierced the surface.

Blood spurted from the image's chest, ran down her sword blade hissing and smoking. The blade itself flared blue; stinking black smoke curled to either side. Dorrin stared, amazed, for a split second. Blood magery even here? She lent her power to the sword blade, augmenting its innate protection with her own, at the same time drawing the tip across the portrait, ripping it one way, then another. More blood surged out, splashing against her personal shield, hissing . . . it died, dried. A red mist rose from the wall behind the portrait, but dissipated when Dorrin called again and again on Falk.

Grimacing, she pulled the rags of the portrait free of its frame, realizing as she did that it had been painted on thin leather, not fabric. The frame itself stank of dark magery; she pulled that, too, free, and one side broke open. Instead of solid carved and painted wood, she found it was plaster, molded and painted to look like wood, over a core of bones and bone fragments . . . of what she did not know and did not want to imagine. On the wall itself, a door, carved with the Verrakai crest and a warning. Dorrin didn't touch it physically, but once more said, "Tangat Verrakai."

The door opened, revealing a small vault. Inside, the shattered remains of an urn with a little brownish red powder that vanished as she looked at it, what looked like a wooden box with inlaid patterns, a discolored scroll, and something beyond wrapped in pale leather. Dorrin left the vault open and walked back, nearer the study door.

"Did you see that?" she asked the sergeant.

"No, my lord. Like you said, you walked through a wall of books, it looked like."

"The room extends beyond. There was magery, and I defeated it." The man looked pale enough already; she did not want to panic him completely. "There's a vault in the wall, with an urn, a scroll, various other items. I do not wish to remove these things at the moment, because Sir Valthan really needs the information in the family birth records, and I haven't found that yet."

"The scroll?"

"Too old. And it should be a book with pages; I saw it as a child." She looked around that end of the office, trying to remember the size and color of the volume. As a child, she had thought it huge, but how large was it really? She found two other record books, one with the breeding records of the Verrakai stud and one with a record of harvests for the past twenty-two years, before she found the one she wanted.

Her family had seemed vast when she lived here, but from the records Haron's plan had been to concentrate power in the family as well as without. Only one of her sisters had survived, and both her brothers had been killed in duels with Haron's sons. Her father had died of a hunting accident; there was a mark beside his name she did not know. Relief flooded her: he was dead; she did not have to worry about seeing that face ever again. In her own generation, cousin had married cousin—to strengthen the magery, no doubt. Stillbirths . . . infant deaths . . . childhood accidents . . . half these listings marked like her father's name, whatever it meant. So the gaggle of children upstairs really were all . . . she'd expected fifty or more.

Yet something about the record book felt wrong. She could easily imagine dishonesty—but why here, in the list of family members, births, marriages, deaths, titles? Was there another record book, hidden somewhere? Or was something hidden here, in this book?

She touched the book with her magery; to her inner sight the pages wavered, as if under water, and a new page appeared, covered densely with a small crabbed script she did not recognize. As she read, she felt the hair rise up on her body: many of those listed as dead—those with the symbol—were not dead but transferred by blood magery to the bodies of others, some Verrakaien and some not. In such disguise, unrecognized, they could go anywhere, work for Verrakai secretly.

Including her father. Not dead, still alive, hidden? At the thought, panic flooded her, the fear she had controlled while in the tower's dungeon. She had not told the Knight-Commander—she had been ashamed, even now, to admit how much she feared him, and why. Her uncle had been duke and also punished her, but her father—he had worn the Bloodlord's hood and mask, he had decreed the torment of her pony and torments even more shameful.

She closed the book and went at once to the door. "I have urgent news for Sir Valthan, which my relatives must not overhear. Tell him we need a safe place to confer."

Dorrin met Valthan in the dairy. Windowless, stone-walled, the dairy felt chill and dank, light from their candle sending tiny dazzles from the water in the channel where butter and milk kept cool. Dorrin laid the book on the small table Valthan's men had set there. "You found something bad?" Valthan asked.

"Many things," Dorrin said. "But this is the worst." She opened the book and pointed to the mark. "These are listed as deaths, with dates and causes listed. But they are not dead. They live . . . in other bodies."

"What?"

"I did not know such evil was possible . . . but with blood magery, and I suppose the help of Liart's priests, they can transfer the souls and minds of Verrakai into other bodies, to work secretly for that traitor Haron."

"So . . . the prince may still be in danger?"

"The prince, yes, but also the realm as a whole. I do not know who the alternate identities are." Her own father, not safely dead but alive—where was he? *Who* was he? She shuddered, forcing memory away.

"How do you know this?"

"There is a page visible only by magery," Dorrin said. "I can try to make it visible to you—" She put out her power again and the page reappeared. "There, do you see it?"

"No," Valthan said, scowling. "What does it say?"

"It gives the dates these people were transferred to another body, and for a few it gives that identity."

"What about those others? Are they now in Verrakai bodies?"

"They're dead," Dorrin said. The page gave part of the ritual by which the transfer was done; it disgusted her.

"Well . . . that's one thing," Valthan said, staring down at the page, through the page he could not see. "What will happen if I touch this? Will I feel the one I can't see?" He put out a finger.

"Don't," Dorrin said. "I don't want to risk it. I need a competent scribe, so I can read this page aloud and send a copy to the prince, but though I have literate men among my cohort, none are skilled at dictation. Do you have a scribe with you?"

He shook his head. "I'm the only one. If you trust me."

"Of course," Dorrin said.

"I mean, I might be one of those Verrakai put in someone's body. I might be about to kill you."

"We can find out," Dorrin said. She read out the phrase that supposedly forced the transferred Verrakai to reveal themselves.

"What was that?" Valthan said.

"Proof you're not a Verrakai," Dorrin said. "Let's get this done—time's passing."

Valthan wrote to her dictation; then Dorrin copied his copy, which matched her memory.

"Do not let my relatives know you have this," Dorrin said. "They might find a way to destroy it, if they suspected its existence. It must go to the prince's own hand."

"A courier?"

Dorrin considered. "Do you have a man to spare? Considering how many prisoners you have and the Verrakai yet at large?"

"Not really," Valthan admitted. "But I expect to meet another troop on the way."

"I still worry that attack on a single courier would be easier than on a troop. If you send one, warn him to stop nowhere but at a grange of Gird—not for water or food or rest."

When they returned to the great hall, the guard had changed to Phelani; Valthan's were out in the stable, readying horses and wagons for the morning's departure. They would sleep there, in relative safety, to be rested for the next day's travel. Dorrin went to the front entrance and murmured the command word that swung the great doors wide. Sweet cold air flowed in, smelling of early spring, the first faint fragrance of healthy growth. She wanted to walk out into the darkness and never come back. She'd done it once; her escape saved her life and sanity.

And she had come back, unwilling, to save those who would not thank her, the innocent among her bitter and resentful family. In her mind she saw the view that darkness hid—the fields, the trees be-yond, the view that should have been as dear and familiar as any-thing in the world. Instead, longing for the Duke's Stronghold stabbed her, the familiar inner and outer courts, sunrise seen from the para-pet, that dinner table with Kieri at its head and Arcolin and Cracolnya across from her. Her eyes stung with unshed tears.

Would she ever feel this was home? A safe place, a comfortable place?

She stared at the gloom until her eyes dried, then turned and went inside.

Before dawn, Dorrin and Sir Valthan ate breakfast in the dining room of the main house, still from rations they'd brought, and Dorrin wrote out another report for the prince, on the conditions she'd found in the keep.

"You'll have to take the tower down," Valthan said. "If it's been the center of their evil that long—"

"I know," Dorrin said. She knew, but she felt a reluctance to de-stroy a work so old, the center of Verrakai House. As if he sensed that reluctance, Valthan put his hand on her arm.

"My lord Duke, I'm serious. They will have built it with blood and bone: it cannot be cleansed. It must be destroyed."

"And will be," Dorrin said. "When I have carried out the prince's commands to find those under Order of Attainder and send them to Vérella. If I spend the weeks it will take to knock the tower down, stone by stone, they will get away."

"But—"

"I will burn out the entire inside, leave it an empty husk," Dorrin said. "That should hold the evil at bay awhile, while I do as the prince wished. Later, I can demolish it."

He nodded. "That sounds well enough." He sighed. "I do not envy you your tasks, my lord."

"Nor do I envy you your journey to Vérella with my poisonous rel-atives." She pushed back from the table. "I will renew my spells blocking their magery and hope those hold until you reach Vérella.

Should you suspect they are regaining their magery, kill them at once. Remember they have powers you've never faced; just one of them held four motionless, including the Marshal-Judicar of Gird."

In the main reception hall, lamps and candles were alight; the women and girls stood in one huddle and the boys in another. Some glared at her, defiant; others cringed. Either expression might be a lie. Dorrin hooked her thumbs in her belt and looked them over.

"Remember my warnings," she said. "The Royal Guard has orders to kill you if you offer any resistance or attempt to use your magery, should my bindings fail." For a moment her mother looked triumphant, but Dorrin smiled, putting into it all the Verrakai arrogance, and her mother's eyes fell. "I do not think they will," Dorrin said. "And to make certain—" She released the power again, first damping their powers, and then a glamour, making them docile, at least for a time.

"Time to go," Sir Valthan said. The Royal Guard urged them out the front entrance. The older women and those with child were put in a supply wagon. The others would walk. They did not complain, but set off down the lane.

CHAPTER EIGHTEEN

"My lord, have you slept at all?" Selfer asked when the others were well away. Dorrin glanced at him. He looked disgustingly bright-eyed for dawn when she knew he, too, had been up most of the night.

"No," Dorrin said. A yawn fought its way past her attempt to hold it back. "Too much to do. Now, too."

"My lord, by your leave—sleep a few hours. We will not let harm come to you."

Dorrin shook her head. "I distrust this sleepiness, Captain. It could be magery—"

"I'll wake you, I swear."

"All right," Dorrin said. "But don't let the men go wandering about—there are many dangers we haven't cleared yet. And now the others have left, move those poor souls from the dungeons into the house—find clothes for them—"

"—and get their names and homes, and find out everything we can from them," Selfer said. "And be sure there's clean water drawn up from the well you specified, and check the state of the pantries and—"

Dorrin laughed, the last thing she'd expected. "And quit acting the mother hen, Captain? All right. I am exhausted. I'll sleep in the dining room."

She woke in late morning when Selfer called her name.

"Yes." She stretched. "What is it?"

Selfer came into the room and closed the door behind him. He carried a tray with a covered dish, two jugs, a bowl and mug, and towels over one arm. He set these on the table. "Something to eat, some hot water."

Dorrin yawned and stretched, while Selfer laid out a simple meal. Dorrin poured warm water into the bowl and washed her face and hands. Her clothes felt greasy, but she was awake. She sipped a spoonful of soup, trusting Selfer would have made sure it wasn't poisoned.

"I feel better," she said.

"Good, because the news isn't. The man you found in the torture cells died. He roused enough to ask after his son, and wanted to see the body. The men carried him in; he smiled when he saw the way we'd laid the body out. He died shortly after that; I didn't wake you then, but talked to the other prisoners and found out who he was. Two are from the same vill; they want to take the bodies there when they're freed. They think they're still prisoners because we're guarding them. Anyway—we have no way to preserve the bodies and I don't know if it's safe to let them—the others—go. It's too quiet; there's no sign of those you're sure escaped."

Dorrin stood, raked at her hair, buckled on the sword she'd laid ready on the dining room table. "Do they understand there's danger from the other Verrakai outside?"

"They think any Verrakai's an enemy, including you, my lord." Selfer straightened the hang of her cloak, as if he were still a squire. "They're scared, they're confused, and of course they're still half-starved and some are hurt. We've fed them; they've had a chance to bathe, and they're in clean clothes, but I'm not sure of your safety, my lord, let alone theirs."

"I must go to them," Dorrin said. "Safe or not—they have no weapons, do they?"

"No, my lord."

"And where are they now?"

"Here, in the main hall where the Verrakaien ladies were."

"What about the servants here in the household?"

"We put them to work—what they say is their usual work. I've had a squad go through the cells, make sure we didn't miss anyone. It would take a river to clean out that dungeon—days, anyway."

"I'm going to burn out the tower," Dorrin said.

"Can you do that without firing the house as well?"

"I hope so," Dorrin said. "The tower must come down, but we don't have time now—burning it out's the next best thing."

The great hall, only that morning full of Verrakaien, now held a few hands of lean, wary prisoners freed from the dungeons. They stared at Dorrin, anger and fear both obvious in their faces.

"You have reason to hate me," Dorrin said. "You can see in my face that I am Verrakai by birth, and you have known nothing but cruelty from my family. But some of you look old enough to remember me— the one who ran away."

"So they said," one of the women said. "I didn't believe it."

"Do not believe me, then, but believe this—" She touched Falk's ruby. "I ran away, I went to Lyonya and was accepted into Falk's service. Since I was knighted, I've served Kieri Phelan, once Duke Phelan of Tsaia and now the new king of Lyonya."

"The Fox . . ." someone muttered.

"The crown prince and Council of Tsaia appointed me here, to take over Verrakai, because they knew the other Verrakaien hated me."

"They should have killed that scum and broken up the domain—" said a man with stringy gray hair.

"Haron Verrakai *is* dead," Dorrin said. "And his brother. All Verrakai, save me, are under an Order of Attainder—do you know what that is?"

They shook their heads.

"For their treason, their lives are forfeit. All will be tried; some may be found not guilty, but most will die." They did not speak or move; their faces showed only doubt and fear.

"I do not know why you were in prison; I do not care. If you were stealing or hurting your neighbors, do so no more."

"Weren't that!" one of the women said, suddenly bold. She took a step forward. "I said only as it wasn't fair all our food was tooken for the soldiers, and someone told the militia, and they brung me here and said I'd find out what hunger was, in them cells."

"It wasn't fair," Dorrin said. "And I took you out of those cells and saw you fed, didn't I?"

. "Yes . . ." It was a grudging yes, but it was agreement, and some of the others nodded.

"It may not be safe for you to go home, with some of my relatives escaped. So I ask if you would be willing to stay here—work here—for the time being. You will be housed, clothed, fed. If you are not willing, I will not hold you here, but I cannot promise you will be safe on your way to your homes—or there—until I've dealt with the other Verrakaien."

"Can we keep these clothes?" asked another woman, holding out a skirt that had obviously belonged to a highborn lady.

"Why not?" Dorrin said. The former prisoners grinned at each other and some began whispering. "I'm not going to wear them." She gestured at her own garb. "I've been a soldier over four hands of years; I need no fancy dresses. But—" She waited until the stir died down. "Remember the danger. If the Verrakai who fled the house see you in the clothes they last saw on their relatives, what do you think they'll do?"

Grins disappeared, replaced by scared looks.

"If I were you," Dorrin said, "I'd be wary of looking as if you'd stolen from the closets. We made the Verrakaien change to servants' clothes, and that left only these fancier clothes for you. Those of you skilled with the needle could remake some of these—you might look like outsider merchants, and not Verrakaien."

"But what about Jen and Tam?" one man asked. "They should be buried in our vill, with their kin."

"How far away is your vill?" Dorrin asked.

"A half day's walk," the man said. "Kindle, we call it, for the fire-oak grove."

Dorrin turned to Selfer. "Captain, is that militia squad up to escorting two bodies for burial?"

Selfer considered. "Mounted, yes, if I send along one of my cohort. We could transport the bodies on pack mules and be there and back easily by nightfall."

"Very well," Dorrin said. "Who is from that vill?"

"Just me and Piter here," the older man said. "Jen was my cousin."

"Then, Captain, find this man something less conspicuous—" The first man was wearing a gray silk shirt, embroidered blue-velvet doublet, a satin scarf around his neck and a black velvet cloak draped over all "—and do what is needful."

Within the half-glass, the two from Kindle were on their way home, with the bodies of their dead and the escort; the other freed prisoners had agreed to stay as servants for the time. Two claimed skill with needlework; Dorrin assigned them to restyle Verrakai finery to more practical garments.

Now she must deal with the younger children, still up in the nursery. That took much of the afternoon, conferring with the nurserymaids and interviewing the children. Dorrin had little experience with children; these seemed normal enough, and she took the maids' word for their character.

Except for one, Restin, a nine-winters boy, whom the maids said had been a rambunctious, difficult small boy but had "improved" after a long illness. She'd noticed Restin doing exactly what he was told—never complaining, never arguing, always mild and biddable.

Always watching her. Something about him made her uneasy, and she could not define what it was except his eyes seemed too adult, too knowing, for a nine-winters boy. Was he actually older, within the Order of Attainder, only pretending to be nine? She called the oldest of the nursemaids out of the room.

"Restin—are you sure he's only nine winters?"

"Yes, ma—my lord. He does seem quite the little man, doesn't he? But it's his way, not his age. Some children, you know, 'specially them as has the death-sickness, they change. The fever, his mother said."

Cold ran down Dorrin's spine. "The death-sickness?"

"It's like they're dying, long afore the crisis. Sickly, weakening. Then the fever takes them. Then the priest prays over them—the only good I ever hear of them."

"Where?"

"They take 'em to the old keep, when the fever comes, to save the other children sickening. Two or three hands of days, it is, and when they come back, they're different. Stands to reason, my lord. It's the same with black-foot and red-spot and lump-jaw, all those ails children get. Like as not the child's changed. Curly hair straight and straight hair curly. Only with death-sickness, they're quieter, easier to manage, more grownup."

They would be, if they were in fact adult minds—adult selves—in a child's body. Adults biding their time. Adults who—she could hardly imagine this—would kill their own children to disguise themselves.

"When was Restin so sick? How often does the death-sickness come?"

"It's mostly before they lose their milk teeth," the maid said. "But sometimes after. Restin—it was five winters back, same year as Lord Carraig died."

Dorrin shivered. Her father's older brother; she remembered them both, too well. Could it be Carraig looking at her from Restin's nine-winters face? "How many of the children here have had the death-sickness?"

"We've been worried about Mikeli; he's pale and not growing well this past year. That's an early sign, often. His mother bade us watch him closely. He's four winters; I can show you—"

"What about older children, the ones sent off to Vérella?"

The maid frowned and began counting on her fingers. "Kosta, he's twelve winters, and Berol, he's eleven. Rolyan, Pedar—it's strange, my lord, but boys get the death-sickness more than girls. I said once to my lady that maybe girls were stronger and she slapped me to the floor. But Syryan, she had it. A right little fireball she was before, all temper all day long, but after as ladylike as you please."

And Dorrin had sent Valthan off with the prisoners thinking the adults would be the worst problem, that most of those children were not yet skilled in magery. Five children's bodies that might—every instinct told her *did*—conceal adult intelligence, experience, and magery.

How long had it been going on? She remembered now one of her older brothers who'd been very sick and afterward seemed different. How many generations? Were some of those minds even older, passed down from one generation to another all the way back to Old Aare?

And what was she going to do about it? Her oath to the Crown required that she eliminate the threat from Verrakai. Carraig, if that's who really inhabited Restin's body, fell within the Order of Attainder. But who could believe that? She had to tell Valthan; she had to tell the prince. And she had to protect herself and the other children from whatever Carraig might choose to do.

"Since Restin is so mature," she said to the maid, "I will want to speak with him in a little. He will better understand the situation than some of the others, don't you think?"

"Yes, my lord," the maid said. "We've made him our helper, you know."

That did not surprise her. Restin, even in the shielded nursery, would be able to use his magery to charm the nurses. "Send him to me after supper," Dorrin said. "I'll be in the dining room."

She found Selfer and explained what she understood. "I cannot be certain without forcing Restin to reveal himself—there's a phrase that may work—but I dare not wait to warn Valthan. They will not have made it to the main road today; we must send a courier."

"What can Valthan do? Did your binding of magery include the children?"

"Yes, it did, but I am not sure how long those bindings will last in my absence. I'm not sure what else might work. Numbweed, perhaps. Its effects might dull the magery. I'll ask—"

In the kitchen, Farin the cook, back at work with additional help from the freed prisoners, led Dorrin to the pantry. "In that locked box."

Dorrin tried the keys she'd found in the basket of things taken from the Verrakai women. One opened the box. Inside were packets neatly tied shut, tiny jars and bottles, and a smaller locked box. The cook pointed. "That there's numbweed to put in wine for the pain of wounds, and that's gnurtz, for calming someone in a fever rage. It dissolves in sib, but not in wine. That box is powdered deathwish, grows on rotting logs in the forest. Only the duke is allowed to use it."

"For suicide?" Dorrin asked. She was sure it was not that, but wondered what the cooks had been told.

"Oh, no," Farin said. "But if someone's dying anyway, in pain, 'tis said a few grains on the tongue will ease it more than numbweed and give an easy death. Not for the likes of us, of course." She sniffed. "Just for the lords and ladies." She went on. "Now, that there is bone-set, you put it in sib if someone's broken a bone and it's said to heal faster. And that's lungwort, steep it in hot water and breathe it for lung fever. Some says mix it with comfortweed is best, but my lady— she that was, I mean—" Another worried glance at Dorrin, who managed a smile. "She didn't like to do that. Now this one is shaved hadjan bark, whatever a hadjan is, something from the south I think, good for proud flesh, they said."

"And you mixed these things with food and drink here?"

"Aye, my lord, all but the deathwish, that we weren't ever to touch." She leaned closer and her voice dropped to a whisper. "My lady that was . . . one of the chambermaids said she had a box like this in her own room, hidden in a hole beside the fireplace, with this and more. They could have mixed things themselves but they wouldn't stir sib where servants could see."

"I see," Dorrin said. She saw too many dire possibilities. "Do you know if this . . . gnurtz? . . . controls the magery of the person with fever rage?"

"Yes, it does," Farin said, nodding vigorously. "They said—my lady that was and the Duke that was—for ordinary folk like us numb-weed was the most we'd need to fall asleep, but gnurtz did the same for them, mind and magery alike. That's why I put a little in the chil-dren's food last night, to quiet 'em like you said." Her brow fur-rowed. "That was what you wanted, wasn't it?"

"Yes," Dorrin said. "That was perfect. Thank you. And to prevent their distress while they're still so confused, I think you'd better con-tinue with it for another day or so."

"As you wish, my lord," the cook said. "Lucky it's just the chil-dren. Wouldn't have enough if it was to hold down that many adults. Trader hasn't come through yet this year."

"Trader?"

"The one brings us this and other things. Gnurtz comes from far away somewhere."

Something else to worry about.

"And for your dinner, my lord? You haven't said what you want. And if I could know what you need for tomorrow, that would help . . . those soldiers you brought with you have their own supplies, they said . . ."

Dorrin looked around the kitchen; all the cooks and helpers stopped at once and stared at her. Through her worry, kitchen fra-grances finally reached her awareness.

"What are you preparing for the children and yourselves?"

"For the children, my lord? Their usual supper: milky porridge, rusks, a honeycake. For the servants, soup and bread."

She remembered the taste of milky porridge and rusks from her own childhood, the hard toasted crusts of bread softening slowly in the milk. Honeycakes, hard as wood, to suck on while waiting for the maids to warm the beds with coals in a pan. If they were annoyed, your bed would be ice-cold in winter.

"I didn't dare put on a haunch of venison for your own dinner, my lord, without your telling me, but I could do a steak—"

"Soup and bread will do well tonight," Dorrin said. "And cheese." Though the cook seemed honest enough, it might be well to eat what the servants ate for a while longer.

The cook looked surprised, but nodded. "And for the Captain out there?"

"The same," Dorrin said. "Dinner for two. Soup, bread, cheese." The soup, now that she was aware of the fragrance, smelled delicious. She walked over to the hearth and sniffed, then smiled at them all and went to find Selfer again.

The funeral escort had just returned; Selfer sent them to the stables to put up the animals. "And be ready for inspection in a half-glass," he said.

"Inspection . . . again?" one of them asked.

"Inspection any time," Selfer said, in a tone that stiffened them all. "At least twice a day until you meet the requirements of a decent militia. I expect those boots to shine."

The Phelani bit their lips not to grin, and led off at a brisk pace. Selfer turned to Dorrin. "Courier's well on his way. Seli will report on the situation in the vill when that lot are cleaned up."

"I think they'll do," Dorrin said.

"With some training," Selfer said.

"Oh, yes. My relatives never liked their servants to learn too much. Easier to control the dull and incompetent, especially the ones with weapons."

"People treated that way become sly in self-defense," Selfer said. "How are you going to teach them honesty at their age?"

Dorrin shook her head. "I can't. But I can reward honesty; greed produces whatever brings reward."

"I hope so," Selfer said. "What did you learn in the kitchen this time? Are we having a real dinner, or more bread and cheese?" He rubbed his stomach and put on a pitiful expression.

"Bread and *soup* and cheese," Dorrin said. "I left it too late for the cook to put on a roast. Tomorrow, Falk's grace, we'll have real food. And I need to see about supplies for the cohort and the militia, too."

"I don't know about the house pantries," Selfer said, "But the granary has plenty of grain and no sign of rodents. Sacks of dried beans, as well. I think one door is for a root cellar but you said not to open any doors without your checking them."

"Tomorrow I'll go with you," Dorrin said, "though if the cooks can enter a door, it should be well enough. I did hear from the head cook that Haron's wife's chamber has a hidden vault with a box of herbs—or poisons."

"What are you going to do about that boy Restin?"

"That man, I believe," Dorrin said. "And if it is, I must kill him."

Selfer looked horrified. "Kill a *child*?" Then he shook his head. "But—if he's not really a child—"

"Exactly," Dorrin said. "I don't want to believe they've done anything so vile as kill a child's soul to give a man a fresh body. But the family rolls—the page I can see with mage-sight—makes it clear they were transferring Verrakai to other bodies. An adult mind in a child's body, with full adult mage powers, would be incredibly dangerous."

"How do we know it was just once?" Selfer said, scowling. "Is there anything you know of that would prevent someone taking body after body, living . . . how long?"

"I don't know," Dorrin said. "I thought of the same thing. I'm sure if it were possible, someone would try it." Bitterness rose in her throat, nauseating. How could anyone engender children just to use them so? "But whether that is possible . . . I don't know, and I don't know how to find out."

"I suppose," Selfer mused, "it's no worse to do it to your own family than to strangers. At least it's not hurting outsiders."

Rage blinded Dorrin for a moment; she fought it down, thought her way through what he meant. "I thought it was worse," she said finally. "Family loyalty . . . but I see what you mean. It cannot be right to bear children just to destroy their futures . . . but the family so vile deserves to lose its own, not impose that loss on others. Though they have, at least some of the time. One of them is a merchant in Valdaire."

"Anyone we've dealt with?"

"I'm not sure," Dorrin said. "All it says here is merchant—not the merchant's name. And a moneychanger in Vérella."

"Vérella! That's not good at all. And no name?"

"No. But if we look for the moneychanger the family used there, I would expect to find him."

"Only men?"

"No. But mostly." Dorrin sighed. Exhaustion weighed her down. Her own, or imposed by that boy upstairs? "This is a long, deep plot," she said. "I never realized that as a child. That they valued cruelty and power, yes—but not this way."

"Not all of them," Selfer said. "You're not like that."

"I hope not," Dorrin said.

"And there might be others, even here. Another girl like you among the children."

"Or boy," Dorrin said. She sighed again. "I have to believe that. I have to look for that, as well as the evil."

"But couldn't you bind this boy's magery and send him under guard to Vérella?"

"If he confesses, when I confront him—but I don't see how I can risk it. Us. The entire domain. If I fail here, the prince and Council will have every reason to invade, raze the entire domain, and kill everyone Verrakai has touched. Innocent people will die, and Tsaia itself could be torn apart."

"Do you really have any doubt that you can kill him? A mere boy of nine winters?"

"Oh, yes. If he is Carraig, then he's no mere boy. He is older than my father was, and had training and experience in the use of his magery for decades before he transferred into this boy. And if he's still older—if Carraig himself were invaded—he may have generations of experience, and power much greater than mine. I have not been able to think of any stratagem he will not have imagined. That's why I want you to remove all Phelani troops from the house—"

"That's crazy."

"No. If his magery defeats mine, your danger is extreme. You must fire the house and all in it, then ride as fast as you may to Vérella. Or—wait—send a squad to Kieri, in Chaya."

As evening dimmed, Dorrin waited for Restin in the dining room, as prepared as she could be. Restin would of course notice every magical preparation, unless the gnurtz dulled his senses enough. She feared it wouldn't.

The boy who came in and bowed politely to her looked as harmless as any boy his age. "You are the new Duke?" he asked in a light tenor.

"Yes," Dorrin said. "I am now Duke Verrakai."

"What happened to the former Duke?"

"He died," Dorrin said. Then, having no desire to drag this out, she said, "Attarik Verrakai, Carraig."

A flicker of eyelid. "Who's Carraig?" in the same light tone. The command to reveal his true identity didn't work—she would have to depend on her ability to detect such transfers.

"You," Dorrin said. "Uncle Carraig, to me. I remember you."

"I'm Restin—" The boy stopped, bit his lip, then grinned, a most unpleasant grin. "What fool made *you* duke, Dorrin? *You* have no power. No one can rule here without it—"

Caught by his gaze, she had no voice, nothing but fear. All the nightmares of her childhood rose in her mind, all the fear, all the misery, all the pain. In the same sweet child's voice, he spoke softly, almost gently. Carraig did that, she remembered, caressing helpless prisoners with his voice as he tormented with his hands. No doubt at all that this was Carraig, not a child pretending another identity. Which meant she must kill him, if she could, unless the gods provided another way. She prayed, for all of them, but felt only a listening stillness.

"I don't know how you found out, little Dorrin. I suppose one of the others told you . . . you will tell me, you know, later. But for now . . . I see you are frightened, child, and that is well. I have had to be so meek with the others, to fool the maids. It's been too long since I had the pleasure of seeing someone truly afraid . . . just sit there, Dorrin, and let me taste your fear . . . I could be in *your* body, you know, ugly as it is. Imagine that. Your soldiers obeying someone they thought was you. That foolish prince—"

Warmth caressed her mind, but it was not his magery. She was not the scared child she had been; she was Dorrin, shaped by the Company of Falk, by Falk himself, by near four hands of years as Kieri Phelan's captain, veteran of more wars than Carraig had seen. She had known a paladin . . . at the memory of Paksenarrion, it was as if Paks were at her side. Her own magery leapt forth, and Restin/Carraig stopped, held motionless.

A dark mist gathered in the air; Dorrin thrust the dagger she'd prepared with deathwish powder into the child's throat and wrenched it side to side. Blood spurted out; the dark mist thickened.

"Ward of Falk!" Dorrin said. The mist hung there, not quite touching her. "Begone," she said. It writhed like a swarm of insects but did not dissipate at once. She drew her sword; it flared blue, as always in the presence of evil, and she pointed it at the thickest area of mist. "Go and never return. Go to the High Lord for judgment, and harm nothing on your way." The words she had learned so many years before, training to be a Knight of Falk, came to her in the old language from no one knew where. "Adakvarteh preklurtz, preklurtz tavin vantish . . ."

By the end of the adjuration, the mist had gone, vanished. Dorrin looked at the child's body, sprawled in its chair, blood still wet on the table, the chair, the floor.

"I'm so sorry," she said. "Ward of Falk for the soul you were born with, and the child who died, and may Falk and the High Lord forgive me this killing, that was not my desire."

Nausea twisted her, two days' worth of disgust and horror and shame; she made it out the front door and spewed on the steps, retching until she had nothing more to lose.

Fine figure of a Duke she made . . . and yet, what could be more appropriate to Verrakai House and its history than vomit on the entrance steps? She stood up, shaky but cleansed, fetched a lamp from the reception hall, and lit the torch that stood ready for her to signal Selfer and the others that she had prevailed.

CHAPTER NINETEEN

They had not gone as far as she advised; they were with her sooner than she hoped. "Ware the steps," she said as Selfer neared them. "I . . . don't like killing children."

"He wasn't a child, if he was what you said," Selfer said. "But I'm not surprised. You do not take delight in suffering or death."

"Flattery?" Dorrin said, smiling.

"No, my lord. Observation."

From someone who had seen her in battle, not only recently but in Aarenis, it was strange testimony but comforting.

"Thank you," she said.

"Are there more such spies here?" Selfer asked.

"Among the children? I'm not sure. I must question the maids more closely. Once I suspected this boy, I didn't test the others with my magery lest he attack one of them then and there." She sighed. "I don't want to panic the children who aren't possessed, or the maids. We'll need to conceal Restin's death, and consider how to handle the body."

"We can't just bury it?"

"There's blood magery here, Selfer. We will need to be sure that every drop of blood is cleaned up, for instance—and burn the rags we clean with."

"I'll have someone—"

"I need to be there." At his look, she shook her head. "No, not from guilt—to ensure that the evil in this house doesn't harm those who come in contact with it." She scowled, looking past him into darkness. "I don't know enough, that's the truth. I never thought I'd be coming back here; I never wanted to know about it, how it works, what the warding spells are. And now that's put you and the entire realm in danger. It's not enough to be disgusted by it—it feeds on disgust and revulsion."

"So . . . what will work against it?"

"Falk and Gird and the High Lord have power against it, but I sense they expect me to do the actual work." Suddenly, for no reason, Dorrin felt lighter of heart. "I suppose that's proper. I swore to be Falk's servant, when I took the ruby. To the gods belong power, and to us the work of our hands."

"Then the first step is cleaning up a mess in the dining room?" Selfer said. "That sounds within human strength."

Dorrin straightened. "Indeed. Set your guards for the night, Captain, and then send me a couple of strong-stomached soldiers."

The blood smell in the dining room was strong but not more than Dorrin had endured many times before in a life of soldiering. The body seemed to have shrunk, as bodies did when not animated. All the adult cunning and malice had gone from the face; Dorrin lifted the body, cradling the head, and laying it upon the table.

"It wasn't your fault," she murmured to the corpse. "They used you, as they used me. You will rest easy in your grave; your soul has long returned to the light, and the Lady will cradle your bones."

She searched along the paneled walls, and found the door that led to a linen pantry. By the time the men came with water and rags, Dorrin had wrapped the body in a linen tablecloth and bound it with brocade curtain ties. "I believe it is safe for burial," she said. "But in the morning, and far from this house. The child who was suffered long before his body was taken; the body should be far from that suffering."

"Yes, my lord," Selfer said.

"I will go up and speak to the nursemaids; they'll be wondering why I haven't sent Restin up to bed."

"You aren't going to tell them?"

"That I killed a nine-winters child? No. Tomorrow I must try to get them to understand what he was, what the death-sickness was, but not tonight. The children who aren't involved need sleep." She yawned. "So do I. I will tell them he'll sleep somewhere else."

"They'll worry—"

"I can't help that," Dorrin said. "It's the business of nurserymaids to worry."

Upstairs, she found, as she expected, the senior maid at the door of the nursery, looking worried.

"My lord, Restin should be in bed—it's past time—"

"I know," Dorrin said. "He is in bed, but not here. He is old enough to have a room of his own, you know."

"Yes, but—"

"He is sleeping," Dorrin said, putting just a touch of power into it. The maid's worried face smoothed. "Yes, my lord."

"Just take care of the others," Dorrin said. "And get some sleep. If the weather's fair tomorrow, you can take them out in small groups to exercise in the garden."

"Yes, my lord." The maid curtsied and went into the nursery, dimly lit by a lamp at either end. Dorrin caught a glimpse of the rows of beds, the little lumps of sleeping children, before the door closed.

She went back downstairs. She didn't want to sleep in the dining room, but she was desperate for sleep. In the end, she slept in the main reception room, in bedding taken from the rooms upstairs, with her own Phelani soldiers on guard.

She woke at dawn, to the low-voiced mutters of two guards wagering on when she'd wake, before or after they'd been relieved for breakfast.

"Before," Dorrin said from her nest of blankets.

"You could've slept another glass or two, Captain," one said.

"*My lord*, Sef; say *my lord*. She's a duke now, not a captain."

The two most inveterate gamblers in the cohort. "I might have known," Dorrin said. "Black Sef and Merik. You two would wake a corpse, arguing odds."

"We was really quiet," Sef said. "Just barely said a thing—"

"I wasn't awake," Dorrin said. "And now I am. That's how loud you didn't talk."

"Sorry, Cap—my lord," Merik said.

"I needed to get up anyway." She felt rested, but dirty, itching with the need to bathe. Today, surely, she could find time to get clean all over. And make real plans for the next days, not just reacting to one thing after another. Somewhere out there still more Verrakai plotted the realm's destruction. "Light more lamps. I'm going to see if the kitchen's stirring."

"It is," Sef said. "I smell sib."

Dorrin could too, now that she paid attention. "Good," she said. "I want hot water." She picked up her pack with its change of clothes, and headed for the kitchen.

There, warmth came from both the hearth and the ovens. Two young cooks thumped at lumps of dough, a row of lumps under a cloth would be ready when the oven heated, a can of sib simmered at the edge of the hearth, and a pot of porridge hung from a hook bubbled even as a red-faced maid stirred it.

"My lord Duke!" Farin bobbed a curtsy. "What do you need?"

"A can of warm water," Dorrin said. "And a place to wash up."

"There's the bathing rooms upstairs," Farin said. Dorrin shook her head. "Well, then . . . the servants' bath, just out there. It's not . . . not fancy . . ."

"I don't need fancy," Dorrin said. "I do need to be clean." She grinned at the cook. "I was a soldier, you know. I can bathe in a cold river, at need. But warm water is better."

"Jaim—bring water cans!" Farin turned back to Dorrin. "A mug of sib, while the water heats?"

"That would be lovely," Dorrin said. She looked around the busy kitchen. Where could she be out of the way while water heated?

"Just there," Farin said, nodding to a corner with a low stool. Dorrin took the mug of sib and sat on the stool, watching. Two more lumps of dough, shaped into rounds, were set next to the others. Farin opened one oven, thrust in an arm, shook her head, and shut it again. The other, she deemed ready. She took down a long-handled wooden paddle from its hook on the wall, and slid it under half the loaves, then swung it around and into the oven with one movement. Dorrin noticed that the others all stepped neatly out of the way without a command, even the youngest.

Work resumed instantly. The young bakers, now they had shaped the last of the dough, cleaned their workspace, took mortars and pestles from a shelf, and began grinding seeds—spices, Dorrin realized, as her nose recognized figan among others.

"Water's hot," Farin said. "Jaim, Efla—carry these out to the bath-house."

The servants' bathhouse had a half-barrel tub hung on the wall, a stone floor with a channel for washing feet, and a stone trough with a plug at one end for washing hands. A leather water sack hung from the plugged pipe that supplied water. Dorrin put her pack down on the ledge above the trough, took down the water sack, and pulled the plug. Icy water poured into the sack; she plugged the pipe again when the sack was full. By then the kitchen servants had the barrel tub down and a stack of towels beside the steaming cans of hot water.

"You may go," Dorrin said; they nodded and withdrew.

She mixed one can of hot water with cold in the barrel tub for a bath, and used the other for washing her hair. Clean and dry at last, and in clean clothes, she felt fully awake, alert.

When Dorrin came back into the kitchen, her dirty clothes stuffed in her pack and water cans atop it, she found Selfer talking to the cook. Servants rushed to take the cans from her.

Farin turned to her. "My lord—your captain suggested meat for breakfast in addition to porridge and bread. We do have smoked ham, of course, and sausages."

Dorrin's mouth watered. "Fried ham. Do you have any eggs?"

"The hens have only just started laying, my lord, and we used yesterday's eggs in the bread."

"That's all right," Dorrin said. "Ham will be enough, with the porridge. And if there's someone who can wash my shirt—"

"The laundry maids heat their water *after* breakfast," Farin said firmly. "If you'll just leave your things in the passage—" Not in her clean and busy kitchen. "Now, my lord, meals for today?"

Dorrin let Farin guide her to the selections the cook really wanted—yes, that haunch of venison for dinner, with baked red-roots, stewed fruit in spices, a steamed pudding, and for midday, a pastry pie of minced meat and vegetables. She touched Farin lightly with her magery—but that commanding presence wasn't a trans-ferred Verrakai, just the cook's own ability.

Breakfast that morning was the first meal Dorrin enjoyed since ar-riving. Porridge with honey dripped in it, fried ham, hot bread swip-ing up the fat from the fried ham. The sun rose into a clear sky, with ground mist along the stream; in the distance, the subtle colors of early spring created a picture of peace and beauty.

She made lists while eating, and after breakfast set about them. With a squad of Phelani, she went back into the old keep, searching from top to bottom with great care. It had been used for storage as well as holding prisoners: the family treasury, the armory, rolls of woolen cloth dyed Verrakai blue, jugs of blue dye, stacks of records. Dorrin had all this carried outside. Some levels were empty; they had once been occupied, some even recently—some beds with feather ticks and blankets still on the frames, chests and wardrobes still holding clothes, a leather purse with three copper coins.

"It's like plundering," Mekli said, staggering past her with a load of old books.

"And just as dangerous," Dorrin reminded him. "I'll be back later. When you get to the lower levels, call me first."

The nursemaids had their charges up and dressed, ready for the outing Dorrin had promised if the day was fair. Dorrin looked them over, this time touching each with a flicker of magery. Her heart sank. There, and there, and there . . . three more children who were not children. Two boys and a girl, seven winters, six, and five.

She should have done it last night, while they were sleeping, but that would have been terrifying for the other children, and the nursemaids . . . now, in daylight, with all of them awake and alert, Dorrin realized it would be hardly less frightening. They would ask her about Restin; the ones who were not truly children, with adult cunning, would soon know he must have been discovered. She tried to think how best to proceed.

Suddenly one of the children—Mikeli, the sickly one—collapsed, falling to the floor with a strange mewing cry, his body jerking, foam at his mouth.

One of the maids ran to him, felt his face. "It's the crisis!" she said. "He's burning with fever. We must get him away from the others." The others hurried over, warning the other children away; children cried out, all was bustle and confusion.

Dorrin watched, wondering which Verrakai was trying to transfer to the child, wondering how to stop it. A bolt of magery staggered her, then another.

It should have been impossible to use attack magery here in the shielded nursery—she'd trusted that shield. Now she felt the leaden weight of that attack; the two boys came toward her, smiling, their power beating at her. Dorrin fought it back, felt the weight ease. She could move; she could think—but what to think? What could she do here, in front of the others?

Trust the light. In her mind, the voice was firm but not harsh. Which light, though? Magery's light was fire; Falk, after his years of toil, had burned out the prison in which he had been kept, cleansing it. Here were children she did not wish to burn. She did not have that other light, the light by which paladins revealed the truth of evil.

Trust me, then. But she still doubted. Was it Falk and the High Lord in her mind, or the Verrakai who had violated children's bodies to take them over? An internal laugh, good-natured, without malice, answered her. Again she thought of Paksenarrion, and seemed to see a ruby centered in the circle she wore on her brow.

She had sworn her life to Falk. She had received her magery back from a paladin and Falk's own Captain-General. With that thought she released whatever kept light from doing whatever Falk and the High Lord wanted. It burst from her, soundless, effortless, unconsuming and revealing. By that light, she saw the adult selves in the two boys nearest her and the girl squatting on the floor behind the others . . . that one pouring magery at Mikeli as he lay twitching across the room.

Saving him had to come first. Dorrin attacked full speed, disabling the other two with one blow each to the head. The other children fled screaming to the corners of the nursery, except for the little girl. She did not even look up, concentrating on Mikeli. Dorrin felled her with a blow, and turned to the maids now huddled protectively over the sick boy.

"These three were making Mikeli sick with magery," she said. "I am taking them away. He may recover now."

"But—but you—".

"He's sweating," one of the maids said. "He's not as hot."

"Stay here," Dorrin said. She carried the little girl, now bleeding from mouth and nose, over her shoulder, and managed to pick up the others and get them out of the room. She shut the door, took a breath, looked around. What now?

Out of the house. No more killing blood here.

Dorrin called for Selfer and explained. "We must kill them—they are not children, but adults using children's bodies—but we must not kill them in the house. Too much blood here already."

"They're so little," he said. "Can it really be—" He looked at her face and then nodded. "You are sure; that's enough for me. Do you want someone else to do it?"

"No. I must." She sighed. "I hate it, but it is my inheritance. I am the legitimate duke—and every duke I know of killed, and killed family members. That is not power I ever wanted to inherit."

"What about the orchard? That is a fruit orchard isn't it? Alyanya's preserve, a place of peace?"

"We can hope," Dorrin said.

Together they wrapped the little limp bodies in linens and carried them out of the house to the orchard, and Dorrin cut their throats. A detail of Phelani dug the graves at one end; it did not take long, since the bodies were so small. Selfer spoke a Girdish prayer for their rest, and Dorrin spoke both the Falkian prayers and the traditional Verrakaien farewell.

As they walked back up the orchard paths, Selfer said *"Children!* How could they use children so?"

"I know. It's disgusting in ways I can't even describe. Those children—the real children—having their lives taken away . . ."

"I was never convinced the Verrakai were evil until I saw this," Selfer said. "I knew you—fought beside you—and if anything you were more committed to good than even Kieri—the king."

"I had memories of this place, and the fear that I would become like them," Dorrin said.

"Not you," Selfer said. "Ever."

"Now that I have the power, I feel its temptations," Dorrin said. "Anyone with power, magical or not, Selfer. You're a captain now—has it started for you, yet? You speak and others obey . . . how does that feel?" She kept her voice light; Selfer had been a good squire and junior captain.

He said nothing for a few paces, then: "I know what you're speaking of. And when I was first a squire, I thought how grand it must be, to have a cohort or a whole company at my command. I felt a thrill of pride, even though I had no right. But the Duke taught me, you taught me, all you captains, that being a commander was not about that. Do I like it, when the cohort does what I command? Yes, of course. But I must command well, for that pleasure to be . . . to be honorable. It isn't all about me."

Dorrin punched him lightly on the shoulder. "So I thought. You are a good captain, Selfer, and we've all seen that coming as you grew into it. But there are temptations at every level of power, temptations to take the easy way. Even Kieri—even the king, that last year in Aarenis."

Selfer nodded, then said, "I didn't know what to do."

"Wasn't anything you could do. We captains couldn't do anything; he was beyond reason for a while. He dragged himself back from being even worse. But anytime you have power, you will have temptations. You know that; always remember it. We are not gods; we make mistakes, we judge wrongly. If you can keep in mind 'I might be wrong'—"

"But doesn't that slow your thinking in emergencies?"

"Indeed." Dorrin kicked at a withered pear on the ground. "It nearly killed me, just now. Trust the gods, trust your experience of Gird, but when you have time, don't trust yourself too much." She stopped; Selfer slowed and turned to face her. "It's not easy, Selfer—it's not ever easy, or it wasn't for me. But if I can do what the prince wants, what the realm needs, what the honest remnants of Verrakai need—it will be by my understanding that I am not always right, and my willingness to admit that, face the consequences, and go on trying."

"I would wonder if it was easier for paladins, had I not seen Paksenarrion's face," Selfer said. "When I was a boy, I heard of them and wanted to be one . . ."

Dorrin walked on. "So did I. But it was made clear to me, in my time in Falk's Hall, that I was not." Another few steps. "We have our own tasks, Selfer. When I knew Kieri Phelan in Falk's Hall—"

"You knew him then? You never said—"

She shrugged. "No reason. He was older by a few years. I admired him greatly; many of us did. The commander of our year spoke highly of him as someone who had followed Falk's path of service—he'd been with Aliam Halveric, as you know—and then through his own merits had been accepted into training."

"Was he the same?"

"Yes . . . not exactly." Dorrin felt her cheeks heating. Like the other young women in her class, she had found him handsome beyond bearing; they had discussed him, in their dormitory, when they thought the sergeants could not hear. Those tough older women had no patience with girlish chatter. From his flaming red hair to the broad-shouldered, fit body, the shapely legs, the . . . she forced that memory back. "When he was young," she said instead, "he was already a natural leader, and he'd been to the wars with Aliam. No one else had actual fighting experience. He had most of us students wrapped around his finger; everyone wanted to be him, or be near him, or both."

"I'm sure you had your own following," Selfer said. "With all due respect, you must have been beautiful as a girl; you're good-looking now."

"I was a mess," Dorrin said. "And I was always in trouble. It wasn't the way my face was made, but how I used it. Growing up here, I learned lessons that made people distrust me, dislike me."

"Well," Selfer said, "people don't distrust or dislike you now."

"Except my own family, and that's nothing new," Dorrin said. "I hope that child lives—"

"Which one?"

"The one who was sickening, being prepared for a transfer. That's what happened—one of the children I'd identified tried to force a transfer. Now we know it's possible."

"Gods! Which one?"

"The girl." Dorrin felt tears stinging her eyes. The girl she might have been, had things been different. A girl who would never have her chance to escape. "I must make it better for the others," she said. "Verrakai must not be a name of terror, treachery, evil."

"You'll do it," Selfer said.

"That's the scariest thing you've ever said to me," Dorrin said. Her heart lifted as they came to the front entrance. The sun seemed brighter; the great doors looked less ominous. "Falk's grace," she said. "If Falk and the High Lord want this done, then surely it can be done."

"And Gird," Selfer said as they came up the steps.

"And Gird," Dorrin said.

A kitchen maid waited for her in the reception room. "Cook says the pastry's still waiting."

Lunch. She had completely forgotten about lunch. "That's very kind," she said. "Where—"

"We's set a table in the servants' hall since them soldiers won't let us in the dining room."

"Fine," Dorrin said. "Lead the way. Selfer?"

The pie, mincemeat and vegetables in a pastry crust, was delicious. Dorrin ate it quickly, anxious to get back upstairs and check on the children. She met one of the nurserymaids on the stairs.

"He's better still, my lord," the maid said. "The fever's all gone; we've never seen the like."

"Is he awake?"

"No, but he's sleeping restful, no twitching. Malin says let him sleep it out."

"That's good. I'm sorry the children couldn't go out this morning, but this afternoon let them play outside."

"In the orchard? That's where we usually take them when it's this cool, out of the wind."

"No, not in the orchard today. It's cool, but not windy—they should be fine in the front of the house."

The children came downstairs quietly, obviously anxious with the house full of strangers and none of the familiar adults about. Dorrin watched them file out the front entrance; none were invaded that she could detect.

Once outside, their reserve gradually leached away and soon they were running around the wide graveled entrance, screeching and playing like normal children. They *were* normal children, Dorrin reminded herself. The nurserymaids watched, trying to keep the children into rough age groups.

After a few minutes, she went back upstairs to check on Mikeli and find out why the nursery's protection against aggressive magery had failed. Mikeli slept peacefully, appearing normal to all her senses. The nursery's protection, a spell controlled at the door, had been turned off; Dorrin turned it back on.

While on that level, she spent the next hour checking room after room for any evil magery and found nothing—the children's floor seemed clear. Down one flight, where the adults had their chambers, was a different matter. After finding multiple death-dealing traps of various kinds, familiar from her time in Aarenis, and spells set to

confuse, injure, or kill, in the first bedchamber she explored, she decided she'd continue to sleep somewhere else.

A soft call from the stairway to the third floor brought her back up.
"He's awake, my lord."

Dorrin went into the nursery; Mikeli was now propped up on pillows, rubbing his eyes.

"Mikeli—how do you feel?"

"Better. Hungry . . . Who are you?"

"I'm Dorrin Verrakai," Dorrin said. "The new Duke."

"Where's Mama?"

"She had to go on a trip," Dorrin said. "But I'm here. If you're hungry, let's go see if the cooks can find you something." She looked at
the nurserymaid. "I don't know what a child who's been sick should
eat—"

"Toast, weak sib, to see how it settles."

"I'm *hungry*," Mikeli said in a stronger voice, pushing away from
the pillows. "I feel . . . different."

Dorrin extended her magery a little. No hint of someone other
than a five-winters child inside, a child thinner and paler than he
should be, but with healthy energy surging inside him.

"Come downstairs with me," she said, standing and holding out a
hand. Mikeli got up and took her hand without hesitation.

"Your shoes, Miki," said the nurserymaid, fetching them and putting them on his feet as he stood on one leg at a time.

CHAPTER TWENTY

O n the way downstairs, the boy asked question after question: what had happened, where were the others, where
were his parents, where had Dorrin come from and why,
what had been wrong with him and why was he better . . . on and
on. Dorrin answered as well as she could, with what she thought
would be good for him to know. That was always less than the full
truth, but she tried not to lie.

In the kitchen, Farin recommended broth and dry bread. Mikeli
drank a mug of broth and inhaled the bread so fast Dorrin was afraid
he'd choke. A little color had come into his pale cheeks.

"Had the crisis this morning, I heard," Farin said. "Fever gone so
fast—is that real, or will he relapse?" She said that quietly, to Dorrin,
across the kitchen from Mikeli.

"I believe it to be real," Dorrin said. "Falk's grace, I call it."

"Falk! I've never heard my lords and my ladies talk of Falk's
grace."

"You will hear me do so," Dorrin said, touching her ruby. "I'm a
Knight of Falk, remember."

The cook gave her a long look. "Does that mean no more of
those . . . with the . . ." She made a gesture, circle and horns.

"No more priests of Liart, no more blood magery," Dorrin said.
Everyone in the kitchen but Mikeli stopped short and almost cow-
ered. "No more," Dorrin said, louder. "I am your Duke, and my word

is your law, but my word is founded on Falk and the High Lord, not those scum."

"But—but I—" That was a kitchen maid by the bread oven, a girl perhaps thirteen or fourteen. Dorrin remembered her as one of those who had carried water for her bath. "I—they made me swear to—"

"Be quiet, Efla!" Farin said.

Dorrin walked over to the girl. "Efla, what did they make you swear?"

Tears ran down the girl's face. "They—they made me swear to him—to Liart—they hurt me and hurt me and I was so scared—"

Dorrin reached out; the girl flinched but Dorrin pulled her closer, into a hug. "Child, the gods forgive such oaths . . . you are not bound to Liart. You can renounce that oath and take a better one." The girl sobbed in Dorrin's arms; Dorrin patted her back. "Efla, listen . . . listen to me. I'm your Duke now. I'm your protector."

Efla pulled back a little, gasping out her story through her sobs. "They—they made me—he—he took me—he put his—and a child— they said it—was really—Liart's—"

Dorrin hugged the girl close again. "It's all right, Efla. They lied. The Bloodlord's servants lie to scare people, and lie to trick them, and lie to harm them. If you have a child inside you, it is the human child of whoever raped you, not a god's child. The Bloodlord cannot engender life."

"Are you sure?"

"Yes. When did this happen?"

"Ten-days and ten-days afore you came. Right before a lot of them left to go somewhere. It was Hagin, son of Jurin, son of Haron who did it. And—and I don't know, and—"

"Come, sit down here." Dorrin led the girl to the stool she herself had sat on that morning. "Bring me a wet cloth," she said to the others. Motion resumed; the others moved around and Farin brought the cloth.

"Wipe your face," Farin said to Efla. "What a silly girl, to bother the Duke with all this. And I still think you wanted it, only you got caught and made up all that about being forced—"

"I did not!" Efla said, with another burst of tears. "I was in the pantry there, I told you—"

"I want to hear all her story," Dorrin said to Farin. "She may have something to tell that will help me clear the last evil from this place. Can you watch Mikeli for me? Will eating too much now make him sicker?"

"Oh!" The cook looked over at the table, where Mikeli was reaching for a pot of honey. "I'll watch him, never fear."

"Now, Efla," Dorrin said. "Can you tell me what happened?"

It was much as she expected. One of the young men had found her in the pantry, late in the evening, when she was finishing the evening audit as assigned. She had been unable to move; he had laughed, fondled her, kissed her, and then forced her to come with him to the old keep, into the dungeon itself. Horrible monsters had been there, dressed in red and black. They'd tortured a kitten in front of her and rubbed her face in its blood. They'd hurt her under her clothes, and laughed at her, and the man—Hagin—had hurt her most between her legs. They'd threatened worse, showing her the tools, the fire, and made her swear eternal loyalty to Liart of the Horned Chain.

"I didn't want to . . . but it hurt so much . . ."

"And now you think you're with child?"

Efla hung her head; Dorrin could barely hear her voice. "I didn't bleed."

"If you are with child, I promise you again it is a human child, not a demon's. Those monsters were human men, in robes and masks . . . not anything but that."

"And the Bloodlord won't come to take me away if I . . . if I unsay it?"

"No. But you can't undo what's done, or unsay what's said . . . you can say differently this time."

"They said we all had to," Farin said. Now she looked worried; the other kitchen help edged nearer. "And once we swore, the Bloodlord would know and we could never get away."

"That's not true," Dorrin said. "Anyone can turn from evil if they want to; the gods act through people—through us." Almost always; Paks had that circle on her forehead through a direct act, but she was a paladin.

Thinking of Paks, she thought of the Duke—the king, she reminded herself yet again. She counted the days . . . was it two or three until the Spring Evener? She looked around the great rooms, dimming as the winds brought a layer of cloud across the sun . . .

nothing like the palace in Chaya, full of color and life. So easy to imagine the bustle of servants, guests, the talk and the laughter, the music—no. That was self-pity, and she would not indulge.

She found Selfer still supervising the removal of salvageable items from the tower. "Shall we burn it now, or hope that's rain enough to keep any flames from the other buildings?" he asked.

"I'm thinking perhaps we should do it on the Spring Evener," Dorrin said. "A day of renewal and also balance, restoration."

"I think you're right," he said. "But if it rains—"

"Barrels of oilberries," Dorrin said. "We've enough oil to burn even the old dry wood. In fact, we can start pouring that on it now. And light it on the Eve."

"We can call it an honor to the king at his coronation," Selfer said, grinning.

"And it will be," Dorrin said. "If I could, I'd light fires for him all the way to Aarenis."

CHAPTER TWENTY-ONE

Valdaire

On the road south, at the head of his cohort, Arcolin half ignored the Vonja agent who wanted to chatter about his new status. His mind ranged ahead to Valdaire and the south, and behind to the north where his domain—*his* domain—waited. He made plans—*his* plans, not that different from Kieri's, but his own. Rain came as it always did; the road was a quagmire where it always was; the cohort stopped in the usual places.

"Gettin' back to it, is he?" he heard over and over. Arcolin nodded and waved without pausing to explain. When they finally made it over the pass and he saw once more the Vale of Valdaire opening below, his heart lifted.

The Duke's great barracks just outside the city on the northeast, originally a caravansary, had been sublet by his factor to another company. Valdaire did not permit troops to camp near the city, so Arcolin found them cramped accommodation in an inn northeast of the main market. His cohort filled every available room; some slept in the stable loft as well. Arcolin went out at once to deal with the business that held them in Valdaire: money and the need to hire captains.

News of Kieri Phelan's new position as king of Lyonya had reached Valdaire as a rumor, widely disbelieved but a good item of gossip. As he chatted with men at the hire-sword hall, everyone had a different version of the rumor, and they all asked for more. Arcolin turned the questions aside and asked his own, interviewing everyone who looked like officer material, talking to the other captains he knew.

"So, Captain, they're saying your duke turned out to be royal-born."

Aesil M'dierra, the only woman commanding a mercenary company, stirred her sib and then sipped it, eyeing him over the rim of the mug. Arcolin hoped for her assessment of the freelance mercenaries hanging around the hire-sword hall. He had a short list of possible captains.

"What have you heard?" Arcolin said, not answering. M'dierra, he knew, would expect some verbal sparring before an answer she could trust.

"The moneychangers' courier, some ten days ago. The one who brings the current exchange rate to the Guild League cities."

"Bannack?"

"That's the one. My senior captain buys him dinner and drinks, and we get the news from the north."

"So," Arcolin said, in a joking voice, "what wild story did Bannack hand you?"

"Kieri Phelan's an elf king's son and he's off to some elvenhome kingdom to be king of the elves. He was stolen away at birth and hidden in a castle—locations vary from across the sea to here in Aarenis." She took another swallow of sib. "I don't believe that; elves can find elves, and anyway he doesn't look like an elf. That story might work over the mountains, but here, no. Kieri is not an elf and though he could be a king's son I can't imagine whose."

"Interesting," Arcolin said. "Always helps to know what rumors are running."

"Fast horses aren't the strongest," M'dierra said. "Now are you going to tell me, or do I have to buy you a meal and pretend to admire your handsome face?"

Arcolin laughed. "Let's share a meal. I'll tell you about Kieri and then ask your opinion of some men I'm thinking of hiring as captains."

"Well enough, but I must reassure my anxious employers that I'm not switching sides just because I'm seen dining with you. Get us one of the side rooms at the Golden Fish, for two full glasses from now."

Arcolin nodded and she rose, a woman near the Duke's age, dark-haired, tall, lithe, though he noted she moved a little more stiffly than she had a few years before. On the way out of the inn's common room, she signaled two Golden Company soldiers, her escort.

His own employer's agent, across the room, saw her leave and came to Arcolin. "What did she say? Who are you hiring?"

"I don't know yet," Arcolin said. "It was just a cup of sib; we're having dinner to discuss business. Speaking of which—" He rubbed thumb and fingers together.

"Oh. Well, I haven't had time to see the bankers today; tomorrow will do, won't it?"

"On arrival in Valdaire," Arcolin said, trying for Kieri's tone.

"But the banks—you don't want to wander around with a sack of gold."

"On arrival," Arcolin said. "And we arrived before noon."

Grumbling, the agent admitted that he did, indeed, have that part of their payment; Arcolin went with him to the Golden Fish, not really surprised the agent was staying at such an expensive inn. On the way, he told Jamis, one of his escort, to fetch a pack mule.

The Golden Fish advertised its elegance with fresh paint on the doorframes and shutters, pots of flowers out front, and two stout door guards alert to keep out anyone they suspected of not having enough money. They ignored the agent, Arcolin, and Arcolin's remaining escort; Arcolin paused and told the nearer guard that Jamis would be coming with a mule to take away the ale he was planning to buy.

"He can't block the entrance," the man said.

"No, of course not."

"In uniform?"

"Yes. Phelan's Company."

"Good enough. S'long as he don't park a mule across the entrance, we won't bother 'im."

Inside, the floors shone with oil; the common room smelled of fresh herbs. The innkeeper came to meet the Cortes Vonja agent, then led them to the inn strong room with its impressively iron-bound door and heavy lockplate. Inside, shelves held labeled sacks and boxes. In the presence of the innkeeper the agent opened a box with Cortes Vonja's city seal on the lid, and counted out the first installment of southern gold, natas and nas with the Guild League and Cortes Vonja mint marks. Arcolin and the agent both signed a paper stating Arcolin's receipt of the money. The innkeeper signed as witness.

"As you see, Captain, I have a good, secure strong room and would be happy to protect your payment overnight, until the banks open tomorrow."

"No, thank you," Arcolin said. To his eye the strong room was not proof against anything but casual and incompetent thieves. Valdaire abounded in such, but also had a branch of the Thieves' Guild. "I have ample guards. I will, however, buy two kegs of your best ale, if you have it to spare."

"Certainly, certainly," the innkeeper said, beaming now.

"And in a glass and a half, one of your side rooms for the evening. M'dierra dines with me."

"Yes, of course, my—Captain."

"You're dining here?" the Cortes Vonja agent said, frowning.

"M'dierra's choice," Arcolin said. "You object?"

"Er . . . no. I just wondered."

"Captain, Jamis is here," Tam said.

"Excuse me." Arcolin bowed and looked around the common room. How long would it take the innkeeper—? But there he was, behind two servants, each with a keg. "This way," he said to the servants, leading them to the front door. As he paid the innkeeper, Jamis and Tam packed the money first, and then the kegs on top of them. Arcolin went on ahead. Kieri had an arrangement for after-hours deposit at his banker's. Arcolin gave the coded knock, a guard opened the door, and when Jamis and Tam arrived, the money went into a vault far safer than the innkeeper's strong room.

"So, when's himself coming down again? Or is it true what I hear, that he's become a king somewhere up north?" Fenin Kavarthin, the banker, gray-haired and a little stooped, secured the vault door while Arcolin looked politely the other way.

Part of the banker's pay was information. "He's the new king of Lyonya," Arcolin said. "That much is true. He's the son of—I think it was the second last king before the one that died this winter, sister of the last queen. But the whole story's long, and I have an appointment."

"So—who's going to take over the Company? And his domain— he had a domain in Tsaia, didn't he?"

"I am," Arcolin said.

"So you're a duke—the Duke—now?"

"Lord of the North Marches," Arcolin said. "Nothing more now; the Council knows I'm from Aarenis. And not nobly born."

"He wasn't either, that they knew about," Kavarthin said. They went up a flight of stairs; Kavarthin paused at the landing. "When will you want the money out, Captain?"

"Some tomorrow, to pay for expenses here."

"You know we still have money Phelan deposited two years or more back. And it's earned. You have his seal and authority—what should I do with that?"

"Send half north with the first Guild caravan, to his usual bank in Vérella," Arcolin said. That had been Kieri's practice: leave most of a season's earnings in the bank in Valdaire, but once the first campaign money was paid, half went north. "Send it to Captain Cracolnya; he's in charge up there for now."

"Not that good-looking woman captain? I thought she was second to you."

"By your leave," Arcolin said, "that's another long story. Tomorrow, if it please you, but now I must go."

A soft mist drifted down as he came out into the street, the afternoon darkening to evening. Jamis and Tam had left with the mule and the kegs, to deliver ale to the cohort. Arcolin checked the hang of his sword and walked swiftly.

For a wonder, the streets were silent on his way to the Golden Fish, idlers urged back inside by mist that turned to drizzle, then to thin rain as he walked. When he arrived, he saw someone leading Aesil M'dierra's horse away from the entrance; she was silhouetted in the doorway. Arcolin stretched his legs and caught up before the door wards closed the door behind her. He handed his damp hat and cloak to a servant and they followed the innkeeper to the private room Arcolin had reserved. It was nicely furnished, the table covered with a clean cloth and set with dishes bearing the golden fish emblem of the place, chairs cushioned with padded leather, a weapons rack on one wall, more sweet herbs scattered on the shining floor.

"Very nice," M'dierra said, sitting in the chair to the heart-hand side; Arcolin took the other.

During dinner, they didn't talk; both had the soldier's habit of eating while food was available. But when servants had taken away the meager remains of the leg of lamb, the pastry stuffed with steamed grain, vegetables, and bits of chicken and pork, the buttered redroots, the bread, and brought in a compote of mixed fruits simmered in spices and honey, M'dierra said, "Well?"

"I didn't see it myself, but I heard it from those who did," Arcolin said, ladling a serving of dessert into the small bowls the servants had put down on fresh plates. "Including Tsaia's prince. You remember Kieri's wife, Tammarion."

"Indeed I do." They both understood the slight edge in her voice.

"At the wedding, he gave her a sword, a sword that Aliam Halveric had found in the forest up there in Lyonya. It was a pretty thing, they both thought, and fit for a lady."

"The one with that green stone?"

"Yes." Arcolin explained what he'd been told about the sword's origin. "I don't know more than that, but I do know that Aliam had no idea whose it was, nor Kieri, and Kieri had vowed not to hold it, when he gave it to Tammarion."

"Why?"

Arcolin shrugged. "I never understood it myself, or why he didn't use it after she died. But it hung on the wall at the fort all those years until the night the Duke's steward and a priestess of Achrya tried to kill us all." He hurried through that part. "Then Paksenarrion rode off with it, having a call from the gods, and the next thing we heard was a summons from the Council for the Duke to come to Vérella along with representatives from the village councils of his domain." Aesil said nothing, but put a piece of fruit in her mouth. "Then I had his letter telling me he was going to Lyonya to be king. And when I got to Vérella, I heard from the prince about the Verrakai attacks, not only on Kieri but on the prince, his uncle, and the Marshal-Judicar."

"The Girdish will be out for blood. What about the other Verrakai?"

"Order of Attainder. And on the Konhalts."

"So Tsaia has three domains up there with no, or new, commanders. Where I come from, that would mean war." M'dierra scowled. "The situation here is unstable too. Has been since the last year Phelan was down here."

"A bad time," Arcolin said.

"Bad indeed," M'dierra said, her voice low. "We did things—"

"We all did things we aren't proud of," Arcolin said. "But now it's your turn. What's the situation, and—most of all—what's your opinion of these five?" He laid his short list on the table in front of her.

She tapped the first name. "What did he tell you about his experience?"

"Served with you for two hands of years, half as sergeant. Decided to go out on his own while he still could."

"Eight years, and two as sergeant. He's not bad, but he's not as good as he thinks he is, and he'll tell you what he thinks you want to hear. He's a competent soldier, less so as a sergeant; too much temper and too fond of ale. An excellent swordsman, though, and capable with several weapons."

"I wondered," Arcolin said. "I thought I remembered seeing him in the ranks that last year."

"You did. Now this young fellow—" She tapped the next name. "He's someone's bastard, won't say whose, but claims he knows. Last season, he took a short contract with Sobanai and they offered him permanent, but he wanted varied experience, he said. I hired him on another short contract, in the fall, to take a cohort on escort duty to Andressat and back; the sergeant said he was diligent and honest. Andressat had some complaint—you know the Count, how fussy he can be. I've contracted to Andressat many times; can't afford to have anyone he won't tolerate, so I let him go, but have nothing against him." She put the list down.

"I need more than one," Arcolin said. "We're short of captains—and I haven't told you about Dorrin."

"Dorrin! Was she killed?"

"No. But the prince and Council have named her the new Duke of Verrakai."

M'dierra stared at him. "What? Dorrin? Why?"

"She's a Verrakai. And she's had nothing to do with them since she ran away to the Company of Falk."

M'dierra said something in her native tongue that must have been an oath, and said, "If you need help up there, Jandelir, consider hiring Golden Company." She was serious; she almost never used his first name.

"I don't think bringing mercenaries over the mountains would calm the situation."

"Perhaps not, but—why are you here, and not there?"

"Contract. And money. We were running short on supplies, with so many troops quartered up there."

"Ah. Well, then—" She looked at the list again and put her finger on the fifth name. "Here's another possible for you. I'd hire him if I had an opening. You don't want the others. You'll want to send someone reliable north, am I right?"

"Yes. Two, if possible."

"My advice: Send this one, Versin, north; keep the young fellow with you. And the Blues let one of their captains go, Talvis Arneson; he lost an eye last year, nearly died of the infection, but survived. Good man, but you know them—won't spend on their wounded. True, he's only got one eye, but every other way, he's worth the chance, especially for training recruits. He's looking shabby now, and living rough, but my captains can find him."

"Send him to me tomorrow, if you will, and thank you for your help," Arcolin said.

"What will you do, without Kieri?"

"What I did before," Arcolin said. "What he taught me. Take good contracts, do the work honestly, treat my people honorably. Stay out of politics."

"And—what have you told them up north about your past?"

"That I'm someone's bastard."

"But not whose?"

"It's immaterial now." Since Siniava's War, boundaries had changed and rulers as well; what had been lay now in ruins, he was sure.

"Is it? Is it ever immaterial? It certainly wasn't for Kieri. If he'd known—"

"Siniava would still rule the South, Aesil." There. He'd used her first name. "You'd have that to deal with, and no Kieri to lead us all against him."

"I wonder," she said. "Men like Kieri seem to bring trouble with them. We need trouble, we mercenaries, but we don't thrive in big wars. No one does." She tipped her head to one side. "Are you still in love with me, Jandelir?"

"I grew up," Arcolin said. "As men do."

"As some men do." She sighed and ran a finger around the rim of her dessert bowl. Her knuckle, he noticed, was scarred and swollen.

"I was young and proud, in those days, intent on having my own company, on proving myself. I saw no profit in you, and that was unfair." She looked squarely at him. "I do not apologize often, Jandelir Arcolin, but this is an apology. I do not think I could have loved you then, even had I stopped to consider what manner of young man you were, but I should have done you that courtesy at least. And later, when I realized it, I should have said so then."

Arcolin could not speak for a moment; all the old longing swept over him once more, then departed. He had loved her; she had loved—or thought she loved—Kieri Phelan; Kieri had loved only Tammarion, and Tammarion had died. If any bard had known all this, it would have made a ballad, but no one did, no one but the people involved. He cleared his throat. "I did love you, Aesil, and admired you as well, and it was years before I gave up the hope that perhaps, someday . . . but you need not apologize, except to ease your own heart."

"And so it is," she said, sitting back and folding her hands on the table. "You are the man I thought you were, once I saw past my own ambition and my own losses. Friends?"

"Always," Arcolin said. "Unless, of course, we're hired by enemies, but even then—"

"We have the Code, and we are content, are we not?"

"We are content," Arcolin said.

CHAPTER TWENTY-TWO

Next day, when Arcolin was coming back from another visit to the banker, he saw ahead of him a gaunt man in dirty, threadbare clothes with a rag tied around his head approaching the inn door. The door ward blocked him.

"Show me your money, or go your way." The door ward sounded both bored and hostile.

"I need to see Captain Arcolin."

"Not likely, beggar—he's no time for the likes of you—" The door ward flourished his billet. The man's shoulders drooped; he turned away from the door, and Arcolin could see that the rag on his head covered his left eye.

"Wait—" Arcolin came closer and signaled the door ward to move back. "Aren't you Arneson, captain in the Blues? M'dierra told me you might come to see me."

"Yes," the man said. "I'm Arneson. No longer captain; they said after this—" He raised a hand to his face. "I was no use to them." The wound that had taken his eye had pulled his face awry as well; Arcolin recognized the damage done most often by a curved blade.

"I'm hiring captains to go north," Arcolin said. "Northern Tsaia, north of the Honnorgat—"

"Where Phelan came from—is he still Duke, or is the rumor true, that he's gone to be king somewhere?"

"Lyonya; he's king of Lyonya now. I'm taking over his domain and Company, with his blessing. I have a one-cohort contract with Cortes Vonja. But come in—it's time for lunch. Eat with me; we'll talk and see if you want the job."

"I'll take any job," Arneson said, squaring his shoulders. "If you think I can be of use. And if you don't—better we talk before we eat. I'm not taking a meal from you, if—"

"Well, then, if you insist—how many years were you with the Blues?"

"Nine fighting seasons. I was at Cha in Siniava's War."

"You were on our right flank, if I remember—"

"No, on your left."

"So you were." Arcolin realized he had already gone past the warped face, the missing eye, to liking the man, wanting him to qualify. "Your company was mostly swordsmen, like ours—did you ever command polearms?"

"Only in training—we trained with them, but rarely used them."

"Same as us, and mostly so our swords can practice against them. Tell me, do you consider yourself fit enough for duty? M'dierra said you were sick a long time. Are you healthy now?"

"Yes, sir. I know my missing eye is a problem, but I'm otherwise whole of body and limb. If you wish to test my sword skills, I'm afraid I must ask for the loan of a sword."

"You wouldn't have lasted nine fighting seasons with the Blues if you weren't a good swordsman. I think you'd better have lunch with me, Captain, because if you're willing, you're hired."

The relief showed through the scar. "I—thank you, sir."

"Come on in, meet the sergeants. They're staying south with me, but they can fill you in—"

"Sir, I'd—I'd rather not—the way I am—"

Arcolin nodded. "You haven't asked about your pay—you're due a signing bonus. We have to get you on the rolls for that—come in for that, and then meet me for supper."

Despite his ragged clothes—he'd probably sold his good ones for food or lodging—Arneson already moved more confidently. Arcolin ordered hot bread and sib. "We have to share bread and salt," he said. "It's our custom."

Arneson smiled as best he could. "I grew up with that. Thank you—I have a pinch of salt."

Arcolin sent Stammel, who had been waiting for him in the common room, to fetch the cohort rolls. As they waited, Arneson sat straight, almost rigid, carefully not looking at the bread. Arcolin knew better than to offer. Stammel brought in the rolls, a quill, and an ink stick and bowl, then withdrew. Arcolin mixed the ink, tested the quill, and turned to Arneson.

"Your full name and your home, where you were born?"

"Talvis Keri Arneson, of Sorellin, but my parents came from the north, from southern Fintha. They were dyers by trade."

Arcolin wrote that in, and had Arneson repeat the familiar oath, changing Kieri's name to his own. Then Arcolin broke the loaf; Arneson shook the meager contents of a paper twist of salt onto it, and Arcolin pushed the pieces together. Joining heart-hands, they turned it over three times and then broke off pieces, each offering one to the other. Arneson signed the book, and they were done.

"You might as well help me eat this," Arcolin said.

His new captain shook his head, but drank a mug of sib and ate half the loaf anyway.

Three glasses later, when Captain Talvis Arneson reappeared, the door ward did not hesitate to let him in. Arcolin, fetched by Sergeant Devlin, recognized only the scar. Clean, shaved, his hair neatly clubbed at the neck, an eye patch rather than a rag covering his ruined eye, in clean clothes only slightly worn, boots oiled, a plain but serviceable sword at his side, he looked nothing like the ragged beggar he'd seemed before. He must have spent the entire advance, Arcolin thought, to look that good that fast.

"Reporting for duty," he said.

"Excellent," Arcolin said. "I've just hired a second captain, who'll be going north with you. He's gone to fetch his things from his lodgings. He has his own mount, but no spare; you'll need to visit the horse yards tomorrow and find a mount and spare for yourself. Our limit for officers' mounts is twelve natas. Right now, I need someone to check with the quartermaster—how close are we to being ready to march? Sergeant Devlin, this is Captain Arneson; introduce him to the quartermaster, answer his questions, and so on."

"Yes, sir," Devlin said. He turned to Arneson. "Captain, this way, sir."

The next day, Arcolin watched his newly hired captains as they carried out task after task he gave them. Arneson, sent to the horse market, came back with three horses—two for himself and a spare for Versin. All three were exactly the kind of sound, useful mounts Arcolin would have chosen for the long ride north. Arneson had had them freshly shod, as well. Versin, sent to market to obtain travel clothes and supplies, returned with a reasonable selection. Burek, chosen to stay with Arcolin in Aarenis, spent the entire day with the sergeants and the troops, supervising drill in a field outside the city. Around noon, one of the troops came to the inn to report that Stammel thought the young captain would do.

"What did you think?" Arcolin asked.

"He's got a funny accent, but he knows his business, sir. Stammel asked him to set us a tactical problem, and he got us working with one of the Free Pikes cohorts. Says we'll do another this afternoon."

"Excellent," Arcolin said. "Tell him that I'd like him back here for supper with the other captains before full dark." He spent the afternoon writing letters to Cracolnya, the prince in Vérella, and Kieri Phelan.

He wondered where the Halverics were; he'd been here three days and heard nothing of them. Had Aliam retired? Then he remembered that Halveric came from Lyonya. Of course he had stayed north, to attend his protégé's coronation. Arcolin let himself imagine, for a few moments, what that might be like. How would elves crown a king? Or would it be just the humans? Nobody had ever explained how that worked, the joint rule of a kingdom, and he could not figure it out. He wished he could be there to see Kieri crowned . . . but he was better here. The Company—*his* Company—needed him.

At supper that night, Arcolin ate with his three new captains. Versin and Arneson had met; Arneson had accepted the additional clothes Versin bought for the journey with the air of a man who knew he had been given charity and knew also he must accept it graciously. He'd changed to a clean shirt and trousers for dinner.

Arcolin kept the table talk to business; time enough for them to share personal matters later. "You two head north tomorrow," he said to Arneson and Versin. "I've written you a safe-passage through Tsaia on the trade road. Ordinarily you'd travel with a northbound caravan, but I need you in the north sooner than that. You'll have to stop in Vérella at least one night; I'm sure the Council will want a report from you on the south. They know I was planning to hire replacement captains here; they'll probably be watching for you. Don't get drawn into political discussions; even if you know something about Tsaian nobility, best not to show it."

He laid out the situation as he knew it, including Dorrin's probable elevation to the dukedom of Verrakai and the Order of Attainder on Verrakai and Konhalt. They listened attentively, including young Burek, who'd be staying with him in the south.

"Are we authorized replacement mounts in case one goes lame?" Versin asked.

"Yes. I've made a list of the people we deal with in every town; I spoke to them on the way south and they've agreed to supply you. You'll have to sign for it, of course. Check in with the moneychanger listed for each town; he will authorize your lodging and, if necessary a mount."

"So we will not need to carry much money," Versin said.

"That's right. Safer than showing gold on the road. The Duke set it up that way years ago, as soon as he could afford it. I must warn you, though, with the Verrakai mess going on, Tsaia may not be as safe as usual, even on the trade road. You will be safer traveling as civilians, but some count's alert reeve, or some Girdish Marshal, may insist on stopping you and asking questions. Show them the pass; everyone on that route knows me and knows the Company."

Arcolin noticed that Arneson ate no faster and no more than the others; he admired the man's determination to hide his poverty. Still, the sooner the man put some weight on his scrawny frame, the better. He called Arneson back as the others were leaving.

"I can tell that you're basically healthy," he said. "But I want our physician to see you, to see if he thinks you need a special diet. Fever, they tell me, does some damage that certain herbs can heal."

"Sir, I'm well enough—"

"I don't doubt you are well enough for duty, but humor me in this, if you will. The road north is long and hard; you will be meeting many travelers who may carry disease. A recurrence of your fever would be bad for both of us. If the physician tells you to follow a certain diet, and it prevents trouble—can that be so hard?"

Arneson flushed. "No, sir. I just—I just do not wish to cause you extra expense."

"I'm certain you won't. Let me introduce you to Master Simmitts."

The physician, as Arcolin expected, recommended that Arneson eat more, to gain at least a stone. He also had specific recommendations for ordering meals at each inn. "This early in the season, traveling north, you won't find fresh fruit. Take a sack of candied plums with you, eat at least three a day. Fresh greens, only lightly steamed, at your evening meal, along with redroots. Cows should be calving; you should be able to get fresh milk and butter. If not, be sure to eat cheese. Fever like you had thins the bones . . ." He was writing as he talked, and eventually handed Arneson a list. "And here's a salve for your scar; use it morning and night. If it doesn't last you all the way, here's the name of a physician in Vérella who will give you more." He took the list back, scribbled another name on it, and handed it over again.

"We have candied plums in our supplies," Arcolin said, as they walked back to the common room. "Be sure to take a sack. I'll be up at dawn; see me before you and Versin leave."

"Yes, sir." Arneson turned to the stairs and went up them with a spring in his stride.

Arcolin watched him go. If he managed only one thing right, he had given that man back hope. He could do this—it was easier every day to talk to people as if he, not Kieri, were this Company's commander. Kieri would be pleased if he did it well. No . . . he would be pleased with himself if he did it well.

Arcolin woke before dawn and came downstairs to find Arneson and Versin both before him—a good sign, though he had planned to be waiting for them.

"Breakfast together?" he said.

"The horses are ready, sir," Arneson said. Versin looked hungry.

"Breakfast," Arcolin said. "Better here than up the pass."

"Thank you, sir," Versin said.

The innkeeper, warned last night of early departures, had porridge ready, bread almost out of the oven, he said, and eggs. He set out bowls of porridge and a pitcher of cream.

"The good thing about the south," Arcolin said, having ordered everything offered, "is how early milk and eggs come in. We leave home with the cows all dry and the hens not laying, and arrive in Valdaire to the full bounty of spring." He poured cream into his porridge; the others did the same.

Burek came into the room, carrying a bowl of porridge with a spoon stuck in it like a flagpole. "The men are up," he said. "Moving their tackle downstairs." He sat down and reached for the cream pitcher. Arcolin made a note to remind him that Phelani were not all men, and the preferred term was "troops."

"Summer, more like," Versin said, as the innkeeper brought a basket of bread still steaming from the oven. Versin broke one open then blew on his fingers. "It'll be sweaty already, down on the plains." He scooped a lump of butter onto the torn side of the chunk, and it melted instantly. He bit into it. "Not that I don't like butter and eggs."

"And here they are," the innkeeper said, setting a platter of stirred eggs and fried ham on the table, along with a bottle of a red southern sauce. "And your plates, gentlemen." He dealt those out, and then hurried off, as Stammel told Arcolin the troops were starting their breakfast line.

Sun gilded the mountains behind Valdaire when they came out into the yard. Arcolin handed over the packet of letters. Arneson and Versin checked their girths, then mounted and rode away. Arcolin turned to Stammel, supervising the cohort's breakfast.

"All good so far?"

"Yes, Captain. That Captain Burek—" He nodded across the yard to the corner where Burek was checking off boxes the first soldiers to finish breakfast were loading in a wagon. "—he's a good choice, sir. Young, but energetic and seems to know his business. Should be a big help to you."

"I certainly hope so," Arcolin said. "What did you think of the others? Or hear of them?"

"Both have a good reputation in the city. There's feeling against the Blues for casting Arneson off without even his death money."

"They did that?"

"Yes, sir. Said they'd use it to bury him if he died, and there was no use wasting it beforehand. Their physician said he was hopeless. His friends supported him while he was still fevered, but after that he wouldn't take charity. Sold everything he had to pay his last bills, and tried to find work as common labor, but most wouldn't hire him, he looked so bad."

"And Versin?"

"Good, solid, experienced—what I'm guessing Aesil M'dierra told you. Doubt you could've found better than the three you signed, Captain."

"Guess I learned something from the Duke," Arcolin said. Then he shook his head. "I've got to remember to say 'the king'; he's not a duke anymore."

"I don't think he'd mind, sir. And when are they giving *you* a title, do you know?"

"Not yet, is what I know. Our prince will be crowned this Midsummer; he might do it then, or he might wait until I come back through in the fall."

"Will we be staying south, this next winter? Or do you know?"

He didn't know; he should be planning for that but his plans went only as far as Cortes Vonja. "We'll see how Burek does," he said. "I have to go north; I would want to be sure Burek is permanent before leaving you with him."

"Oh—of course, sir. That makes sense. Only I heard from one of the Clarts that the Duke's factor who handles the winter quarters rents them out early—we wouldn't need the whole place, but to reserve part of it . . ."

Someone Arcolin hadn't thought to visit. What else had he forgotten?

"Captain Burek!" he called.

"Yes, sir?" Burek jogged across the inn yard.

"I've got a last visit to make here in town. Finish all this—" He waved at the yard where some men were still eating and others were packing up. "—and if I'm not back, start them on the road, ordinary pace. I'll catch up."

Paltis, the Duke's factor, lived across the city; Arcolin rode, to save time, after assuring the innkeeper he would be back to pay any final charges. Paltis was enjoying his own breakfast when Arcolin was shown in.

"Captain Arcolin—it's been several years! I heard you'd brought a single cohort down."

"Did you hear that Duke Phelan is now the king of Lyonya?" Arcolin asked.

"That? A rumor, of course. Just because he hasn't been here a couple of seasons—"

"No, it's the truth. It happened a few tendays ago, not long before I started south."

"How did he conquer it? Were you in the battle?"

"It wasn't a battle." Arcolin explained again how it had come about.

"What does this mean for his property?" Paltis asked. "Will he want to sell it? I've had offers. And who will pay the taxes?"

"The court of Tsaia has appointed me to take over his domain, with his blessing," Arcolin said, handing over the relevant documents. Paltis bent over them, lips moving as he read. "I'm here to see you about our winter quarters. We will need some of the space this coming winter."

Paltis looked up. "But—but I just told the Blues they were first on the list."

"I believe, if you check the contract you had with Kieri, that our Company is always first on the list."

"Yes, but—but you haven't been here, and if he's no longer the legitimate owner—"

Arcolin let his voice chill. "You've dealt with me before, as his senior captain; you have before you his word in his writing—and the authority of the Council in Tsaia—that I am now authorized to use any of his property as he himself would. I claim precedence to the winter quarters and if you wish to remain factor . . . you will comply. Else I'll see a judicar this very hour."

Paltis drooped, as Arcolin expected. "Maybe—maybe the Blues can squeeze into the other two-thirds."

"In addition," Arcolin said, "the Blues are not approved at all."

"But they pay well," Paltis said.

"They treat their wounded badly," Arcolin said. "I will not have them mingling with my people."

"Your people?"

"They are now," Arcolin said. "And I intend to take care of them. Cancel whatever agreement you have with the Blues; tell them the owner's back in the south and needs the space."

"But—what about the rest of it—surely you want to lease some of it—"

"I'll decide that later," Arcolin said. "Our contract's with Cortes Vonja—you can send me messages there, if you need to."

"The Blues will be angry." Paltis looked worried.

"Only if you tell them why I don't want them. And surely you have more discretion than to tell them that, don't you?" Arcolin put a little menace in his voice; the factor stepped back a pace.

"Of course I wouldn't, Captain."

"If you say what I told you, that the owner required the space, and your contract with the owner requires you to release it, they may be annoyed, but they won't be angry with you. It's in the contract; you're a man of business; you hold to contracts."

"Yes . . . that's true. Well, then, what about renting to caravans for short-term in the summer? I've done that; they stay only a few days, on their way north or south, and they clean up after themselves." Paltis looked at Arcolin, glanced away. "It covers the cost of a watchman, their fee does."

Arcolin knew the Duke had allowed caravans to use the winter quarters during the campaign season. "You may do that for this season," he said. "But no long-term contracts. I may require the space some years. Deposit the rental fees at Kavarthin & Sons, as usual."

"I will," Paltis said, bowing. "Of course I will." Something about his tone made Arcolin doubt him.

Arcolin rode across the city, more familiar to him than Vérella, noticing the changes two years had brought. Though the market square stalls were open for business and traders cried their wares, he sensed tension, and few children played there, where they'd been always underfoot before.

He decided to pay a last visit to the banker's—they opened when the market did—and ask his opinion of Paltis.

"Oh, Paltis is good enough of his type," Fenin Kavarthin said. He offered Arcolin a mug of sib; courtesy required taking at least a sip. "He makes his profit from his commission, as I'm sure you know, and so he wants to lease to the wealthiest he can find. Brings in a trickle to the Duke—my apologies, Captain. To you now—after the tax the city takes, and his fee."

"How often does he deposit here?"

"You're doubting him, I see. I cannot help you, if you wonder whether he's stealing from the Duke—from you. I never see the contracts; he keeps those. All I see is what he sends to the account. He leases for the entire winter season and I can expect a deposit for the reservation fee, then on arrival, the day before Midwinter Feast, and the Spring Evener. Summer leases are variable—some caravans rent the place for only a night, some for a hand of days. I may see a deposit four or five times during the summer."

"But you aren't sure how many summer contracts he makes, or what he charges—?"

"No. That is not my duty." Kavarthin pressed his lips together.

"Quite," Arcolin said. "I meant no discourtesy."

"Those not in our field sometimes think it extends to anything having to do with money," Kavarthin said. "I am not offended that you ask, but making clear where our responsibility ends. We keep your money safe."

"For which I am grateful," Arcolin said. "On another matter—are you still affiliated with the Merchants' Guild? We heard rumors in the north that some banks are now refusing reciprocity."

"We have our agreements. Things have changed since you were last here, but in Cortes Vonja . . . if you want to deposit funds with Kostin, he has been reliable so far. Our greatest concern now is that some Guild League cities are minting inferior coins. Cortes Vonja and Pler Vonja, so far, have not done so. Should you wish to send funds here, I would advise a heavier guard. Travel on the Guild League trade roads is not as safe as it was five years ago."

"Thank you," Arcolin said, draining his cup of sib. "Thank you for your advice."

"If you want someone to check on Paltis—"

"Not at this time," Arcolin said. "It's just that it's been several years since anyone went over the accounts with him."

"Just so. One of my sons, grown up in our business, can be hired for that work. There are others, of course, and I will not say he is better than others or it will seem a father's favor, but because this bank handles the money of several mercenary companies, he is familiar with military finances."

"I will consider that, Master Kavarthin. Perhaps it will be as well to wait until we return—"

"If you truly suspect your factor has been cheating you," Kavarthin said, "it would be well to catch him out before he changes his records."

Arcolin considered. "Perhaps so, but my cohort marched this morning. I must be with them by midday, at least, or they will worry. You yourself consider him good of his kind—"

Kavarthin sat back and folded his hands on his stomach. "It is my experience that everyone handling someone else's money faces the temptation to borrow a little of it from time to time. Even we bankers. We have a guild, as you know, and within that guild, for the good of all, we have rules and checks to keep our reputation secure. Factors have no guild. If owners of property are here, and use their factor merely as a convenience, another servant to run errands for them, most are honest. But in cases like this, where the owner is far away and may or may not appear once in a year . . . well, factors are only human, after all, and they can come to feel that they do more of the work and receive less of the profit." He coughed, a soft dry cough that conveyed more of his opinion of factors than the state of his lungs. "I am not saying—I will not say, because I do not know—that Paltis has been dishonest. But there has been talk that Paltis might have indulged himself."

That was clear enough. "Perhaps I should speak to your son before I leave," Arcolin said. "And yet, I must leave soon."

Kavarthin pushed himself up. "Just a moment, if you can spare it." He went to the door of his office and called. "Stepan!"

Arcolin had met one of Kavarthin's elder sons, Arpan, a few years before. Stepan clearly came from the same mold. He bowed politely to Arcolin and looked at his father.

"Captain Arcolin is a little concerned about the activities of his factor, Paltis," Kavarthin explained. "He must ride this morning; he has a contract with Cortes Vonja. I suggested he might engage your services to look over Paltis's contracts, since he cannot stay in Valdaire himself."

"Certainly," Stepan said, looking at Arcolin. "I would need a letter from you, Captain, giving me authority to speak to Paltis, and some idea of the terms of his contract with you—or, it would have been with Duke Phelan, would it not?"

"Yes," Arcolin said. "That contract is still operable, though. The Duke had me cosign it."

"That's good, but you should make a new contract as soon as possible. Sometime this summer, at least. I understand you're in a hurry, but if you could just give me that letter."

Arcolin felt as if he'd stepped into a quagmire. Not only was it taking longer than he'd told Burek, but finances always affected him that way. One of the reasons he'd never seriously considered having his own company was his distaste for the money side. Well, if you fell into a swamp, the thing to do was climb back out. "I'll be glad to," he said.

A glass later, he had produced the documents Stepan wanted, and agreed to pay his fee to investigate the matter. Stepan promised to send word of the audit when it was complete. Old Kavarthin looked entirely too satisfied, he thought, and rose to go—this time for certain.

Kavarthin walked with him to the door. "It's been a difficult few years," he said. "You know what it was like, the season you defeated Siniava. It's become more difficult, especially in the south and east. There's been reason why people who were scrupulously honest before might be less so now."

"I'll keep that in mind," Arcolin said.

"And if I were you, I'd ride with that sword on my hip and not under the saddle flap," Kavarthin said, nodding at Arcolin's horse, being walked up and down by a bank servant. "And wear your helmet."

"On the trade road?"

"Indeed."

CHAPTER TWENTY-THREE

At the inn where they'd been quartered, Arcolin paid the innkeeper's last charges and heard that the cohort had marched off three full glasses ago. Once out of the city gates, he considered putting on his helmet, but the morning was already warming; he wanted to feel the breeze on his head. He checked the hooks—yes, he could free it quickly at need. He legged his mount to a canter on the dirt path to the left of the trade road and its drainage ditch. If only Tsaia had roads like this, it would take six days less to move a cohort north and south.

Traffic on the road this close to the city seemed sparse for the time of day. He saw one small flock of goats herded toward the city on the other side of the road, and an oxcart on the road itself, driven by a farm woman, a small child alongside the ox with a goad. In the cart, a stick cage held geese, their long necks poking between the bars. They honked indignantly. He passed a moderate-sized caravan heading east, a half-glass after he left, with guards armed with bows atop each wagon. He waved; the guards raised their bows in salute. Ahead, the road curved around a hill slope covered with trees; Arcolin knew from past years that a trail easy for horses cut through the trees and met the road again, saving some distance. It was also an easy place for bandits to ambush a lone traveler. He'd taken it often enough before when in a hurry . . . but not today. He passed the fork in the trail, noting fresh hoofprints and a pile of droppings where it entered the trees.

He kept to the path beside the main road, slowing to pass a group of foot travelers and give them greeting. Three men, two women, one older than the other, four children, all with packs and staves. His horse, eager as always to run, tossed its head; Arcolin legged it to an easy canter again. The morning's problems blew away as the breeze brought him the fragrance of blossoming trees; his horse pinned one ear and quickened stride. Arcolin grinned. This one, of all his mounts, most loved to run, and he'd held it to a foot-pace all the way south. He took one hand from the reins to steady the hilt of his sword and closed his legs.

The horse bolted in great leaping strides, not quite bucking, then flattened out, running fast enough to bring tears to his eyes. Arcolin caught a blurred sensation of movement to his left, but they were past it before he registered the sudden appearance of five men on horseback and the flash of sunlight on drawn swords. Hooves thundered behind; he could not tell how many. His horse pinned both ears and quickened again. Arcolin switched hands on the reins and drew his own sword, though he doubted any bandits had mounts as fast as this one.

Then he remembered the foot-travelers. Were they there merely to slow riders like him, or were they in danger? And what about that caravan? Surely its guards would be enough to hold off a few brigands. He glanced behind. Two riders, kicking hard, but their horses could not keep his pace. More behind them turning back to the westbound path. A quick glance at the road showed nothing ahead; behind, when he looked back again, he saw dust rising, saw one of the brigands lean out to strike at someone on the ground.

Arcolin sat back, hauling his mount down; the two chasing him yelled in triumph. He swung his mount to the right, jumped the ditch between the footpath and the road, and reversed back down the road, passing the brigands before they could change direction. He heard his pursuers' horses grunt as they too jumped and the clatter of their hooves behind him.

The odds weren't good, Arcolin saw, as he neared the altercation on the footpath. One of the women was on the ground—dead or injured, he couldn't tell. The men, trying to fend off armed horsemen with walking staves, showed some training, but the four brigands were ahorse and armed with swords. He reined in as he passed the fight and jumped back across the ditch on the Valdaire side. Two of the brigands had noticed and turned to meet him. One of his pursuers tried to jump the ditch, but his horse refused, and plunged uselessly in the muddy bottom.

Arcolin charged straight at the fight. The two facing him spread apart; Arcolin reined for the one nearer the trees, then, with a shift of his weight, sent his horse at the other, who had committed too early to attack his flank. One stroke of his sword took the man's arm. His own horse squealed and bucked, as a clang reminded Arcolin where his helmet was—on the saddle instead of his head. He heard the solid THWACK as his horse's hind hoofs connected with the brigand's horse.

Now he was in the thick of it, hoping the foot travelers would realize he was on their side, but with no time to explain. No time to retrieve his helmet, either. He felt like a fool, but the helmet had saved his horse an injury. He parried a sword stroke meant for one of the travelers. One of the men, using his staff expertly, managed to unhorse a brigand; the other woman smacked the downed man on the head. If he could only get them in order, they were now four to four, but—he parried a stroke aimed at him, and on the backstroke came so near the brigand's face the man flinched back and accidentally reined his horse away. Arcolin shifted his weight and signaled his mount. His horse reared, hopped forward, and struck the rider with front hooves, knocking him out of the saddle. The man's sword flew from his hand, and his horse bolted away.

He couldn't reach the man on the ground with his sword, but one of the foot travelers could. Four to three now. One of the men knocked the brigand trying to climb out of the ditch back into it.

The remaining two brigands reined their horses around and, kicking vigorously, rode at speed into the woods. Arcolin listened to their receding hoofbeats. His own mount was breathing hard, finally, sweat showing on its neck. He looked around. The man whose arm he'd severed sprawled on the ground, unconscious or dead—his horse had slowed to a stop some distance away and was now snatching nervously at grass on the verge of the path.

Arcolin rode over to the ditch, where the last brigand was trying to catch his horse. The horse moved faster in the muddy ditch bottom than the man, and finally scrambled out on the near side; the man managed to grab its tail for help up the slope, then pulled himself into the saddle from the off side, as Arcolin rode toward him. The man smacked his horse with the flat of his sword, and kicked; the horse threw a tremendous buck, then another and another, and the man flew off, landing with a loud thump. Arcolin was off his horse and had run him through before the man caught his breath. Then he saw the leg bent at the wrong angle and realized the man would have been no danger.

"We owe you thanks, sir." One of the travelers came toward him, staff still in a defensive position. "It would have gone hard with us—"

"You use your staves well," Arcolin said. "Are you Girdish?"

The man beamed. "Yes, sir. All of us, and the children, too. And Tamis there—" He nodded at one of the others. "He was in the Foss militia two more years than I was." He paused. "You're one of Phelan's captains, aren't you? I saw a Phelani cohort pass by a while ago. Haven't see one for the past few years; wondered if they were ever coming back."

"Yes, I'm Captain Arcolin," Arcolin said.

"So the Red Fox is back, is he?"

"No, not Phelan himself," Arcolin said. "When you get to Valdaire, some of the rumors are true—he's king of Lyonya now. I'm leading the Company."

"Liss is hurt bad," one of the other men said, coming up. "She won't be able to walk."

Arcolin led his horse closer. The woman on the ground had a lump on her head, but the worse injury was to her leg, trampled during the fight. The younger woman knelt behind her, supporting her shoulders to give her a sip of water.

"There's a caravan headed east a ways behind me," Arcolin said. "If we get you over onto the road, they may be able to help."

His horse jerked up its head and looked back eastward. Arcolin looked along the road and saw a horseman approaching at speed, carrying a maroon and white pennant. Closer yet, he saw it was Sergeant Devlin, on one of the spare horses.

"Captain, what's happened?" Devlin asked.

"Brigands," Arcolin said, waving at the bodies on the ground. "Six of them attacked these travelers and me."

"He came back to help us," one of the men said. "Without him—"

Devlin looked at Arcolin, then pointedly at Arcolin's mount with the helmet still hooked to the saddle. Arcolin grinned and shook his head. "No time," he said. "This woman's got a broken leg; she needs a physician. We're a glass or less from Valdaire: ride in, tell the city guard what happened, and ask for a cart for them—"

"We don't have money for a cart," the man said.

"You're still in Valdaire's domain," Arcolin said. "You can call on them for aid, since they haven't cleared out those brigands." To Devlin he said, "I'll stay here until you return, then have you stay while I ride on to the cohort. I know they'll be worried, but we can't leave this party unprotected. If the caravan will lend me a few guards when they get this far, I'll go ahead then."

"At once, Captain," Devlin said. He rode off at a canter. Arcolin unhooked his helmet, felt the slight dent where the sword had struck, felt inside—no change in the liner—and put it on. He checked the man who'd lost an arm—dead already from blood loss—and the two the travelers had downed. One still lived, unconscious; Arcolin finished him. Technically, he was due a bounty for proven brigands killed within the city's outbounds, but he had no need for it, and these travelers did. He explained it to them.

"I don't know what the current rate is, but I know the bounty's still in effect."

"But you killed some of them—"

"I have pay," Arcolin said.

Before Devlin returned, the caravan appeared, trundling slowly along the road. Arcolin jumped the ditch with his mount again, and waited for them. They did not slow at first, but the caravan master climbed off the first wagon to speak to Arcolin.

"What is it? Someone in your colors rode by telling us there was danger ahead."

"Brigands here—that party there has an injured woman, and we killed four of them—two got away into the woods."

"So we keep moving and warn others, eh?"

"Yes, but I want to hire a couple of your guards to ward those travelers until the city sends a cart out for her. I need to go ahead and tell the cohort why I was delayed."

The caravan master chewed his lips a moment. "Well. You are Phelan's captain and you did give us warning. I can let you have two, but they must follow as soon as others come to help. And it will cost you a nata each."

"Here." Arcolin dug into his saddlebags and handed the man two natas.

"Jori! Baltis! Come down here." Two guards slithered down from the loads atop their wagons. "These are good men," the caravan master said, as they approached. "Four years with me on the road, and Jori knows wound care, as well." He turned to them. "Stay and guard those people until help comes," the caravan master said. "They fought off a brigand attack; there might be more."

"The bounty for the four brigands killed so far goes to the travelers," Arcolin said.

"Understood," the caravan master said. He turned and jogged toward the front of the caravan, now three wagons ahead.

With the guards, Arcolin crossed the ditch again, this time on foot; his horse made no difficulty, hopping the deepest muck at the bottom and scrambling up the bank in two heaves of its hindquarters. It was dry again, breathing normally.

"These men will stand guard with you until a cart comes for her," he said, nodding to the woman. "I must go now."

"Gird's grace go with you," they all said in a ragged chorus. Arcolin mounted and turned his horse eastward again, letting the horse roll into a strong canter.

He caught up with the cohort at last, to the obvious relief of his new young captain; by then his mount was willing to walk quietly along as he explained what had happened. He did not mention leaving his helmet off; that story would be all over the cohort as soon as Devlin returned, he was sure.

The rest of the march to Cortes Vonja was uneventful as they followed the familiar trade road to Fossnir and Foss, then the river branch that led down the Immerest to Vonja and Silwan. The eve of the Spring Evener found them near enough Fossnir to see the bonfires on the city towers; Arcolin wondered where his old companions were. He imagined Kieri presiding over a formal celebration—blooding a ploughshare, perhaps, or a spade—and then lighting the ceremonial fire. If elves did that sort of thing. Dorrin, he was sure, would have a bonfire. As captain of the cohort, he cut his hand and blooded his own blade, then touched it to the others'. The next morning, the sun rose indecently early—with the others he had stayed up singing most of the night—and they went on.

Burek, though much younger, had all the qualities Aesil M'dierra had claimed, and Arcolin saw nothing in his manner that should have set off even the prickly Count of Andressat. Burek's speech and behavior were both mannerly, respectful of all, without indicating any weakness. His sergeants liked him; Stammel, usually noncommittal about new officers, sought Arcolin out to commend the choice.

When they reached Cortes Vonja, the city militia commander, a man Arcolin remembered vaguely from the last year of the war against Siniava, explained why the militia needed help.

"It's not like it was before," he said. "No more campaigns of city against city, each one knowing why and when. Now it's wandering troops, no allegiance but to themselves, some with a grudge against a city, and some without, but all hungry. Trade's down—I'm sure you know that from over the mountains—and caravaners expect cities to patrol the trade roads and keep the brigands off 'em. There've even been attacks between here and Valdaire, if you can believe it."

"I can," Arcolin said. "I was in one. Brigands attacked a party of foot travelers in broad daylight, right beside the trade road, still in Valdaire's outbounds."

"With your cohort there?"

"No. I was riding alone, having been delayed leaving the city."

"But you got away safely, I see," the man said.

Arcolin felt a prickle of irritation. "We killed four of them," he said. "The foot travelers were good with their staves."

"You—pardon me, Captain, for my assumptions. I had forgotten the reputation of the Duke's Company. You stopped to aid. That is exactly the attitude we need from the troops we hire, and so few have it—"

Arcolin, who remembered the Cortes Vonja militia scattering in disarray, said nothing, but their commander flushed a little.

"Well," he said, and made a face. "Here we are, again. We have the trade road to patrol, and fewer men to do it with than back in your day. Our farms and outlying towns are being attacked—mostly those to the south and east. Cortes Cilwan says the same, and Sorellin."

"What about Andressat?" Arcolin said.

"The Count has accused us of letting brigands get away to harry his borders. He hasn't told us of any other problems."

"Is there concern that any of these brigands are part of an organization?"

"Well . . . the Duke of Immer, he that was Alured the Black, does say he should by rights take toll of the roads, even these up here. But Immerdzan's a long way away."

Arcolin looked at the map the commander had laid out. "One cohort can't patrol that much territory—better to seek out your brigands and try to break them up."

"Exactly. But our people have no idea where they're hiding. From Andressat's complaints, possibly in the rough country below the downs."

Arcolin visited Kieri's banker before returning to the cohort, to ensure that he could transfer funds to Valdaire as they had before, and then spent the rest of the day with Burek going over the maps the militia commander had given him.

"Someone here must know who the brigands really are," Burek said. "More than two years—they're getting support from somewhere or they'd be dying out; the problem would be smaller."

"My guess would be Alured the Black," Arcolin said. "Did you ever meet him?"

"No," Burek said.

"He's ambitious and cruel," Arcolin said. "Easy to offend, but also a natural leader and a reasonably good field commander. My guess is that he wants it all—all Aarenis."

"Not that different from Siniava," Burek said.

"Quite so. Something none of us recognized when we made alliance with him. We needed his aid, we thought, and Siniava's evil was so obvious . . ." Arcolin shook his head. "We erred. It wasn't until after Siniava's death, when we went downriver with Alured as we'd pledged." He pushed the memory of those days from his mind and dragged it back to the problem at hand. "I think I'll have Stammel send a couple of our best gossips around the taverns tonight and see if we can find out anything, but we'll march tomorrow down this way—" He pointed.

"The brigands will find out we're asking questions," Burek said.

"If they don't already know the details of the contract, I'd be surprised," Arcolin said. "They'll have spies in the city, of course. And they'll be trying to find out things from our men. That's a game all sides can play. We have some very good players."

The five Phelani soldiers who started their evening at the Flowing Jug brought a momentary lull to conversation and an anxious look to the owner's face. Peering past them, he said, "Is that whole mercenary company coming into the city?"

"Just us," Devlin said, grinning broadly. "Sergeant said we'd done so well, we could come in and fetch him back a jug. We'll each have a mug, to start with."

"Here's a table," Jenits said. "We could eat—"

"You don't think of anything but food," Tam said.

Devlin leaned on the counter, ignoring their familiar and well-rehearsed opening. He tapped a Cortes Vonja nata. "I'm buying this round," he said and pushed it across.

"*This* round?" the owner said. "And shouldn't you take that jug back to your sergeant?"

Devlin laid a finger along his nose. "He doesn't know which tavern we went to, does he? Happen we'll need to visit them all, to find one with ale good enough for our sergeant."

Three rounds later, the little group left that tavern, had a noisy argument in the street, split up, and the pair swaggered into the Blue Pig demanding drink while the trio joined a circle of gamblers playing Leg and Hand at the Cat and Crow. Each complained bitterly about their former comrades and dropped carefully planned nubbins of gossip about the Company. The trio, accused of cheating by the other gamblers, were invited to leave by the tavern's security, quarreled again on the doorstep, and staggered off in three different directions. The pair, meanwhile, had struck up a friendship with a young woman and after serenading the tavern with an off-key rendition of "Sweeter than the Honey-Bee" were thrown out. They had their quarrel four doors down and like the others sought further adventure on their own.

Torre's Necklace shone far to the west when they returned to camp, sober and well supplied with gossip.

"I'd forgotten how much fun this is," Tam said. "You'd think they'd learn."

"We do it best," Devlin said. As the most cat-eyed of them, he led the way. "Trade secrets passed down from generation to another."

"If any of it was true," Jenits said.

"The bits we all heard will either be true or what someone's passing as truth," Devlin said. "But wait until we get to camp."

In the light of the lamps in Arcolin's tent, Tam's idea of fun showed up as bruised knuckles and a cut on his forearm.

"What happened?" Arcolin asked.

"It became necessary to show fight, Captain. For the honor of the cohort—"

"Specifically," Arcolin said.

"Oh—it was after we separated. I was supposed to be staggering drunk, and someone believed it. If he hadn't breathed so loud, he might've hit me with that billet, but that and his breath-stink revealed him—so I ducked and he hit the wall where my head had been. The cut's from his friend."

"And?" Arcolin said when Tam seemed to have stopped.

"Well, Captain, you know it's not safe for civilians to have weapons they don't know how to use, so I tried to make the streets safer by disarming them. But sometime in the altercation the one with the club split the skull of the one with the knife, just as the one with the knife sliced the one with the club. I'm lucky to have got off with just a cut."

"The night guard arrived, didn't they?" Arcolin said.

"Yes, and I explained very carefully," Tam said. "They thanked me for my intervention, but suggested I might want to return to camp. It was all polite."

"I'm sure," Arcolin said. "Did you by any chance hear anything useful?"

"Yes, Captain." Tam's expression changed from one of false innocence to that of a competent soldier. "I thought the fellow at the first tavern was overanxious about us, though we were just drinking quietly and saying how good it was to be back in the south, where it's warmer and the food is better and the girls prettier."

Arcolin glanced at the others. "You agree?" They nodded. "Go on, Tam," he said.

"I noticed there weren't any girls in the tavern, the way they were three years ago. We used that as an excuse to move on, and that's when we split into three and two. I was with Jenits. We went on to the Blue Pig. It was more like it had been, there: three pretty girls, two of them from down the street, where there's a house. They all kissed Jenits, but he's younger than me."

Jenits, Arcolin noticed, turned red.

"One man asked if we'd been hired to chase bandits, and we said yes, and he said good luck in a tone that didn't mean it. Made the Trickster's sign where he thought I couldn't see. Jenits said he'd rather chase women than bandits, and the girls were all over him."

Most of the stories were the same, but for Devlin's. He had abandoned the pretense of drunkenness as soon as he was alone, and walked to the east gate of the city, where—on the pretext of trying to find some soldiers who'd overstayed their leave from the camp—he chatted with the gate guards. Then he'd gone outside the walls and walked back around the long way, noting which windows still showed light at the wall.

"I nearly ran into something," he said. "Some men standing around a hole in the ground . . . and out came another, and handed over a bag of something that clinked."

"A tunnel," Arcolin said. "Think you could find the entrance again by daylight?"

"Certainly, Captain. By daylight or dark. I've no doubt it's concealed, though."

Arcolin considered telling the militia captain about it, but he'd been hired for a different job and past experience with Vonja suggested it would be more profitable to let the Vonjans deal with any smuggling themselves. Likely some of the militia were involved.

CHAPTER TWENTY-FOUR

Chaya

At the heart of Chaya towered the King's Grove. Ten of the tallest trees grew in a circle around a mossy mound where the coronation would actually take place. Kieri had been told of it, and forbidden to go near it. Now—on the morning of his coronation—he looked out the window to see the trees massed beyond the palace walls. Already he heard a distant bustle in the palace, and soft scuff of those who would bathe and dress him coming along the passage . . .

Kieri came down the steps of the palace in his coronation robes over new clothes from the skin. Before him, the Council that had sent Paks to find their king; on one side his uncle Amrothlin, the elven ambassador, and on the other the Captain-General of Falk. Immediately behind them, two King's Squires and Paks. Behind them, the other Siers and lesser nobility, including Aliam and Estil—he'd insisted they be part of the procession, over Aliam's protests. Merchants and crafters, too, this time over the protest of his Council, but he wanted everyone. Even—along with all the other ambassadors and envoys—Hanlin of Pargun.

Palace staff lined the way to the gate, and beyond was a crowd, held back by a green rope in the hands of rangers in russet and green. Kieri would have walked faster on his own, but measured his pace to that of the Council.

Left out the gate . . . along the street . . . and then an abrupt turn into a narrow lane winding between and around great trees, in a dim green coolness. The fragrance of sunlit meadows, of spring flowers, vanished into the rich, complex odors of forest.

Finally, the King's Grove. The ground rose slightly under his feet as they approached tree trunks wider than houses; the path lifted over knotted roots, dipped between them.

He felt the taig here, far more strongly than he ever had; the flavor of each individual tree, its essential being, touched him. Ahead, his Councilors lurched and scrambled, the oldest helped by the younger, but to Kieri the path felt smooth, welcoming. On either side, great boles rose, furrowed bark shaggy with moss and tiny ferns near the ground, but higher showing multiple shades of red-brown, lavender, green-gray, where lichens patched the bark. A rich fragrance enveloped him, complex and enticing.

Beyond the trees, the ground rose smoothly, the path marked out with round white cobbles on moss and grass intermixed with tiny flowers, pink and white and blue. The top of the mound rose to the height of two men, level there with a single stone on it. The Council paused, then split into two lines, each moving to the side. Only the most senior, Sier Halveric, led the way up the mound. Kieri followed, and the Captain-General of Falk and the elf ambassador moved with him. Behind him, he could hear his Squires and Paks, but the others, he'd been told, would join those marking the human half of the circle.

As he climbed, he could see files of elves lining up on the other side of the circle. With every step he felt the same strangeness he'd felt in the battle on the way . . . the hairs stood up on his arms, his neck, and the sunlight pouring into the center of the opening acquired a silvery shimmer. Every leaf, every flower, seemed to glow from within. More fragrance rose from the moss, from the grass, as if the earth itself breathed welcome and delight. And now he could see the Lady of the Ladysforest, bringing with her the elvenhome light, with her attendants behind her. He came to the lip of the mound's flat top and saw the stone, a polished slab inlaid with the flowing patterns elves favored.

Trumpets sounded. Kieri stiffened. He had seen no musicians . . . and yet the sound seemed to come from everywhere.

"Present the king-to-be," the Lady said. "Is he acceptable to all?"

"Great and gracious Lady," Sier Halveric said, "this is Falkieri Amrothlin Artfielan, seed-son of Falkieri, fourth king before, and born-son of his elven queen. The Council of Men accepts him as king, with joy."

The Captain-General bowed. "The Company of Falk accepts him as king, with all joy, in the name of all his human kindreds."

"I present him to the Lady Flessinathlin of the Ladysforest," said the elf ambassador. "He is known to us, as my Lady knows, and I will ask: Is he acceptable to the elven kindred?"

"The Ladysforest accepts him, with all joy. Let the elfane taig witness, and the forest taig witness, and the people of this realm witness: All accept him."

Kieri felt his eyes stinging.

She bent her gaze on him. "Come forward, Falkieri my beloved grandson, and make those pledges that bind our peoples together. And accept the blessing of the Singer, the High Lord, and all gods who serve the good. It is time."

The Halveric and the elf ambassador stepped aside, and Kieri went forward alone, to stand across the stone from the Lady. "Your dagger," she said, drawing a slim silver knife from her waistband. Kieri handed her his dagger—new, like the rest of his outfit but the elf-blade at his side—and took hers.

The words—he had learned the words of the pledges—but speaking them in chorus with her, in that mix of light, in that place, he felt them piercing his heart. "I, Falkieri Amrothlin Artfielan, pledge my life to this realm, to the welfare of all its people of every race. I pledge to renew and protect the taig to the end of my ability . . ."

And as they spoke, Kieri followed the Lady's lead as she pricked her finger with his blade, and he pricked his finger with hers, and the mingled drops of blood fell on the stone, in the exact center of the design on its upper surface.

Kieri had never seen elf-blood before; he had heard the phrase "silver blood" but had not known what it meant—now the silvery glints danced in that drop, and when the drops landed, they shone a moment on the surface, then disappeared. In that moment, a lance of light shot upward from the stone, bright even in the sunlight. Kieri felt for a moment that he had been clasped in strong arms and given a knight's buffet. Then he was standing, blinking against the afterimage of intolerable brightness, and the Lady across from him blinked back.

"The gods have blessed you indeed, Grandson," she said. "I think we may safely say the pledge was witnessed."

Kieri found it hard to speak. "I . . . did not expect that."

"It is not usual," she said. "Only a few coronations have had such a response from the stone. But now—you need a crown on that head." She gestured.

The crown was of green-tinged gold, a circlet of leaves—each one unique. On it were set rubies dark as blood. It sat lightly on his brow, as he came back down the mound, this time on the elves' side of the circle, walking arm-in-arm with his grandmother. Together, they circled the mound, and the courtiers of both bowed low, then mounted the hill again. There they bowed to one another, and the Lady said, "It is your day, Kieri; make your procession and then I will join you for the feast."

Kieri went back down the human side, this time to cheers. Now his Squires led the way, and the whole Council walked behind. Back down the lane, and into the city, its streets lined with cheering crowds. Banners hung from the windows, flowers were thrown down before him. He'd seen triumphant processions before; he'd walked in some. This was different, and not just because he was now king. He felt around him—behind, where the King's Grove lay, and ahead, where the forest curved around the far side of the city, and beneath, where the waters trickled through stone to emerge as springs nearer the river—the taig, stronger than ever. His awareness seemed to deepen with every step, and yet it did not distract him from his people, pressing as near as the rangers allowed.

He would walk, he knew, the bounds of the city, ending again at the palace gate. "Bounds must always be walked to dawn first," Belvarin had explained. "It is not the direction of the circle, but the direction of the first turn that matters—it must be the shortest way to the rising sun and the elvenhome kingdoms." Now they were nearing the city's margin, with forest beyond gardens and orchards. A cloud of birds rose singing from the trees—tiny birds, brilliantly colored, fluttering like butterflies. They swooped nearer, flew in a spiral over his head, and returned to the trees as the procession turned toward the river. Butterflies then took over, out of the gardens and orchards, arching over the lane, then settling on his shoulders and arms as lightly as air, as if he wore a cloak of jeweled wings. As they neared the river side of the city, the butterflies lifted away, and out of the water meadows rose flying creatures as brightly colored as the birds and butterflies . . . glittering gauzy wings, metallic greens, golds, blues, scarlet. Kieri put up his hand and one landed there long enough for him to see it clearly. Great green eyes, a body boldly striped in black, gold, and green, with a green tail. The head cocked toward him; he could see tiny jaws move. Was it talking? He could hear nothing, but the creature looked as if it were listening.

It was a long walk, and his new boots—comfortable enough that morning—were far less so by the time they reached the palace gates again. He could smell the fragrance of roast meats and bread, but next he had the ritual visit to the royal ossuary, and spoke vows into that listening silence, to those who had given him bone and blood, vows no one else would hear.

He came up again to find the feast spread in the King's Ride, long tables stretching away into the distance. On either side, the trees rose up; he could feel them, feel their roots below the cushiony sod that welcomed his feet. His place lay at the farthest table, with the Lady, and that led him past the others, where men and women—and not a few children—bowed as he walked by.

At the head table, set across the line of other tables, he left a seat between himself and Aliam Halveric, and bent his knee to the Lady. She had withdrawn her glamour, as someone might fold in a cloak, but he was aware of the line of it connecting her through ground and air to the elvenhome kingdom she ruled.

"You are happy, Sir King?" she asked. He heard real affection in her voice.

"I am," he said. "Still somewhat mazed, though."

She chuckled. "So I would think. Bards elven and human will make songs of all this for a thousand years. Your paladin looks well."

"She is not *my* paladin," Kieri said. "She belongs to her gods."

"Ah, but you were her . . . there is no word in human language that I know . . . I believe you were there when Ardhiel told her the story of the harp growing?"

"Yes . . ."

"Well—you are one of those who can grow people. It is not the same with individuals, of course, because unlike a tree, humans have choices they can make."

"It was not my doing," Kieri said, watching Paks come up the line of tables, laughing and chatting with people. "She was extraordinary from the start. I wish you could have met my wife, though . . ."

"I, too, Grandson." She turned to face him and for a moment he saw compassion in her face. "You had children, and lost them. We both did. It is my dearest hope that the Singer grants you another love, and I know—because of my losses—that new children will not replace the old in your heart."

Just as Kieri felt tears sting his eyes, Paks arrived at the table and came to his side. "Sir King? Are you well?"

"Very well," he said, swallowing the tears, bitter and salt together. "Sit here between Aliam and me, will you not?"

"Of course, Sir King." She sat, and as they ate, she chatted more with Aliam than with him, giving him space to talk to his grandmother. The afternoon wore on with music and song and—as he had promised Kirgan Marrakai—dancing.

At one point, the Pargunese envoy, Lady Hanlin, paused beside his chair. "I see not *all* the beautiful girls are in Pargun," she said, with a sly grin. "But some are. I have nieces, you know." Then she passed on, smiling and chatting with anyone who would speak to her, and smiling pleasantly at those who would not.

"If all Pargunese were like her," Aliam said, leaning across, "we would have far less trouble with them."

"We would have different trouble," Kieri said. "Open enmity is easier to recognize."

"I do not believe she intends evil," said his grandmother. "And I believe I would know."

"Then I suppose she wants to marry me off to a Pargunese girl," Kieri said.

"Perhaps. It is a traditional way of cementing friendship between peoples, though—" She paused, one eyebrow rising. "—it does not always work. Especially if one does not wish it." Then she smiled, a smile that seemed to fill the entire world for a moment. "But I must not lessen the joy of this occasion."

The next two days were filled with Lyonyan traditions: showing the coronation gifts—now covering many tables—to anyone who wanted to walk past them. Guild processions wound through the city, ending at the palace with a presentation to the new king. Twice, small children escaped and got lost somewhere in the palace; these were quickly found and restored to their parents. Three times, adventurous adolescents tried to sneak upstairs, only to be foiled by alert guards and escorted outside the palace walls. In all this, Kieri had no time for a long talk with Aliam Halveric, and Aliam and Estil had not come to the palace since the coronation itself. On the third day, he sent a message and asked them to come. He was sure the Council would not meet that day, even if he convened them; everyone was tired by now.

When they were announced, Kieri led them upstairs to the royal suite.

"I'm still not used to this," Kieri said, waving his hand at the room. "This and all that goes with it. I wasn't trained for it."

"You'll do well," Estil Halveric said. Aliam grunted, running a finger along the carved back of a chair. "It's nothing but a larger domain, after all . . ."

"Oh, it's not the responsibility," Kieri said, though he felt the weight of it hovering over him. "It's this—this palace, this ceremony. Your steading, Aliam, or mine . . . comfortable enough, beautiful—yours anyway—but no more luxury than anyone needs. This is . . ."

"Royal," Estil said, with a touch of firmness. "Royal, like you, Sir King."

"I'm not—"

"You are," Aliam said. "You are, and you always were, and this is your house—you belong here, and you will adapt to it sooner than you think."

"I must not forget," Kieri said, turning to look out the window. "I must not let it . . ." He searched for the right words, could not find them. "You always said, Aliam, that a soldier must never get too used to comfort—"

"So I did, and it's true."

"But this—" With him, they looked around the sitting room of the royal suite. Soft cushions, upholstered chairs, another one of those incredible carpets figured with flowers and vines and trees and birds and butterflies . . . "This, if I let it—"

"You won't let it," Estil said. Kieri saw the sparkle of tears in her eyes. "Kieri, Kieri—you are not that kind of man. You were not that kind of boy. That is why you will be a good king—are a good king already. This is all due the king's majesty: it is meet and right, the measure of a royal house, but you will not dishonor it by thinking it is yours alone. Trust yourself, Kieri."

"I . . . am not sure. When I think of how I got here . . ."

"It's my fault," Aliam said. "Those years of not knowing. If only I'd figured it out, and how to go at proving it—"

They had been over that before; Aliam had fallen at his feet, begging forgiveness, when he first arrived. Kieri shook his head. "It is *not* your fault. I told you, Estil's told you—if your king and your wife can't convince you, who can?"

Aliam smiled, but the smile touched only his lips; his eyes were still sad. "If you will quit thinking you aren't worthy of this, Kieri, it will ease my mind considerably."

"At least you aren't calling me Sir King every moment," Kieri said. "The day you quit calling me Kieri—at least in private—I'll really worry."

"We must go soon," Aliam said. "I can't leave the Company to themselves for too long . . ."

"Are you going south this year?" Kieri asked.

"Not me," Aliam said. "I might send Cal in my stead, but he's taken over much of the work at home. We have potential contracts—but I'm getting old to go back and forth over the mountains."

"You are not old," Estil said, punching him lightly. "You are fat and not taking enough exercise, that is all."

"We can take care of that," Kieri said, grinning. "At least while you're here. You should see the royal salle—in fact, come with me now—"

Kaelith, one of the King's Squires, stood duty at the door to the suite, and led the way to the royal salle, but on the way they were interrupted by Sier Halveric.

"My pardon, Sir King, but I thought you would wish to know—now that the stables are no longer full of guests' horses, the royal mounts have been brought in, including those gifts given at your coronation. Master of Horse would like your word on which to keep at hand."

"We should go today," Aliam said. "I'm sure we're taking up stalls you'll need."

"Not to worry, Aliam," his brother said. "I moved your mounts to my own yard."

"Stay, Aliam," Kieri said. "You've always had a good eye for horse-flesh; you can help me choose."

The royal mews rang with the sound of hooves and whinnies; Sier Halveric introduced the Master of Horse, Sir Ganeth, a lean man Kieri could just remember bowing over his hand during earlier cere-monies. He wore the ruby of a Knight of Falk on his collar.

"Sir King, I know you have heard comments about the color of our horses—and as you are half-elven, it is important for you to under-stand that the two have different preferences in color. Do you your-self?"

"I was taught to value conformation and performance over color," Kieri said.

"Quite right, quite right. And yet here we must also consider color. The elves, Sir King, prefer horses of water and air, what you proba-bly call grays and blue roans, like your mount Banner. Men prefer horses of earth and fire, what you probably call bays and chestnuts and red roans. In recent years, the royal stables ran heavily to earth and fire, by the will of the Council—" Here he glanced sharply at Sier Halveric, who shrugged.

"With only humans attending Council regularly, they would natu-rally lean towards those colors. Everyone knows grays are tempera-mental . . . perhaps you have to be an elf to understand them . . ."

"The first horse I ever owned was a gray," Kieri said. "A Marrakai-bred, and one of the best I ever rode. Banner is of the same breeding."

"Sir King, you are half-elven. Perhaps it was that—"

"Perhaps. But let's look at these—" Kieri waved at the stalls. It was not the moment to point out that the Royal Guard of Tsaia chose grays for their ceremonial mounts because they looked good with the Tsaian royal colors.

"We have an indoor school," the man said. "If you would prefer, there is a royal box . . ."

"Indoor school?" Kieri had never heard of such a thing.

"The elves built it," Sier Halveric said, with just the faintest edge to his voice. "Their horses are . . . flighty . . . or so our stable personnel insist."

"I'll just walk along the stalls first," Kieri said, hoping to stop that in its tracks. "Come on, Aliam, Estil, let us see some horses."

The Master of Horse moved up just off his right shoulder. "Sir King, this first row begins with the horse you rode from Tsaia—"

"Banner, yes." The horse put its head out. Kieri rubbed its face, glancing in to note the clean, well-laid straw, the wrapped legs, the horse's shining, satiny coat. Whatever the stable help thought of grays, they had treated Banner well. "You like it here, Banner, eh?" The horse tucked its nose and he chuckled.

"The rest of this row are what we consider traveling mounts worthy of nobility: horses you might ride about the kingdom as you visit the steadings. The former king had not ridden for years, and his favorites had, in the meantime, aged to the point where I questioned their endurance for long travel. I chose to retire them, and seek younger animals, but if you wish to see them, I will take you to their pasturage."

Kieri wondered what to make of that. He had always chosen his own horses, after that first one, often buying Marrakai-bred, as with Banner. He wondered how someone else's choices would suit him. "How many horses would you think I need for such travels?" he asked.

"I'm not sure," Ganeth said. "I was not Master of Horse to the king before the former king; I do not know how such decisions were made."

Kieri had to admit he had not seen such a collection of near-perfect horseflesh anywhere, not even in the royal stables in Vérella. Under the covered arcade, a row of bay and chestnut heads looked out over stall doors. Two, three, five . . . ten? He stopped counting. Who needed so many horses? Kieri walked along slowly, letting each sniff his hand, and casting a practiced eye over their conformation.

"You'll want to see them in action," Ganeth said.

"Indeed yes. And then try them out."

Ganeth smiled widely for the first time.

"But where are the grays?"

The smile disappeared. "They're in this row . . . through here . . ."

Backing on the first, this row of stalls held grays and two blue roans, all looking out of their stalls like the bays and chestnuts . . . but these wore headstalls and were all tied to a ring just outside the stalls. "Why?" Kieri asked.

"The grooms feel safer," Ganeth said.

"The horses don't," Kieri said, looking at the row of fretful heads tossing this way and that, jerking the halter ropes. "Easy," he said, approaching the first. The horse pinned its ears.

"He nips," Ganeth murmured.

"He won't nip Kieri," Estil said.

Kieri appreciated the sentiment, but he wasn't sure. "Easy," he said again, with the same tone he'd used on horses and injured soldiers for years. He reached for the tie; the horse reached for his arm. Kieri bared his teeth and grunted; the horse in the stall wrinkled its nostrils tightly and pointed its muzzle away from him while he untied the line from the ring, and reached up to unfasten the halter. The instant it felt the halter loosen, the horse whipped around and kicked the stall door. The other grays jerked at their ties.

"You see how it is, sire," Ganeth said. "They must be tied, for the grooms' safety."

"How long have they stood tied like this?" Kieri asked. "Today, I mean?" He did his best to keep his voice level. The horse in the stall had its nose in a water bucket, the swallows running up the underside of its gullet visibly.

"Since the stalls were mucked—they were all taken to water at dawn bell, and walked in the row while their stalls were cleaned and relaid."

Kieri glanced in. The gray pinned one ear and lifted a hind hoof. "Oh, settle down," Kieri said; the ear swung forward and the gray went on drinking. The stall was bedded just like the others; the horse bore no lumps or marks of misuse, other than being tied for hours in one position. To the others he said, "I'm going to untie them; their movement won't be true in the school if they've been standing tied that long."

Ganeth bowed, and excused himself to have the horses saddled for presentation in the school. Soon the sixteen bays and chestnuts, plus

Banner, lined up in the school for Kieri's inspection. Every one showed the sound, useful conformation needed for a travel mount; all were up to his weight. They had a different look than the Marrakai-bred horses he'd ridden most, the head a little longer. He remembered that from his time at Falk's Hall. "These are all excellent," he said to the horsemaster. "Where did you find them?"

"Many are gifts from your nobles' breeding," the horsemaster said. "The grays mostly from your elven relatives. Will you see them in action now?"

"Yes," Kieri said. "But from the saddle. I'll ride Banner to warm myself up before I try them. Aliam, I'll depend on your eyes on the ground for anything I miss."

"The usual criteria?" Aliam asked.

"Yes . . . you know my horses and my style of riding; you know what suits me as well as I do, I daresay."

The grooms saddled Banner with Kieri's own saddle, the fox-head insignia still on the skirts, but now with a saddlecloth in green and gold, with the royal insignia embroidered on it. He wondered what had happened to the familiar maroon and white cloth.

Kieri walked Banner around the riding hall, watching as the exercise riders mounted, noting which horses shifted or showed any sign of discomfort or tension. Most did not. They lined out behind him; he turned Banner to the center, and watched, saying nothing, but noting every detail of their movement. Walk, trot, canter: the riders were expert, the horses well schooled. It came down to minor points . . . the length of overstride at free walk, the cadence at trot, the steadiness.

"Aliam?" he said, swinging down from Banner as the horses lined up again.

"That one." Aliam pointed. "I think he's a little short-strided for someone of your build. A good horse, no doubt, but he'd suit your Captain Cracolnya better. Those four—" He pointed at them. "About perfect for you, I'd think."

"I'll start with the doubtful one," Kieri said. "It's only fair to give each a trial." But after he mounted, he knew his eye and Aliam's had been correct: the horse was better suited to another rider. On long rides, that short stride and quicker cadence would be tiresome for him.

He spent some minutes with each horse, assessing feet, legs, disposition, and finally movement. "The four you chose I certainly want," Kieri said finally. "Of the rest, I will reserve judgment until I've seen and tried out the grays."

"But surely there are enough—"

"As you said, the elves prefer the other colors—and this realm is jointly ruled. I must have some grays other than Banner in my stable."

The horses he had not dismissed were taken to one end of the hall, and a line of grays and blue roans entered, all saddled and ready for trial.

"You know horses sense tension and fear," Kieri said to Ganeth. "Have you exercise riders who are not afraid of grays?"

"Some," Ganeth said. He gestured, and three came forward, a woman and two men. "Arian is half-elven, a ranger come to assist during the coronation celebrations. The others, Kiel and Surn, have some elven blood."

Arian grinned. "Not only that, Sir King: word spread that you might be seeking new King's Squires, some with elven blood. Several of us found reason to come to your coronation."

Kieri chuckled. "Word spreads fast. Well, Arian, I will decide when I've seen those who want to serve. For now—let's see how you ride."

The three mounted; Arian rode as if born in the saddle; her mount also looked to be a near-match for Banner in stride length. "What do you think, Aliam?" Kieri asked.

"She rides really well—oh, the horse. Definitely one for you. So is that one—" Aliam pointed at the third horse in the group. "The second one's not as good, I think."

In another half-glass, Kieri had found six grays that suited him. "Keep the others," he said to Ganeth, "as mounts for my Squires. Arian's right: I do intend to have more Squires and they must all have good mounts and reserves, for I intend to use some of them as couriers."

"Very well, Sir King," Ganeth said.

"And Arian, you can tell the others I will begin interviewing those who wish to serve as King's Squires tomorrow. They should meet me in the salle at sunrise."

"Thank you, Sir King."

On the way back to the palace, Estil said, "Now, that's a nice young woman."

"I'm not marrying a child," Kieri said. "She can't be more than twenty-five at the most. Find me someone nearer my age, and still able to bear, since all anyone cares about is an heir."

"It's not all I care about," Estil said. "I want you to be happy."

"And in the meantime, I want to talk to Aliam—and you, of course—about the defense of the realm."

CHAPTER TWENTY-FIVE

Aliam listened to Kieri's concerns with the same attention and intelligence he had always shown. "I've said the same to my brother for years," he said. "But the Council's so set against a standing army—though you're wrong about the effectiveness of the forest rangers. And I would not want to march my formations into the face of the Royal Archers' blackwood bows, either."

"I know that Pargunese woman says she wants peace," Kieri said, "but she doesn't rule Pargun. Their king does, and after we killed his men in that battle in Verrakai country—and the border skirmishes we've had—I still think attack across the river is a possibility."

"I agree," Aliam said. "And I agree you need something more substantial up there, but how can you move rangers from the west while Tsaia's still dealing with Verrakaien and Konhalts? How secure is that border?"

"Precisely why I wanted to talk to you," Kieri said. "If you're not taking troops to Aarenis, what about lending them—for a fee of course—to the Crown?"

"And insult the Royal Archers?"

"It's not an insult," Kieri said. "They don't know our kind of fighting . . . I could send them north as well, to back up the rangers there. That might even give us reasonable coverage of the shore between the towns. Put a cohort or two in the rear, ready to respond in any direction—"

"It's not a bad plan," Aliam conceded. "But you won't get the Council to agree."

Kieri grinned. "I realized that, when I was talking to them before the coronation. But now . . . I'm not just someone they agreed might be, or could be, the king. Now I'm the crowned king, and under the Compact, they will all have to oppose me if they want to stop me."

Aliam looked worried. "Kieri, I know you can do it—but—think what it looks like. You're proposing to give me, an old friend, a contract—"

"Because there is no one else, Aliam. Surely you see that. I don't want to bring in foreign troops, or I'd hire my old Company. You're Lyonyan already. And you're the only one here."

"They are eating our reserves," Estil said. "We haven't had them all at our place in years—never, really, because after the Company got that big, Aliam wintered some of them in the South."

"I can't make a profit out of it," Aliam said. Estil stirred but said nothing; he went on. "If I do it for cost alone—their board, their salaries—and if I do not command it myself, the Council may agree that it is fair. Otherwise I fear they might turn against you, Kieri, and you are the best—I think the only—hope this kingdom has."

"It will be helpful to get them out of our storerooms, to be sure," Estil said.

"Let me talk to the Council," Kieri said. "From what you say, you should go back to your home, and I will move as gently as I can, and still get anything done. But you should hear something by the half turn. And if you choose to send troops south, instead—"

"No," Aliam said. "I think not. I really don't feel like another trek over the mountains and back."

"Well, then. Let's to more pleasant things—tell me about the family."

Next morning, Kieri arrived at the salle with Aliam, Astil, and Varñe to find more than four hands of men and women in forest-ranger green and russet waiting for him, Arian among them. Carlion and Siger, who'd been warned some applicants might come, eyed them with professional disdain.

"There's too many to assess at once, Sir King," Carlion said. "If you're to get any training this morning, that is. I'd rather take groups of four."

"We'll rotate them," Kieri said. "And to save time—Siger, take the others to the stables, and tell Sir Ganeth I want a riding assessment on both grays and browns. Carlion, when you're through with the first four, send them to the stables, and Siger will send you another."

"Will you want to spar with them all, Sir King?"

Kieri shook his head. "I haven't time today; I have a Council meeting after breakfast. Today Aliam and I will work together."

Kieri and Aliam went on into the salle and let Carlion make his choice of the first four. They began with stretches and other exercises that soon had Aliam puffing.

"You used to run me ragged with these," Kieri said. "Is Estil right? Have you been sitting around too much?"

"She thinks so." Aliam grunted as he clambered up from the floor. "But I'm getting older—see how much balder I am? It's all right for her, but my joints ache."

"You told us the best cure for aches was more exercise," Kieri said.

"So it is, for the young," Aliam said. "Or maybe I am just lazy. This morning, I will say, it does not hurt as much. King's grace, perhaps?"

"You were never lazy," Kieri said. "And the grace your king wants is a good bout—" He opened the storage bin and tossed Aliam a banda and practice sword, and took one for himself.

Aliam's swordwork was as good as ever, though perhaps a touch slower, and he was quickly tired, but recovered between rounds. He and Kieri traded touch after touch.

"All you need is more practice," Kieri said, as he finished. "If I were your physician, and not your friend, I would bid you work daily with your armsmaster."

Aliam shook out his arms. "And as my friend?"

"The same, but with concern for your health. If you stayed here longer—"

Aliam shook his head. "I cannot. Cal is competent, but I need to be home—there is much work to be done. You know how land is, especially with so many feeding from it."

"That, we hope to change—but I understand." Kieri looked around the salle. The second four, now fencing in the middle of the salle, were three men and one woman; Carlion paced about them, watchful.

"You will have King's Squires enough," Astil said, on the way back to the palace.

"Do you regret deciding to retire?" Kieri asked.

"No. I was glad to come and serve again—and so I always will be at need—but my life now is at the farm with my family."

"I would like you—all of you current Squires—to help evaluate these applicants," Kieri said.

"You have said you plan to use Squires more, and differently," Astil said. "Can you explain, Sir King?"

"I will write it out for you," Kieri said. "But it includes acting as couriers to carry messages and envoys to foreign courts when haste is needed. Think of the tasks those who came to seek me found necessary—weapons skills, woodscraft, palace manners, diplomacy. I need Squires who are flexible, able to act independently, as well as intelligent and hardy. And I want to include part-elves; we need to bring the peoples closer together."

After breakfast, Kieri bade farewell to Aliam and Estil, then convened the first Council meeting since the coronation. The Siers looked wary and he wondered if Aliam's brother had told them his plans. But their concern, it seemed, was different.

"Sir King, with all respect—how far into summer will we need to stay in Chaya?" That was Sier Davonin. "Growth time is here; I have duties at my steading I would carry out, if I am no longer needed. And truly, I believe you need our advice less than when you came."

"What is your custom?" Kieri asked.

"A few of us stay in Chaya," Sier Belvarin said. "When the former king was well, three or four, who met perhaps once a tenday. The rest lived on their estates—"

Kieri hoped his expression didn't change. No wonder the realm had been sliding into disarray if that was all the attention its rulers paid it.

"We have had meetings every day since you came, but for the coronation and days of celebration," Sier Tolmaric said. "I knew things would be different, but—"

"My pardon, Siers," Kieri said, before Tolmaric said something he might later regret. "In my ignorance and my need I have overworked you. But I wished to be fair, to assure you that I would not thought-lessly overturn all your cherished traditions, or ignore your advice. You are correct, Sier Davonin, that I no longer feel as lost and inca-pable as I did, yet I do not believe you want a king who ignores you and does not listen to your concerns."

"Quite so," Davonin said. "But as your understanding of us has grown, so also our trust in you. I, for one, am content to let you ask for my advice, should you ever need it, which I increasingly doubt." She gave Tolmaric a sideways glance.

"Well, then," Kieri said. "Let us say I will release those who do not have specific duties here—as Sier Galvary does, and Sier Halveric as well—within the next few days. I still have one matter, on which I know you all have strong opinions, and I would not seem to be evad-ing you when I act on it."

"You said 'act' and not 'ask,'" Sier Carvarsin said, scowling.

"Indeed so. And we might as well come to it now. I'm still con-vinced Lyonya needs a stronger defense."

Scowls all around, except from Sier Halveric, who merely looked grave.

"As I told you before, we have unrest to the west and a known enemy to the north."

"The lady from Pargun spoke to me of peace between us," Sier Davonin said.

"And to me as well," Kieri said. "I believe she may be sincere—"

"*May* be! You consider her a liar? That sweet old woman—" Sier Tolmaric bristled.

Kieri stared him down. "Siers, I have seen many old women who could poison an enemy with sweetmeats while swearing eternal friendship. You are all honorable; I am sure none of you would say one thing and mean another, but my life has been spent among those who thrive on conflict and controversy. I found Hanlin of Pargun de-lightful, and I am sure many of you feel the same—but even if she is sincere, she does not rule Pargun, and she did not claim to speak for their king, who has long hated me. I remind you that Pargunese troops entered Tsaia to kill me on my way here—"

"That could be the Verrakai's fault," Belvarin said.

"So it could," Kieri said, "except that they must have had the king's agreement. Would a king well-disposed to Lyonya have

cooperated with a plot to kill its new king?" Before they could answer that, Kieri went on. "Along the river, we have only three towns
with any defenses at all; the rest is forest and small holdings that
could be easily overcome—"

"You think Pargun will invade?"

"I don't know," Kieri said. "But north of the river, in Tsaia, they
have tried repeatedly. Often, when defeated at one site, they've
launched a second attack at another."

"The Lady will not be pleased to know you talk of war," Amrothlin said.

"I will not be pleased if I fail in my duty to protect my land and
people," Kieri said. "And I talk of war only to prevent it—in the
words I used before, to give the lamb a safe haven from the wolf, as I
am now the shepherd. It is my duty to see the danger and protect."

"I am not so sure," Amrothlin said, "that protection is all you
intend. You have fought Pargun before, more than once, but under
another's command. Perhaps you only want the chance to do so
unchained—as sheepdogs, loosed, may turn on their sheep."

Now all the Council looked really scared. Kieri stared at Amrothlin, until, amazingly, the elf looked away. "If you truly think that of
me, Uncle," he said, "then you must question the Lady's reading of
my heart and her judgment in approving my kingship. That is a matter you may take up with her, if you wish."

"You brought this up now so that you would be our crowned king,
not our king-elect, didn't you?" Carvarsin said. "Now we cannot
naysay you, unless we all agree."

Kieri looked at the Council again, one face at a time. "That is true,"
he said. "But consider this: If it is not by Falk's Will and the High
Lord's will that I am here, despite so many ill-chances, then I challenge you to explain why I am alive and in this seat. Why, when you
were desperate for a king and sent a paladin to find one, I was there
to be found, and proved by the sword." He nodded to it, hanging on
the stand. The jewel in its hilt flashed as if he'd touched it. "You
swore you would accept whoever she found, and both when she first
presented me, and again at my coronation you swore you accepted
me. If you are so light in your thoughts that you would twice for-
swear yourselves before you grant the crown, why should I stay to be
the plaything of your passions?"

A moment's stunned silence as the councilors chewed that through.

"I support you," Sier Halveric said, and slapped the table. A ragged chorus of slaps followed his.

Kieri looked at the two elves. Amrothlin shrugged. "It is not for me to accept or not accept: that is our Lady's place, and she has consented. But do not push our Lady to the brink of her patience, Falkieri my nephew. Wiser heads than yours are at risk."

"We are all at risk," Kieri said. "I seek to lessen it."

"And unfledged birds seek to fly by falling out of the nest," Amrothlin said.

"I shall endeavor to grow feathers enough before I fall," Kieri said. To his surprise, Amrothlin laughed and so did the others, if a bit nervously.

"What, then, is your plan?" Sier Davonin asked. "For I am sure you have one."

"We have unstable peace," Kieri began. "It is unstable because only a river divides us from an enemy."

"We have river forts," Sier Galvary said.

"If the Pargunese were unwise enough to attack the river towns, the forts might hold them off. But why would they not go around the towns?"

"The forest itself—"

"Is a partial protection, but is also my responsibility. It would be better to find a way to live peaceably with the Pargunese. That is not something I expected to say, ever, as I was convinced the Pargunese had no interest in peace, but I am advised that I might be mistaken. If they are not interested in peace, then we have much to do before the land is safe from invasion."

"You speak of an army."

"Yes." Kieri sighed. Through long association, the humans of Lyonya had absorbed many elven—he dared not call them notions— about conflict and war, most of them, to his mind, inaccurate. He had been where they had not. "The rangers are excellent at what they do, patrolling the forest and keeping our people safe from brigands and the occasional raid from Tsaia—something we won't have as much of with the old Verrakaien gone. We have the small city militias in those river forts, and the Royal Archers . . . but we do not have a force fit to meet even a single cohort of Pargunese, should they take it into their minds to invade."

"But why would they?"

"Me," Kieri said. "I warred with them on the borders of Tsaia; I killed one of their Sagons myself, and only realized much later it was their king's brother. Moreover—and I found this out only recently— it's possible their quarrels with us and with Tsaia come from very old wounds. The elves say their ancestors were driven out of their lands by magelords of Old Aare—they came to Pargun and Kostandan looking for refuge and then met what they saw as old enemies across the river."

"Where did they come from, then?" Halveric asked. "I thought they were of mageborn origin themselves, probably crossed the river from Tsaia."

"Not according to my elven tutor," Kieri said, nodding at Orlith, who sat silent and still in his place. "He won't say more than that they came from across the eastern ocean, and the same who tormented me tormented them until they fled."

"Do you believe that?" Belvarin looked at Orlith and Amrothlin, then back at Kieri.

"In essence, yes. About the details, I don't know. But if they had reason to fear and hate the Tsaians—the magelords, I mean, and know some of them moved here—and they've had me as their enemy these four hands of years and more, that could well be enough to bring an attack. We are less defended than my stronghold in Tsaia. That's full of trained soldiers, and they've learned to let it alone."

"So you want us to raise an army to make peace?" Belvarin said. The edge of scorn in his voice emphasized the apparent contradiction in that.

"I want us to raise a defensive army to make invasion less likely until—gods willing—I can convince the king of Pargun that I do not wish war."

"Raising an army's hardly likely to do that," Belvarin said.

"Not raising one is likely to have our roofs fired over our heads," Kieri said. They looked worried at that, as he intended. "It is true, I went to war year after year, and hired out my company to fight—but some of that, Siers, was garrisoning forts, defending and not attacking. I know what it takes to protect our river border; it will not be the muster of such an army as could invade Pargun." He paused, meeting every Sier's gaze. "I have no intention of going beyond the bounds of Lyonya with troops ever again."

"But will Pargun believe you?"

"Not at first. But with time." Maybe. He still had doubts—no, he still had the firm belief that Pargun was up to no good and would always be up to no good. But either way, for the sake of his realm, they needed more than scattered rangers.

"So what do you think we need?"

"I want to move half the rangers off the west border—remember, that force was doubled because of concerns about Verrakai aggression—and use them to keep watch on the river. The Royal Archers have the potential to be a useful force—I've been observing them—but they've not actually fought for a generation or more. Yet we're paying them. I want to give them some formal training in combat arms, and have them paired with rangers."

"Will that be enough? That's not so bad; it costs us nothing more than it does now."

"It will cost us more," Kieri said. "Even an idle army is expensive, and moving one about more so. But that is not enough. We need two or three cohorts of trained, competent soldiers—ideally, as mounted infantry."

"We don't have the resources—" Galvary said.

"Or the men."

"Or anyone to lead—"

"Right now," Kieri said, "you have a company perfectly suited to Lyonya."

"What?" They all stared at him.

"Aliam Halveric's company. He is not taking it south this year, he told me. It's smaller than it was; he didn't take it south last year either, and some of his troops moved on, to find other employment. Most of the ones who stayed are from Lyonya originally. They're well trained and experienced in all kinds of warfare. Far better than hiring foreigners—I've been the foreigner hired, so I know that for a fact. Far better than starting from scratch with raw recruits. We should ask Aliam for the loan of them this season and through the winter. If he wants to campaign them again next year or the year after, we'll have time to plan for replacements."

"I know he's your friend, but—isn't that—I mean, shouldn't we
have—"

"Others? Of course we should. We should have a small, but efficient, standing army under my colors. But it takes almost a year of
training, and then a season of combat, to produce seasoned troops. If
Pargun attacks this fighting season, Halveric's is what we have available. All the other mercenary companies are in the south already."

"Your own?"

"I hope so. I told Arcolin to take a contract if he could—troops are
expensive to keep idle—and at least one and maybe two cohorts of
mine should be on the road to Aarenis right now. Besides, I would not
bring my—my former—cohorts here except in an emergency. They're
not Lyonyan. They're foreign, just like Golden Company or Clarts or
any of them."

They looked at one another, avoiding Sier Halveric's gaze until he
spoke. "It's like a gift to my family," he said. "Let me provision
them—as a gift to the Crown."

"That is generous indeed, Sier Halveric," Kieri said. "But too much
burden for one family. Suppose you half provision them, and let me
know if you run short for your own people."

"Thank you, Sir King. It will be an honor to serve the Crown."
Halveric looked around, challenging the others. One by one they as-
sented to asking Aliam Halveric to hire out his company to the
Crown, for use in the north.

"Sier Galvary, if you will draft a formal request from the Crown, I
will sign it and it can be sent tomorrow."

One by one the invited foreigners came to pay their respects before leaving; the lady of Pargun, uninvited, also came and
made the briefest of farewells. Kieri interrupted Kirgan Marrakai's
obviously memorized speech to ask him about the night of the assassinations.

"I hear you were actually there, Juris. Dine with me, if you are not
leaving until morning; this is something I should know."

"If you will, Sir King." The young man scowled briefly, then
looked up. "It was a dirty business."

Alone with the kirgan that evening at dinner, Kieri let the young man tell the tale as he would. Like most Marrakaien, Juris told a story well. Kieri could feel the prince's shock at the news of Verrakai treachery, the young men's eagerness to do something decisive, the older men's steadying influence.

"They kept wanting us—Mikeli and me—to sit down, think things through. And we finally did. Roly had gone to bring maps so we could see where they might attack the palace. And then Verrakai came in—" Juris took a breath. "No one knew he could change appearance. I thought for a moment it was my father—and before I realized the truth, in that moment he had us all, silent and motionless as stones." Another pause. "We could do nothing. We had to watch, Mikeli and I, while he took a sword out of the Knight-Commander's rack and killed him where he sat, and then the Marshal-Judicar, and still we could not move. He told us he would kill Mikeli next, then me, and put the sword wet with Mikeli's blood in my hand. If it hadn't been for Roly—" He told the rest in a rush, down to the death of Verrakai's brother in the stableyard. "I didn't see that, but I heard." He paused again. "It wasn't anything like it is in the tales."

Kieri managed not to chuckle at that; Juris deserved better. "It never is," he said. "And you never forget your first serious fight, even if it doesn't go badly."

"I always thought—we all did—we'd do better. We're trained from childhood—"

"You're alive," Kieri said. "You and the prince, and your enemy is dead. Yes, you lost friends, but you did well."

"My father said that. It doesn't feel right, though."

"No, and it never will," Kieri said. "That's part of being the kind of man you are—you're Girdish and that means just winning is never enough."

"How did you deal with it?"

A Marrakai approach—direct as a sword thrust. Kieri answered as the question deserved. "Looking back, I was an arrogant idiot for half a year or so, trying to pretend it didn't bother me; Aliam took me out back of the camp one day and chewed me up one side and down the other. Said not admitting what I felt was as bad as dragging around long-faced as some did."

"It bothered you less, in time?"

"Yes, or I could not have stayed in soldiering," Kieri said. "But still—if someone I care for dies, it hurts. It's supposed to hurt."

"The others—our friends who weren't there—they don't seem to understand—"

"They will when they've been where you've been, and gods grant that it's not exactly the same. Be patient with them. You and Mikeli and your friend Roly will always have a bond they do not have, but don't rub it in."

"No, Sir King. I won't. Thank you."

As the days passed, more applicants for King's Squire service came in from outlying areas. Kieri had them all assessed and then, as time allowed, interviewed them one by one. All who had been rangers were hardy and skilled, but some found they did not like the prospect of living in a city or palace. They preferred the green aisles and solitudes of the forest. Those whose training came from other sources varied in their abilities; some humans were not fluent enough in elvish, and others, trained in weaponry only at home, lacked the fighting skills Kieri knew his Squires might need. A few were too quick of temper.

At last Kieri had four hands of applicants who had passed every test he devised, and who all—to his mind—would serve equally well. With the other Squires who did not wish to leave his service, that made five hands and one. Most had been rangers, as the rangers had provided the only part-elf applicants.

Organizing the Squires' service might have taken longer if Garris, the eldest, had not offered to take over that task. "I'm getting a bit old for the rest of it," he said to Kieri. "You can dismiss me, if you want, but I do have experience, and I can save a clerk's wages doing the paperwork for you."

Kieri had been wondering how to suggest that Garris might want to retire; this was the perfect solution.

"Thank you," he said. "That's a weight off my shoulders. I suppose we need a ceremony."

"Of course," Garris said. "Pledging an oath to the king—that's when we get the gold bands. I'll organize that, when I find out how long it will take the tailors to make up the uniforms."

Kieri took the list of names off to the office he'd now established, and stared at it, reminding himself which faces went with which names. He was amused to find that he remembered the women's faces best; everyone's hints about marriage and heirs must be affecting him. But these women were too young, like Paksenarrion, like the young women trailed past him at his coronation. As Tammarion would be, if she came to him now as he had known her first. He tried to imagine Tamar as she might be now if she had lived: there would have been silver in that golden hair, though in memory she was always young.

That thought hardened his resolve to find someone older to marry; it was not fair for someone like him—his age, his experience—to marry a woman scarcely out of girlhood. In the ceremony a hand of days later, he was pleased to find that he remembered all the names and faces, male and female, and that he could look on his Squires as he had once looked on first-year soldiers.

Shortly after that, Paks bade him farewell and rode away, this time eastward. He knew better than to ask why—she would not know, herself, until she reached whatever goal the gods had given her. His new Squires, mixed with the experienced few, began their new duties. He sent couriers to Tsaia—one to Verrakai lands to find out how Dorrin was faring, one to Vérella, with messages both for the prince and to send on south to Arcolin, and one to his former stronghold.

CHAPTER TWENTY-SIX

Aliam's response, when it arrived some hands of days later, was the first contingent of troops, a half-cohort with Talgan, one of his junior captains, at its head. The palace steward brought Kieri Aliam's letter and Talgan's word that they planned to camp in the river meadow near the palace.

Kieri unfolded the stiff parchment. Aliam's handwriting, he noted, had not improved with a year off fighting.

> *My Lord King:*
> *Greetings and prayers for your good health. Your request was far too flattering to us but comes timely, as you know. Caliam is needed here, and the boys are all too young to command, but the captains I send are known to you and competent. If it pleases you to tell Talgan what you want done, he will send word for the rest. I have two hundred I would be grateful if you could find employment for, and another hundred could be spared.*

Something about Aliam's tone bothered Kieri, but he couldn't quite understand it. Of course Aliam and Cal would stay at Halveric Steading—no need for them yet, at least. He headed for the kitchens, where he found the steward talking to the cooks.

"What have we for tonight's dinner?"

The cook started listing the meats; Kieri held up his hand. "That's ample," he said. "We have fifty hungry soldiers to feed out of this kitchen tonight—can you do it?"

"Yes, my lord king!" The head cook looked happy at the thought.

"Good. They'll have marched most of the day; they'll be hungry. Plenty of meat and bread, anything else you can cook in a glass or two." He nodded, dismissing the cook, who turned at once to the assistants.

"Have a horse saddled," Kieri said to the steward. "I'll ride out presently to speak to Aliam's captain."

The camp, when he came to it, looked a proper camp: they had not dug ditches or made a barricade, but the tents were set up in neat rows, and a safe fire pit already flickered, though no pots hung over it.

"My lord king," Talgan said, going down on one knee. Kieri remembered him only slightly; he had been Seliam's replacement, but Aliam had always praised him.

"About your provisions," Kieri said. "I see no pots on the fire."

"Mm . . . yes, my lord. We . . . came away in a hurry. We have only hard travel rations."

"You will eat well tonight. The palace kitchens are at work on it. Send a squad to the kitchens in a glass."

"Thank you, my lord king. If I may—it's good to see you again, sir, and we were all glad to hear about you."

"Thanks, Talgan. How are the Halverics, down south?"

"Very well, sir, though we were crowding them, all of us there together so long."

"I had the same problem in the north," Kieri said. Talking to Talgan, he felt himself sliding back into that world he'd left. "But with the gods' aid, Arcolin's got them down south again. I would have taken them myself—" The memory of all those trips to Aarenis went through him like a knife blade—the sights, the smells, that view coming down into the Vale of Valdaire with all the south open before him and every opportunity. He pushed that aside; it was not his world anymore.

"I'd think being a king a lot more pleasant," Talgan said, relaxing.

"I don't have to wear armor in a Southern summer, at least," Kieri said, laughing. "That last year—it's a wonder Aliam and I both didn't end up skin and bones from sweating off so much weight."

Talgan grinned, then sobered. "Well, my lord king, Lord Halveric said to ask you for orders, and then let him know what you wanted of the rest. I'm to send word."

"Do you have Lyonyan maps in your tent?"

"No, my lord."

"Well. I should have brought them. I'll get you one later. Let's go sit down and I'll do my best to explain."

Kieri laid out his plans for the northern defense. "I can use two full cohorts easily. How soon do you think they could move?"

"A few days," Talgan said.

"I've already sent the Royal Archers north," Kieri said. "After you've provisioned here, you should position your group about a half day from the river. I've marked that on the map I'll show you. I'll send Sier Halveric to you in the morning to discuss provisioning."

"Shall I send a messenger back for more, Sir King?"

"No," Kieri said. "I have a new courier service of King's Squires. I'll send one of them, and you can have one with you, to use as a messenger here in case of any emergency."

As he wrote out the message for Aliam, he wondered if his first letters, sent even before the coronation, had reached any of their destinations yet. He still thought of travel times between the north and Valdaire.

Cortes Vonja, Aarenis

Arcolin led the cohort south, away from Cortes Vonja, on a narrow road bordered on either side by fields where young grain stood knee-high. As they approached the first village, they saw people running out of the houses to hide from them.

"Surely the Cortes Vonja militia told them we were coming," Burek said. "They must know we aren't brigands."

"Unless the Cortes Vonja militia's been robbing them," Arcolin said. "Or someone else in uniform. I wonder if the brigands are uniformed and the militia commander just happened not to tell us."

"Surely not."

"Cortes Vonja had a bad reputation," Arcolin said. "We'll find out. I've been here before; if the village headman's still around, he'll recognize our colors and come talk to me."

By the time they'd reached the little village square, an older man was hobbling toward them, leaning on a stick.

Arcolin held up his hand and the cohort halted. "Is it Maenthar, my old friend?" he called to the man.

"Is it really the Fox's company, come to start the war again?" the man asked. "I am Maenthar, indeed. Friend? That depends."

Arcolin dismounted. "And I am Arcolin, as you see. If it depends on me, we are friends still." He reached out his hand. The man hesitated but finally reached forward and touched his fingers, then put his own to his chest and forehead; Arcolin did the same.

"I thought you must have died," Maenthar said. "They said the Fox was gone forever, back over the mountains to the north, and we were forgotten."

"Never forgotten," Arcolin said. Something was seriously wrong here; Maenthar had always been friendly and open before. "Even if I had stayed north the rest of my life, I would not have forgotten you and yours."

"Me alone, now," Maenthar said. He spat, barely a polite distance from Arcolin's boots. "Before you wake memories better left asleep, I will tell you. My family died—two sons taken by the Cortes Vonja militia and both died in battle, they told me. One killed here, with my wife and daughter, while I was away to the city, summoned to be told of the other deaths. I have no love for soldiers now, Captain, though I remember you gave us aid that time."

"I'm sorry," Arcolin said.

"And they say it's because the Fox left and went north, and left the land aflame with war. War grows no grain. He started it; he should have ended it. Let the hungry eat, I say, and kill no more."

"Before," Arcolin said, "you had wanted Siniava dead."

"So I did," Maenthar said. "He was a bad man and his raids threatened us. But now—there are many bad men, all with swords and torches. More bad men with swords than good ones, is what I see. And no peace to grow the grain, but the taxes still go up."

"We were hired to put down brigands," Arcolin said. "The ones that rob you and spoil the grain."

"It does not matter whose boots trample the grain," Maenthar said, in the same hard voice. "The grain gives no harvest, whoever marches across it. We nearly starved, in the great war, and we are still hungry. If you tell Cortes Vonja what I say, they will arrest me and have me torn in the square. And I no longer care."

Pity filled Arcolin's heart. He remembered Maenthar's open, smiling face from before, his wife who made such good sweetcakes and sold them on market day, his daughter who had peered at the troops from the window of their house until her mother pulled her back inside.

"I have no reason to tell Cortes Vonja," he said. "I only wanted to assure you that we would do your village no harm; we but march through, and perhaps, by ridding you of brigands, we can ease your burdens."

"Bring back my wife and children from the grave," Maenthar said. "I would have no burdens a man could not bear, if they lived again." He looked away a long moment; Arcolin waited. Then he said, "I apologize, Captain. It is not all your fault, but you are the first I could tell. In the city, they threatened me with a trial for treason because I cried out when they told me my two sons in their army were dead. It was too much, to come back and find the others dead as well, and a hand and half more from the village."

"It is too much," Arcolin said. He did not try to stop the tears that flowed. Let the man see he was genuinely moved.

Maenthar was crying too, now. "I tried. I held the village together as best I could—I thought it was over—but then they came from the city and told us we were lazy scum, for sending less grain. I told them we had fewer workers and they said—those men in velvet and fur, with gold chains at their neck—they said work harder."

"Maenthar—" Arcolin put out his hand again, and this time Maenthar gave his freely. "It is hard," Arcolin said, remembering the loss of most of his cohort at Dwarfwatch. "I am sorry, that is all I can say."

"I believe you," Maenthar said. He ducked his head, swiped at his face. "I will bear you no ill will, I swear it."

"Nor I you," Arcolin said. "If sharing your anger with me eased your heart, I am glad."

"The brigands have not bothered me much here," Maenthar said, this time softly. "They have come through, telling us not to see them, and they've stolen a hen or two, and loaves Casra had set on the windowsill to cool, but they stayed on the road."

"They were bold to stay on the road," Arcolin said, as softly.

"Oh, they're bold enough. But I told my people to do as they said, and it would be as well if my people thought I had done the same."

"If you need to berate me all the way out of the village—" Arcolin said.

"I will," Maenthar said. "But this time it will be an act." His smile was rueful but genuine. "Two things: They talk of the old kings coming back, and their leader—of this group at least—has a tattoo on his heart-arm he touches when he speaks of someone called Ibbirun."

"Thank you," Arcolin said. Ibbirun . . . the Sandlord of Old Aare. By repute, the Sandlord was evil, either akin to, or another name for, Gitres the Undoer. He raised his voice, then, for any villagers who'd crept to the backs of the houses to hear. "Well, Maenthar, I'm sorry you feel that way. We were friends once, and I hope will be friends again. We never did you injury, and we intend no injury now."

"Just go away, that's the best thing you can do for all of us," Maenthar said just as loudly; his voice once more edged like a scythe. "Stay out of the fields; give the grain a chance. And keep your men from stealing, if you can."

"*My* men don't steal," Arcolin said coldly. "As you should remember." He took the reins back from Burek and mounted, nudged his mount into motion, and the cohort followed.

Once they were well out of the village, Burek said, "That was instructive."

"Did you hear all of it?"

"Should I have?"

"It depends. I need to know—if you did, I needn't repeat any of it."

"Yes, sir, then I did."

"Cortes Vonja politics," Arcolin said. "Duke Phelan always thought someone high up there was in league with Siniava, but couldn't prove it. What if that same person has transferred allegiance to Alured?"

"Would Alured believe it?"

"He might. Or he might let whoever it was believe he believed him."

Burek rode in silence a few moments. "Field tactics are easier than politics."

"With one cohort compared to a city, yes. But men are men, either way."

"Do you think that . . . Maenthar . . . will tell the brigands about us?"

"I hope so," Arcolin said. "It will be better for him and will not hurt us. Even if one of his people spied and saw him being friendly, our past friendship excuses it and we were never alone together."

Burek blinked. "Did you think of that at the time?"

Arcolin laughed. "We both did, I'm sure. In past years, Maenthar would've invited me into his house for a cup of sib, at least. He had good reason not to, as I had good reason not to take him aside."

"You . . . think of more things than I do," Burek said. "I thought I knew what a cohort captain's job was."

"In twenty or thirty years you'll know more," Arcolin said. "Sooner if you're the fast learner I expect you are."

Toward the end of that day, they had passed through another village and set up camp in a pasture beyond it. Arcolin had spoken to the headman of the second village, a young man he did not know. The headman bowed and promised anything Arcolin might want, if only he would not ravage the vill.

"We don't attack villages," Arcolin said. "We are on hire from your city, to drive away brigands who rob you and damage your fields."

"We have no brigands here," the man said. "I've heard they have problems south of here."

That night, well after dark, two men approached the camp and asked to see the commander. Arcolin chose to see them outside his tent, asking them to join him at the campfire where cooks were heating water to wash the cookpots.

"We wanted to talk to you privately," one of them said. His gaze shifted back and forth; the other stood hunch-shouldered and silent. "Don't you have someplace we can go?"

"No," Arcolin said. They looked at the tents, and back at him; he held his expression and finally the speaker sighed.

"Well, sir . . . knight, you must be, I guess. It's like this. That boy Stef, he's afraid to say, because them brigands threatened him and his wife—she's that big with their first, due by harvest."

"So there are brigands."

"Aye. They come every four hands of days and take toll, and then the damned city militia, that doesn't stir itself to help us, comes to take taxes. And if you goes after them, sir, they'll think we told and they'll be down on us. Burn the fields no doubt. You can't stop 'em. No one can; there's too many."

"More than us?" Arcolin asked.

"They said so," the second man said. "They said we had to tell you the wrong way, if you made us answer."

"You haven't told me any way yet," Arcolin said.

The first man grinned nervously. "Well—we was thinking, maybe it would be worth something."

"If they come and find natas in your house," Arcolin said, "they'll know you took money from us and then they're most like to send the whole village up in flames."

"Oh, I wasn't thinking natas," the man said. "Maybe a few coppers? Maybe two each?"

"I'm thinking nothing," Arcolin said. "We'll just go on the way we think is best, good or bad. You can tell the brigands you told us nothing."

The man gulped; his throat moved as he swallowed. "But he said—"

"Who?"

"I told you," the second man said. "I told you we shouldn't."

"Shouldn't what?" Arcolin said.

"Don't you say anything!" the first man said.

"Oh, give over, Ari," the second man said. "It's not going to work, and we can't be worse off for telling him the truth. He has the men with swords, after all." He turned to Arcolin. "It's our headman. He wanted us to find out what you knew, and then send you into an ambush. Ari's right: they threatened him and he gave in."

"Who carries the messages back and forth?" Arcolin asked. "You? Either of you?"

"I do, sometimes," the first man said. "There's more than one of us."

"One of them comes to meet you somewhere outside the village? Or inside?"

"Outside."

"And you're supposed to report after this meeting, aren't you? They know you're here."

"Yes," the second man said, when the first hesitated.

"Well, then," Arcolin said. "Tell them we don't trust you, would not pay you, and intend to stay on the road, not go haring off across the fields like a bunch of novices."

"Is that true?"

"I'm telling you," Arcolin said. He gave a covert hand signal, saw it picked up and passed along. In moments, Stammel was just in view at the far side of the fire, but well back. Arcolin stood abruptly, as if out of patience. "Take these two to the perimeter and send them away," he said to the nearest soldiers. "Tell the sentries I don't want them lurking around the camp." He threw out his hand, as if tossing them away, then turned and went into his tent. Would they go back to the village, or would they go to meet the brigand? He trusted that either way one of his own expert scouts could follow without detection.

Burek was still up, copying the day's notes onto the map. Arcolin looked over his shoulder. The younger man had neat handwriting, the writing of someone who had been schooled early. "I'm almost done," Burek said.

"I'll take the first watch," Arcolin said. "If there's trouble, it'll come after the turn of night. One of us must be fresh, and if we're lucky I'll have a report coming in within the turn of the glass."

"Thank you, sir," Burek said. Another few minutes, and he sat back, fanning the map with his hand to dry the ink. "That's all, I think." Arcolin looked again.

"Very good. If I get a report before your watch, I'll add it myself."

Burek followed him outside and disappeared in the direction of the jacks; Arcolin began a circuit of the sentry posts. This was their first truly hostile camp, though after the attack on the road, he had insisted on a camp defense even under the walls of Cortes Vonja. Here they'd erected a barrier of bramble and stakes.

Arcolin heard nothing he should not hear—their own animals munching grain in their nosebags, the familiar night sounds of the south—grassfrogs, treefrogs, various insects, a night-bird singing in the distance—were what they should be at this time of year. A light breeze eased across the camp, moving away the smells of men and armor, fire and food, and bringing a hint of cow dung, sheep, and the stronger smell of spring grass and herbs. He greeted each sentry, took a report, and went on to the next. At the sunrising post, opposite the camp entrance, he met Devlin, making a circuit the other way.

"All's well summer-side, Captain," Devlin said.

"All's well, winter-side, Sergeant," he said. They each continued their respective circuit, meeting again at the camp entrance, sunsetting.

"A quiet night," Devlin said. "But watchful, I think. Or maybe I've been away too long."

"I threw two rocks in the water," Arcolin said. "I'd like to hear a splash."

As if in answer, a distant cry broke through the gentler night noises. When it cut off, not a sound came from frogs, insects, birds, for what seemed a long time, then something went "crrrrick . . . crrrrick . . ." again.

Stammel appeared out of the darkness. "Trouble?" he said to Arcolin.

"I don't know yet." They waited another while in silence, and then Arcolin said, "I hope that wasn't one of ours—" He stopped abruptly as one of the horses stamped, then snorted. Then he heard the foot-steps running this way and laboring breath.

Devlin, Stammel, and the sentries kindled more torches; Arcolin squinted into the gloom and could just make out something moving, coming nearer. He hoped it was his people, but he couldn't yet tell.

Then they were panting up to the entrance, gasping the password, with a dark form trussed up in a Phelani cloak between them. "Stupid clods of dirt-grubbers." That was Vik, the wiry redhead who had been one of Paks's close friends. "If they'd just said what you told them—but they didn't, and the brigands killed them before we could do anything."

"And who's this?" Arcolin asked. The bundle appeared to be breathing, or trying to.

"The live brigand," Tam said. "We didn't think he ought to go back and tell his friends that someone had attacked them out of the dark. Might be bad for the villagers."

"And we thought you might want him," Vik added, dropping his end of the prisoner with no concern for the prisoner's welfare. "He must live on rocks; he weighs as much as a bullock."

"Is he wounded?"

"A knock on the head is all," Tam said. "He should live, I think, but it was dark." Arcolin had his doubts. Tam's fist had killed men before.

"He was breathing when we wrapped him up," Vik said.

"Stammel, take charge of the prisoner. If he lives, we'll see what he has to say when he wakes up. Devlin, check the perimeter again and let's set an extra guard on the stock. Tam, Vik, come with me."

Their report was brief and simple: The two men from the village had gone through the village and then out in the fields, where they'd met two other men. They'd been asked about the cohort; they'd first answered as Arcolin suggested, but when challenged, they'd elaborated.

"One of them said they weren't afraid anymore, because you were going to get rid of all the bandits. The other threatened those two— it was ridiculous. There they are, no weapons, no reserve force, and they're challenging men they must know have killed a dozen times, more."

"I'm surprised they were killed quickly," Arcolin said.

"The dead brigand had a temper," Vik said. "Whipped out his sword—one of those curved ones from the coastal region—and had the head off the first man, so the second brigand ran the other one through."

"We didn't realize in time," Tam said. "They had just this little light, and it was the shine of the sword that we saw, too late. Then they started arguing with each other, and we got to them."

"Who yelled?" Arcolin said.

"This one," Vik said, with a jerk of his head toward the camp. "We got the first one, but this one yelled, and then Tam hit him. Twice."

"He didn't hold still," Tam said, scuffing one boot in the ashes. "And he still had his blade."

"So," Arcolin said, "in the morning I get to explain to the village headman that two of his friends were killed by brigands right under our noses?"

"Not right under, sir," Vik said. "Way off there, where there's that block of woods."

"They might think their two stumbled on a brigand and killed him, after he wounded them, and then they died," Tam said.

"The one with no head helping his friend stab the brigand, you mean?" Arcolin asked.

"He could've thrown a rock, before," Tam said. His brow wrinkled. "See, he hears something—he throws a rock, it hits the brigand, who cuts off his head, and then his friend—"

"Without making a sound, manages to stab the brigand with his nonexistent sword while being stabbed. Of course. I'm sure the village will see it that way. I, on the other hand, am aware how easy it is to kill an unarmed peasant with any decent blade. I don't suppose you brought it along?"

"Only one," Tam said, producing it from behind his back. "We left only one brigand, so we could leave only one blade."

The curved blade had a deadly elegance; Arcolin hefted it with care, not only for its edge but the stench of death on the blade. He handed it back to Tam. "See that it's clean, and wrap it so no one gets cut. Then get some sleep, both of you."

In his tent, Burek snored lightly, deeply asleep; Arcolin made his own notations on the map and in his log, then went out to walk the perimeter again.

CHAPTER TWENTY-SEVEN

At the change of watch, Arcolin told Burek what had happened.

"I slept through that?" Burek looked ashamed.

"No harm done," Arcolin said. "I may sleep through the next little problem. Wake me if you need me."

He woke to the smell of breakfast cooking. That meant it was near dawn or after; the tent wasn't as dark as it had been. He had one boot on when Burek poked his head into the tent. "Sir—good, you're awake—"

"What is it?"

"The man died, and I thought you should know before the villagers found him—"

"Found him?"

"And the scene, I mean. He died about midwatch, so I told off a squad to take the body back to where the fight was. I thought that way we didn't have to explain why we had his body here."

Arcolin had a quick mental vision of four of his soldiers, two lugging the dead brigand's body, over the fields in the dark. He could imagine the track they'd leave on the dew-wet grass—

"I worried about the track they might leave," Burek went on. "But Stammel said the grass was dry enough, just be back here in a glass or less. And they were, and dewfall came after that."

Arcolin pulled on his other boot and stamped down into it. "Good thinking," he said. "I suppose you had them take his weapon back with him?"

Burek stared, then flushed. "No, sir—I didn't think of that."

"Never mind," Arcolin said. "They'll think someone stole it, or there was a third brigand."

"Do we march today, after all this? The brigands must be near."

"We march, because we're not supposed to know the brigands are near." And with luck they could be packed and on their way before the villagers found the dead men. "We know nothing, we heard nothing, we saw nothing . . . they told us no brigands were anywhere around and they'd had no trouble, so . . . we go on being ignorant."

Burek grinned. "Stammel thought you'd say that."

"Stammel is a wise man," Arcolin said.

By the time the sun had cleared the trees beyond the fields, they were ready to march, leaving behind only flattened grass: the jacks filled in, scraps of food burnt to char and then the fire pit watered down and raked, the brambles pulled into a pile. Burek had arched his brows at the care taken.

"Leave a mess behind, find a worse mess when you return," Arcolin said. "Duke's saying; I expect he learnt it from Aliam Halveric. Farmers don't like their fields and pastures damaged, and they'll find ways to cause you trouble the next time you come through."

Burek thought about that for a moment, then said, "Dead men aren't a mess, then . . . ?"

"Not if it's nothing to do with us. They'll think it does, but more like we drew trouble down on them, the brigands spying on us. That reminds me—" He turned, just as Tam came up with something wrapped in a cloth. "Ah—thank you, Tam."

"It's really pretty, Captain," Tam said.

"It'll go in the Company records as split between you and Vik," Arcolin said. "It'll be the end of season, most likely, before you see a copper out of it."

" 'Sfine, Captain. I just wondered."

"And remember—no talking about it, anywhere we go."

"No, Captain. I'll tell Vik." He paused. "I can tell Vik, can't I?"

"Tell him not to talk about it. Nothing happened. That's the important part. Nothing at all happened."

Tam grinned, saluted, and hurried off. Arcolin unwrapped the cloth. The grip of it was made of some intricately carved bone or tooth—he didn't want to meet the animal with such teeth—inlaid with gold and silver. No guard but a narrow flange of metal where the two met, and the blade itself had the waterflow pattern that meant the best steel.

"Rich brigands," Burek said. "Or they've been robbing rich men."

"Rich men with exceptional taste in weapons," Arcolin said. "And this one's seen considerable use." The carving had worn down almost to the inlay, just where a hand would put the most pressure. He wrapped the cloth around it again. A shout came from behind the wagons, in the direction of the village. Several shouts. Arcolin loosened the cord of his saddle roll, pushed the wrapped weapon into the center, and retied the cord.

"Try to look stupid," Arcolin said to Burek. "Whatever you do, don't smile. Mount up." He mounted his own horse, and turned it out of the lane, where he could see what was coming.

The rest of the cohort, now in marching formation in front of the wagons, were doing their own best to look stupid. Hurrying up the lane toward them was yesterday's village headman and two others, waving their arms. Arcolin knew the wagon guards would stop them.

"Stammel, a hand with us, and start the rest down the road."

"Captain." Stammel named five, who fell out and lined up beside Arcolin and Burek. The others filled in, Stammel gave the command in a voice that could probably be heard in Cortes Vonja, and the cohort marched off, in perfect step. Behind them, the first wagon's driver slapped reins together and yelled at the mules; harness creaked and harness rings jingled as that wagon, and then the next, followed.

"With me," Arcolin said, and nudged his horse forward, toward the approaching villagers.

Faced with two armed men on horseback and five armed soldiers afoot, the villagers straggled to a halt, breathing heavily.

"What's amiss?" Arcolin asked.

"You—you can't leave—I demand—you killed four men!" the headman said.

"We did not kill four men," Arcolin said with perfect honesty. "And you are not authorized to place demands on me—my contract is with Cortes Vonja, in whose outbounds your village lies."

"I will report you to the city as thieves and murderers," the head-man said, less breathless now.

"Then I will report *you* as an arrant liar," Arcolin said. "We stole nothing and we did not kill four men. We camped away from your village, as you requested; we left our camp clean and ready for use again as pasture. We brought our own supplies; we had no need to steal."

"Two men from the village came to see you last night. I know they did."

"They did indeed. Did you send them? Did they tell you that I sent them away? I do not deal with such as they—men afraid of the light, who whisper in the dark."

"They're dead," the headman said. "They never came back from your camp, and this morning they're dead, over there—" He waved in the general direction Arcolin knew was right. "You must have killed them—we have no weapons to take off heads."

"You said four were killed—who were the others? And why were four of your people wandering around at night?"

The headman glanced at the other two men, who were still stand-ing slack-jawed, staring at the soldiers. "They—we don't know—maybe from another village—"

"They spoke to me of a robber band, as if they knew where it was—why not robbers?"

The headman paled. "We—we don't have robbers here. I told you that."

"But you do have four dead men. And one with his head cut off, you said. Would farmers from another village have swords?"

"Nay," one of the other men spoke for the first time. "They don't have swords no more than we do. But you folk have swords."

"So we do," Arcolin said. "But we were camped here last night, and you say the dead men are over there somewhere." He waved in a direction slightly different from what the headman had indicated.

"Not that way, but there," the second man said, eager now to cor-rect him and pointing very specifically. Arcolin looked in that direc-tion.

"Where?"

"There's a mound, maybe sun-hand away, and there's trees on it—it's not level so no use to clear it for a field."

Arcolin translated this from peasant estimates of distance to those used by the Company. "And you found dead men there?"

"Aye, that I did. I been sent to track the headman's bull that broke out last night, and once we were past the ploughland, my dog, he picked up the smell of blood, and I couldn't call him off. It might've been the bull's, after all."

"And you found four dead men," Arcolin prompted.

"Yes, and one with no head—it turned me right up, sir, it did indeed. That was Aren, married to m'wife's third sister, and her baby coming any time. Noki, the other, he's m'cousin by m'father's sister, her husband, they has four, the youngest still at breast . . ."

"What about the two you didn't know?" Arcolin asked.

"Never saw them before," the headman said. He glared at the other man.

"That's not right," the third man said. "You spoke to that one with the big sword yourself, that time he come to the village to buy a goose, he said."

"Be quiet," the headman said. The other men said nothing, but from the sly looks, Arcolin knew they were enjoying the headman's discomfort. "They don't know, sir. They mistook his face. I never saw either of the others, and I still say it must've been you—or one of your men—that killed them."

"I know it was not," Arcolin said. "Do you think soldiers who have marched all day have nothing better to do than run around the countryside all night finding wandering peasants to kill?" The headman opened his mouth but Arcolin went on. "It's clear to me that your two villagers stole your bull, took it away to sell to someone, probably a whole group of robbers, and there was a quarrel. The robbers killed your men, and then perhaps another quarrel, and the others made off with your bull, leaving four dead men behind. It's nothing to do with us, but you might consider that two of your men knew more about robbers in your area than you did."

"But—but you can't just leave—" the headman said, as Arcolin lifted the reins and his horse took a step backward.

"My orders from the Cortes Vonja Council are to keep on the move until we drive brigands away," Arcolin said. "Now they've got meat and know we're in the area, they'll be away from here. And your two who were in league with them are dead. Go back to work." He backed his horse another three steps and spoke to Burek and the men. "Come now; we have work to do. Let these farmers do theirs." He turned his horse in a showy spin and rode off, not looking back until he was sure they were out of earshot. Then he saw the farmers still standing in the road, the other two apparently haranguing the headman.

"That went well, sir," said one of the five marching alongside.

"I wonder what he's going to tell his brigand contact," Arcolin said. "The next one, I mean. What a whey-faced little wiggler he is, too. I'm afraid that village is in for trouble, unless those two force a new selection." He looked at the sky. The dawn's limpid blue had faded to a harder sheen. West, wisps of cloud like wing feathers appeared high up. Sweat tickled his scalp under his helmet.

"Rain later today or tomorrow," he said. "Good thing it wasn't last night."

"Do you really think they stole the headman's bull?" Burek asked.

"No," Arcolin said. "I think the headman's bull doesn't exist. We came through the village—did you see any bull yesterday?"

"Could've been out with the cows."

"Could have. Except we passed cows with a cowherd and two dogs: no bull. I make it a practice to look in the pens in villages we pass, in case we're accused of stealing livestock. The headman's house—second on the left—had a stone-walled pigpen. Sow and litter of piglets on one side; a boar on the other. A fenced pen for cows, but no bull. Most of these villages share a bull between two or three of them. There was a bull in that first village we passed yesterday."

Burek shook his head. "I've been with two other companies, and I never knew a captain to notice more than whether the village had enough to feed us. I'd heard the Duke's Company was different."

"The Duke always said you couldn't tell which information was important until you needed it," Arcolin said. "And we spent years down here, you know. I had time to learn."

"I will learn," Burek said.

Not, Arcolin noted, *I'd like to learn*, or *I want to learn*, or *Teach me*, but *I will learn*. He hadn't had such a promising junior captain since Ferrault. He wondered suddenly if this was how Kieri had felt after hiring him. He remembered saying almost exactly the same thing, the first time Kieri explained why he'd done something.

"I'm sure you will," he said to Burek. "Now, tell me what you notice about the fields we pass."

Burek looked to either side. "Ploughland once," he said. "Furrows grown over with grass—and grass that grows in damper places. Cowpaths . . . it's pasture here. Rougher than behind us."

"Easier to conceal people and animals in, wouldn't you say?"

Burek looked again. "Not as flat as it looks at first," he said. "Yes—that—" He pointed to a sinuous line of thicker growth in a slight hollow. "That could be a hidden stream."

"When I was here last," Arcolin said, "this, where old furrows show, was ploughland and that over there was grazed short. There's a spring in there somewhere—it's boggy across the way—but a good gravel-bottomed pool. That's where they watered the village herds, back then. But I don't see a regular path to it now. The population's down, from that war, but you'd think they'd still use the water. Now they're watering cattle upstream from the village. That's not good practice."

"I noticed that, yesterday," Burek said. "I didn't know this other water was here."

"Land hereabouts, the water runs generally east—wiggling north or south, but meeting the Immer downstream of Cortes Vonja . . . it's all in the Immer drainage. My guess is someone else is using that water now. Someone who knows a trail through the bog on the far side, so they can come to the village through the woods to the east."

They were almost up with the cohort now; Arcolin waved; the wagon guards signaled ahead and Stammel halted the cohort for them to catch up. The soldiers moved back into their places, and Arcolin spoke to the teamsters and guards.

"We're being watched," he said. "I want everyone alert, both sides and behind—notice everything and I'll take your report at nooning and evening. That headman was lying; the others were scared."

Once in the lead again, Arcolin changed the formation, putting out flanking scouts for the first time. "We need the practice," he told Stammel. "I don't think anyone will attack today, but just in case."

"Mounted or afoot, sir?" Stammel asked.

"Mounted, so we don't slow," Arcolin said. "Stay in sight. I'm most interested in who's watching from near the road, and in assessment of the cover."

"Notice the animals," he said to Burek, when they were moving again. "The scouts are out far enough that they shouldn't disturb rabbits and birds nearer the road. We should see a little movement of animals into the cover beside the road, but anything moving out of cover toward the scouts means something else is in there."

Nothing showed for almost a glass, in Arcolin's estimation. The pasture land continued to roughen; along the line of the unseen stream, brush thickened to a line of scrubby trees. Then, as that bore away eastward, a flock of pink-fronted doves racketed up and away, and downstream of them, another.

Arcolin held up his hand; the cohort halted. "They'd need some-one closer," he said to Burek. On the right, ahead, the ruins of what he remembered as a herder's night-shelter canted sideways; next to it, a thicket had grown up where he remembered a small cattle pen. "There, for instance. Let's see what happens when our flanking scout gets closer."

The scout, checking position on the cohort, had reined in; Arcolin signaled her on. "Watch the horse's ears," he told Burek. Another five strides, and the horse lifted its head, ears pricked.

"It's seen something," Burek said.

"Right," Arcolin said. The scout loosened her sword and rode on. Two more strides, and four crows lifted from the thicket, cawing. The scout glanced back. Arcolin signaled again; she turned her horse a lit-tle away and held position.

"One hand to flank," he said quietly to Stammel. "Two hands with me. We want him alive, if we can." To Burek, he said, "Come on—we'll try to cut him off." He drew his sword and legged his horse to a hand gallop. Burek caught up with him; they passed the ruin and thicket. Be-yond, an ungrazed field had grown up in tall grass and patches of scrub. Arcolin looked to the left—no sign anyone had crossed yet.

"He's probably got a crossbow," Arcolin said. "And he'll probably shoot at us. But if we make him run, he won't be very accurate."

"There," Burek said, pointing to the right. Arcolin, too, saw grass move against the breeze.

"Good eye," Arcolin said. He legged his horse into a gallop, trust-ing Burek to follow. The movement ahead quickened. Arcolin yelled; his horse flattened out, crashing through the tall grass and weeds for a point ahead of the movement. He could hear Burek behind him.

The grass stilled—the man was getting ready to shoot. Arcolin shifted his weight; his horse threw a flying change, veering sideways, then another and then he saw the man, struggling to span his bow again. One jump, and Arcolin's horse was there, skidding to a halt; Arcolin swung his sword, knocking the crossbow from the man's hand. Burek pulled to a halt on the man's other side, as the man snatched a short curved blade and swung at Arcolin's horse.

Burek rode closer, tried to hit the man with the flat of his blade, but the man whirled, and Burek's horse took a cut on the chest, and reared. One hoof caught the man's arm; Arcolin swung his cloak over the man's head as he staggered, blinding him, then leaned over and hit him as Burek had planned. The man dropped. Burek was off his horse and leapt onto the man's back and pulled his arms back before he could struggle. Arcolin looked back. His tensquad was making its noisy way through the weeds now, halfway to them. He waved to the scout, calling her in, and saw her pass the signal to the hand of men headed for the ruin. Burek's horse stood quietly, for a wonder, head drooping. Had the blade been poisoned?

He dismounted and walked over to the horse. A bad gash, gaping open, but not life threatening in itself. He took the reins. "Burek, that blade may be poisoned. When the tensquad gets here, try to keep our prisoner from cutting himself on it."

"Is my horse all right?" Burek asked.

"I'm not sure. He's quieter than I'd expect." Arcolin looked the horse over. No other injuries. Sweaty, but they'd galloped and the day was increasingly hot and humid. The horse blew into his hand; Arcolin sniffed. "What's he like? You've had him long enough now."

"Solid, I'd say. Sound, well trained. Not as spirited as yours. By his teeth, two years older than the seller told me; I got a nata knocked off his price for that."

"We'll hope it's just a quiet disposition," Arcolin said. Blood dripped freely from the wound; horses always bled a lot, in his experience, and could lose much more blood than a man before falling over.

Devlin arrived with the tensquad; in moments they had the prisoner yanked upright, the cloak off his head, and trussed. Arcolin warned them about the blade, and they left it for him to examine. Burek came over to his horse. "It's bad . . ."

"The surgeons can sew it up, if he's as quiet as you say. You'll

have to ride your spare." Arcolin gave the reins of both horses to
Burek and went to look at the blade. Like the other, it had no guard
but a simple flange; the grip was less ornate, made of wood carved
into ribs. The blade was smeared with horse blood; Arcolin sniffed.
Under the smell of blood was the odor of something else. He picked
the blade up by its grip, and handed it to Devlin. "It's got something
on it, probably a contact poison. Wrap it up and bring it along."

The prisoner meanwhile had said nothing, made no attempt to escape. Arcolin looked at him, and was reminded of the men in Alured
the Black's camp. Darkly sunmarked, as expressionless as a carving,
no fear in his eyes, he might have been standing sentry somewhere
instead of being bound in hostile hands. He had an old scar on his
face, and doubtless more elsewhere on his body. Arcolin looked him
up and down. No change in expression at all.

"Get him back to the road," he said. "Send the surgeon." Then he
turned to Burek. "How's he doing?"

"Bleeding's slowed," Burek said.

"We don't want to be here too long," Arcolin said. "I'll leave the
scout and five with you. I need to go see our prisoner." He mounted.
"Hand up your saddle; I'll see someone saddles your spare and brings
it out to you." He went back to the road in an arc, checking the road
ahead of the cohort for anything suspicious. The flanking scout on
the far side waved a clear, and Arcolin rode back down toward the cohort. Stammel, as he expected, had set up a temporary perimeter,
wagons in the middle.

"Prisoner's tied to a wagon wheel," he said. Arcolin handed down
Burek's saddle.

"He'll need his other mount," he said.

"Will the horse make it?" Stammel pointed to one of the men, who
took the saddle and went to get Burek's spare from those tied to the
last wagon.

"If the poison wasn't strong enough. If he can walk fast enough to
keep up with us." He hoped it would. They would not easily find a
replacement in southern Cortes Vonja; it wasn't good horse country.
He dismounted and went to look at their prisoner. The man was staring straight ahead, ignoring everything or pretending to.

"I'm sure you recognize the uniform," Arcolin said. "That scar on
your face is at least three years old; you would have seen us before."

No response, not the flicker of an eyelid.

"Some men prefer death to life, and that's a choice any man can make," Arcolin said. "You will shortly have that choice. You can tell me one of three things: who your leader is, where your leader is, or who hired your band. Or you can die. Think about it."

"Ya'kint make muh," the man said, without looking at Arcolin.

"I won't try," Arcolin said. "But I will see you dead before midday if you don't." He turned away.

"I'll die," the man said.

"Your choice," Arcolin said over his shoulder.

"Better you than them," the man said, more softly.

"Them?" Arcolin said, turning back.

The man spat toward the left. "You been here before—you figure it out. How you do it?"

"Kill you? Sword to the neck, how else?"

The man's brow furrowed. "You do it quick? Even if I don't tell?"

Arcolin's memories of the last season in Aarenis rose to choke him. "Yes," he said.

"You one of them Girdish?"

"Yes."

"Well, then—go on. Do it now. I got nothing to think about and nothing to live for."

Arcolin looked at him a long moment, but the man stared past him, unresponsive again. He drew his sword, aware of many watching eyes—the veterans of the last trip to the south in particular.

"This man has chosen to die," he said, loud enough to be heard. "He wants a quick death, and I have promised it. Gird's grace on him, Tir's honor for his courage, and the High Lord forgive what he has done and tried to do." He stepped to one side; the man continued to stare ahead. One swing of his sword and it was done; blood spurted and the man's head fell forward. "I'm sorry," Arcolin said softly to the man's departing spirit.

"What should we do with him, sir?" Stammel asked.

"Bury him," Arcolin said. "Let his fellows find that we gave him that much honor."

"Very good, sir."

The soil was deep and soft; it didn't take long to dig a grave, and they rolled him into it and covered it over before the others returned. The injured horse plodded along, barely at a foot-pace. "It's the numbweed," the surgeon said. "It'll wear off by sunset. Wasn't as bad as it looked, barely into the meat. Should heal clean."

"There was something on the blade," Arcolin said.

"Worse for men," the surgeon said. "Would've felled you, left you barely moving, easy prey. Horses are bigger; it would take more than you could get on one blade. He'll be slow today, possibly stumble now and then, no more. Walking will do him good. I'll look him over again when we stop at noon."

The cohort moved on, the injured horse tied to the first wagon. Arcolin glanced at Burek, now on a stocky roan. He had the inward expression of a man arguing with himself. Arcolin cleared his throat, and Burek looked up. "We're not going to make it two villages down the road today," he said. "We lost two sun-hands to that bit of excitement."

"I'm sorry," Burek said. "My horse—"

"It wasn't your horse," Arcolin said. "We needed to clear that lookout point. Is that the first horse you ever bought yourself?"

"Yes. Well, I bought them both at the same time." He patted the roan's neck.

"Our surgeon's experienced. If he says the horse will live, the horse will live."

Burek took a long breath. "I believe him, but—horses don't have choices."

"I'm not sure," Arcolin said. "We train them, yes, and we expect them to go where we direct, but they come with minds, and they choose to trust us or not." He kept scanning the road, the land to either side, checking the scouts for signals. Burek looked aside now, obviously doing the same.

"Where will we camp, then?" he asked.

"We have a reason to be slow," Arcolin said. "We got one of their spies; they would have more than one. If they go looking for their man, and find all that blood, they may think we have wounded. I think we'll camp before we reach the next village."

"Less than a day's march?"

Arcolin smiled. "We'll find a nice obvious fallow field. Send a party down to get water, have them talk about wounded men. We should cut their trail there; if they aren't using the stream for hidden access, I'll be very surprised. Look at the sky."

Burek looked up. Clouds had thickened, the early feather-clouds followed by a thicker layer moving from the west. "Rain by morning," he said.

"And they won't expect us to move," Arcolin said. "We make camp early, a good strong barrier, then put the men to rest. Come dark and the rain—well, we'll see what word we get from those we send down to the stream."

By midday, the sun was hidden behind the gathering clouds; the light dimmed and haze blurred the line of woods. The ground rose a little to their right, a low hump, and the road curved a little to the left. "The stream turns here," Arcolin said. "There used to be a wide flattish area—there—" He pointed. "More than one company camped there, years past. You can still see the outline of a ditch."

A damp gust came from the west, bringing out all the smells of the land. Arcolin turned in the saddle. "The old campground," he said to Stammel. "Rain's coming; we'll stop here and set up before it starts." He raised his arm; the scouts raised theirs; he signaled them to stay in place for the time being.

By the time the first wisps of rain touched the canvas, the camp was completed: a line of fresh stakes in the old ditch, whose perimeter was too large for one cohort to defend otherwise, an inner perimeter of brush, the jacks trench, the enclosure for the animals. Arcolin had a shelter rigged up for Burek's horse, poles roofed with brush. The water party returned from the stream to report a beaten trail, hoofmarks and bootmarks both, on both sides.

"There's a branch off, up a sort of gully. We only went a little way up it; as far as we went, the tracks stayed in it."

"No reason for that but staying hidden," Arcolin said. "Thanks, Donag." Rain pattered again on the tent. "Get some rest now." He turned to Burek. "If you'll update the map, I'll do the perimeter round. Then we should both rest; it may be a very long night."

Soft curtains of rain blew across the camp as Arcolin made his way to the first sentry's post. This was no brief shower; it was going to rain for the rest of the day or longer. Though it was only early afternoon, the woods were no more than a dark blur in the distance.

"Think they'll attack, Captain?"

"Not immediately. When they think rain and darkness have made us careless, probably."

"I won't be careless, sir."

"I know, Seli." Arcolin grinned at him, and went on to the next post. As he passed the enclosure for the horses and mules, he checked on Burek's horse; the surgeon was there, feeling around the wound.

"As I hoped," the surgeon said. "He's fine—walking won't hurt him, but he shouldn't be ridden or do anything fast. I put more numbweed on it; he'll rest better."

"I'll tell Burek," Arcolin said.

"He's been here," the surgeon said. "I just sent him back. First horse, is it?"

"Yes," Arcolin said, remembering his own first horse. He had cried when Arrow broke a leg in a ditch trap, hurt more by that than by his own broken arm. No horse since had been the same. "The first one's always the best."

CHAPTER TWENTY-EIGHT

"We're inviting attack," Arcolin said to Burek when they met again in his tent. "With brigands, you can hardly ever bring them to pitched battle. They live by ambush and trickery; they are not crazy enough to come out of their hiding places at a challenge, even if they have a force large enough."

"But we don't know how many there are," Burek said. "What if they have superior force?"

"Supply," Arcolin said. When Burek looked confused, he explained. "Brigands must eat, the same as a regular army. They get their food by stealing it, or by scaring peasants into giving it to them. Where peasants are well fed, brigands are few. Too many for the comfort of travelers on the road, but too few to worry us if we're alert. These brigands have made deals with the villages, that much is clear. But the villages still have food; none of the people look pinched, any more than those we passed coming into Cortes Vonja on the trade road. How many extra men—hungry men—can a village supply?"

"If they're a clandestine invasion, though, could not their commander be importing food for them?"

"That's possible for a few, much harder for many. We moved multiple companies around Aarenis, that last year against Siniava. We used every wagon, every road . . . we left evidence everywhere of the size of our force. It's true we've been here only briefly, but I see nothing like the mess just a few hundred men leave when they inhabit a countryside." He took another swallow of watered ale. "The cohort will rest until dark; so must we. If they come, it will be after dark, first a probe to see if we're alert, and then, if we're lucky, an attack."

Arcolin woke to the smell of cooking; torches lit the center of the camp. Someone had lit the candle on his desk; it had burned down a finger-mark. Rain still fell, the persistent soaking rain he remembered. Burek stirred; Arcolin considered letting him sleep another half-glass, but already the younger man's eyes were opening. "Sir?"

"It's dark, and supper's almost ready. I'm going out; come when you're ready."

The sentry posts, unlighted and placed so the sentries would not be silhouetted against the central fire, had just been relieved. Arcolin spoke briefly with each sentry, low-voiced in case someone had crept close in the wet darkness to listen. They would be stiffening if they had; he himself had spent more than one wet night creeping up on someone else's sentries, and it was a cold, miserable job. As his eyes adjusted to the darkness, he could just make out the outer perimeter.

Coming back to the fire, he noted light glowing from the tent that would—if anyone had been injured—have been the sick tent, and a shadow within, bending down. So Stammel had already thought of that—no real surprise. He found Burek at the fire with the last of the soldiers.

"Do we eat here in the rain, sir?"

"No. In the tent, as the others are—they just aren't lighting all the tents. It's standard with us. The darker it is, the harder for the brigands to keep track of time."

Burek nodded; they carried their supper back to Arcolin's tent and ate by candlelight. The glass emptied before they were through; Arcolin turned it and marked the turn in the log. Burek took the dishes back to the fire. Arcolin went outside again to regain his night vision. Stammel had gathered a few men near the fire to sing for a while.

It was two turns of the glass, and the singing had dwindled to nothing, when the first warning came, a rhythmic tap on the tent. Burek looked up; Arcolin nodded, and snuffed the candle. In moments, their eyes adjusted. Over the way, the "sick tent" still glowed faintly with the candle inside it. Arcolin had planned for attack from either the stream side—which offered attackers the best cover on approach—or the road side, which offered attackers better ground position. "Or both," he'd told Burek and Stammel. "It'll tell us something about their training." True brigands, in his experience, were more likely to come up from the stream—easier navigating from their usual route of travel. Trained troops able to navigate in the dark would cross upstream of them and take the road itself . . . a longer march, and technically difficult, but they would not be attacking uphill. A clever commander might try both. Rain and a little wind would cover the sound of either. The rain drummed lightly on the tents, made its hissing and pattering sounds on the grass and trees. It should cover the sounds of their movements from the attackers just as well.

A stifled yelp came from the downhill slope . . . someone had staked himself, Arcolin thought with satisfaction. Unless it was meant to lower their guard, direct their attention to the stream side of camp. He moved to the road side, peered into the wet dark. A veteran grabbed his arm, fingers working in the Company finger-talk. Someone at the inner barricade had heard noise on the road.

Arcolin pulled the man closer and whispered in his ear. "Torches on my signal."

The double tap of understanding; he knew the signal would be passed to those with the flints. Moments crept by. Was that a squelching in the mud ahead? Breathing? That was certainly a human grunt, as someone stumbled or stubbed a toe. Now he could just sense movement, darker shades in the dark. He clapped his hands, once. Movement he had not been certain of seeing stopped.

In that moment of stillness, the torch bearers pulled oiled leather covers off the oil-soaked torches, snapped sparks onto them from flint and steel, and more than half the torches caught light, just as a yell from the stream side jerked his attention that way. But he was not fooled, nor were the veterans: as the torches flared, the enemy in front of them, eyes gleaming in the light, were clear to see. They wore dark cloaks, but glints through them suggested mail underneath. They wavered a moment, but a sharp command from the rear sent them forward, yelling. The front rank tore off their dark cloaks, threw them onto the bramble barrier and tried to run across it; Arcolin's troops made short work of them, but those following did not stop. The penetration was narrow; Arcolin peered into the rain-sparkled darkness to estimate how many there were.

Behind him, he heard more fighting, across the camp. Burek's voice, Devlin's—apparently there the enemy had hit a wider front. In front, Stammel and the first two files were engaged at that one penetration, holding it back with ease. Arcolin signaled the torchbearers, who leaned their torchpoles out beyond the barrier—there he was, the enemy commander.

"I'm going out," he said to Stammel. "Follow me!"

"Captain, are you—?" But that was as far as Stammel got before Arcolin was moving, catching the first two standing on the much-flattened bramble barrier by surprise with his longer sword. Behind, he heard the files coming, as he raced toward the gleam of the enemy commander's helmet. The torchbearers almost caught up with him, so the light gave him just enough reflection to follow as the enemy commander turned and tried to slip away into the darkness.

"Look—!" came a shout from behind, just as someone rose from the darkness and lunged at him. Arcolin felt a blade scrape against the mail over his ribs and struck out with the buckler on his left hand. Nothing; the fellow had rolled aside. Arcolin whirled, searching in the uncertain light as Stammel and the others came up beside him.

"Got him!" someone said with satisfaction.

"I saw their commander," Arcolin said to Stammel, half-ashamed now of the impulse that had sent him to chase the man. "I thought he was close enough to catch."

"He might have been," Stammel said. Neither of them mentioned the other possibility, that it was a planned ambush. They looked at the dead man in the torchlight. Arcolin took the narrow, wave-curved blade from his hand.

"Southern work. And those other two blades we found were south-coast. Could have been sailors' blades."

"Indeed, sir. Alured never got this far north and west, did he?"

"Not that I know. Siniava, maybe. These could be escapees from his army . . . but I think not."

"Back to camp," Arcolin said. They were scarce three hundred paces from it, and on the way back found no more enemy until they reached the barricade, with the bodies of those who'd attacked it. By then the hubbub on the far side had ended as well.

"Thirteen," Burek said when he came to report. "They came up the slope pretty quietly, and laid cloaks over the brambles, then thought to scramble over, but we were ready."

"Any guesses how many more?"

"About that many ran away downhill as soon as the torches lit. Might have been more behind them; I couldn't see that far."

"We killed ten on our side—they chose a narrow front and a column attack, just what this cohort knows how to handle. They fought competently, though it was the wrong formation for them. More than ten got away, when we went after them. Their commander, to my sorrow. None of our people killed or wounded—what about you?"

"One dead, two wounded, all first-years," Burek said. "Gan ran out over the barrier—young idiot."

"There's always one," Arcolin said, and caught a look from Stammel. Well, he deserved it.

"The wounded are Peli and Aris. Surgeon says Peli will be back on duty in two days; Aris will be out at least three."

Arcolin winced. Novices were most at risk in their first battles; that's why the cohorts went to war ten percent or more over strength, but it always hurt. And this was the first time he had been in complete command—he had chosen the contract, he had chosen the route and the camp and its defense. He pushed that away—commanders who could not accept risk were as dangerous to their people as those who ignored it. What his troops needed now was his approval.

"We came through this very well." Arcolin cocked his head at Burek. "So—how do you like the way your command fights?"

"Very well. I'd heard, of course, but seeing it—it's no wonder you were—are—considered one of the best companies in Aarenis."

"Good. I'll need a report from you—talk to Devlin if you're uncertain—on the demeanor of each of the recruits on that side. Our tradition is that recruits may be promoted after their first battle; if they aren't promoted after their second, we dismiss them. This wasn't a full battle, but we'll be promoting some of them anyway. I saw three on my side, for instance, who did extremely well."

"Were the enemy as many as you were expecting?" Burek asked.

"Within the range, but enough to suggest outside aid," Arcolin said. "An attack force of about forty—they probably left some behind—the nearest villages would be not only under their control but stripped bare if they lived only on the land. And a competent commander."

"So—now we look for the supply route?"

"Exactly."

The rest of the night passed quietly; Arcolin checked with the surgeon and saw that both the wounded were sleeping under the influence of numbweed. The rain stopped sometime before dawn, though the clouds and ground mist impeded visibility almost as much. Arcolin looked at the obvious track the enemy had made going up and down the slope to the stream.

"Armor up," he said to Burek, back at the tent. "We're going to scout the stream, on horseback to save time, while the cohort breaks fast."

They rode up to the road first, looking for traces, but rain after the attack had washed away any traces between the camp and the road.

"Do you think they came on foot?" Burek said. "To coordinate, covering more ground . . ."

Arcolin shook his head. "I think they came at least partway ahorse. I'm hoping to find some evidence, and perhaps the horses will help us." At that moment, his mount lifted its head and pointed its ears to the right, toward the stream. "Like that," Arcolin said. He felt his mount's sides swell and tremble, precursor to a whinny. He tapped the horse on the neck. "Quiet, you."

Burek's horse was looking the same direction; Burek slipped off and clamped the horse's nostrils. Far to the east, Arcolin heard a distant whinny, then others nearer, from the direction of the camp. "At least three horses," Burek said. "No . . . four, five . . ."

Arcolin raised his brows. "Are you that keen of hearing?"

"No, Captain. I spent years on a horse farm. Someone over there has a mare, and walked her past a stallion . . . that was the first whinny. They wanted to find out where our horses were."

"Well . . . they don't know we're here, then. That's good." Arcolin rode on, attending to his horse's reactions and to the look of the ground. There . . . a pile of wet, rained-on horse droppings. And there—a round hole, another, that could have been made only by horses carrying riders in the mud. The trail to the stream showed clearly when they came to it. Rain could not disguise the hoof-chopped leaves, the place where horse after horse had skidded a little on a steep downslope, creating a hillock at the bottom, the pock-marks of many hooves in the mud.

"Can you estimate how many?" Arcolin asked.

"Not more than a dozen, I think," Burek said. He dismounted and looked more closely. "It's muddled—they used this trail both ways, rode back over their tracks. Shod horses and barefoot both . . . this track's distinctive, an unusual shoe. This . . . here's a barefoot horse with a bad flare on the right fore. Much work in this muck and it'll go lame." He walked up and down the track while Arcolin held his horse, bending now and then to measure a track with his hand. When he came back he held a shoe, bent nails hanging from it.

"This one will definitely go lame if they don't have a farrier," he said. "I still think ten to twelve, and that they rode double on the way in—the few good tracks I could find pointing to the road were much deeper, even after the rain." He put the horseshoe in his saddlebags and remounted. "The horses aren't that good. By the hoofmarks, most have some problem. Bought cheap at a horse fair, I'm thinking, and overdue for hoof work."

Arcolin reined around and they headed back for the road and camp. "I had no idea you were so knowledgeable about horses."

"It's why I tried a cavalry company first," Burek said. "I thought my background would be useful there."

"Why not horse breeding or training?" Arcolin asked.

"I didn't want to stay in one place," Burek said. "And besides—I also like swords and fighting." They were up at the road by then. "I had the chance, sir . . . to stay, to become a horsemaster . . . but it would be the same thing the rest of my life, year after year. I had seen the local militia drilling, and later saw the armies come through, in the war against Siniava. Including this one."

"Where was that?" Arcolin asked. "We covered a lot of ground that last year."

"Andressat," Burek said. "That's why the Count made complaint of me, I'm sure, when I was sent back there with troops he'd hired. I'd hoped he wouldn't recognize me as a man grown, but he did, or someone else did, and told him."

Arcolin had hoped Burek would mention Andressat and clear up that mystery; he had not expected this. "You were a horsemaster's son?"

Burek nodded. "Though there were rumors, my looks being different than my father's. At any rate, I grew up in the stables and fields of Andressat's stud. As I grew older, the Count approved my work and named me successor to my father. The other prentices said it was only because my father was not my real father, and said things about my mother—and then there was a fight, and I was punished for it. So I ran off for a few days, and when I went back, the Count declared me outlaw and I left forever."

"Are you angry with him?" Arcolin asked.

"Not anymore. At the time—I was sixteen perhaps—I thought it was unfair and hated him heartily, but he did me a greater favor than he knew and I'm grateful for it now. I like horses and I know a lot about them, but I found my true calling when I left."

Arcolin looked at him. "Did you ever see your family again?"

"No. My duties with Golden Company sent me nowhere near the stud, and I was still hoping to go unnoticed. I sent messages—twice—but with no answer. Likely they were glad to be quit of me. My father never understood wanting to swing a sword."

The camp was in sight now, busy and orderly, the thorn barrier repaired, sentries in their daytime locations.

"We have a choice," Arcolin said. "We can spend the day pursuing them—though they have a good lead and know the ground better than we do—or we can move on and see what the next village tells us. Or we can sit here, as if planning to stay awhile. What would you do?"

As Arcolin expected, Burek was able to lay out reasons for and against each choice. "I don't think I'd pursue them," he said finally. "Too much chance of ambush, and on ground they know, they can move faster than we can. Staying—they'll move away, won't they?"

"They may move some of their force away, but they'll need to keep an eye on us," Arcolin said. "What I would worry about, given their use of poison so far, is whether they have the means to poison the water. We hurt them; that makes some men hot for revenge." They had come to the camp entrance by then. Arcolin dismounted and led his horse to the horse lines. Burek followed, handed the roan to one of the grooms then went to see his other mount. It whuffled at him and he leaned to check the gash on its chest then breathed into its nostrils.

"So we move?" Burek asked on the way back to their tent.

"Yes," Arcolin said. "After the promotion assembly."

The newly promoted privates fairly glowed with pride—they were the ones actually engaged against the enemy—and the remaining recruits looked ready to attack any number of troops if only they could earn promotion. Arcolin glanced back as he led the cohort away from the camp, well pleased with their appearance. It still felt strange to have no one over him—no Kieri Phelan to approve what he had done, or correct his errors. It felt strange to have no other cohorts, too. He imagined himself coming down next year with another cohort to join this one, perhaps Cracolnya's, to give him archery support.

The day brightened as the morning wore on, clouds lifting and thinning. The scouts reported nothing alarming; the next village, as they neared it, looked placid enough. His horse pricked its ears, and mules brayed ahead. Mules? The peasants here did not use mules, but oxen, in their fields.

In the village, he found two wagons blocking the way. Four armed men stood before them, obviously frightened but determined, a motley group with a tall skinny black-haired man on one end. Behind them, an obvious merchant and someone who might be an assistant or family member.

"Who are you?" one of the armed men said.

"Duke Phelan's Company," Arcolin said. "Hired by Cortes Vonja to restore peace to the countryside. And you?"

"A merchant of the Guild," the merchant said, coming forward. "How many are you? Enough to lend us escort on the way to Cortes Vonja?"

"No," Arcolin said. "That is not our contract. However, we fought off a brigand attack last night, and you should have fewer problems on the way north than before." He looked the merchant, his guards, and his wagons over carefully. What was a Guild merchant doing out here, so far from major transport routes? "Where are you from?"

The merchant frowned. "That is Guild business," he said, "and none of yours."

"I must insist," Arcolin said, with a gesture to his cohort. "You have four men; I have a hundred."

"Sibili," the merchant said. "I come from Sibili with silks and tiles, oilberries and wine."

"So you came through Andressat?" Arcolin said.

"No. It is too hard to get the wagons up that damned cliff at Cortes Andres, and that's the only crossing. We followed the war road to the east and curved back around." "War road" must mean the way armies had taken through the forest Alured had once guarded, and then north . . . Arcolin tried to remember just where it went. Was this story plausible at all?

"Where did you hire your guards?" Arcolin asked.

This time a guard answered. "Me in Sorellin, two years back; I'm Arnen. Them others, I hired. One of our regulars got sick in Sibili, so Pedar—" He flicked a thumb. "—he's from Sibili. Meddes comes from some vill in the Immervale, and Kory from Valdaire, he says." Arcolin looked at each man; he would not have hired any of them.

"And what's the cargo?"

"What Master Rieran says, I suppose," the guard said. "Haven't seen it m'self, but to keep count of the bales and barrels and make sure no seals is broke."

"As you can't bear witness to it, we will have to check," Arcolin said. He looked at the merchant. "Master Rieran, is it? I'm Captain Arcolin. We have no intent to plunder, but we must account for your cargo—we were told the brigands we seek were being supplied from outside."

"You think I—how dare you!" Rieran puffed up like a rooster; Arcolin ignored that. The man was pale-faced and sweating, not red . . . he was feigning indignation.

Arcolin looked back at the guards. "Step aside, gentlemen. Sergeant—?"

They moved aside without demur; Stammel and a tensquad herded them out of the village, to sit in the shade of a tree under guard. They gave up their swords without protest, and in return Arcolin saw them provided with water, bread, and cheese.

"Likely they are not involved," he said to Burek. "Though the guard leader seems none too bright, and might have hired foolishly. Now for the merchant—"

The wagons did indeed contain bales of silk, boxes of painted tiles, and barrels of oilberries, goods worth aplenty in more northern markets—but while riding around the first wagon Arcolin smelled something the merchant had not declared. He flicked his fingers to

Devlin and again when the second wagon yielded another smell that did not belong. He said nothing aloud, but had the wagons unloaded there in the street, his troops keeping back curious villagers, who might well want to snatch a few oilberries.

Devlin found the latch to the false bottom in one wagon; Vik found it in the second. One held sacks of unground southern grains, sides of dried salt meat, dried salt fish . . . though packed round with herbs, the smell could not be hidden. The other held weapons . . . more of the curved swords, short-stocked crossbows ideal for use in wooded areas, hardened leather armor, some strengthened with metal plates or mail.

"Well," he said, looking at the merchant, now fishbelly white and trembling. "This looks like smuggling, not trading. Who are these for?"

"I don't know," the merchant said. "I—I didn't know about that. I swear it; I'm an honorable member of the Guild. One of the guards must have—"

"I wonder what the courts in Cortes Vonja will say," Arcolin said. "They do not look kindly on those in league with their enemies."

"Enemies!" The merchant nearly squeaked. "There is no war— there are no enemies—you—it can't be treason—" That last in a wail. Arcolin looked down from his horse until the merchant collapsed in a heap, shaking. Then he dismounted, drew his sword, and walked over to the wretch.

"You know I could kill you here, and tell them in Cortes Vonja I executed a traitor and they would give me gold."

"Please . . . I have a family . . ."

"Then, for your family's sake, tell the truth. Who hired you to bring these things here in secret?"

"I—I can't. He'll kill me; he'll kill us all."

"That may be," Arcolin said. "But I will surely kill you if you do not. You follow Simyits, do you not?"

"Y-yes."

"Then chance comes as it comes. Your chance now is life, if you tell me who hired you, or certain death, if you do not. What does Simyits say about chance?"

"It was by following chance that I ended here," the merchant said, raising a tear-stained face.

"You could always change your allegiance and choose a better god," Arcolin said. "There are many."

"Don't let them hear," the man said. He looked at the villagers. "Make them go away."

"Why? Is one of them a spy who will tell your master?"

"It could be. Please . . . I will tell you, but not here."

"Get him up," Arcolin said. Two of the soldiers pulled the merchant to his feet and half dragged him away, closer to the cohort. "Now," he said to the merchant.

"The Duke," the merchant said. "The new Duke of Immer."

"Alured, you mean," Arcolin said. "Once pirate, then brigand, now Duke?"

"Who's your assistant? Your choice or his?"

"My nephew Harn. I wanted my son, but he—the Duke—has my son hostage. Harn isn't . . . he isn't very smart, sir. Captain."

"When were you due at the Guild Merchants' Hall?"

"A hand of days, sir."

"Where did you offload the supplies to the brigands?"

"Next village north, sir. Well, just south of it. There's a sort of old barn there, and a thicket grown up around it. We camp there overnight; they come and take their supplies. They're honest, at least; I've never lost a thing to them, though I take my hard coin into the village and have dinner with the headman and leave them to it."

"How often do you come through with supplies?"

"Me? Three times a year: Sibili to Cortes Vonja, Cortes Vonja to Sorellin, then down the Immerhoft Vale to the coast, Aliuna or Immerdzan, then west to Sibili. But there's others, I was told. I don't know who they are." He looked back at the wagons and villagers then lowered his voice even more. "Look here, Captain—I'll give you every coin I have, I swear, if you'll only let me go . . ."

"After the village has seen what you carry and what we would be letting go by—do you think that secret would last?"

"Last long enough for me to get home and take my family away, aye."

Arcolin shook his head. "It would never work. And I don't break contracts. No, you must go to Cortes Vonja for judgment. If you tell them you were coerced, they may show mercy." He doubted that, and was sure the merchant did too, but it was the only good outcome.

"You will ruin me," the merchant said, gasping. "The Guild will strike me from their rolls; even if the courts are kind, I will be ruined—marked forever—"

"I am not ruining you," Arcolin said. "You are the one who chose to deal dishonestly. Now quit sniveling and get back to your wagons." He followed, signaling Burek to his side. "We need to get these wagons and their cargo to Cortes Vonja. The brigands know it is their supply train; we can expect them to attack, even though their numbers are reduced. If indeed this is a widespread plot, as it seems, they may be able to call on neighboring bands. My first thought was to split the cohort and send you back with twenty or thirty . . . but it's a solid three days with these wagons, if you push the pace, and there are too many places where wagons are easily ambushed."

"So we're all going?"

"Yes. The question is what to do with those guards." He nodded to the little group under the tree. "Very likely one or more of them are part of the conspiracy, told to watch the merchant for any attempt to inform on it. The others may be honest or may not. I do not like killing men without cause just because they work for someone dishonest. Hunger drives men to many deeds they would not do if they were not ruled by their bellies. But the cohort is my first responsibility; a traitor among them puts all at risk."

"Are you asking me?" Burek said.

"I am thinking aloud," Arcolin said. "And you may have some ideas I have not thought of."

"Disarm them, bind them in the wagons?" Burek said.

"Disarm them, of course. Bind them . . . I had thought to have them walk, but then they could still call out to the brigands, if that was their intent. I don't want them in the wagons; they know where the secret compartments are, and they could rearm themselves."

"Wait—the poison they used on my horse—a little of that would make a man weak and slow, the surgeon said. Would a little of it in food do the same for them? Make them drowsy, even put them to sleep?"

"It might." Arcolin nodded slowly. "I'll speak to the surgeon on the way. We need to get these wagons reloaded and make a start—the longer we wait, the more chance of attack. I'll speak to the village headman."

The headman in this village was a stout gray-haired woman with arms that looked strong enough to handle a pike. Arcolin introduced himself.

"I thought you lot were the tax collector again, and we just paid the spring tax three hands of days ago," she said.

"No, we're here to deal with brigands, give you some value for that tax you paid."

She spat sideways into the street. "Value! The only value them in Cortes Vonja cares about is what lines their pockets."

"Tell you what," Arcolin said. "I must take the contraband with me, but I think some of it might spoil by the time it would reach Cortes Vonja. It's my choice, under my contract. Could you make use of some salt pork and a sack of grain?"

"We could make use of all of it," she said, staring at the stack of grain sacks and meat.

"I'm sure you could," Arcolin said, "but so could my men."

"What you want for it?" she asked.

"Nothing more than you've done," Arcolin said. "Maybe, some other day, some information on brigands in your area."

"What'll they do if they finds we tooken it?"

"I don't know," Arcolin said. "If you want, we can take it all with us."

She looked around at her villagers, whose expressions made it clear what they thought.

"We'll take it and thank you," she said at last.

Arcolin put two sacks of grain and most of the meat aside. "If I were you," he said, "none of this would look like what it is, by dark."

"Trust me for that," she said. Then, to his surprise, she bent and kissed his hand.

Soon the reloaded wagons were on their way north at the best pace the mules could manage on the soft road, the unhappy merchant perched on the driver's seat of the second. For the time being, the five guards, disarmed and hands bound, walked behind the wagons, closely followed by the rear guard.

Four wagons, two of them heavily loaded, made a mess of the road, which here was scarce more than a lane. At every turn of the glass, they had to rest the mules and horses. By nightfall they were abreast of the previous night's campsite. Arcolin shook his head and pushed on. That open field was too easy, when the brigands now knew its secrets. A few hours north, the road would firm again, even after the rain, and he hoped the brigands would be waiting, instead, at the place they usually got their supplies.

The jingling harness and grunts of the mules and horses, and the creak of wagon wheels made more noise than the soldiers afoot; Arcolin blessed the sharp breeze that came up just after sunset and blew the sound away west, where he hoped the main mass of brigands weren't. Moving at night was risky, but it was as risky for the brigands, and every distance he made north improved their chances of reaching Cortes Vonja without an attack.

Before the middle of the night, he halted them on the road, now firmer, to rest until dawn. Stammel came to him after they halted.

"Captain, that tall caravan guard, Kory—"

"What about him?"

"I think I know him; I think he's that bad recruit who poisoned Corporal Stephi, the one Captain Sejek had branded and whipped. That scar on his forehead could've been a brand. His name was Korryn then. Kory's close enough."

Arcolin had never seen the man; he started to say that there were many tall, lean black-haired men with scars, but this was Stammel. "Are you sure?"

"Almost, sir. None of 'em talked much, but he said nothing at all. He never looked straight at me, but little glances out the side of his eyes, like."

"Well . . . after he left he's none of our concern. If he's satisfied his employers—"

"That's true, sir, but I wonder who his employer really is. Not that merchant, I'll wager."

"He harmed Paks, I remember that—but now we think it was Venner who gave Stephi the drugged ale, not Korryn." Stammel said nothing. Arcolin sighed finally. "What do you think he's doing, then?"

"Nothing good, sir. And loose, he'll be eager to hurt us, for that punishment. There's hate in his eyes when he looks at me. Devlin thinks the same."

"He was there too, wasn't he?" Arcolin sighed again. "We can tell the Vonjans what we know of him, but we'll need proof. It's been—what?—five years or so?"

"Sejek used the sea-ink dye on the stripes, sir. Made sure it was in deep. It should show."

"Well. I'll tell the Vonjans, when we get to the city."

CHAPTER TWENTY-NINE

D awn revealed familiar country, thickets and brush to the east along the line of the stream, and rising ground, rough pasture, to the west. Arcolin allowed the cooks to make a hot breakfast; he drank his sib in the saddle, watchful. The five guards had caused no trouble so far, making no attempt to escape when taken to the jacks; they ate their porridge without comment. The surgeon had advised against dosing them, so Arcolin had their hands bound again for the day's march.

On the firmer ground, and after a rainless day, the road withstood the wagons' passage reasonably well; they passed the old night shelter by midmorning, and came to the village outside which they'd first camped. Suddenly a figure appeared, running for the woods; Arcolin waved his mounted scout on and sent Burek to follow. Shortly they came back with a bound captive, blood running down his face from a clout on the head.

"You criminals!" the man said. "You can't do this!"

"Evidently, we can," Arcolin said. Up close, he recognized the village headman. "You know who we are; you had no business to run from us—except to signal the brigands in those woods over there."

"I wasn't—I just saw a—a loose cow."

The scout—Arñe, today—sniggered audibly. "Didn't see a cow, Captain."

"You scared it into the bushes with that horse," the man said.

Arcolin dismounted, walked up to the man and leaned into him; the man flinched. "You are a liar," he said. "I have authority from Cortes Vonja to depose any village official I find in league with brigands. You lied to me before; I let it go, out of mercy, but this time— no. To Cortes Vonja you go for trial, and I do not think you will return."

"My—my wife—my children."

"You should have thought of them before," Arcolin said. "You have put your whole village in peril."

"They gave us half a ham once," the man said, hanging his head.

"I just gave sacks of grain and six hams to a village that stayed true," Arcolin said. The village hadn't been true, exactly, but at least they hadn't lied to him.

The villagers, creeping to the doors of their huts, hissed in wonder; the man groaned. Arcolin looked around; the whole village was probably complicit, but hearing of reward for good behavior, maybe they could find one honest man or woman.

"Truss him well and put him in the wagon," he said to Burek, then remounted. They were moving again shortly, and in another two days had reached the outskirts of Cortes Vonja without incident. Arcolin left Burek in command of the camp outside the city, and with a small escort rode in to deliver the news to the Council.

When he came back, he found a troop of Cortes Vonja militia drawn up outside the camp, their commander arguing with Captain Burek.

"What's this?" Arcolin said.

"We're here to take charge of the merchants' wagons and any prisoners," their captain said. "Your junior officer is refusing to hand them over, on threat of force."

"Quite right," Arcolin said. "Captain Burek has done what he ought. It is for the Council to decide who takes charge—"

"It's our duty," said the Cortes Vonja captain.

"Not this time," Arcolin said. "I've just been to the Council; their orders are that *we* escort the wagons into the city, to the Merchants' Guild Hall, for the legitimate cargo to be recorded and readied for delivery or transshipment."

"You don't trust us?" The captain bristled, turning red and gripping the hilt of his sword.

"I have no opinion of your trustworthiness," Arcolin said. "I but transmit the orders of the Council, as given to me but a half-glass since. Would you argue with your own Council?"

"I—no, but any levy on illegal cargo is ours, by right."

"That is a matter between you and the Council," Arcolin said. "As the contents of my contract with the Council is between the Council and me. Here—see the Council's seal on this?" He nudged his horse up to the other captain's mount and pulled out the freshly written and signed orders. The man scanned the page, scowling.

"It is most irregular!"

Arcolin shrugged. "I would not know. What I do know is that my orders came from the Council, as did my contract, and I am bound to follow them." He looked at Burek. "Burek, I want two tensquads for escort into the city, all veterans, and Stammel for sergeant. You will command the camp. I will send the escort back as soon as the wagons have been unloaded at the Merchants' Guild Hall—none of our men have leave to carouse. I should be back by nightfall, after reporting to the Council again."

"Yes, sir," Burek said. Stammel, close behind him, was already choosing his people.

Arcolin turned back to the Cortes Vonja captain. "We will not need your help," he said. "But I thank you for the offer."

"It is no matter of mine," the man said, "if the Council chooses to use foreign rabble instead of its own loyal troops." He turned his horse rudely, rump toward Arcolin.

"At least they can count on us not to run away," Arcolin murmured, remembering a particular battle that spawned at least two songs popular with mercenary companies.

"That was the Vonja militia, not Cortes Vonja," the man said over his shoulder.

"My pardon," Arcolin said, bowing slightly. "I misheard the story."

"You—!" But he legged his horse into motion, forcing his way through his own troops and calling "Follow me!" One near Arcolin rolled his eyes and shrugged. Arcolin grinned at him.

"They appeared as soon as you were through the city gates," Burek said. "Demanded the cargo, demanded the prisoners. I didn't know for sure—they were in the city uniform—"

"Cortes Vonja is not overfond of paying its debts," Arcolin said. "Duke Phelan had trouble with them a few times. I learned a lot about writing contracts as he revised his with them. Pler Vonja's as bad; Sorellin's actually reasonable, for a city run by merchants. Anyway— if their militia take charge of the merchandise and.contraband, the count would be . . . different, let's say."

"They'd steal it?"

"They or the Council proper. Say that half those swords didn't appear . . . the Council has the use of them, either for their troops or as raw steel to be reforged into the pikes they prefer. They're not likely to short the count of the actual merchandise, as our merchant is a Guild member, and at any rate it is not due us."

"What is due us?"

Arcolin grinned. "After much argument and complaint, I followed Kieri's lead and had the contract specify that all contraband weapons are ours, and five eighths of any other contraband . . . but everything taken from brigands is ours, without limit."

"Ready, sir," Stammel said. The merchant's wagons were hitched and loaded; Stammel had placed two on the driver's seat of each, two at the rear, with the rest surrounding the wagons on foot. The merchant, the five guards, and the headman from the village, all with hands bound, were on foot between the two wagons.

"Excellent, Stammel," Arcolin said. "We'll be off, then."

At the city gates, the guards were reluctant to let so many armed men in, until Arcolin showed his orders from the Council. As he'd expected, the appearance of that many uniforms in the city street opened a wide lane for them; though people stopped and stared, no one tried to come near the wagons on their way to the central square.

The Merchants' Guild Hall, on the main square and across from the Council Hall, had an inner court large enough for a dozen wagons— three were there already, unloading. Several of the Council were waiting when they arrived, and the Cortes Vonja Guildmaster came out of the Hall in his formal robes a moment later. Arcolin told Stammel to unbind the merchant and have him stand forth.

The Guildmaster examined the seals of the bales, boxes, and barrels, and called Guild servants to unload them. "Your record," he said to the merchant, who pulled it from under his robe and handed it over. The Guildmaster thumbed down the pages.

Arcolin turned to the senior Councilor present. "By your leave, I would send my soldiers out of the city, but for my personal escort."

"Indeed," the Councilor said. "They will need a pass at the gate—" He pulled out a tally and bound it with an orange ribbon. "There. You could go with them, and we could send you a report."

"No, thank you," Arcolin said. "I prefer to wait and be sure the captives tell the truth of our dealings with them." Though true, that was not his only reason: he wanted to be certain the cohort received its fair share of the bounty.

"Oh—of course."

Arcolin went over to Stammel, who had the tensquads waiting in formation. "Here's a token to pass the gate," he said. "Tell Burek to find an excuse to come looking for me in about two glasses, with an escort of five—that's the most they won't question. I have plans for those swords the Council may not like."

"Should he bring a wagon?"

"No. I intend to find a weaponsmith to turn them into spares for us, if the metal's good enough. I can hire a cart, but I want a guard."

"Yes, Captain." Stammel took the token, turned and barked an order at the troops, and they marched, boot heels ringing on the stone.

Arcolin sent one of his escort with his horse, to find a farrier.

"Is something wrong?" one of the Councilors asked.

"Loose shoe," Arcolin said. "It might hold another few days, but best get it done while I'm not on the road."

"Prudent," the man said, nodding his approval.

The tally of the merchant's goods took a full glass. At the end, the Guildmaster spoke to the Councilors. "This merchant has discharged his duty to those who entrusted goods to him; he has delivered all bales, all boxes, all barrels on his record, and by the testimony of this man—" he looked at Arcolin, "this is the same record the merchant had when he was accosted. Of clandestine cargo I have no knowledge."

"Then let us see," the Councilors said.

Arcolin climbed into first wagon. "If you come close, you can smell the meat," he said. They came, sniffed, and nodded. "As I told you, I gave some of the food to the village where this was found."

"How can you be sure they won't just give it to the brigands?"

"They were hungry themselves," Arcolin said, without mentioning the tax collector. "I expect they ate it all that night, or most of it. Send someone up and I will show them the latch to the false floor."

"Let the merchant show it," the Councilor said, sending a dour look to the merchant, who complied. Sacks of grain . . . sides of salt pork . . . piles of salted dried fish . . .

"This was not on your book," the Guildmaster said, scowling at the merchant. "You know the Guild's rules."

"Yes . . . but my family . . ."

"We are not here to hear excuses; we are here to determine the truth. You know it is forbidden to carry wares you have not recorded."

"And false-bottomed wagons?" Arcolin murmured.

"Oh, no," the Guildmaster said, aside. "That's not a problem. A merchant may be carrying treasure that must be concealed under another load, even as that load is delivered and another picked up. But it must be recorded and available to any Guildmaster along the way."

The mercenaries' share of the food came out remarkably evenly— five of eight bags of grain, ten of sixteen packets of dried fish, five of the eight remaining hams. Arcolin smiled to himself; he had gifted the villagers with an amount that made division later easier. The next wagon, packed with bundles of the curved swords, was another matter.

"Five-eighths," the Guildmaster said. And to the servants, "Unwrap those and start tallying."

"No," Arcolin said. The servants paused, confused. "By contract, all captured weapons belong to the Duke's Company."

"But you already have weapons."

"Yes," Arcolin said. "But by contract, those weapons, in that wagon, belong to me. And so do two of the mules and half one wagon, but I'm willing to trade that for four mules." The Councilors sputtered. Arcolin waited a precise moment and said, "Or their value, as of today, in the horse market. We can take them down and sell them, if you like."

"But—but—"

"It's in the contract," Arcolin said, sticking his thumbs through his belt and leaning back, the very picture of confidence. He had learned that pose from Kieri Phelan, and suspected Kieri had learned it from Aliam.

"You are as bad as Kieri Phelan," the senior Councilor said.

"I take that as a compliment," Arcolin said.

"And you have a copy of the contract and we have already certified that it is correct. Do you want half a wagon or the two extra mules?"

"Mules," Arcolin said. "We must get off the roads to catch these brigands—and that means pack animals."

"You killed twenty-three of them—how many do you think there are?"

"One for every one of those swords," Arcolin said. "And your merchant said he came through twice a year, not always with the same cargo. He avoided Andressat, took what he calls the war road. You might want to consider a permanent guardpost on these lesser roads."

"That will cost a lot," the Councilor said. "We could hire you for that, I suppose . . ."

"Not all year, and that's what you need. You can't stop a trickle of individuals coming in—not with the forest land you've got—but you could stop serious supply, by blocking the roads. That will force them to come to the villages for food, and when they do that, it'll be easier to catch them."

"What are you going to do with all those swords? They're not the style your people use."

"Depends on the cost to remake them to our pattern. If that's too expensive, I'll sell or trade them to one of the mercenary companies that uses a similar design, or have our armorer beat the steel into lumps and sell that. The steel's good enough; it's not the best, but serviceable for blades or tools. What I won't do is let them get into the hands of the brigands."

"Our troops couldn't use them?"

"Your troops use polearms. Their blades are daggers—daggers could be cut from these swords, I suppose, but the cost, unless you were credited with the value of the metal removed, would be high. As well, for close formation fighters—as your militia is, and as we are—the curved style of blade is not as effective. For brigands, it's ideal, if the quality's good enough."

"I'm sure any of our smiths would be pleased to work with you," the Councilor said.

"And if we have metal to sell, or need their assistance, I will certainly come here and not somewhere else," Arcolin said, answering the unspoken intent.

Burek rode into the Merchants' Guild court. "There you are, sir! I'm sorry to intrude, but I need your authorization—"

"If you'll excuse me—" Arcolin bowed to the Councilor, who nodded.

"Stammel said you'd need me," Burek said. "But I do have something for you. A packet all the way from the north." He pulled out a leather purse and handed it over.

Arcolin untied the cord that held it closed, broke the seal and unfolded it. Inside was Kieri Phelan's familiar handwriting. Arcolin scanned the first paragraphs, realized the letter was so densely packed with information he could not absorb it hurriedly. He glanced at the Councilors, who were obviously watching for something they could interpret, folded the letter back into its leather case, and nodded to Burek.

"You did right to bring me this. I will deal with it later; the immediate need is to secure our share of the goods seized. We have four pack mules; we will need a couple of carts just for the rest of the day."

"Right away, sir," Burek said. He looked at the mules, still harnessed to the wagons. "Which mules are ours?"

"The team hitched to the second wagon," Arcolin said. He had noticed that this team worked better together than the other and seemed less skittish. They were not matched in color—two were dark, one an odd pale cream color, and the last a flea-bitten gray—but their stride length was the same. The other team, matched seal browns, were not as efficient. To the Councilors, he said, "Those four—all right?" They nodded.

Burek turned to his escort. "Those mules—we'll be taking them."

"But not the harness," the Councilor said. "The animals only."

"All accouterments attached to their bodies," Arcolin said. "That includes harness."

"Sir! You—" began one Councilor.

Arcolin shook his head and the man stopped. "Be glad I don't consider the wagons accouterments attached to their bodies. The clause was written for just this situation: an animal without its saddle or harness is merely another expense."

The senior Councilor gave a harsh bark of laughter. "He has us there—I was thinking it meant halter and lead, but the way it's writ-ten, he's right."

"Go ahead," Arcolin said to the men who had paused, watching this exchange.

"Very good sir." The men began unhitching the mules.

"I'll go find us carts," Burek said.

"The far end of the market," Arcolin said, pointing. "When I was here before, I saw a row of carters down there."

"We use our own mules?"

"Yes. Pay the full rate, but explain we want to try out new teams. And if you find a couple of extra pack saddles at a good price, pick those up too."

In the time it took Burek to return with word that he'd arranged carts and pack saddles, the Guildmaster had called upon two other Guild merchants to form a jury to pass judgment on the guilty mer-chant. They had agreed with the Guildmaster—Arcolin wondered if they ever disagreed—that the merchant had broken the code in more than one way, and deserved to be stripped of his membership. They brought out a fat book—a list of Guild members—and literally cut his name out, with a small sharp knife. Then they ripped the badge off his robe.

"Your name will be removed from every list in every Guild League city," the Guildmaster said. "The penalty for falsely claiming Guild membership is public whipping and a brand. Do not think you can pass yourself off as a Guild merchant any longer. You are nothing to us, a mere peddler."

The man wept; Arcolin felt pity for him, but not much.

The Guildmaster turned away and went back into the Guild Hall; the Councilors told the city guardsmen to take all the men into custody.

Arcolin sent two of the men now holding mules to fetch the carts; Burek went with them. The others took the packsaddles, and, strip-ping off the harness, saddled them. The senior Councilor looked at Arcolin. "I thought they were soldiers—but they know the ways of teamsters and grooms?"

"Soldiering requires many skills other than sticking someone with a blade," Arcolin said.

"Our militia commander claims he needs grooms and teamsters as well as troops to move his forces about."

"I'm sure he does," Arcolin said, buffing his nails on his shirt. "After all, your militia are tradesmen and craftsmen who serve but two years unless there's a war, isn't that right?"

"Yes—but what has that to do with it?" The senior Councilor frowned.

"There's scarce time in two years to learn to handle a pike in formation, maneuver, and fight. We train recruits for a full year before they see battle, and they are with us, many of them, for the rest of their lives. All these can groom, saddle, and harness horses or mules; they all ride; they all dig ditches and build barricades."

"But that takes time away from weapons practice, doesn't it? Wouldn't they be better if they did that only?"

"No," Arcolin said. "They need all the skills I mentioned, and more, to do the work you hired us to do. A tailor does not merely sew cloth pieces together, like a housewife patching a shirt."

"True. So . . . how long will you stay in the city?"

"I expect to march again tomorrow morning," Arcolin said. "Unless more of the horses need shoes reset. If you have more questions for me, Burek can take them on, and I can catch up."

"What can you tell us specifically about these men?" the Councilor asked.

Arcolin shrugged. "The village headman knew about the brigands and lied—tried to tell us they had no problems and knew nothing." He told the rest of what had happened that day and night, and then why he had captured the headman.

"And you saw him—"

"We saw him run from the village as we marched back through, and captured him. He gave some tale about a stray cow; his excuse the first time was a stray bull."

"No doubt our city guard will hear about a stray calf," the Councilor said. "But the others? You said they were the merchant's hire; would they be complicit in his crimes?"

"They could be," Arcolin said. "They offered no resistance when we told them to stand aside, but few men, criminal or not, will oppose their single sword to a hundred. One I am fairly sure has a criminal past, the tall black-haired man with the scarred forehead—"

"Ugly brute," the Councilor said. "But I suppose that scar proves he's really a soldier, at least."

"Not if it's a brand that's been cut over to obscure the design," Arcolin said. "I never saw the man myself, but my senior sergeant, when he was on recruit training one year, saw a recruit branded for multiple crimes. My sergeant thinks this is the same fellow. If it is, he will not have changed his ways."

"How can we tell?"

"Have your guards strip him. If he has well-marked stripes on his back, not just white scars, that's a strong suggestion, with the scar on his forehead. It was a fox-head brand once."

"What about the others?"

"The merchant said he hired one, and that one hired the others. I didn't talk with them on the way here; as long as they didn't give trouble, that was enough for me. They were under guard the whole way. I'd talk to the merchant."

"Oh, we will. Now the Guild has withdrawn protection, we will have out of him whatever he knows."

"Indeed." Arcolin heard the noise of cart wheels and hooves. Burek came in, leading his horse and the men with the carts and the carter.

The men loaded sacks of grain and hams into the carts, and when the carts were full lashed the last bundles of swords to the packsaddles. "If you do not need me presently, I should get back to the camp," Arcolin said. I am at your service, should you call."

"Go on, then," the Councilor said. "We must examine the merchant and the others; we may send for you later today, and perhaps you would care to dine with the Council this evening?"

Arcolin rode back to camp well pleased with the day's business. The matter of the mules' harness had been an afterthought when he was working out contract details in Tsaia; he had not thought of harness, but of saddles and bridles. Still, "all accouterments, tack and the like, attached to the bodies of said animals" certainly did include harness.

His quartermaster examined the supplies with the suspicion of one who had found pebbles in the bottom of a grain sack before. "Mixed grain, sir. This here is wheat, right enough, but this other is spelt, and this is some grain I don't know. Not bread-quality grain, but should make mush of some kind."

"Not poisonous, though?"

"No. I think I saw that red grain in the far south, when we was here before, but I never tried it."

The salt meat and fish went to the cooks. The Duke's Company had never developed a taste for salt fish, so that, Arcolin decreed, would be used first. "Start it soaking," he said. "We have a river of water here, and it's a market day. Fish stew." There were groans, but only for effect.

To Burek, he said, "We need a good solid arms practice today. Basic drills, then file against file, then pairs of files. We're about one-third novices, and they tend to sloppy shield-work."

"Yes, sir."

"If they call me back to talk to the Council, I'll need a few for escort, but otherwise, make sure everyone cycles through. Those not drilling can work on camp chores. I'm going to be looking at those swords with our armorer."

When they'd opened all the bundles, they found a mix of blades, some new-forged and some obviously hard-used. Most were heavy blades with a slight curve, the type Arcolin knew as falchion.

"Good for cutting a way through undergrowth," the armorer said. "If we're going into the forest, these might be useful, though I don't like the lack of a guard."

"Can you put crosshilts on them?"

"Yes, but not as fast as a city smith with a full-size forge and some boys. If we cut up some of the worst and sell the metal, it'd pay for the new guards, if they're simple."

"How long, do you think?"

"Half-glass to a glass for each—another day or two here, for all of them."

"We can't stay here that long—we'd need a trustworthy sword-smith and I'm not sure I trust any of them in Cortes Vonja unless we were here to supervise."

The armorer grinned. "That's a captain's problem, that is. What about their militia armorer?"

"They'll charge enough to get the cost of the swords out of us. I need someone honest and reasonable. Well, let's look at the rest."

"This one's Halveric Company," the armorer said. "Same design as ours, just about, with that extra little curl to the guard and the H stamp on the pommel. Haven't found any of ours yet, and I'd better not. If Halverics were down this year, they'd pay us to get this back. They usually clean up a field better than that."

"Then it came out of someone's pay. Let's see . . . these are longswords . . . someone's officers? Do you know this mark, Captain?"

"Sofi Ganarrion's . . . he won't be happy about this. Well, unless it's to do with the marriage. Officers' swords, not the dress ones. Someone sold them to pay for something—gambling debts, like as not." Arcolin picked one up, tapped it with his fingernail. "Not bad steel at all, but Burek and I both have better. Might do for a spare."

"We don't want these, do we?" The armorer's face was drawn into a scowl of disgust, as he pointed to five jagged-edged curved blades with hooks at the tip.

"Gods, no! Hammer them into a lump and we'll sell the lump."

"Might want a Marshal or Captain to say a prayer over them first," the armorer said.

"That bad?" Arcolin leaned closer; a wave of malice made him stagger; the armorer caught his arm to steady him. "You're right. I'll send someone. We should get that taken care of tonight."

The rest of the weapons were daggers and some simple knives of various lengths, useful more as camp tools than weapons. "Knives to the cook tent," Arcolin said. "We'll let them decide which they want. That one"—he pointed—"is stout enough to cut leather; that could go in the tack kit. I'll see about getting us a Marshal."

He sent Burek on that errand, and went to his tent to read the letter from Kieri.

CHAPTER THIRTY

Arcolin sat in the folding chair, the letter on the table—Kieri's table, around which he and Kieri and Dorrin had sat so many times—and opened the letter.

My dear Jandelir,

Forgive the hasty note—all I had time to write and not all my thoughts—upon leaving from Vérella. I can think of no one better fit to take charge of the Company than you, my friend. I had never thought to leave it, but since I must, I know I leave it in the best possible hands.

I am certain that by now you have heard more of what happened, including the sacrifice made by Paksenarrion. I do not know when you will have reached Vérella or what news will then have been received there. She is alive and hale, beyond all our hopes. We were attacked by Verrakai and Pargunese before reaching Lyonya, nearly overwhelmed until my relatives, the elves, arrived. Yes, I say relatives and elves. You will understand how I felt when I found that my grandmother—my mother's mother—is an elf. All the jests I ever made have come back to haunt me.

My hope is that you found a contract and are receiving this in Aarenis. Should you have any problems with my banker or other persons with whom I worked, this letter should, in addition to what I sent before, be sufficient to prove that you are entitled to all that was mine. I mean that literally, Jandelir. My old life is over; I must commit to my new realm, or I will not do it justice. You can be trusted, I know, to deal justly with my—no, YOUR other captains and with those in my former domain—which I hope Tsaia will confer on you permanently.

You are ever welcome at my court in Lyonya, and if I can do aught to make this easier on you, you have but to ask. I think of you sitting at the same table, somewhere in Aarenis, reading this on a quiet evening—too hot, perhaps, for comfort.

Take care, old friend, and be not surprised by what may come. I never expected to be a king. Who knows what the gods will send you?

Falkieri Artfielan Phelan

Arcolin read the letter twice, feeling tears sting his eyes. Kieri had never expected to be king; he himself had never expected to inherit the entire company and domain. It was . . . ridiculous.

And yet the finality in the letter, Kieri's determined turning away, the lack of questions, of any request for information, made it all real. Kieri had gone away—for a good reason—and left him a gift worth— he could not guess how many crowns or natas. A gift beyond price . . . and the greatest part, Kieri's trust that he could—no, he would—nurture it as Kieri himself had done.

"Well," he said aloud, to the person who was not there. "I will do that. I will."

He refolded the letter and put it back in its case, tucking the case under the blanket of his camp bed.

Outside, he heard the sergeants scolding some hapless recruits for being lazy and slow with their shields. It had been days since he himself drilled; he walked to the area the sergeants had laid out.

"Captain!" Devlin called. Arcolin waved, pointed to the stack of bandas, and took one, shrugging into it, then put down his longsword to pick up a short one and a shield. The sounds died down; Stammel shouted at them, and the thuds and clangs speeded up again.

They had finished the warm-up drills and were well into file-on-file. Arcolin signaled Devlin, who made space for him on the second row and told one of the others to stand out. Short-sword formation work wasn't his usual way of fighting, but he practiced it regularly anyway—Kieri had done so, on the grounds that a commander might need to fight in formation in a tight spot. With only one cohort, that chance might come oftener.

"Shield position," Devlin muttered. Arcolin shifted his shield a hand to the left. Devlin called the front rank to drop back through the second; Arcolin managed the side-step to open ranks and then close again. Now he was in front; the front-rank center of the opposing side made a tentative poke at him, easily blocked, and Stammel yelled.

In a few minutes, Arcolin was sweaty and had two new bruises, one for missing a parry and one from holding his shield at the wrong angle. He could feel the mood of the cohort better this way—they liked it when the captains got dusty and sweaty, too, and they particularly liked it when they took some lumps. Devlin called a shift to the right; Stammel, anticipating, moved his group, too, but Arcolin saw an opening and gave someone—Tam, he saw—a hit in the ribs that would bruise even through the banda.

Then he heard Burek call his name; the sergeants called a hold, and the noise stopped. Arcolin moved out of the formation with a wave to Devlin; Burek and a Gird's Marshal were riding up to the drill field. Arcolin pulled off the banda, set the short sword and shield down, and picked up his longsword, sliding it into the hanger then wiping the sweat off his face.

"There's a rumor from up north that your Company's gone Girdish because a paladin visited you," the Marshal said. "I'm Marshal Harak, and we'd be pleased to see you at the grange."

"Not entirely Girdish," Arcolin said. "It's a long story. One of our soldiers—from this cohort, in fact—did become a paladin, but not everyone's Girdish. I put no pressure on anyone to change faiths, if their character's good. But there's a grange building back home, in the stronghold, and a Marshal living in Duke's West."

"That's good," Marshal Harak said. "Some things happened that last year of Siniava's War—"

"That none of us are proud of, yes," Arcolin said. "I'll not argue that. Did Burek tell you our problem here?"

"Something about bad blades—Siniava's, do you think?"

"I can't tell, but definitely evil. I felt the malice myself. We want to destroy them, beat them into lumps, but our armorer thought we should have a Marshal or Captain present."

"If the malice is strong enough for you to feel, then yes, you need help. Let us go."

In the armory, the armorer had set the bad blades far from the others, near his forge. He had a fire going and his tools set out.

"These are the blades, Marshal," Arcolin said.

"Bad blades indeed," Marshal Harak said. "You did well to send for me. Let us see . . ." He took out his Gird's symbol, freed the chain from his neck, and dangled the symbol above the blades. Arcolin was not sure, but fancied he saw a sickly yellow-green glow gather between the blades and the medallion. "Oh, that's nasty," Harak murmured. "Gird won't like *that*." Still holding the medallion, he held out his other hand. "Armorer, lay one of those blades on the anvil, and give me a hammer, if you please."

"Marshal?"

Marshal Harak grinned. "My father was a smith; I'm no master of the craft, but I know the use of a hammer."

"But the steel's cold." Gingerly, the armorer reached out with tongs, snatched a blade from under the steady swing of the medallion, and laid it on the anvil. Then he gave the Marshal a hammer.

"And Gird is not. We will need the fire, I know that, but this is more in the nature of the clout you give a mule or horse that's not paying attention, before you teach it." Marshal Harak lifted the hammer in his right hand. "By the strength of Gird Strong-arm, by the fire of the High Lord's altar, be still!" He brought the hammer down on the blade. It squealed like an ungreased wagon wheel; the blade jerked sideways, narrowly missing the Marshal's leg.

Arcolin shuddered; Marshal Harak laughed, repeated his abjuration, and slammed the hammer onto the blade again. This time it merely shivered and the sound was less, more that of someone shaking a saw blade. Again the Marshal prayed and hammered, and this time the blade lay still. The Marshal handed the hammer back to the armorer, took the blade, and shoved it into the fire. Then he picked up the next and repeated the process.

When he was through, he went to the bellows and began working them. "Your turn now," he said to the armorer. "I'll pump for you. If you were taught the Runes of Sertig, now would be the time to recite them."

The first blade was glowing. As its wooden handle burnt away, the armorer yanked it from the fire with tongs, laid it on the anvil, and hammered vigorously, muttering in dwarvish. The barbs and jagged edges sank back into the parent metal. When that blade cooled, he thrust it back and took another. When all were done, he took the first, bending it around the horn of the anvil and then pounding that bend flat. The Marshal meanwhile plied the bellows at the armorer's command, sweat pouring down his face, and talking in jerky phrases.

"Those had to be . . . Siniava's blades . . . special troops. If you'd heated them . . . the forge would . . . explode. Takes Gird's power . . . or Falk's . . . or a dwarf if you can find . . . to call on Sertig. If you find . . . more like that . . . must master the demon inside first . . . before the fire . . ."

"Will they explode an ordinary fire, a campfire?" Arcolin asked.

The Marshal nodded. "Ordinary fire . . . they fly out to kill. And the fire . . . goes wild. Buried . . . they work through . . . the ground . . . seeking blood prey." He coughed in a gust of smoke, then spat. "Siniava . . . was not a good man."

"Who put the demon in the iron, I wonder," Arcolin said. "What if someone is still making blades like these, though Siniava's dead?"

"That would be . . . most unfortunate . . . if you find such . . . send for me. Dangerous."

"The metal's safe now?"

"Only fire sprites like forge-fire," the Marshal said, stepping back from the bellows and wiping his face. "And Sertig, of course. These were pure malice, hammered into the metal by—I would guess—an artificer-priest of Liart." To the armorer, he said, "If you have other stout arms to pump the bellows, the metal's now safe enough without me here."

"Of course, Marshal," the armorer said. "I'm sorry, I just . . ."

"No apologies needed, but in a camp full of healthy young soldiers, I see no need to sweat longer than I must to let you work safely."

"Come out in the cool, Marshal," Arcolin said. "Have some refreshment."

"My thanks." The Marshal walked with Arcolin to the edge of the temporary drill field, where Burek was now organizing the troops for supper. "It's been too long since I saw these colors in the south. You and Halveric Company were the core of resistance to Siniava and even before that . . . the whole Mercenary Code, I understand, began with your Duke and the Halveric."

"Yes," Arcolin said. "Aliam had set out years before what he thought was right, and taught Kieri, so when Kieri formed his own company, that's how he fought."

"Well, I'm glad to see you back. I suppose with the Duke now king in Lyonya, the Halverics won't be back at all . . ."

"I don't know," Arcolin said. "My thought was that Aliam stayed in Lyonya this year for Kieri's coronation. He is older, though, and he might send a son with his company later."

"Or disband it, if he has no need for the money. You will need an ally, Captain, to maintain the Code; other companies have fallen away from it since Siniava's War."

"So I understand," Arcolin said, thinking of Andreson. The theft of the wounded man's death fund still rankled. "Golden Company will stand with us. I met Aesil M'dierra in Valdaire and we agreed."

"That's good. It was one thing in which you mercenaries led the militias, your Code, and I would see that way spread, if fighting must."

The Marshal refused Arcolin's offer of wine. "I am too hot," he said. "Small beer would suit me better, or water alone, if it was not drawn from the river."

"Not ours," Arcolin said. "We have no beer, but we do have good water." He himself dipped a jug of water and set out two mugs and the Southern flavorings: a lump of dark honeycomb, a box divided into compartments each with a different spice. "I, too, am thirsty," he said, "though I think drilling was not as hard work as what you did on the bellows. I should have called one of the soldiers in sooner."

"No, indeed." The Marshal had added a chunk of honeycomb, a sliver of dried lemon, and some dried mint to his mug, then poured in the water. He took a sip and smiled. "It was necessary that I control the bellows until I was sure the evil in the steel had vanished. As long as it was there, it tried to seize the wind and blow the fire into a storm. Gird strengthened my arms to resist." He drank again, and again, emptying the mug and pouring it full once more. "It was not hard to work the bellows fast enough—the difficulty was slowing and stopping."

"What then should we do, if we find more such blades?"

"They cannot catch fire by themselves; keep them away from it. Keep them away from other iron or steel; I do not know that the evil in them can spread of its own will, but I do not know it can't, either. They were near other steel in a wagon, were they not? When I've cooled off a bit more, I'll examine the other swords you found, and ensure that none of them are contaminated."

None were, but the Marshal noticed the Halveric sword. "That's unusual, isn't it?"

"Yes. Halverics were always careful with their arms."

"Hm. It's not new, either. What's this mark?"

Arcolin had not examined the Halveric sword closely, being more interested in the danger presented by the bad blades. The Marshal pointed out the small CH stamped into the undercurve of the flared pommel.

"A Halveric family member, perhaps?"

Arcolin's skin rose in goose-prickles. "Caliam," he said. "Aliam's son who was captured."

"Killed? Wasn't he the one at Dwarfwatch?"

"No. That was Seliam, his younger brother. He was killed, but his sword was recovered. Cal's sword wasn't."

"So it would have been one of Siniava's prizes?"

"Yes," Arcolin said.

"Hmmm. The Halverics are Falkian, are they not?"

"Yes."

"Then you should let me take it to the Captain of Falk here—have him bless it—before you return it to the Halverics. There's an aura of terror clinging to it—"

Arcolin looked away a moment, then met the Marshal's gaze. "No wonder. Caliam will father no more children. Our people found him beaten, bound, squeezed into a crate like a pig for market . . ." The old anger rose; he pushed it down.

"He fought bravely through the rest of the war, I heard," the

Marshal said. Arcolin nodded. "Then Falk would want him to have it back again, without the pain. May I?"

"Certainly," Arcolin said. "I'd intended to send it back to the Halverics in any case, but having it blessed by a Captain is a happy thought." He took the blade, found a clean cloth in which to wrap it, and handed it to the Marshal. "I should write a note to accompany it—perhaps if you stay to supper—"

"Captain!" That was Burek. "There's a messenger from the Council; they bid you to the city."

The Marshal laughed. "So much for supper," he said. "No, do not apologize. Shall we ride up together?"

In the long summer evening, they rode back to the city, Arcolin's escort behind them. The guards at the gate passed them through without question. "Where is the Field of Falk?" Arcolin asked. "Or is there more than one?"

"Only one; we outnumber them, with three granges. In the northeast quadrant, a little north of the east gates. My grange, should you wish to visit another time, is in the smiths' street, near the main market."

"I will do so," Arcolin said, "though I planned to march south in the morning; I will be back later. And here—I must make offering—" He reached into his belt pouch.

The Marshal held up a hand. "No, Captain. Not now. We worked together to defeat an evil; we did not exchange blows. Your contribution will be gratefully received another time, but not now."

"You certainly gave enough blows," Arcolin said. "That work—"

"Is well repaid by seeing good metal lose its evil taint. No, I know what Gird requires, and this day Gird requires no offering from you. Another time, I am sure he will." The Marshal grinned, touched his riding whip to his head and reined his horse down a side street before Arcolin could say more.

The Council had gathered in the Council chamber; Arcolin recognized most of them from years past. Another boon he owed Kieri, for Kieri had ensured that his captains—especially the senior captains—met senior officials wherever they had a contract.

"My pardon, sirs, for appearing in such disarray," Arcolin said. "We had a situation that demanded my attention all afternoon."

"And a Marshal's attendance, we understand," one of them said.

"Indeed so. Some of those swords we captured were spelled, with evil intent. Fortunately, my armorer noticed before putting them to the flame. Marshal Harak said that had he done so, a magical fire would have burned up the forge and killed many."

"Now?"

"Now, thanks to Marshal Harak, that evil is gone; those blades have been destroyed, and the metal is safe to trade, he says. But it took us some turns of the glass. I am in no fit state to dine with you gentlemen, so if that was the reason for your summons—"

"In part," another Councilor said. "And I for one will excuse you from that, if the others will." He wrinkled his nose slightly.

"I would as soon dine with a mercenary fresh from battle as with someone too dainty to stand the smell of honest sweat," said another Councilor angrily. He was a big burly man, probably, Arcolin thought, from one of the construction guilds.

"Gentlesirs," the chairman said, tapping a crystal bell with a little rod. "You will not quarrel here, surely. Captain, my pardon for our behavior. If you wish to dine here, and would prefer more formal attire, I am sure that among us we have both bathing facilities and suitable clothes. If on the other hand you prefer to return to your company, that is both understandable and acceptable to me—and I assume to all." He glared around the table; no one spoke. "Now, Captain, there are a few other matters of which we must speak. One is that fellow Kory. You say that you personally had not seen the man who received the Duke's punishment, but that one of your company had—by any chance, is that person one of your escort?"

"Yes," Arcolin said.

"The man insists he was never north of the Dwarfmounts. He does bear marked scars on his back, however, and it's clear the scars on his face come from multiple injuries. Yet we would not condemn him unless it can be proved. We would speak with that person who might have another way to recognize him."

Arcolin stepped to the door of the chamber. "Sergeant Stammel—" Stammel came into the room, calm as ever.

"The Council wants to know what you know of the guard we captured, Kory . . . you think he's really someone who was our recruit years ago."

"Yes, sir. Korryn, he called himself then. I signed him up myself, and wish I hadn't. Good swordsman, already an expert, tall and strong, a bit arrogant as young men are who learn early to handle a sword. Told me he was a duke's son's bastard and would've been acknowledged but that his mother angered the duke, who turned her away, with her son. That's how he got his first training, he said. Had been earning his keep as a door ward but wanted a real career."

"Did he say which duke?" Arcolin asked.

"No, Captain. He wouldn't say; said he'd promised not to. I liked that. Seemed to show a sense of honor. I was wrong about that. He was a complainer and quarrelsome. Sometimes we can train that out of them, as you know, sir, but this time we didn't. He was always bothering the women, wanting to bed them."

"Are you sure you recognize him? What makes you think it's the same man?"

"It's not just his size and hair—not even just the scar. He had a distinctive way of moving—especially when fighting, but even just walking or running. He gestured with his hand, something like this—" Stammel demonstrated. "—when he talked, especially when he joked about something. He had a way of sweeping his hair back with his left hand—" Stammel demonstrated again. "Aside from that, when we shaved him—for Captain Sejek had decreed he be *tinisi turin*, I remember a birthmark on his groin, left side I think. Small, dark. But what about whip scars—were they found?"

"Indeed," the chief Councilor said. "But he claimed he always scarred dark, and we do not know what the dye you used would look like after so many years."

"I gave him the last five lashes myself," Stammel said. "And I know exactly where I placed them."

Some of the Councilors shifted back in their chairs, Arcolin noticed. Stammel was not a large man, but every fingerbreadth a veteran soldier: hard-bodied, steady, with strength beyond the obvious muscles.

"Do you whip soldiers often in your company?" one of the Councilors asked.

"No, sir," Stammel said, answering before Arcolin could. "Recruits we mostly clout if they need it. Soldiers get their pay cut, and maybe a few lashes if they do something really bad. But what this Korryn did—plotting to get another recruit in trouble, putting some kind of poison in a corporal's drink, beating a fellow-recruit who'd refused to sleep with him and then lying about her—saying she'd attacked the corporal—that was bad enough for a whipping. Then he fought, tried to kill one of the village council. Bad enough to kill him outright, if he'd been a regular, but as he was a recruit he got off light."

"Doesn't sound like it," murmured one of them.

"Don't it, sir?" Stammel asked, head cocked a little. "He nearly ruined one of the best recruits we ever had—nearly got her condemned to the same punishment—and then Stephi, a corporal—got him in trouble, too. Stephi was so ashamed of what he'd done that he got careless, thinking of it, and was killed next campaign year. If it'd been my choice, I'd have killed him then and there. But Captain Sejek, he wanted an example made."

Arcolin didn't interrupt, but when Stammel finished, he said, "The recruit the sergeant speaks of is now a paladin of Gird. She fought three campaign seasons with us, including the last of Siniava's War. If she had been killed, I myself would have died in the north, along with the Duke who is now king—she, as a paladin, saved us, and she is the reason Kieri is now a king."

"That may be, but we must be certain."

"Of course," Arcolin said, with difficulty keeping the edge of scorn from his voice. He was convinced now, by Stammel's explanations, but some people were never satisfied by facts they had not themselves discovered.

In the end, Stammel and Arcolin followed two Councilors and several clerks to the city's prison. There, in the lamplit governor's office, Kory was brought before them. He looked the worse for wear, with fresh scrapes and bruises and one sleeve ripped to the shoulder; his hair had been tied back close to his head, so his scar was clearly visible. In daylight it had been just a mass of pale scar tissue, shiny. But in the lamplight, as he ducked his head, the shadows suddenly showed the shape of the brand under it all, the fox head.

Without waiting for permission, Stammel walked up to him. "Well, Korryn—you don't seem to have learned much in the past hand of years."

"You!" The man glared. "If it weren't for you, I'd have had a decent place in the world."

"You always were a braggart," Stammel said. "If you'd put the effort into honest work you put into bragging and bullying, you probably would have had a decent life. I'm not the one who made you a liar and a coward."

"I'm not a coward," Korryn said. "I'm just not stupid enough to bow and scrape to the likes of you." He spat at Stammel; Stammel put up a hand in time, looked at the spittle, and then wiped it down Korryn's own shirtfront.

"Your noble father—if indeed you had such—would not be pleased with his bastard," Stammel said.

"Would he not?" Korryn grinned suddenly, a different grin. "I think he would—" His arms struck out, the broken chains of his bonds smashing the two guards in the face, and then his hands closed on Stammel's throat. "I have looked forward to this a long time, Matthis Stammel."

Arcolin felt a pressure on him like a load of sand: he could not move. He knew at once it was some enchantment.

"It was my honor to serve as the body for one greater than I could ever be," Korryn said. "And to have an audience—that is best of all."

Stammel, Arcolin saw, could not struggle; his face darkened to a dusky purple, then bluish. Korryn dropped him, a limp heap, to the floor, then pulled a blade from one of the motionless guards.

"Which should I kill first?" he asked in a light tone. "The captain who never knew me and yet was quick to condemn? The Councilors? The guards? Such a puzzle . . . who will suffer most from watching others die and being unable to stop them? My pretty captain, I do believe—" He stroked Arcolin's cheek with the flat of the guard's sword. "But do not worry, Captain—before you die of shame, I will have my fun with you, too. I think the guards first, as they are such mindless cattle they might escape my spell."

He did not turn, but backed around behind the guards, slitting the throat of one; blood sprayed out, soaking Stammel's body. The other, he gutted from behind, slowly, watching with obvious delight those who could not move to stop him. "In favor of my lord Liart, and my lord Ibbirun, I give this blood and this pain," he said. "May they grant me power to serve them better." He dipped his hand in blood and then walked around, smearing blood on all their faces.

"I think one of you must become my next body," he said. "And I think—looking at these flabby merchants, and the paunchy governor of this prison—it must be you, Captain. It closes the circle, you see. To have *you* become the secret enemy . . . that is a sweet revenge indeed, even though he whom you injured—the man you *thought* you injured—gave his life to me, I will revenge him."

Arcolin, consumed by horror, prayed to every god he knew for help. It was as the prince had described; he could not move at all. Did that mean Korryn was a Verrakai? How could that be? He felt his muscles straining against the smothering force. The prince had been rescued by the unexpected arrival of a friend, but no one was likely to interrupt the Council questioning a prisoner in the prison governor's office.

Korryn bent over the governor's desk and drew the sword tip across the governor's forehead; blood dripped down into the man's eyes; he could not blink it away. "Your guards are disgusting," he said. "Your cells are disgusting . . . *you* are disgusting." Korryn's back was turned; Arcolin struggled harder; struggled to get his hand to his sword hilt, but he could not, though he did feel his fingers trembling against his trousers. Korryn sliced the governor's cheek, talking all the time, his tongue as fast as the blood running down.

Then Stammel, blood-drenched, crawled out of the welter of blood and guts, dagger in hand, and stabbed Korryn behind the right knee. Korryn screamed; his leg collapsed and he fell sideways, clutching at the desk. In that instant, Arcolin could move; he drew his sword and struck through Korryn's neck before anyone else moved. The head rolled off the end of the desk and hit the floor with a wet thump. Arcolin wrestled his sword out of the edge of the desk.

"I said he bragged too much," Stammel said, his voice raspy. Two great bruises stood out on his neck.

Behind Arcolin, two of the Councilors had fainted, untidy heaps on the floor; the other, gasping but still conscious, staggered to the wall and slid down it.

"You're—"

"Alive," Stammel said. "The governor . . . ?"

Arcolin looked at the man now slumped face-down on the desk, moaning. "We need a surgeon," he said. Opening the outside door, he called for guards and surgeon, heard shouts in answer, and turned back. Stammel had pushed himself to his feet; his expression now was blank; his eyes stared at nothing.

"Stammel?"

CHAPTER THIRTY-ONE

"I can't—don't let it— Stammel lurched forward. "He's still—he's in—NO!" His eyes showed red, where they should be white, red as fresh blood; he fell into Arcolin. Arcolin tried to hold him up, but the guards' blood on him was slippery, still wet; Stammel sagged, falling to the floor just as more guards arrived from outside.

By now the Councilors had roused; one managed to stagger outside, retching. Another stared wide-eyed at Arcolin, unable to answer the guards' questions.

"Prisoner got loose, killed the guards, attacked the governor and my sergeant," Arcolin said. "I killed the prisoner. Surgeon for the governor; he's cut but should recover. I need another for my sergeant—" Under his hands, Stammel burned as if with fever, his muscles shivering.

"But how did it happen?" the first guard asked, looking around. He had a sergeant's insignia but seemed too confused to direct the others; they all stood in a huddle, like sheep startled by blood smell.

"Get the Councilors out of here," Arcolin said. Nobody moved. "*You!*" he said to one of the guards. "Help that man outside. Yes, that one. You!" to another. "Help the one in red." To the sergeant he said, "Did you call for a surgeon?"

"Uh . . . yes . . . sir . . ."

"Then get more guards—you need to clear this room so the

surgeon can work on the governor. Get a Marshal, too—Marshal
Harak, in the smiths' street."

"A—a Marshal?" The sergeant was still staring around as if dazed,
though the two men Arcolin had spoken to had obeyed. Arcolin
stood up abruptly; the sergeant flinched.

"Sergeant! Wake up! Did you hear me?"

"Y-yes, sir!" The sergeant's eyes finally focused.

"Tell your men to clear this room of bodies and blood," Arcolin
said. "Send one for more guards and a Marshal." But one of the
guards who had helped a Councilor out was now yelling outside; he
could hear a distant clamor of running feet. The sergeant gave a
shiver, then began giving orders, sensible enough, if slow. Arcolin
knelt beside Stammel again. Stammel's eyes were open and he was
breathing, but he did not respond when Arcolin spoke to him.

More guards arrived; a surgeon followed. "Get that dead man out
of the way," he said to Arcolin. "All that blood, he can't live."

"It's not his blood and he's not dead," Arcolin said. "He was strangled, but not killed; it's the guards' blood."

"He looks dead," the surgeon said. He reached down gingerly. "He'll
be cooling by now—well, he's not. That's odd. He's probably going to
die, though, from the looks of him. He's in my way; move him."

Arcolin stared at him, too angry to speak for the moment, and the
surgeon gestured to two of the guards.

"Come here and drag this fellow out of the way."

"Stop," Arcolin said; the guards stopped as if struck on the head.
He glared at the surgeon, who was already bending over the governor, ignoring him. "Fetch a door or something," he said to them. "My
sergeant is not dead, but injured; he doesn't need to be dragged."

"Yes, sir," said one. They both left and came back with a plank three
handspans wide and half again as long as Stammel. "This do, sir?"

"Yes," Arcolin said. He took Stammel's shoulders and head himself, and helped the men lay him on the plank. "Lift him," he said. He
took his hanger and scabbard off his belt and used the belt to lash
Stammel gently to the plank. "Give me your belts," he said to the
guards, and added them around Stammel's chest and legs.

"We wouldn't have let him fall," one said, scowling.

"I think he's been spelled," Arcolin said. "If he starts thrashing,
the belts may give time to set the plank down."

"Oh . . . spelled. Well, then . . . where to?"

Where to indeed? Arcolin had no idea where to, other than Marshal Harak's grange. He picked up his sword in one hand, the hanger and scabbard in the other and followed them outside. In the square, others were gathering—guards, citizens—and the councilors, recovering from their shock in the soft evening air, were talking rapidly to one another. He heard hoofbeats, wheels grinding, axles squeaking, and a carriage drove into the square. The councilors looked up at the noise, and saw him.

"Captain!" Councilor Janchek came over to him. "You saved us all! We cannot thank you enough—" Janchek looked at the men with the plank, at Stammel's bloody body. "Your sergeant—he died, then?"

"He's not dead yet," Arcolin said. "And *he's* the one who saved us all—he distracted Korryn enough to weaken the spell that bound us. I need that carriage—" He pointed.

"But—but that's the chairman's carriage—and he's—he's all bloody—"

"He's worth more than any carriage ever built," Arcolin said, grief and rage swamping deference.

"Sir—Captain!" His escort, left behind at the Merchants' Guild Hall, came jogging into the prison courtyard.

"Gird's grace!" Arcolin looked them over. "Vik—take my horse; ride at once for the camp and bring our surgeon to Harak's grange. Smiths' street. Tam—find Marshal Harak's grange. Tell him we're coming there. If you see him on the way—just find him. It's Stammel; he may die." Those two took off at a run, no questions asked. The other two moved over and took the plank from the local guardsmen. "Orders, sir?"

"Into the carriage with him."

The Councilors in their cluster made no more complaint; Arcolin only realized he still had his bloody sword in hand when he tried to climb into the carriage.

On the short drive to the grange, Stammel's condition didn't change. Still that fixed unseeing stare, still the heat rising from him as from a stone left in the sun.

Marshal Harak was waiting outside his grange, Tam beside him. "What is it? What happened?"

"I think it's a spell," Arcolin said.

"And what about you?" Harak asked. "You're soaked in blood."

"Not mine," Arcolin said, as he helped lever the plank out of the carriage. "And not his. Korryn—or whatever was in Korryn's body—tried to strangle him. He fell. We were all spelled helpless; we couldn't move. Korryn killed the guards—that's the blood and gut stench—and Stammel crawled out of that welter when Korryn's back was turned and stabbed him. That broke the spell for a moment; I killed Korryn. Then Stammel—" His voice shook; he fought to steady it, and told the rest.

They had Stammel in the grange by then. Harak pulled two benches out, bade them lay the plank across the benches, and called for his yeoman-marshal. "You say he said something was trying to invade him? And he was refusing?"

"That's what it sounded like to me," Arcolin said. "But it was just those few words."

"I think you're right," Harak said. "And I don't like it. This Korryn you speak of—" His yeoman-marshal came into the main part of the grange, drying his hands on a towel. "Wait a moment," he said to Arcolin. And to his yeoman-marshal, "Eddin—we need water, a lot of it, and towels. And bring the relic over here, if you would."

Eddin, Arcolin was glad to see, was no youngster, but a steady-looking man who might be thirty or so. "Yes, Marshal," he said, going first to a niche in the far wall and coming back with a small knife—a stone blade in a wooden haft. Then he was off at a jog, buckets hung on a pole across his shoulders, to the well down the street.

"Now tell me," the Marshal said. He had laid the little knife on Stammel's forehead and put his hands on Stammel's shoulders.

"Korryn was a recruit we had years ago—" Arcolin began. He repeated what Stammel had told him.

"Tell me about the attack."

Arcolin related it in as much detail as he could; Eddin came in with the water in the midst of that.

"Stop a bit," Harak said. "I want to keep contact with him, but we must get this blood off him. You all must strip him, and then wash him of all this. I will hold his head; we'll wash that last, when I can hold his shoulders."

During that bloody business, Arcolin held his tongue. They unbuckled the belts that held Stammel to the plank, unfastened his clothes, peeled them back, and then, with the help of the Marshal and yeoman-marshal, turned him side to side to get them off without having to cut them. Under the clothes, much less blood, but Stammel's skin was flushed as if with sunburn and hot to the touch. His muscles still trembled; his eyes were still open and blank, the whites blood-red. They washed him, front and back, careful to clean off every smear of blood.

"Now his head," the Marshal said. "Eddin, place the relic on his breastbone, right over the heart, and do you take your place across from me." Without ever taking his hands completely off Stammel, the Marshal moved to his heart-hand side, and Eddin to the other; they knelt, heedless of the bloody water on the stone floor. Arcolin took a clean towel and bathed Stammel's face, his hair, cleaning the blood out of his ears, the crease at the back of his neck. The bruises from Korryn's grip showed dark against the red of his skin. "Be sure to get the blood off the plank," the Marshal said. "We're going to move him to the platform when he's clean."

Arcolin wanted to ask why, but instead wiped the plank with a fresh towel.

"Good. Now—we all go to the platform. Slowly, so that Eddin and I can keep our hands on him. You, Captain, keep your hand on his forehead as they carry the plank."

As they neared the platform, Arcolin felt something—a cool touch of some kind—on his skin; he shivered. He felt struggled, fearing it was another evil attack; the Marshal glanced up at him. "Gird's grace, Captain. It is but Gird's grace; do not fear."

"I—I didn't know—"

"After what you've been through, I don't wonder. Everyone step up, now, and do not be alarmed if it makes a noise."

The platform made no noise, however. "Now, Captain," the Marshal said. "We need a sheet from the back—there's a narrow corridor with doors to small rooms. The third on the left is clean linens. Bring us two sheets, if you will."

Arcolin found the linen closet without difficulty and brought back two clean, folded sheets that smelled of the fresh herbs kept with them. At the Marshal's direction, he laid one on the platform; the others lowered the plank until they could slide Stammel off onto the sheet.

"Do you know what's happening?" Arcolin asked. "What bespelled him?"

"If that fellow Korryn was invaded by a demon—if he invited one in, for some reason, and he seems the sort to do so—it might be seeking another host. Stammel, weakened by injury, would be easiest."

"Korryn said something about willingly giving up himself to one greater than himself," Arcolin said.

"That would be a demon," the Marshal said. He slid his hands up to Stammel's head and cradled it. "You go where I was, Captain. Both hands on his chest, above and below the relic. You others—" he said to the two soldiers. "One of you take each an ankle. What we need now is the power of those who love this man. He refused the invader; he is still trying to fight it off. We must help. But if he loses the fight, Captain, you must be ready."

It took Arcolin a long moment to understand; he felt the blood draining from his face. "You don't mean—kill him? Kill my own sergeant?"

"If the demon wins, we must. You and I both; you with the sword, and I to ensure the demon invades none other."

"But surely you can save him—you, the relic—"

"I hope so. I cannot promise. Demons do not die when the bodies they take over die. Sometimes they fade, after a while, and if the person is strong enough, in body and will, then . . . but usually with some residual injury."

Arcolin stared down at Stammel's face, the face he knew so well . . . the absolutely reliable sergeant he had depended on for so many years. All that honesty, all that courage—could it be lost so easily, and would he have to—his mind shut that out. "Stammel," he said, as if Stammel could hear. "Matthis . . . don't give up. We're here."

"He's not Girdish, is he?" the Marshal asked.

"No. He follows Tir."

"When your people arrive, we'll send one of them for a Captain of Tir. Keep talking to him, Captain, as if you expect him to hold a position. He may hear you; it cannot hurt. You others as well, or if you can, pray for strength for him. I will add my prayers."

Arcolin leaned close; he could feel the heat rising from Stammel's body. "You are the best, Stammel," he said. "You are the one we all rely on. Hold now—hold hard. I trust you, Stammel; you will not give up; you will not let evil win. If Paks were here, she would say the same. You trained a paladin, Stammel; she knows you are the toughest and best . . ." He murmured on.

It seemed an age before Vik arrived with a tensquad and the cohort surgeon, who immediately began giving orders. "Two of you—get this mess cleaned up at once," he said. "You see buckets; you saw the well. Now." Just like every surgeon he'd ever known, Arcolin thought. The surgeon came up to the platform, bowed, and stepped onto it. "What's amiss here?"

"A spell, possibly a demon trying to get control of him," Arcolin said. "The Marshal hopes he'll have the strength to withstand it long enough." He looked past the surgeon and said "Vik—the Marshal said to find a Captain of Tir."

"At once, sir," Vik said, and turned on his heel.

"Those bruises were made by hands," the surgeon said. He pulled down Stammel's jaw. "His tongue's swollen." From his bag he pulled out forceps and grabbed Stammel's tongue, pulling it forward. "At least he'll get more air. What a fever! Not natural, you say?"

Arcolin glanced at the Marshal, whose eyes were closed, and answered instead. "No. It began when I killed the man who choked him."

"Um. Heat promotes swelling; we need to cool him, especially this throat." He touched it gently; for the first time Stammel groaned. "I'm sure it does hurt, Sergeant," the surgeon said, as if Stammel were conscious. "You're lucky you have such muscle here—a finger's breadth to the side, and you'd be dead for sure. I need clean water, clean cloths."

Arcolin told one of the others where to find the linens.

"I don't deal with magery," the surgeon said. "No physical wounds other than the throat?"

"None," Arcolin said.

"That's good, but this fever . . . I don't know how to counteract it other than cool wet cloths. And I don't know what cooling will accomplish. Some fevers need to run their course. Ah—" He took the towels and water the troops brought, wet one, waved it in the air to cool it, and laid it on Stammel's throat. "And we must close his eyes— they'll dry too much this way." He pulled the lids down and weighted them with a wet cloth. Arcolin felt relief at the disappearance of those blood-red eyes, yet he hated the sight of Stammel with a bandage like the blind wore.

"Here's the Captain of Tir," Vik said from the entrance, now darkening as the evening drew on.

The Captain, in the usual black cloak, the iron symbol of Tir at his breast, bowed as he came into the grange. "Peace to this grange," he said in a deep voice. "I ask Gird's grace to enter."

The Marshal opened his eyes. "Gird's grace to you, Captain, and my thanks for your arrival. We have here one of yours, in the grip of a demon, I believe. A brave man, who saved others this day, and now lies stricken."

"He does indeed." The Captain hesitated before mounting the platform and bowed again. He knelt beside the Marshal. "How long has he been like this?"

"Since early evening," Arcolin said. "The man who was the demon's host strangled him and left him for dead before killing others he'd spellbound. But Stammel was not quite dead and struck the blow that lifted the spell from us; I beheaded the fellow . . . but then apparently the demon attacked Stammel."

"Stammel," the Captain said. "He is known by name to many of us as a soldier of good repute. It would be dire indeed if he fell to a demon."

"Can you save him?"

"I do not know. I will try; it is up to Tir—and Gird," he added, with a nod to the Marshal.

"By your leaves," the surgeon said. "*I* would treat this fever with cool water."

The Marshal and Captain exchanged a glance; both shrugged. "It cannot hurt, I suppose," the Captain said. "But if it is a demonic fever, I don't expect it will help, either."

"The gods made bodies to follow certain rules," the surgeon said. "If it is clear thinking and determination he needs to resist the demon, he will do better if he is not burning with fever. Fever drives men out of their minds; it is how we are made." With that, the surgeon set up a relay, whereby he handed hot cloths from Stammel's fevered body to those who passed them to the door, where they were dipped in the coldest clean water that could be found, then brought back, waving in the breeze to cool them more, and laid on again.

Arcolin went back to talking, encouraging Stammel with everything he could think of: memories taken from their years fighting
together, reminders of times Stammel had held a line, prevented a
rout, answered one demand after another, always faithful, always
steady, dependable . . . he knew the Marshal and Captain were
praying, knew the surgeon was doing his best to cool the fever,
knew vaguely that his troops, across the grange, had finished cleaning, scouring the stones, then drying them. Some had come to the
platform to pray with the Marshal.

Evening slipped into night; someone lit candles around the grange.
Those who came to stand in the doorway murmured to the troops, and
then more came, and more. The slow dark hours passed with all of
them working over Stammel, with Stammel—as Arcolin could sense—
fighting to hold off what fought to take him over. Arcolin's back ached;
his knees burned from the platform, but he dared not shift his position.
Anything he changed might be the wrong thing, might lessen Stammel's will to fight. Stammel's lips were dry and cracked now; his
tongue, held forward by the surgeon's forceps, looked unnatural, a fis-
sured dry stone. The surgeon reached over and squeezed a little water
onto Stammel's mouth. His tongue glistened a moment then looked dry
again. The surgeon squeezed a little more, enough that a tiny trickle
ran down the back of Stammel's tongue. His throat moved.

"That's good," the surgeon said, as if to himself. "Now I can try
more . . ."

Arcolin realized that the surgeon had done this before, but he had
scarcely noticed. Now he met the surgeon's eyes.

"If I can get water into him, it will help with the fever," the man
said. "And you, Captain—you look like half a demon yourself. When
did you last drink something or move?"

Arcolin shook his head. "Doesn't matter," he said.

"Oh, gods take the lot of you," the surgeon said crossly. "If Gird
and Tir can't save him, you kneeling there turning into a lump of
stone won't do it. You need to move, and you need to eat and drink
something."

The Marshal and Captain had turned to look at the surgeon when
he spoke; they now looked at Arcolin, at each other, and nodded.

"You must," the Marshal said first. "You have the cohort to look
after. Let someone else take your place, and refresh yourself."

How could anyone take his place? But he saw Vik, sober-faced, and Tam, and others who knew Stammel as well, if not for as long as he had. He nodded, realizing then his neck was so stiff he could scarcely nod, and motioned to Vik, as the nearest. Vik helped him up, and then knelt in his place; Arcolin staggered, coming off the platform, and his people caught him, held him, thumped his shoulder.

"Bathing room and spare clothes back there—" the Marshal said. "Water, bread . . ."

Arcolin made it back to the bathing room, where a butt of water sat on its stand, the spigot over a shallow tub with a plug in the bottom. He stripped off his filthy blood-stiffened clothes, and dipped a half bucket of water over himself. The cold water woke him up; he took the lump of soap on a ledge and washed carefully—blood contained tiny demons, the surgeons always insisted, that brought disease. Then a rinse, then out to pad wet-footed across to the Marshal's own rooms—the small office, the simple bedchamber with its clothespress. Coarse gray trousers, too short for his long legs. A blue shirt that looked too big for the Marshal—perhaps it had been inherited. It was long enough for his arms, but twice as wide as he needed. A soft lump that turned out to be gray woollen socks with a hole in one heel, rolled into a bundle. He sat on the Marshal's bed to pull on his boots, and realized he had not cleaned them. He walked out to the main room carrying his boots and his filthy clothes, sock-footed, feeling the chill of the stone through the hole in that left sock.

The surgeon turned to look at him. "Did you eat? Did you drink something? Did you visit the jacks?"

He'd forgotten that. He started to drop his clothes and realized he had no idea where the jacks was.

"Back corner," the Marshal said, anticipating his confusion. "And your surgeon's right. Eat. Drink."

"Here, Captain; I'll take those." One of his troops—Bran, he thought—took his boots and clothes, and patted him on the shoulder as if he were a tired horse. He felt like a tired horse. He turned back to the side passage, found the jacks and used it, found water and drank a little, found a half loaf of bread and managed to haggle off a piece because he'd left his dagger, with his belt and all, out in the main room.

His imagination revived, horribly, with the water and food; he saw himself having to tell the troops that Stammel was dead, and by whose hand . . . having to tell Burek . . . having to find another sergeant, only no one, no one in the world, could replace Stammel, not really.

No one can replace anyone.

He jerked upright, eyes open, only then aware he'd slumped over the little wooden table in the Marshal's tiny kitchen. How long had he slept? Was Stammel—? He tried to get up but could not.

Rest. You are not the only one.

Rest? He had no time to rest. And only one what? But even as he tried to rise, darkness came over him again.

When he woke, it was to hear voices nearby, voices he should know, but could not understand at first. Gradually sense came back to him. He was no longer at a table, but stretched on a bed; daylight came through a window, morning light by its color, by the feel of the air. He opened his eyes. Overhead was a plain plastered ceiling; the bed wasn't his—wasn't in a tent, but in a room, in—in the grange? He looked around.

"Sir." That was Devlin, by the door, red-eyed. Arcolin felt his heart sinking; he wanted to close his eyes and be somewhere else.

"Yes," he said instead. "I'm sorry—I fell asleep—"

"He's still alive," Devlin said. "Still fighting. But Captain Burek wants to know if he should start the cohort on the road today." He cleared his throat. "I—we brought you clean clothes. There, sir."

"Right," Arcolin said. He pushed himself up. The clothes were on a chair; his boots were clean and polished; his sword—no doubt clean—in its scabbard on the hanger on the belt. Sleep had done its work; he was awake; he was not as tired. He ached, nonetheless, in ways he had not known he could ache. He went to the bathing room, stripped, poured another half bucket of water over himself, dried, and dressed again in uniform. Went to the jacks, came back.

"Sir, are you going to stay—?"

Arcolin shook his head. "I cannot. We have a contract; I cannot neglect the rest of you—you are *all* my people, not just Stammel. Gods know what Stammel is to this cohort—to the whole Company— but you know what he'd say—"

Devlin said it, in a mock-Stammel tone.

"Right," Arcolin said. "And Dev, I can't let you stay either. You're the only active sergeant now; I need you. We'll leave some here, to help out. One corporal—which?"

"Arñe," Devlin said at once. "Because she was Paks's good friend. It might help."

"Good. Is she here?"

"No, sir."

"I'll send her. We can't afford to leave a whole tensquad: pick five. Range of ages, anyone with good stories to tell."

In the main grange, five of his people were around Stammel, along with the surgeon, a different Marshal, a different yeoman-marshal, and the Captain of Tir. "Where's Harak?" Arcolin asked, just as Harak appeared in the entrance, with a third Marshal.

"I'm glad you slept," Harak said, before Arcolin could say anything. "If you'll trust us, I swear by Gird and the High Lord we will care for him. Everything. He's still fighting; the fever's a little less, your surgeon says. I think we've convinced him we'll keep up the cooling cloths. They do seem to help a little. The Councilors came by, wanting to talk to you, but I sent them away. You'd been in a fight · yourself—"

"Nothing like his," Arcolin said.

"If he recovers," Harak said, "it will be several tendays—perhaps as long as Midsummer—before he's fit to return to you—if he can. I will send word, if there's anything—"

Arcolin went to the platform again. Seli was at Stammel's head, whispering to him. When he saw Arcolin he moved aside; Arcolin laid his hands on Stammel's head—would it be for the last time?— and said, "Stammel—old friend—hold that line! Hold it, until the enemy's gone. I will be back; I swear it. Friends are with you."

"I have Girdsmen enough for the chores," Harak said. "Your people are needed elsewhere, but for four or five, if you can spare them, to keep talking to him, reminding him who he is."

"Yes," Arcolin said. "Sergeant Devlin—your choices?"

"Corporal Arñe, Little Tam, Bald Seli—he's here, Doggal, Suli—she's only a first-year but she was promoted in that fight—"

"I remember," Arcolin said. "Good choice. So we have someone here to watch with him now, and we'll send the rest back. Marshal, I thank you for your hospitality, but I cannot let it stretch to feeding and housing five of my soldiers without compensation." He dug into his belt pouch and pulled out a handful of natas. "Here's a start; I'll stop by my banker on the way out and make sure he knows you can draw on the account as you need. Captain—" The Captain of Tir looked up. "My thanks, and Stammel's, for your prayers." To the rest of his people, Arcolin said, "All you Phelani but Bald Seli, come with me now. Time to go—"

"Sir . . . !" It was more protest than anything else. Arcolin shook his head at them. "Could he be in better hands? Can any of us pray like three Marshals of Gird and a Captain of Tir? Stammel will have our prayers as we do our duty; he will have five of the Company with him at all times. Sergeant Devlin has chosen them well. Form up!"

His horse, rested, fed, saddled, stamped outside; Vik held the rein while he mounted. "Devlin—take them back to camp; tell Burek to start out. Once more I must finish a few things in the city before I follow."

"Sir, with all due respect . . . put your helmet on this time."

Arcolin unhooked it from the saddle and put it on, fastening the chin strap. "Thank you, Sergeant," he said, torn between grief and pride. "You're absolutely right." At the end of the street, he turned toward the street of moneychangers, and heard his men marching away.

CHAPTER THIRTY-TWO

I t was noon before Arcolin made it out of Cortes Vonja. In addition to visiting Kostin the banker, where courtesy demanded he accept a glass of cordial and nibble a few of the seed-crusted cakes while ensuring the Marshal would have access to Company funds, he had to visit the Council chambers once more. They insisted on having one of their clerks take down his story of the previous day's events and were inclined to blame him for not warning them of Korryn's magical abilities. He set them straight, and they finally agreed that he could not be blamed for not knowing what they and their guards had also not seen.

Now, in the heat of midday, with the sun beating down on his helmet, Arcolin set his slower mount off at a steady amble. He had left the speedier chestnut in the city, for his people to use if they needed to contact him. The cohort was long out of sight; they would be—if Burek had them moving as briskly as he hoped—between the first two villages.

Away from the city, the countryside was just as hot but smelled better. Fat cattle grazed in the water meadows near the river; beyond that, a patchwork of grain fields in brilliant greens, orchards in darker colors now the flowers had fallen. In a few, early cherries were turning color, red as blood. Along the hedgerows, brambleberries flowered in shades of pink and rose; boneset and heal-all raised their white and blue clusters; myriad other flowers—yellow, pink, red,

blue—made the hedgerows a ribbon of color. Arcolin noticed the
beauty, but his mind was fixed ahead on the cohort and behind on
Stammel.

Within a half-glass, dust showed where the cohort might be, just
beyond the village he could see. His horse pricked its ears and quickened its pace a little. Arcolin squinted, but could not make out the details under the dust. He heard nothing; the wind blew across the
road, not along it.

As he came to the village, no one fled. A woman hanging washing
on the bushes outside her cottage barely looked at him; children ran
beside him a short way, then went back to whatever they'd been
doing. It was too hot for the two dogs he saw to give chase; each
barked from its own resting place under a berry bush, but without
getting up.

Now he could see a little better . . . wagons, with horses tied behind. Burek had mounted scouts out on the flanks, as he should; at
that distance, he could not see the colors, but the formation was
enough. In spite of his worry about Stammel, his heart lifted. This
was his place; these were his people; of course he had to be here. He
nudged his mount out of the amble into a canter. The guards on the
rear wagon raised a shout . . . and then he was within easy hail.

"Yo, Captain! How is he?"

Arcolin reined in. "The Marshal thinks the fever may have
dropped a little. Where's the surgeon?"

"Asleep in the first wagon, Captain."

"Good. And the others—?"

"The same. Captain Burek said he wanted them ready to fight
later." The slightest tone of uncertainty there.

"Exactly right," Arcolin said. He lifted the reins, and his mount
picked up the fast amble again, past the first wagon, past the pack
mules loaded with sacks of grain, past the cohort—smaller than it had
been—Devlin alone at the head of it, and then Burek, on his roan.

"Sorry it took me so long," he said to Burek as he came abreast of
him. "First the bankers, and then the Council. Would you believe
they thought it was my fault Korryn attacked? When they were the
ones who'd insisted on an examination?"

Burek shook his head. "Vonja," he said.

"Yes, indeed. I'd rather deal with Foss Council any day."

"How is he, sir?"

"Still fighting," Arcolin said. "Three Marshals and a Captain of Tir are with him; they've pledged the resources of both grange and camp to do everything they can. I don't know—" He took a breath. It would not help Burek or the cohort to hear him say they could not go on without Stammel. He should not even think it. "I've been thinking about who to make temporary sergeant and corporals. With Arñe back there, we're short on both. I'll talk to Devlin, of course, but I wanted to ask your thoughts."

"Mine?" Burek looked surprised, then thoughtful. "I haven't been with them long enough, is my thought. Let me think. There's Jenits . . . he's always right there, doing what he should and more. Volya's another good one, but you have many good troops. And I'm not sure—besides that—what to look for."

"You're on the right track with Jenits," Arcolin said. "It's not just being good with weapons, or obeying orders. We have long-time veterans who are steady as stone in a battle, reliable when someone else is giving the orders, but will not stir themselves without. What we need in corporals is someone with the potential to be a sergeant, and what we need in sergeants is someone who can see what needs to be done and do it—or know who to tell. It's not age and experience; you find youngsters with the ability to see and the will to do, and older ones too. We may not have formal battles this season, but if we did you'd see that our sergeants and corporals also keep order in battle. Exhorting, encouraging, reminding recruits what commands mean. So they must be steady, able to stay calm in any situation."

"I don't think all companies choose them that way," Burek said, frowning slightly.

"No, they don't," Arcolin agreed. "But it works for us, and it worked for Aliam Halveric. Some companies won't let women into those positions, which is silly. One of the best sergeants I ever had— no shame to Stammel—was Dzerdtya. She didn't want to be a captain, she said when offered the chance at knight's training, but you could not ask a better cohort sergeant. We saw that in her from the first tenday of her training."

"She retired?" Burek asked.

"She died," Arcolin said. "At Dwarfwatch, along with my junior captain Ferrault. She and Stammel I would place at the top rank.

Different personalities, but everything you could want in a sergeant."
And the cohort had survived Dzerdtya's death; it would survive
Stammel's, if that came to pass.

"My father said I was crazy to become a soldier," Burek said. "He
was content as horsemaster, and thought I should be, but I said you
could die of a kick to the head or a bad fall."

"Crazy or not, I'm glad to have you here," Arcolin said. "You did
well keeping the cohort in order while I was in the city."

His horse threw up its head; so did Burek's roan. Arcolin raised his
hand and signaled halt; behind him the cohort stamped its halt; far
behind, two horses snorted. One of the forward scouts came into
view, waving for attention. Arcolin checked his flanking scouts; both
had halted, waiting for orders. He waved to the forward scout to
come in and report.

"Captain—that village where we took the headman—the brigands
must've attacked. There's smoke—looks like two cottages burned—
no sign of that herd of cows."

"They probably attacked the night after we went through," Arcolin said. "Any sign of the villagers?"

"Could be bodies on the lane, I didn't go closer to count."

"They massacred the whole village?" Burek said.

"Probably not," Arcolin said. "Probably killed a few, took a few
prisoner to do work in their camp, and sent the rest away with
threats. They want to scare their food supply, not destroy it." He
looked at Devlin. "Devlin, come up the road with me a bit."

Out of earshot of the cohort, he said, "We may be fighting later
today or tonight. Who do you want for sergeant and corporals?"

Devlin shook his head at first. "None of 'em's ready to be
sergeant—but I have been thinking—"

"Well, think faster. They may have set up that village as a trap and
it's less than a glass away."

"Yes, Captain. In that case . . . Jenits as sergeant. Kef and Sim as
corporals. They're all young, so they won't mind being bumped back
when we're back to normal." His look at Arcolin pled for reassurance
Arcolin couldn't give.

"Or when we have more time to consider," Arcolin said. "Good
point. Go tell 'em; let them know it's temporary." So far, he told
himself.

Devlin pulled Jenits up to the front, then Kef and Sim, and told them what they'd need to do as they continued on to the village. Arcolin sent additional scouts out.

They all smelled smoke now, wisps of it still rising from ruined cottages. The headman's cottage—a ruined heap. The one next to it, and the one across the lane, also burned. Heaps of rags that were, as they neared, clearly bodies . . . three men . . . four women . . . two children. The other cottages, still whole, were tight-shuttered in the midday heat. A trampled track across the young grain showed which way someone had come and gone.

Arcolin raised his voice. "If anyone is hiding here: Your former headman is under sentence in Cortes Vonja for aiding the brigands who did this to you. You have no safety here while the brigands prosper; you should go to the city, or a village where you have relatives."

No one answered, but he was sure there were listening ears, whether villagers or brigands.

"Do we follow them?" Burek asked.

"Not where they want us to," Arcolin said. "They've had plenty of time to set up a good ambush on land they know far better than we do. We'll go on south and then cut east where I hope they won't see us doing it. But we will bury these bodies and make sure the village well's clean. Someday people will live here again." He looked at the sky. "If we do all that, we might as well camp in the village tonight."

By nightfall the dead had been decently buried, and timbers and stones from the ruined cottages arranged in a barrier to protect a perimeter around the remaining buildings. Arcolin insisted on checking inside each of the cottages. "Not for survivors," he explained to Burek. "For brigands waiting to attack us." They found neither people nor food.

Somewhat to Arcolin's surprise, they were not attacked that night, and made an early start the next morning without incident. They passed through the village where they had found the merchant and his wagons before; the headwoman grinned at them and waved as they approached.

"We have one friend," Burek said.

"As long as we bring gifts," Arcolin said. "You ride on; I'm going to talk to her."

"I knew you'd come back," she said, when he reined in beside her and dismounted. "What did them in the city do to that fellow with the wagons?"

"The merchant? Threw him out of the Guild. Confiscated his wagons and his merchandise."

"Them brigands is mean, angry folk," the woman said.

"Angry?"

"Yesternoon, it was, when they come riding down the road like a pride of princes. Smelled of smoke and death; I had all my people hidden. Said they was hunting the one as told the Fox army—they mean you—how to find their supplies." She grinned wider. "I told 'em you didn't need anyone's help; you'd done no more than walk past the wagons and you knew about the false floors."

"Did they find the gifts?"

She shook her head. "Gifts, my lord? I never saw no gifts, nor did anyone else. Nobody gives us gifts; the tax man takes away and so do them villains, I told 'em so. They looked in my house, walked in like they owned it, but o' course I have nothing of theirs." She leaned close. "We had full bellies that night, my lord, all the mush even the childer could stuff down, and our hogs had the rest. Wasn't a single extra grain here when they searched, nor anything but what they expected. And it was good warning you gave us, not to store any. They was looking for that red southern grain in our jars—stirred every one and found only what we grow here, wheat and spelt."

"When did they come?" Arcolin asked.

She thought a long time, spreading one hand to touch her fingers, then shaking it to cancel the count; he wasn't sure she knew how to reckon days. Finally she said. "It wasn't the night we feasted, or the night after, or the night after that, but the next day."

"Thank you," Arcolin said. "And now—do you know where the outbounds of Vonja are? We're bidden to stay within them. Is there another village within the bounds farther on this road?"

She shook her head. "I don't know, my lord. There was one before Siniava's War, but I heard it had been destroyed, and I haven't left here since I got back. There's our hog-wood just to the south of us— and there's a sort of ford over the creek in about a sunhand's walk, but your wagons may have trouble with it. The pigherds say someone should have repaired it. That other village was most of the day's walk at one time."

"Perhaps we should look," Arcolin said. "Thank you, for your time. I am sorry I have no grain for you this time—but this—" He handed her two of the copper coins southerners called pages.

"Thank you, my lord. You was kind before and these'll hide easy, if them brigands come back."

Beyond the village, the lane deteriorated even more as it led into the woods. The wheelmarks of the merchant's wagons showed clear, and old ruts with them, but certainly wagons passed this way only a few times a year. Soon the trees shut out all sight of the village behind. The road twisted back and forth as they climbed a low rise. Around one turn, they came on a sounder of swine, the herdboy trying to prod them off the way, but two were intent on something on one verge, rooting determinedly, and the boy's stick made no difference to them. A prick from the tip of Arcolin's sword was another matter; with an annoyed grunt, the two trotted off down a woods path after the others; the boy gaped at Arcolin, then ran after them.

Down the other side of the rise, they came to the stream the headwoman had mentioned, the remnants of a gravel ford now scattered by many a spring flood, and mucky holes on both banks. Rough-trimmed timbers along both sides showed how the merchant had managed to get his wagons across. But with only seven men altogether? Arcolin rode out into the stream and looked upstream and down. On the right bank of the stream, a game trail wide enough for humans ran alongside the stream, and when he looked closely—yes, rain-softened boot marks.

"Checkpoint," he said to Burek. "The ford's been deliberately made more difficult. They'd meet the wagons from the south here—check the cargo—help them across—and then meet them again at that village—must be closer to their camp." He chewed his lip, trying to think out the logic of it. How was the merchant paid? Wait—those two sacks of coins he'd found in the false-bottom of the first wagon, under the sacks of grain. They had not been marked with the seals of the Moneychangers' Guild. Would a merchant carry so much of his own money after he bought goods and before he sold them? Arcolin had first thought of that money as a bribe . . . but if the brigands hadn't taken it—why not? What if, instead of a bribe, the brigands had added it to the load?

"Burek, when I was in Valdaire, my banker told me some Guild

League cities had started minting bad coins. Did you hear anything about that?"

"Yes, sir." Burek rode his horse into the ford. "M'dierra's company got some; she was furious. It was while I was with that cohort in Andressat. She had the rest over in Cilwan, and her banker refused about twenty percent of the payment. She had a row with the Count of Cilwan—it was Cilwan-minted coins the banker refused—and the Merchants' Guild came in on his side, until the banker gave a public demonstration. The coins were counterfeit, all right. The natas were the weight of nas, lead-cored. The Count blamed merchants for bringing in counterfeit, swore up and down his mint was honest. The merchants were furious and blamed the Count; the Moneychangers' Guild backed M'dierra's demand for the rest of her pay. But Cilwan's not the only mint to turn out bad coins—there's been complaints of other mints, too."

Arcolin felt stupid. "I should have looked at our merchant's coins more closely. They looked fine to me, but now I wonder—why was he carrying so much money, not as an agent of the Moneychangers' Guild?"

"Were they all southern mint?"

"I didn't even see that," Arcolin said. "Some were gold, some silver . . . I did see a Cortes Vonja mark on a few on top."

"Seems unlikely all the mints would start minting bad coins at once," Burek said. "Though it's a way to stretch a treasury until people figure out there's plenty of money and few goods."

"But . . . if someone else were making the false coins—sending them to various cities—that would cause trouble, as in Cilwan." He looked around. Nothing to see, nothing to hear but the gurgle of water over the ford. "Alured, I'll wager. He wants the Guild League broken; he knows it financed the last war . . . if the cities war against each other, if the merchants can't trade as they have . . . he could move in with more than brigands."

"I don't see why he isn't happy with a dukedom," Burek said.

"Nor I," Arcolin said, with a sigh. "And our immediate problem is these brigands and tonight's camp."

Burek flushed. "Sorry, sir—"

"No—that wasn't a correction. Thinking long-term is what made Phelan successful, but while thinking long-term we must not lose track of today's duties. Let's get these wagons across—we may have to unload them—and try to reach that village—ruined or not— tonight." He cast a last look at the bootprinted game trail before turn- ing to the cohort.

Devlin's choices as junior sergeant and corporals had already shown their ability and energy in the previous night's camp. Now Jenits in particular pulled almost equal weight to Devlin. Arcolin, re- membering the brash youth of Jenits's first campaign year, the last of Siniava's War, watched the serious, determined young man organize his two files quickly and get the second wagon unloaded even before Devlin had the first one ready to cross. And it was Jenits who sug- gested using the spare horses and the four mules to move cargo across the stream alongside the wagons.

More quickly than Arcolin expected, they were across, the wag- ons reloaded, and on their way. The next village site, when they came to it, looked clearly deserted—the cottages no more than tum- bled stone walls pierced by saplings and weeds. It had backed on the woods, with fields before it . . . fields now growing up in weeds and bushes, even young trees. The village well, surprisingly, had a few flowers, barely withered, on its curbstone.

"Someone uses this," Devlin said. "And it smells clean."

"Dip a bucket," Arcolin said. The wellhouse and axle were gone, but the stone edging was remarkably clean. Someone was maintain- ing this well—someone who cared about the *merin*. The bucket came up with clear water that smelled fresh. Arcolin dipped a handful— it tasted as clean as it smelled.

He took the bucket and walked around the well, pouring a thin stream. "Thanks to the *merin* of the well, for the good water," he said aloud. "We honor the Lady and her handmaidens. No harm will come to this well by our use." Then he turned to Burek and Devlin. "We'll camp here tonight. A solid defensive perimeter. When my tent is up, I want to talk to both of you."

While Devlin organized the camp, Arcolin rode out into the fields a short way, weeds brilliant with yellow, blue, and white flowers up to his horse's belly. Ample cover for a force to approach on that side, the old furrow ridges and hollows concealed by tall vegetation. He saw no sign of disturbance, off the wagon track, but with the thick growth he knew he could miss such signs easily. He rode across the wagon track and there, near the forest edge, found a well-traveled footpath running just along the margin, between field and wood. Well-traveled, but not by many, and the only footprint he found was bare.

In the last year of Siniava's War, he'd seen the like: peasants driven from their villages, eking out a poor living in the edges of woodland, hiding from everyone. A clean well would be a boon to them. And such people would not welcome brigands any more than soldiers. If he could convince them to talk to him, he might save the cohort time and blood.

He rode back to the camp, now bustling as his people dug a ditch, cut stakes, and laid out the campsite itself. All were at work but the sentries and the scouts he'd assigned to patrol beyond the perimeter, even Burek. As he dismounted, he caught a glance from Devlin; he nodded, tied his horse to the tail of a wagon, and went over.

"Problems, Sergeant?"

"Not exactly," Devlin said. "But—I have a feeling."

"So do I," Arcolin said. "There's a lot more going on than some brigands bothering farmers or merchants. Is the feeling about this place, or more than that?"

"I wish we had two cohorts," Devlin said. "Or all three. Marching through the woods today—I don't know, sir, I just—it's been a long time since I felt like we were a small group."

"We are a small group," Arcolin said. "For what it's worth, I had the same feeling. I'm half inclined to go back tomorrow, just patrol in the open land closer to the city. But I think it's as much having Stammel gone, and the five we left there, as real danger. You're having to bring along juniors faster than ever and we're down six, including a sergeant and a corporal."

"I know we've lost only one in combat," Devlin said. "It's just . . ." He shook his head.

Arcolin clapped him on the shoulder. "We'll talk when camp's made."

As soon as the camp was set up, Arcolin called Burek and Dev into his tent. "We're in over our heads," he said quietly. "There's much more going on here than some leftover homeless peasants and soldiers from Siniava's War."

CHAPTER THIRTY-THREE

Cortes Vonja

Matthis Stammel burned in a fire that had no beginning and no end. It had been before he could remember. Voices he dimly remembered called on him to hold a line he could not see, to stand in the fire, to endure . . . Don't give in, they pled. Don't quit. Young voices, older voices . . . he had no way to answer them, to ask what, why, who? Something—some*one*—dire held him down in that fire, someone who demanded that he give in, give up, let go, die. Someone who promised ease and rest if only he would retreat.

He fought with every fiber of will and strength to do what the voices asked, but the other one, the interior one who needed no voice to speak, demanded surrender. He wanted to ask the captain . . . ask the Duke . . . if he couldn't please, just for a moment, have someone else take his place. He had not heard their voices for a very long time. The last thing the captain had said . . . the captain trusted him. The captain trusted him to hold.

He could feel his flesh burning away to nothing, the blood in his veins bubbling. His breaths, when he was aware of them, burned his throat; fire blazed in his lungs. Why am I not dead? he cried silently. The unspeaking one in his mind promised he would be, dead and cold, if only he would surrender. It was too much, too long, for anyone to endure. The unspeaking one agreed, offering hope, offering a dream of green grass, shade, cool water, if only he would let go, let the other take control.

He was so tired, tired of the pain, tired of the struggle. Wherever this was, whoever the enemy was, no man lived forever; no man could fight forever. The voices he knew faded, returned, faded . . . one came again, a girl's voice, trembling, begging him . . .

"You promised to tell me more about Paks," she said; he could barely hear her over the crackling that was his bones in the fire.

Paks. What Arcolin had said. What the girl—he struggled to think past the burning, past the pain, past the pressure that bore in on him, the dark presence that held him down—who was the girl? Paks had—had gone into the thieves' lairs, in Vérella . . . she had endured five days and nights. How long had he endured? Forever, the dark presence told him. And it will go on forever unless you yield. He struggled—was it really forever? The girl was still murmuring to him. "The Marshal says it won't last; the demon's weakening . . ."

Demon? Was it a demon he had inside him? Stammel strained, trying to see, feel, somehow know what—who—it was. Fire—fire and smoke, and a shadowy something, the first actual, visual image of his enemy. Pain seared him, worse than ever, but this time he had a focus; he concentrated not just on holding on, but on attacking, pushing back at it. He still did not know how or when it had come, but he was not—*not*—going to fail the Duke, or his captain, or Paks or his other recruits.

He heard the voice more clearly now—not Paks, but another of his recruits—he could not think of her name or see her face, but he knew he had known them. Flames licked him again, white-hot as always, and he cried out. This time he heard himself cry out, felt the hands that held him . . . and something cool and wet on his burning lips, his parched tongue. The pressure inside swelled, but this time, as he fought it back, it retreated a little. He reached out, in that shadow-world of fire and smoke, grasped at it, and squeezed . . . squeezed as it struggled and fought in its turn, as it shrank, shrank to the size of a wasp—and with one last bone-piercing pain, stung like a wasp and was gone.

Silence, after the roaring of the flames, but for the very human voices he heard around him. The pain . . . was gone, as if it had never been. He could feel some hard surface under his back, wet fabric on his body. He was cool at last—too cool, cold and wet and shivering suddenly in reaction.

"Fever's gone," came a gruff voice. "And he's breathing."

Stammel took a breath. Easily, as if it had never been different, cool air moved into his nose, filled his lungs. No burning. No smoke. Hands touched him, gentle hands pulling away the wet cloth, drying him, laying something soft on him.

"When do you think he'll wake?" came the girl's voice, from somewhere near his head.

"I don't know," the gruff voice said. "And I don't know what he'll be like when he wakes. That fever alone—that many days—such fevers can leave men reft of sense and speech."

But he was not senseless. He did not know where he was, or when, or what had happened, but he would know—he would remember—he was sure of that.

He tried to speak, to say that, and though he felt his tongue move in his mouth, the sound that came out was a rough, animal noise, nothing like words.

"Let's see if he can swallow," the gruff voice said. "Lift his shoulders, one of you."

Someone held his head; someone else slid a strong arm under his shoulders and lifted him to rest against a living, breathing human. A cup came to his lips; water flooded his mouth. He swallowed, swallowed again.

"That's good," the gruff voice said.

"Sergeant—it's me, Arñe," said another voice, older than the girl's. "Are you all right now?"

"Of course he's not all right," the gruff voice said. "He's been battling a demon for days. Let the man rest . . . we'll get him to a bed now . . ."

Stammel felt himself being turned, lifted, carried somewhere . . . he didn't care, as long as it wasn't flames. He slid into sleep without realizing it.

W hen he woke again, he could hear someone breathing in the room with him. He felt clean, rested—a sheet lay over him; he moved his legs, and whoever it was stirred. "Sergeant? Can I get you something?"

It must be night, it was so dark, and they had left someone with him—and it had been dark before. He must have slept the day around. But fear ran a cold finger down his spine.

"A light, first," he said, rejoicing in the sound of his voice—his own voice, sounding like himself, and ignored the fear.

The hiss of indrawn breath told him a truth worse than fire. He felt himself trembling, tried to sit up and could not. "It's not . . . dark . . ." he said.

"No, sir," the girl said. "It's broad day outside, and—and I must tell the Marshal you're awake." Her feet scraped on the floor—a stone floor, by the sound.

"Wait," he said. He was not ready to face anyone else. "Is there water?"

"Yes, sir. Just a moment." He heard the small sound as she picked up a jug, then the water falling from the jug to a mug—clay by the sound—and then her footsteps coming to the bed. It had to be a bed; her footsteps were below him, and the surface felt like a bed. "I—I don't know—"

"Take my hand and put it on the mug," he said. This close he could smell the familiar uniform; she was one of theirs, a soldier. Probably a first-year, from her nervousness. Her hand on his was firm, callused—definitely one of theirs—and she pulled it up, set the mug firmly in his palm and waited until his fingers gripped before she loosened her grip, but only to guide his hand toward his face.

"Should I lift your head?" she asked. He could hear the tension in her voice.

"Probably," Stammel said, trying for a lightness he did not feel. "Or I may spill it." His arm was trembling with the effort—he hoped that was the reason.

She lifted his head and guided the mug to his lips. He drank, a cautious swallow first, and then drained the mug. "That was good," he said. "Now tell me—what happened? Where are we?"

"The Marshal said I shouldn't tell you things," she said.

He remembered Paks saying something about her time in Kolobia, how annoying it was when people wouldn't explain. "Perhaps you should find the Marshal, then," he said. She eased her hand out from under his head, set the mug back on something—a table?—with a little clunk, and went out. The door was on his right . . . her receding footsteps told him of a passage.

A current of air from his left suggested a window; the smells with the air—rotting vegetables, human filth—meant a city. Had he caught a fever and been left behind? But he knew better than to drink tainted water or eat the foods most likely to give men fevers.

He tried again to sit up, but he felt dizzy and sick. He lay back, feeling for the side of the bed, for the wall. He had these few moments—for he heard heavier footsteps, booted footsteps, coming down the passage—to prepare himself, to master the turmoil he felt.

"Suli—your private—said you were awake. I'm Marshal Harak. I saw you at your camp, but we did not meet."

Harak. The name meant nothing to him, but a memory came of the Marshal who had come for the Captain, and later ridden away with him . . . and he himself . . . he had been . . . the memory faded.

"Suli said you could not see."

"It's dark," Stammel said. His voice was firm, at least.

"I'm going to look at your eyes," the man said.

Stammel felt the warmth from his body, the breath on his face.

"Your eyes are bloodshot, as if you'd been slugged," Marshal Harak said. "They were like that when your captain brought you here. Do you remember anything about that?"

"No." Stammel struggled with a darkness as black as the flames had been white. "Only the fire. White . . . hot . . ." Sudden nausea twisted his gut. "I—I need the jacks—"

The man called out; other footsteps came running; the man's strong arm heaved him up and another grabbed his arm and put it over a shoulder. The two men half dragged him out . . . through another door, to a room he could smell. He heaved, felt the stuff come out his mouth, smelled it, felt the splash on his bare chest. Again . . . again . . . they supported him; he was too weak . . .

When that was over, they wiped him down with wet cloths, and carried him back to the room . . . he could still feel his own warmth on the bed when they laid him down. "Drink this," the Marshal said, holding the mug to his lips. This time the water had some herb in it, not numbweed's bitterness but something . . . he wasn't sure.

"You're alive and sane," the other man said. His was the gruff voice he'd heard before—how long before? "I am Verstad, a Captain of Tir, and I tell you, soldier, you have fought long and bravely to come through so hard an ordeal. Though your captain brought you here, the Marshal has granted me the right to tend you alongside Marshals—"

"I'm in a . . . grange?" Stammel said.

"Yes."

"Gird has no quarrels with Tir," the Marshal said. "And your captain said you followed Tir."

"I do. I . . . did." Stammel struggled to keep his voice level. "But if I am blind—"

"Tir does not despise the wounded, and that includes the blind," the Captain said.

"But I can't fight—"

The Captain grunted. "You fought off a demon without sight or movement . . . I would not call you helpless."

"I . . . don't . . ."

"If you remember anything, now or in the next days, it would be good to tell us about it," Harak said. "We know only what Captain Arcolin told us happened, not what happened inside you."

Stammel lay still a moment. "I want to know why I can't even sit up."

Again Verstad grunted. "That would be because you lay for days in a high fever without eating and with only the little water we could drip into your mouth, the flesh melting from your bones: your clothes would be loose on you now. Anyone is weak after a long fever. You will have to rebuild that muscle."

"I must—I have to be able to get to—to the jacks myself!" He hated the sudden whine in his voice, as he lost control of it, his diaphragm seized in a cramp.

"You must eat and drink first," Harak said. "Has the nausea passed?"

"Yes." One word at a time he could manage in close to his normal voice.

"Then we start feeding you. Or rather, your own soldiers will. And you consider giving thanks, Matthis Stammel, for your captain's quick wit in bringing you here, and the days and nights your own people have watched over you."

"I—do. I am . . . I am just . . ."

"Mazed, still. Very well. We'll see what some good meals do for you."

The others were all embarrassed; he could hear it in their voices. Suli alone was not, though still clearly timid with him because of his rank. He finally asked her why his blindness bothered her less.

"My uncle Saben," she said. "He was kicked in the face by a cow; he had an infection in one eye that spread to the other—it nearly killed him—but after, when he decided to live . . . he was still my uncle, you see. He still knew everything he had known. He could still tell when one of the animals was sickening, by the sound of its walk, or its smell, better than my father. The dogs knew his whistles; I would take him out to the hill, and tell him where the animals were, where the dogs were, and he'd work them the same as ever. And you aren't even scarred as he was."

"And now that you've left home? What does he do now?"

"My little brother, who has no desire to leave the farm, is learning his whistles and goes everywhere with him. You did not think I would leave before I was sure—?"

"No. No, Suli, I know you would not. I'm sorry."

"It is hard, the first year, my uncle said. He thought of finding a ledge, and stepping off into the air. One night he went out into a storm, when everyone else slept. He was sure he knew how to feel his way to the cliff, even in the storm . . . but the gods led him round, and his dogs found him, herded him just like a sheep, nipping his heels when he faltered. I remember waking the next morning and we all went out to look for him—there were his tracks, around the cow-byre and then in . . . he was in the straw, with both dogs on top of him."

"So you will not let me find a ledge—not that there are many in Vonja—" Stammel put the thought of bridges and the Immer-est's swift current out of his mind. Suli would be disappointed in him.

"*You* would not go looking for ledges," Suli said. "Not a sergeant in the Duke's Company."

In the night—the true night, not the night of blindness—the dreams and memories came. He was not always sure which was which. When the grange was quiet, and the night breeze changed the scents that blew in, he lay, sometimes dozing, sometimes truly sleeping, sometimes wakeful. Now he remembered most of the day it happened, remembered the soldiers drilling, the trips in and out of the city with Arcolin. He could almost see the.faces, the places. Marshal Harak—his face would not come clear. That last ride into the city . . . he could almost feel the saddle between his thighs. Arcolin had called him in to speak to the Council about . . . about something. Someone.

One night it burst in on him. Recognizing one of the caravan guards as Korryn, his fox-head brand camouflaged with more scars. His own testimony to the Council—the Council's request that they go see the man in prison to be sure of his identity. And Korryn had said—something—and then hands at Stammel's neck, choking; he had fallen—unconscious—found himself under bodies, a welter of blood and guts, with Korryn free, and everyone else motionless. Arcolin's hand, near his sword, had been trembling with the effort he made to move.

But he, Stammel, could move, and he had struggled out from under the bodies, stabbed Korryn, and Arcolin had struck at once . . . and then . . . and then . . . like a blow inside his head, he had been stunned, and the fires began.

He woke, aware that he'd cried out and was soaked with sweat.

"Sir?" Suli, as always, was first to his side.

"Bad dream," he said. "Just a bad dream."

The fires, he'd been told, were the demon's invasion. But Korryn . . . that was not a demon, inside Korryn. He was sure of that. It was something else, something less than a demon, something . . . almost human.

What humans had powers to hold men still? Arcolin had told him what the prince said of the assassination attempt. The Verrakai had such powers. Magelords. But if Korryn had been a magelord, had such powers, why go for a soldier?

※

At first Stammel could totter only a few steps to the jacks, leaning on someone's arm. Then he made it out to the grange itself. His soldiers applauded. He tried to grin; he hoped it looked normal. Day by day, days he found it impossible to count without light, he pushed himself for more, knowing from years of training that his body would respond. All the way to the front entrance, where he stood gasping for breath, feeling the sun on his face. All the way back, one hand on the wall to guide him. Around the interior, still touching the wall, until he could find his own way to the jacks, to the bathing room, to the little kitchen.

※

As Stammel became more able to navigate in the grange on his own—as long as he kept one hand on a wall—he was aware of discussions carried on just beyond what his people thought he could hear . . . but now, concentrating on hearing, he could hear all too clearly sometimes.

Arñe, doing her job as corporal, made sure they kept the grange clean and fetched whatever anyone needed—"We must not be a burden on the grange," she said, perhaps more often than necessary. In truth, they weren't busy enough, and soldiers needed to be kept busy. They polished everything that could be polished, to the point where Stammel heard the yeoman-marshal complain that he had nothing to do. Arñe arranged what drill she could but lacked space, since this city grange had no barton, and the street outside was busy dawn to dusk, noisy with the sound of smiths at work. Stammel could distinguish the solid whang-whang of the ironsmiths from the lighter tink-tink-tink of whitesmiths.

Some hands of days after he'd wakened, Stammel laid a hand on Bald Seli's shoulder and came into the grange on a drill night for the first time. The big room was full of strangers, all talking, it seemed; it smelled of sweaty people and stale breath. Seli eased him onto a stool near the entrance.

"Go on," Stammel said, when his people came to greet him. "All of you—go drill with them."

Marshal Harak opened the drill with a prayer, then set his yeoman to doing basic exercises. He didn't introduce the Phelani; by that Stammel knew they had been there long enough to become familiar to the locals. By the grunts and groans, Stammel could guess which exercises Harak assigned, though the names were different; his muscles twitched a little as he imagined doing those stretches and bends. After a few minutes, Harak told them to fetch hauks. Someone dropped one; it rattled on the floor. Someone else laughed; Harak growled at them in the same tone Stammel himself used.

Then came the tap-tap of the simple beginning exercises, with Arñe—Harak must have asked her—counting the time. In his mind he could see it; his body remembered every move. Someone—there, across the room, fourth row, near the front—was off-beat, constantly late. Arñe said nothing; she must be waiting for Harak to comment.

As she speeded the count, the slow one continued to lag, off the beat. Stammel opened his mouth and shut it again. It was not his place to correct another man's unit. He hoped it wasn't one of his people. Finally Harak said, "Gan, you're behind. Pick it up."

"Sorry," a man said. Right location, Stammel thought, pleased with the accuracy of his hearing. "My arm's sore, Marshal."

"You think an enemy will slow down because it's sore?" Harak asked.

"No, but . . . I'll do better."

But once more the tap of this man's hauk was slower than the others, and slowing down. Stammel itched to correct him and before he quite realized it, he stood. The count stopped.

"Are you all right, Stammel? Do you need something?"

"I need a hauk," he said. "It's time I started training again." As he expected, there were mutters of *But he's blind* here and there in the room.

But from the Marshal, only silence. Then, "Of course, Sergeant.

They're on the wall to your right. Five strides across the entrance, ten to the corner, turn left and about ten strides—"

That was a challenge—he might have sent someone to be a guide—but also recognition. Stammel put his hand on the wall and set off into the dark; the wall disappeared—the entrance. Five strides . . . and the wall reappeared, solid stone he was glad to bump his fingers on. Ten—he felt the wall ahead before he reached it, a looming presence he did not know how he perceived. But it made turning the corner easier. In three strides he was abreast of some of the yeomen; he could feel the heat of them, and smell them, and hear their breathing. Another five strides, and two . . . and under his hand was a rack, mostly empty, but—as he felt his way along it—the well-worn handle of a hauk. He hefted it, then found another. They felt heavy, but he told himself that would be good, after his long illness. He heard a soft sigh that seemed to come from everyone in the room.

"Best come forward," the Marshal said. Stammel stretched out one arm, so the hauk brushed the wall, and went toward the Marshal's voice until the Marshal said, "Far enough. You're even with the front rank, two strides from the platform. Gan—move over and make room. Keder, help the sergeant line up."

"That's me," a voice said, from behind and to his left. "Take three steps sideways left, that'll put you about right, and I can help if you need."

But Stammel had been opening and closing ranks since he was a recruit; his body knew how to move sideways and his three steps, Keder told him softly, put him exactly right.

"You may resume," the Marshal said, and Arñe's voice, much closer now, started a slower count than it had. He lifted the hauks and beat time with the others. Beside him, Gan lagged a little, then caught up. Stammel supposed the Marshal's eye was on him. Perhaps he considered having a blind man at the head of the line was a good example. As Arñe picked up the speed, Stammel concentrated on correct form, on precise timing. Up, across, forward, back, together in front, together behind . . . he began to wish he too had done the stretches and bends. A muscle in his back twinged; he ignored it. It was a healthy twinge.

On six, they should be tapping hauks with the person beside

them—but Gan was never there when he was. He himself was on count, he was sure.

"Gan—you missed your tap!" the Marshal said.

"I don't want to hurt him," Gan said.

"Don't worry," Stammel said. "I'm not easily hurt." There was a moment of silence, and then the Marshal again.

"Gan, if you don't keep time, I'll bring you up here and drill you myself."

That got a muffled chuckle from the others; apparently it was a familiar threat. The next time Arñe called six, Stammel's hauk tapped another on his left. His tap was strong, the other's weak, and the hapless Gan dropped his hauk. "Keep going," the Marshal said. "Gan—recover on three . . ."

Stammel's arms ached; the palms of his hands stung. He ignored that, too. Nothing was as bad as the fire, and it had been years of training, he was sure, that gave him the endurance to survive. He would not quit until he fell over.

The Marshal had other ideas. When the group moved into line-against-line, and Stammel turned about to face the man behind, the Marshal stopped him. "Sergeant, your captain put your health in my care. You have done enough for a first drill. Rest now."

In truth, he was trembling, but he hated it, quitting in front of the yeomen. He took it as an order, instead of his own will. "Yes, Marshal," he said, and without a reminder found his way back to the rack to put his hauks away, and—left hand on the wall this time—made it back down the grange, across the terrifying space where he had no wall to guide him, and found the stool he'd been sitting on by barking his shin on it.

He had at least started. He would come back somehow, some way, however long it took. Though what he could do as a blind man—a blind soldier—he could not imagine.

CHAPTER THIRTY-FOUR

Vérella

Camwyn, the prince's younger brother, mounted his horse, first in the procession, and led his friends to the training ground. Today, it would be mounted drill without weapons—not nearly as exciting as knocking the heads off straw-stuffed figures—but at least his brother the prince let him out of the palace. Eight Royal Guards rode with them, in case of attack, and the Royal Guard senior riding instructor, carrying a bundle of flagged sticks to mark points on the field.

Camwyn had missed all the excitement when Verrakai attacked his brother; it was all over by the time the palace guards came to warn him . . . and arrest Egan Verrakai, Duke Verrakai's grandson, until that moment one of his own friends. Now Egan was imprisoned, under Order of Attainder, and Mikeli would not relent.

The training field opened out before them as they came through the gates. Camwyn felt like spurring his mount into a gallop, but he had promised Mikeli he'd obey.

"Line up there," the instructor said. "Straight line, and I want every horse square to it. Guard, place your mounts there—there—and down there." He rode on, leaning over to place the first stake.

No one argued with him. Boys who argued spent the rest of that lesson on the ground with a shovel and rake, putting horse manure into a sack and dragging tools and sack around the field while their friends rode. Even princes. Camwyn's horse lined up neatly, but pawed at the ground. On his left, Beclan's horse shifted its rump from side to side; on his right, Aris's danced in place. By the time the instructor rode back up the field, the turf under the line of horses was scuffed and torn. He stopped in front of them.

"Gentlemen! I told you a square halt. Yet your horses are writhing about like worms in a bucket."

"He won't hold still!" Beclan Destvaorn said.

"Neither would I if you were sitting on my back like that," the instructor said. "Your toes are out; you're playing a tune on his ribs with your heels; you've cramped his neck with that death grip on the reins, and you're sitting on the small of your back, not your seat."

Camwyn, attending to his own posture, suddenly realized that his right heel was snugger than the left; he relaxed that leg a little and his horse quit pawing. "And you," the instructor said, pointing his remaining flagged stick at Camwyn. "Your seat bones weren't evenly weighted and you were digging him in the ribs—good that you fixed it, but you shouldn't have done it in the first place. That's the same mistake you made on your first pony."

Camwyn felt his neck getting hot, but the instructor had already moved on to the next of them, Aris Marrakai. Aris, Camwyn thought, put on airs about his father's horses, admittedly some of the best in the kingdom. Camwyn relaxed, prepared to enjoy the next bit.

"You're letting your horse dance without warming up properly—surely you, son of the foremost horse breeder in the realm, know better."

"Yes, sir," Aris said. "I don't know why he's doing it."

"Do you not, indeed? Then I will tell you. You—" The horse leapt straight up, twisted in the air, and came down in a series of enormous bucks. Camwyn's horse threw its head up and skittered sideways away from Aris's mount; all the horses reacted. Aris rode the first few bucks with a skill Camwyn envied—Aris was the best rider in their group—but soon lost his rhythm. The instructor had ridden his own mount close, and tried to grab the horse's rein, but it squealed and lunged, teeth snapping.

"Dismount! Now!" the instructor said. Aris flew into the air, launched as much by the horse as by his own will, and the instructor plucked him neatly by the back of his tunic as the horse ran squealing down the field, bucking and kicking. "All dismount!" the instructor said. Camwyn and the others did so. Aris, pale-faced, stood staring at his horse, now standing lathered and trembling at the far end of the field, snapping at its own sides. The Royal Guards closed in cautiously. As they watched, the horse lunged toward one of them, but fell to its knees, and then, jerking, to its side. Aris took a step in that direction, but the instructor stopped him.

"Did you saddle your own mounts today?" the instructor asked.

"No," Camwyn said. "They were in their stalls, saddled, when we got to the stable. And we were on time!" He glanced at Aris, who stared down the field, eyes glittering with unshed tears. "Aris—I'm sorry—"

"Unsaddle them now. No—first spread out. Camwyn, to that corner. Two horse-lengths between you. Then unsaddle them. Check the saddlecloths, but do not touch anything you find."

"Should I—? Please, sir, let me—"

The instructor's voice softened. "I'm sorry, young Marrakai; it's too late. And I'd not risk you—let the Guard remove the tack."

Camwyn's own mount, another Marrakai-bred bay, had quieted. He unfastened the girth, pulled the saddle off, and set it on the ground; the horse stood quietly, as it should. He looked at the sleek bay back . . . with a lump on it. Lump? He reached out to feel it, and just stopped himself. "Sir?" he called.

The instructor rode over, took one look at Camwyn's horse, and hissed through his teeth. "Don't move," he said. Camyn stood still. "It may not have bitten yet," the instructor said. "Drop the reins, come hold my horse." The instructor was already dismounted. Camwyn took the reins as the instructor spoke quietly to his horse, drawing a dagger from his belt.

"What are you going to do—" Camwyn began, but the dagger was already moving, the lump flying away from the horse's back.

"May be too late already," the instructor said as Camwyn's horse shuddered and jerked its head; sweat broke out on its neck. The instructor stroked across its back with his gloved hand. The horse flinched, pinned its ears, and cow-kicked. Before Camwyn had time to ask another question, the instructor had cut its throat, dancing away from the flailing hooves as the horse fell, a torrent of blood pouring out.

"Sir!" Camwyn said.

"Poison," the instructor said. "Yours and Marrakai's; now we'll see the others."

None of the other horses showed any lumps, nor did the saddles or saddlecloths. The instructor checked carefully; the boys tried not to look at the dead horses, or at Camwyn or Aris. Camwyn, still leading the instructor's horse, walked over to Aris.

"He said poison," he said.

"I heard." Aris, usually so ebullient, spoke so low Camwyn could hardly hear him.

"Who would poison a horse?" Camwyn said. "And how?"

Aris swallowed hard before answering. Camwyn realized he was trying not to cry. "Verrakai," he said. "To kill you, or maybe me, or both. Or because the horses were Marrakai-bred."

"But they're all dead," Camwyn said. "The bad ones, I mean, and Egan's in prison."

Aris looked at him. "If they were, our horses wouldn't be dead. No one else would do it, but one of them or someone they controlled." A tear rolled down his cheek; he scrubbed it away. "I'm sorry, it's just— he was my first, that was mine alone."

"I didn't know," Camwyn said.

"I was there at his foaling," Aris said. "My father—helped me do the things you do with foals, to teach them trust. I was in Fin Panir for most of his training, but when I'd come home, I'd help. And then when I came here—Father let me bring him."

Camwyn didn't know what to say. Aris had not been his closest friend, in the group of boys who took instruction with him, and he himself had ridden a succession of palace ponies and horses chosen and trained by someone else. "I'm sorry" was all he could think of.

The other boys were saddling their horses. Down the field, two Royal Guardsmen, dismounted, were taking the saddle and bridle off Aris's horse.

The instructor came back. "The other horses appear safe to me. This attack was aimed at you, Camwyn, and at Aris—and your families, of course." He cleared his throat. "It would be best if you continued with practice; you are of an age where learning to continue in your duty past any difficulty is important."

"You can't just—with the dead horses lying there?" Camwyn bit his tongue and apologized.

"On a battlefield someday, you may face worse than this," the instructor said. "So may your mounts. We all hope war stays far away, but I would be remiss in my duties as your instructor if I let you all trail back to the palace like a litter of whipped puppies. Gird has given you a challenge: will you meet it?"

"Yes, sir," Aris said, before Camwyn could say anything. Camwyn nodded.

"Then we are but one horse short. Camwyn, you take mine. Beclan, Aris will ride your horse for a few minutes. You come with me to the center of the field. Ride two by two, that way, at a walk. Do not let your horses put a hoof in the blood or foam from the two poisoned ones."

The instructor's mount, a faded roan smaller than his own charger, moved off in a walk with complete equanimity. Camwyn concentrated on his posture, on giving precise signals, and was almost unseated at the first turn when the horse spun in a quarter circle.

"Lightly, lightly," the instructor called. "You're yelling at him; try a whisper."

As the lesson went on, with students changing horses every circuit of the field, until finally pairs were changing horses while trotting together, Camwyn felt better. When he was on the ground, following the instructor, hearing every comment, he began to see things he'd never noticed before. Riding the different horses, having to adjust his seat and his aids to them, he tried to apply those things in a way he hadn't before.

Finally it was over; once more they stood in a line, and this time the horses were quiet. The instructor looked them over. "Well done," he said. "You young men—" It was the first time he'd ever called them *men*. "—are worthy of your fathers. You learned a hard lesson today, one I would not have chosen for you. But I warn you—what happened today may happen again. You, as lords' sons, are all in danger. From now on, you must go early to the stables, as a group, and as a group inspect every mount, and all the tack, before mounted drill. Of course all the grooms are being questioned, but you're old enough to take some responsibility yourselves. I have sent to the stables for two horses, for Camwyn and Aris; when they come, we will go back, in proper order, as if nothing had happened. I will report to the prince and Council."

Four more Royal Guardsmen arrived with the two led horses, a roan and a gray; they carried fresh saddlecloths. With them came a Marshal. The instructor checked the saddlecloths, the saddles, and then drew aside to speak to the Marshal while the two saddled their new mounts.

"You will be knights someday," the instructor said, when he returned to the group. "Ride like that, through the city, and not like chattering boys."

Camwyn felt no desire to chatter; Aris rode beside him, grim-faced now, looking ready to kill someone. He was reminded that Aris's older brother, Juris, was his own older brother's best friend. Instead of talking, Camwyn sat tall, imagining himself as Camwyn Dragonmaster, for whom he'd been named. Of course, he was Girdish, but the images of Camwyn, sword in hand, confronting the Father of Dragons were far more dramatic than those of Gird with his cudgel. He scolded himself for daydreaming, hoping no one had noticed, and watched the people in the streets as they passed. Was one of them a Verrakai agent? Servant? What would he do if someone rushed at him?

In the royal mews, the stablemaster met them. "My lords—I had no idea—"

"Enough," the instructor said. "These boys have other lessons now. Let them go, and then we'll talk."

Camwyn wanted to stay and listen, but his escort and his tutor were there as well, and Duke Marrakai had already collected Aris.

"To the Council with you all," Marrakai said. He looked as grim as Aris. "We want it all down before you've forgotten or talked each other into something that you didn't see."

Camwyn had found Council meetings boring before, the times his brother the crown prince made him sit through one. He'd not been to one since the assassination attempt. This one proved different. He and his friends were held in an anteroom and ordered not to talk, while one by one they went in to tell their stories to the Council. Those who finished were whisked away by tutors, older siblings, parents before they could report on what it had been like.

Camwyn expected he and Aris would be first, since their horses had been poisoned, but instead they were last, and Camwyn went in before Aris. He had to relate the entire morning's events, from waking up to the instructor killing his horse.

"Are the horses usually saddled and waiting in their stalls?" asked Duke Mahieran.

"No, sir," Camwyn said. The Duke usually ruffled his hair and called him a young scamp, but today his uncle treated him with cool courtesy. "Since Midwinter, we've usually had to groom and saddle them ourselves, but sometimes the grooms do it."

"So you were not surprised to find the horses ready?"

"Not really. It's easier that way, anyhow."

"And did you check the saddle?"

"I tightened the girth before mounting, and looked at the stirrup straps and girth for soundness, but I didn't feel under the saddle-cloth. The horse showed no sign of discomfort; its eyes were bright; its nostrils . . . everything seemed normal."

The Duke led him through the rest of it—mounting, riding out to the drill field—step by step. Camwyn described the horse's behavior. "They were all shifting around—not just mine, who was pawing. It's spring, and we haven't been out for days—"

"What was Aris Marrakai's horse doing?"

"Prancing in place. I heard Aris talking to it—we're not supposed to, in drill, but he was trying to calm it." Camwyn went on to tell the rest as clearly as he could.

"What did the lump look like? Part of the horse or something on the horse?"

"On the horse," Camwyn said. "Like—like one of those mud nests some wasps make, but only this big . . ." He held his forefinger and thumb apart. "Maybe as thick as my thumb. Dull-colored, flattened some where it was under the saddle."

"You saw nothing, no lump, under the saddlecloth before you mounted?"

"No, it was under the saddle, right in the middle of the back. I wouldn't have seen it."

"Someone put it there," Duke Serrostin said.

"That's obvious," Duke Mahieran said impatiently. "Camwyn, when the instructor knocked it off the horse's back, did it break apart when it landed? Did you see anything come out of it?"

"No," Camwyn said. "I was holding his horse here—" He gestured. "—and the lump went that way, where I couldn't see. Do you know what it was?"

"No," the Duke said. "I'm sure we'll find out. You may go now. And this is not a topic for gossip, is that clear?"

Camwyn looked at his brother, but Mikeli's face was blank as a closed door. No invitation to stay . . . Camwyn walked out, as Aris was ushered in; their eyes met briefly, Aris's still angry.

Camwyn's tutor and guards awaited, and he spent the rest of the time until lunch on the history of the Girdish wars, a period when the Marrakai—allied early with Gird—had gained importance. Camwyn had worked out most of the battles with his collection of miniature soldiers, and tried to impress his tutor with his perfect knowledge of the terrain, opposing forces, and tactical quirks of each, but his tutor concentrated on the unexciting areas of family genealogy, law, finance, and religion.

Lunch came while he was still struggling to untangle the lineages of Mahieran, Serrostin, Verrakai, Marrakai and their vassals during the Girdish wars. Camwyn preferred to consider merely their alliances—Girdish, anti-Girdish, and neutral—but his tutor insisted on his noticing who married whom and which branch of a family chose which.

After lunch in his own quarters, surrounded by palace guards and a hovering taster, Camwyn joined the others again in the Bells training hall for weapons drill. No time to talk there; the armsmaster kept them busy and breathless until all Camwyn wanted to do was fall to the floor and gasp. After that a lesson with the palace Marshal on the Code of Gird, and finally a bath and supper. With his brother and several of his brother's friends, including Juris Marrakai. And Aris.

"I share your grief," his brother said to Aris, taking him by the hand. "And yours," he said to Camwyn, taking his. "By Gird—we could have lost you both today!"

He led them to the table and sat them one to either side of him. Camwyn looked across at Aris. He had not eaten with Mikeli and the men since their father died; he'd still been in the nursery then.

"We join the Council after dinner. Just for talk—" Mikeli looked at them both. "No more questions—or not as formally, anyway."

"Do you know yet what it was?" Aris asked. "Juris won't tell me anything." He glared down the table at his brother, who grinned.

"The Marshal and instructor believe they do, but are reserving that knowledge for the time being."

"It was wicked," Aris said.

"Yes," Mikeli said. "But we will not talk of it during dinner. We have other things to discuss with both of you."

Camwyn sat up at that.

"After the meal is served," Mikeli said. He nodded to the guard at the door; servants came in with food, and the taster sampled each dish without incident. The servant withdrew, and the prince forked a slice of roast goose onto his plate. The others served themselves.

Camwyn ate steadily. Mikeli would talk when he was ready, not before, and the food—more varied and richer than what he was usually served—delighted him in spite of the situation.

Mikeli put down his fork. "Camwyn, you and Aris are not as close as Juris and I, I think. Is that not so?"

Camwyn nodded, his mouth full of roast goose.

"The attack on you two might be because someone thinks you're like Juris and me—or because you're my brother and Aris is a Marrakai—or because you were both riding Marrakai-bred horses today. Duke Verrakai planned to put blame on Juris for killing me . . . whichever Verrakai did this might have wanted to put blame on the Marrakai for your horse's behavior."

"But his horse died, too," Camwyn said.

"Yes. Perhaps they hoped both of you would be injured or killed when your horses reacted to the poison." Mikeli sighed. "Cam, you've never been that interested in Council meetings and such."

"No . . ."

"And your tutor says you like anything military better than anything about politics or finance—"

"I don't like all the gossip," Camwyn said, ducking his head.

"At your age, neither did I," Mikeli said. "But I knew I would be king, and must learn why it mattered. Camwyn—you know how close to death I came. And if I had died, you are my heir. You and I are our father's only living children."

"Why me? Rothlin's older and he knows more. If there's an emergency he'd be better—"

"Because that's the way it's done. Roth only gets the crown if both of us die, and that's after Uncle. Cam, I haven't pushed you much; I remember too well how I hated giving up my boyhood interests. Now I can't wait any longer. I need you; the land needs you." Mikeli stopped there and looked at him.

Camwyn felt a stab of fear. Mikeli was serious . . . he had not let himself think much about the assassination attempt. He hadn't wanted to imagine his brother sitting helpless with a magicked sword coming at him. Now he let himself imagine Mikeli dead, and someone telling him, and having suddenly the whole weight of the kingdom on his shoulders. He couldn't do it—could not—and yet . . . and yet he was named for Camwyn Dragonmaster. Did that count for nothing? Was he like an infant's toy, given a hero's name but capable of nothing?

"I did not know," he said, to give himself time.

"No, any more than I did when Father died. I don't blame you, Cam, but now I need you. I need a brother who may be a king after me, and will be a help to me while I live. I had hoped the menace was over and you could have a few more years—but it's not, and you can't."

Camwyn tried for the feeling he'd had riding back from practice— solid, sober, knightly. He glanced at Aris. The younger boy's face lit up. Egan Verrakai had said Aris was a cocky upstart who thought he was the equal of his elders. That he was pleasant around Camwyn only because he was currying favor. But since Egan had . . . left . . . something had changed in the boys' riding group. Aris hadn't acted differently than any other boy his age assigned the duties of page or squire. Now Aris's smile warmed his fear. "I'll do my best," Camwyn said.

"I want my friends to know you better, and you to know them," Mikeli said. "And I want to know your friends, as well. That doesn't mean you and Aris have to become like brothers, as Juris and I are, but we need all of you, for the struggle that's going on."

The rest of the meal passed quickly; the older ones talked of things Camwyn didn't fully understand, but he tried, instead of ignoring them. The older men of the Council, the young men's fathers and uncles, continued to treat him and even Aris as if they were adult, equals. They talked of affairs of the realm without explanation, but Camwyn found it easier to follow a conversation between Duke Serrostin and Duke Mahieran on the movement of funds between

Vérella and Fin Panir than to listen to his tutor. Aris, he noted, was quicker to ask questions, willing to risk his father's correction or his brother's scorn—which didn't come as often as he'd expected.

Egan had always insisted that lords must never show ignorance, never admit they didn't understand, but the Marrakaien—now that he could watch Juris and Aris together with their father—all seemed as comfortable asking questions as answering them.

"What do you think?" Crown Prince Mikeli turned to his uncle and the other Council members after the younger boys had left.

"I think we're damned lucky they're alive, either of them," Duke Mahieran said. "That was a close call this morning; Gird's grace their instructor knew what to do."

"I'm asking about Camwyn," the crown prince said. "Is he what you'd expect—what we need?"

"Hard to tell what he's really like, after something like this . . . he seemed quiet . . . a little stiff . . ."

"He's lost his best friend," Duke Marrakai said. "It can't be easy, knowing the Verrakai boy's in prison, under charge of attainder. Aris said Egan was always with him."

"And I didn't do anything," the crown prince said. "I thought—if Cam liked him, that might ease the tension with the Verrakaien."

"Egan didn't like Aris," Juris Marrakai said. "He didn't want Camwyn and Aris to be friends. Though in all fairness, Aris didn't like Egan either. I don't know who started it."

"I do," Count Destvaorn said. "And unfortunately it fuels our suspicions of Egan Verrakai. He told tales of Aris, and some of them were not true. I heard him; I scolded him; he apologized. But later I heard through a friend's son that he was spreading the same tales again. And tales of me, as a Marrakai friend who could not be trusted."

"I worry that Cam's loyalty to his friend could overcome his good sense," Mikeli said, helping himself to a handful of shelled nuts.

"After the attack on you? And on himself today?"

"I hope not, but—I don't know, my lords. This business today frightened me, I don't mind admitting. We were warned some of them could take other bodies, and to keep watch, but—a groom? A stableboy? How can we tell?"

"Dorrin Verrakai has some way to tell—she found some, she reported," Duke Marrakai said.

"And we've heard nothing from her since—"

"Except reports from the Marshals in Harway and Darkon Edge that things are better. No specifics," Destvaorn said.

"We could send someone to ask, but she's surely coming to your coronation," Duke Marrakai said.

"I am not sure," Mikeli said. "If she's battling renegades over there, she may not come."

"I would send her a very clear invitation," Duke Marrakai said. "A royal courier. We will all feel better if we see her again and can be sure of her loyalty, and you can also ask her advice."

CHAPTER THIRTY-FIVE

Verrakai Holding

The prince's courier cantered up to the house on a lathered horse at midafternoon. Dorrin, riding out of the stable yard at the same time to visit the nearest village, reined in.

"My lord Duke," the courier said. He was a tough-looking middle-aged man with a courier's tabard over his clothes, sweating heavily in the early summer heat.

"Be welcome," Dorrin said. She had had no word from Vérella since hearing that the Verrakaien she'd first sent had all been executed. What now, she wondered? One of the stable hands who had followed her out to close the gate came running when she waved. "Maddes here will walk your horse cool; come inside and have something to drink. You will stay the night, of course."

"I can't stay that long," he said. "If you could lend a horse . . . I should get back to Harway tonight." He had dismounted, and now unbuckled one saddlebag, pulling out a velvet pouch. "This is for you, from the prince's own hand."

"I haven't a horse that will make Harway tonight," Dorrin said. "And you must not camp alone on the way. I cannot guarantee your safety."

He looked at the house, where a servant was just visible coming out with a tray and the ritual bowl of water. "I'm supposed to hurry—"

"From the look of you and your horse, you did. But you could not clear Verrakai lands by dark, and surely you know I am still hunting down errant kinsmen. You are a royal servant; you are owed my protection. Go in, rest, be welcome to what I can offer until I return. I must go now. Two legal matters await me, urgent ones that I promised to deal with today. My people will see you fed and rested; I will be back by dark."

Dorrin rode off, along with a tensquad of Phelani. The cases were complex, a tangle of Tsaian law and traditional practice, some of it Verrakaien and some apparently local, from ancient times. She had discussed them with the village leaders but the people were adamant that only the Duke could settle matters and only in there, in the village.

It might even be an ambush attempt set up by her missing relatives, designed to lure her away from the house. She could not be sure. Nothing had been seen of the missing young men, nothing heard, according to what she'd been told. But she had promised to come and give judgment in the place the dispute had arisen, and her people needed her.

As she approached the village, a clump of villagers awaited her— more than she thought lived there. Dorrin reined in.

"Good afternoon, Lord Duke," the eldest said.

"Good afternoon, Elder Sennet," Dorrin said. "You have a case; I have come to hear it. May the High Lord grant me wisdom to see the truth and judge rightly. Falk's grace on you and all here."

"The case is . . ." The elder looked meaningfully at the oldest woman.

"Our lord Duke's birthday," the old woman said, grinning broadly and showing how few teeth she had left.

"What?" Dorrin looked from her to Sennet.

"We wanted to thank you, my lord," Sennet said. "You sent us back our dead, back then, and you taken no more for the dark tower, not from any village we asked, and so we wanted to thank you."

"And I knew it was your birthday," the old woman said. "On account I was there when you was born, a-helping in the house, I was, and it was seven tendays and a hand after the Lady's Evener, which it is this day, my lord. So I told Sennet, that's the best day to thank the Duke, it's the Duke's Lady's Day, it is."

"Maerin!"

"Well, it is. 'Tis no shame to say it."

They looked frightened now. Dorrin understood: mention of the Lady of Peace, Alyanya, had been forbidden in her childhood and she supposed that had continued. She herself had left the villagers to what beliefs they chose, except that she had sent word to make no more sacrifices to Liart of the Horned Chain.

"Lady's grace on you, Maerin," Dorrin said. "For your kind thought, and on you, Sennet, and the rest of you." Their faces relaxed and a murmur passed through the crowd. She dismounted; Sennet pushed a boy forward to hold her horse.

A lane opened in the little crowd: they had placed a board across two sections of tree trunk for a bench, and gathered flowers to decorate it. Dorrin sat down; the board tipped only a little.

"If you permit, my lord," Sennet said. A little girl held a wreath of flowers and field herbs, some drooping already with the heat. "A Lady's Day crown."

Dorrin bent her head; the child, barefoot and with a strong smell of pig about her, put the crown on her head; Dorrin felt the stiff stems of wild rosemary prickle through her hair. "Thank you," Dorrin said to the child. In that face, she saw no hint of Verrakai cunning; the girl smiled and stared until Sennet touched her shoulder and guided her back to her mother.

"And now," Sennet said, "Cheers for our Duke and best wishes for her life—the Lady's grace to her!" The crowd gave cheers, somewhat raggedly, and when that trailed away another child's voice could be heard.

"Kin we eat *now*?"

"Hush, Larn! Be still. The Duke will speak."

Without that cue, she would not have known what came next. "Sennet, Maerin, you have surprised me very well. You wanted to thank me for the very little I have done; I must thank you all, every one of you, for the great things you have done. You have done your work in the shadow of terror; you have welcomed one you had reason to fear. Who could do more? I shall try to be as good a duke to you as you deserve." The faces of those nearest her were intent, hopeful.

From the back of the ground, the child's voice came again. "But Ma . . . I'm *hungry*!"

Dorrin laughed. "And right now, you need your duke to say the best way to celebrate a Lady's Day is with her bounty—let us eat!"

They had brought out their poor best for her; when she saw the little meant to feed them all, she felt ashamed to take one bite. She had seen them tending flocks and herds, these past tendays.

"Them's *your* sheep, my lord," Sennet said, when she asked. "Your sheep and cows. We didn't have no right to take one of them."

"Is it not Alyanya's rule that guests and hosts share the wealth of both? Send someone, Sennet, and bring back a sheep, or two—enough to roast on the fire and give everyone enough and more." She thought a moment. "And if there are fruit trees or berries, outside the house garden, that you thought reserved for my use—use them now."

"Does the Duke want to choose the sheep?" Sennet asked. "The flock's penned just outside there—" He pointed beyond the houses.

"Nay," Dorrin said. "I trust you, as you trust me. Alyanya's blessing on it, and be sure there is plenty. Let the children eat, meanwhile."

Sennet nodded to several of the men, who slipped away toward the sheepfold, and to several women, who went the other direction, whether to garden or woods, Dorrin did not know. The others watched her as she waited.

Her magery nudged: she could enlarge the feast without even those sheep. She did not, knowing that all they had seen of magery meant death and torment for one of their own. As she looked around, she could not help comparing the village to others she'd seen, from Kieri's domain to the Immerhoft Coast.

This was hers; she was responsible for this—these houses barely more than mounds of sticks, roofed in bundles of old grass, not even proper thatch. In this season she should have seen kitchen gardens bursting with flowers and vegetables, trees hung with ripening fruit. Instead, meager gardens whose plants looked stunted, much smaller than those at the big house. Only a few trees, and little fruit on them. Ragged, dirty children, ragged clothes—stream-washed, she guessed, to honor her, but—

"Where do you get your water?" she asked Sennet.

"There's a well, but it's . . . it doesn't give good water now, not since—" He gulped and looked away. "We go to the stream—it's a sunhand away. I know, my lord, I know we're not as clean as they in the house—"

"Let me see your well," Dorrin said.

He led her to the well; one side of the old stone coping was gone.

A few withered flowers lay on what remained and the ground around it. Sennet paled. "I'm sorry, my lord, the children will believe in the *merin* and put flowers . . ."

Dorrin could smell the stink of blood magic from where she stood, ten paces away. She went closer. "Someone cursed it."

"It was—" Sennet gulped. "It was the old Duke, my lord. Said the likes of us had no right to water like that, said we was lazy. Please don't be angry, my lord . . ."

Anger filled her as water filled a bucket. "It is not you I am angry with," Dorrin said. "And those I am angry with are dead." As they deserved.

"We tried to get the stones out," Sennet went on. He still sounded scared. "But twice when we sent someone down with a rope, more stones fell and killed—and we did not want more to die."

"You did not ask me for help with this," Dorrin said. "I will ask you—will you permit me?"

"What can you do?" Sennet said.

What could she? She had no idea, but that the magery was tugging, shoving, telling her something. "I am not sure," she said. "But will you let me try?"

"You are the Duke," Sennet said. "I could hardly stop you."

"True, but you are the elder here. If I can get the stones out, can you rebuild the wall?"

"If the Duke permits—but my lord, there was also—the blood."

Naturally, there would have been blood.

"Did he sacrifice something here?"

"A—a woman, my lord. A woman with child, near her time."

Dorrin shivered. Most potent sacrifice, she had been taught, for this kind of magery. "I must go down," she said.

"No, my lord! No, we don't want to lose you! We can do without the well."

"You cannot," Dorrin said. "It cannot be left unclean; it is why your gardens bear so little. Not just the lack of water, but the presence of so much malice. I know this is not what you intended, Sennet, but it is my judgment—and you invited me here to give judgment—that this well must be cleansed, and to do that I must go down."

He looked horrified; she left him there and went back to her escort.

"Find me stout ropes," she said. "And I need you all to lift and lower on my command."

"My lord?"

"It is urgent."

The only ropes in the village were gray with age and frayed—no time to ride back to the house for better. Dorrin loosed her magery enough to mend them, and led the escort back to the well. Everyone who had not gone for more food now stood around it, a careful distance away.

"Back more," Dorrin said. "I do not know how good my control is, and you all know it takes magery to heal mage-dealt wounds."

They backed until most were behind their pitiful hovels. Dorrin took off her cloak, her armor, all but her shirt and trousers and boots, her sword, and her ducal chain of office. "I'm going down that well," she said to her escort.

"You're not!" More shock than refusal. "Let one of us—"

"None of you have magery," Dorrin said. Her heart pounded; her skin felt tight. "My uncle cursed this well, and with it, the village; I am going to heal it or die in the attempt, but I need people I can trust on the ropes. I may be able to move the stones by magery—or not. I've never done this before. Make me a sling and some loops for climbing."

They had used ropes like this in the Company, tying in fixed loops for hand- and footholds, making slings for lifting and lowering burdens and people. Dorrin checked the knots and again touched the ropes with magery. They should be sound . . . she went to the well and sent some of her light into it. The well had been made long ago, lined with hand-cut stone. That stone was still sound, tightly knit in place, in part by its revulsion at what had been done to the water. No water showed, only the jumble of stones thrown down from above. She sensed below them the evil intent that had killed a woman and her unborn child to spoil the well.

Dorrin touched Falk's ruby. "Lord Falk, help me," she murmured. She would try to move that one, there at the top—she sent her power down. The rock screeched, twisting, and jammed deeper. The one next to it broke in two, and the broken piece landed on top of it. A gout of malice surged out of the well; Dorrin staggered, but threw her power at it, imagining a net, and then a scythe, to cut it loose from what was left below. A writhing half-visible shape outlined by whirling dust rolled about her, knee-high. Dorrin drew her sword and touched its glowing blade to the mass . . . and the mass vanished.

"That was . . . interesting," she said.

"Was that . . . it?"

"Not all, I think." She looked in. A sullen menace filled the well now; she could sense it sinking lower as she let her magery strengthen. She tried to move the rock fragment now on top; it rose so fast it almost hit her in the head, bursting out the roof over the well and then landing with a jarring THUNK just short of a cottage wall. Again she sent a scythe stroke of magery to sever the power that propelled it, and again dispatched the remnant that threw up a cloud of dust in its struggles.

"It's too dangerous," Black Sef said.

"Too dangerous to try that again," Dorrin said. "Some of those rocks are much bigger. I will have to go down."

"Today?"

"Today. It will be stronger tomorrow, now it knows someone's trying to destroy it."

CHAPTER THIRTY-SIX

O nce she was down below the rim, the heat was even worse, stifling. The stench was both physical and magical: stagnant, polluted water, blood and death and decay, sour and sickly sweet all at once. The walls seemed to be closing in on her; the thick, stinking air clogged her nose, her lungs. Dorrin reached out with her free hand and stroked the old stone lining. "You want to be clean," she said to the stone. She had only a few phrases of dwarftongue, and wished she'd learned more; a dwarf would know how to comfort this stone. "You are dross," she said, one of the few words she remembered. Strong, it meant. Healthy. Brave. "Help me," she said to the stone. She felt something change, just a little; the smell of clean stone touched her nose. "Help that broken stone, if you can; it was once whole, as you are, and clean."

At the bottom, in the dimness, she made her light again. The stones there seemed locked in a hopeless jumble, each blocked by others, each blocking others. No way at all to put a rope sling around any of them and lift. Dorrin created with magery what she hoped was a secure lining for the entire shaft, in case the stone lining had been undermined. Then she put the tip of her sword on the stone below her foot and poured magery into it . . . lift slowly, she thought.

The stone rose, and with her standing on it, came slowly, steadily, up out of the well until she could see out, step out, off the stone and onto the ground. The stone followed her sword; when she pushed a little, it sank to the ground an armspan from the well. She withdrew her magery and then her sword, then nodded to her escort and they lowered her again.

One after another, the stones obeyed her magery, and one after another she stacked them ready for rebuilding the well's coping. She found under one the body of a man, desiccated, shrunken to skin over bones. She touched it, brow, eyes, mouth, and spoke Falk's prayer of dismissal and Alyanya's blessing. Lifting it in her arms, she carried it up, standing on the stone on which he had lain, not noticing that this time the stone rose at her command without the sword's touch. She laid the body on the ground, heart full of sorrow.

She found another body a layer below that and brought that, too, to the surface. The next stones were harder. Here the malice returned; the stench of blood and death intensified. She felt squeezed in a vile embrace, struggling to breathe, to move. Nedross, she remembered. These stones were nedross, evil in essence. Paks had been trapped under nedross stone, tormented.

The thought of Paksenarrion brought hope, an easier breath. Her magery flashed out, beyond her control; she felt the clash of two magicks as the blow of a thunderclap; she staggered and fell as the stones beneath her shattered, crumbled, disintegrated entirely to dust that plastered her face, clogged her nose. The dust vanished even as she choked on it. She was standing on a rough uneven surface of dry rock, not hewn stone. At her feet, a bloated stinking shape—the dead woman and child, magically preserved in gross decay. Pity filled Dorrin's heart; hot tears ran down her face. Not only such a death, but to be locked into this shape forever—

Not forever. Dorrin fell to her knees. Power and compassion in that unseen voice. Falk? Gird? The High Lord himself? She did not know; it did not matter.

She reached out her hand and touched the stinking corpse. "Be free," she said, speaking words she knew she must say. "Be free, go home, heal . . ."

The corpse turned to dust, bright as sparks in the dimness, and the sparks flew upward to the distant light. Now Dorrin saw bones only, the bones of the mother, the bones of the unborn child, fragile as slivers of dry grass, all lying loose, the ligaments that once bound them gone with the rest.

She had nothing to carry them in but her shirt. She took it off, and one by one she picked them up, the mother's bones, the child's bones, and laid them on the shirt, then rolled it into a secure bundle she could carry. She looked around the now-empty bottom of the well to be sure none were left, then felt the rough rock itself. Dry. Dry as those bones had been. At one side, a cleft that might once have been a spring to feed the well. She put her fingers into it. Dry.

"I don't know what else to do," she said, squatting there in the bottom of the well. "If it was blood that cursed the well, my blood will certainly not heal it."

Silence followed her words. The stench had gone with the corpses; what she smelled now was dry stone and her own sweat. She waited, listening, and finally pushed herself up, tucking the bundle under one arm. "Falk? Alyanya? If you have advice—"

Nothing. Nothing but the feel of a few grains of dust still in her mouth, annoying. She worked up a gob of spit, and spat them out; the spit landed near the dark cleft, sat there glistening a moment, then disappeared. Dorrin found another grain of sand under her tongue and spat again, in the interests of sport trying to hit the same spot. Again it hit, this time spreading a little before it vanished.

It was hopeless. All she had done was give the village back its dead, to bury or burn, whatever they did with bodies. Scant comfort, and what they needed was water, clean water . . . again tears came to her eyes, a misery so great she could not hold back her sobs. Her family legacy: poisoned traps, a painting that bled in a frame of bones, a ruined well, dry filth where once there had been clean water. The tears ran down her face, dripped onto the rock, formed a runnel that trickled into the cleft . . . and spread, a thin film that thickened, widened . . . Dorrin stared, her tears drying, as the water rose, first just wetting the stone, then deeper, deeper. It touched her boots; she put out her hand . . . it moved, rich with life and health, wetting her palm, rising around her hand.

Drink. She obeyed, cupping a handful of water and sipping cautiously. Clean, cold, teeth-aching cold . . . she clutched the bundle of bones and stood.

"Thank you," she said aloud. "Falk's grace, Alyanya's bounty—"

The surface of the water rippled and it rose even faster. Dorrin retreated up the uneven rock surface; it was a hand deep now at the cleft, lapping at her boot where she stood. She reached for the rope, but before she touched it, the water surged up, lifting her with it so fast that all she could do was try to hold the bundle of bones out of it. She was halfway up when she realized how this was going to look—the first female duke in generations, rising out of a well sopping wet and half-naked—but had no time to do more than start a chuckle before she was once more at ground level.

The villagers and her escort had come closer with every successful lift of a rock; her escort had the presence of mind to throw her cloak around her. Dorrin handed the bundle to Sennet.

"These are the bones of the woman and child," she said.

He looked down; none of the villagers was looking at her. "My lord . . ." he said in a choked voice.

"Your well once more gives water," Dorrin said. "By the grace of the gods."

They all fell on their knees, still staring at the ground. A whiff of roasting mutton came from the village clearing. One of her escort had taken off his own shirt and offered it to her. Dorrin shrugged into the sweaty shirt, put her formal armor back on. No one had moved. This was ridiculous . . .

"There's a sheep on the fire," Dorrin said. "Weren't we supposed to have a feast to celebrate my birthday?"

Sennet looked up cautiously. "Yes, my lord, but—"

"I know I have brought you three of your own to lay to rest, but can the feast still go on? It would be a shame to waste the sheep."

Dorrin could not read all the emotions that ran across his face; he still held the bundle of bones.

"We . . . we can . . . but it's different . . ."

Others were rising now; some hurrying off in the direction of the cooking pit, others to their houses.

"I cannot stay much longer," Dorrin said. "A royal courier arrived just as I was leaving; I must find out what the prince wants. I would share food with you before I go, if that suits you."

"Oh, my lord Duke—" He was crying now. Another man came and took the bundle of bones from him; a third helped him up.

" 'Tis good water," one of the women said. She had dipped a waterskin into it without Dorrin noticing, and now took a swallow.

"Efla!"

"Well, it is. If the Duke brings water, shouldn't we use it?"

"You should ask," Sennet said, with a glance at Dorrin. "It's the Duke's water."

"It's the land's water," Dorrin said. "And it is returned to you by the gods' grace; all I did was what they told me, to free it from a curse. But Sennet is right: as it is, with the wall broken, it is not safe. You should build the coping wall again, before a child falls in and drowns. It should not take long, I think?" She looked at Sennet.

"It will be done at once," he said. "Aren—Tamis—" Men nodded and moved to stones Dorrin had piled. "And yes, my lord, we will share food with you. The men can set stones loose for now and mortar them tomorrow, will that do?"

"Quite well," Dorrin said.

CHAPTER THIRTY-SEVEN

The sun was almost down when she rode away, her own shirt—washed hastily in water from the well and spread to dry—on her back once more, her trousers almost dry, her boots still squelching a bit with every step. She had tasted everything; she had been hugged by grimy, bright-eyed children, thanked again and again by every adult. Her escort said nothing until they were well away from the village.

"What happened down that well?" Black Sef asked.

"Much that I don't understand," Dorrin said. An evening breeze wafted across the way and chilled her legs in the damp trousers.

"Did you know you could do all that?"

"No," Dorrin said. "I just knew I had to do something."

"I didn't know magelords could move rocks."

"It's in the Chronicles," Mattis said. Dorrin remembered he was Girdish. "Some battle, a magelord took the water from a river and made it come out a well and it drowned people."

"That's water, not rocks," Black Sef said.

"Bucket of water's as heavy as a rock," Mattis said. "Lifting's lifting." He looked at Dorrin. "Captain—uh . . . my lord—if you could lift yourself and a rock up, why did we have to lower you down on the rope?"

"Would you step off a cliff if you had friends with a rope to lower you?" Dorrin asked, then legged her horse into a canter.

She came to the house just before dark. A strange horse grazed in the front field. Her belly clenched: trouble?—but the house was silent, light glowing from a few windows. Closer, she could see it was a red chestnut with a star and white stockings behind.

"You?" she said to the horse. It raised its head, flicked an ear, and blew a soft whuffle. "You are *Paks's* horse—"

A stamp of hoof. Dorrin understood that Paks belonged to the horse, not the other way around.

"There's a comfortable stall in the stable," she said. The horse scratched an ear with a hind hoof and turned away, walking down toward the stream. Dorrin heard a chuckle from her escort; she shrugged and rode on into the stableyard, her heart lighter at the thought of seeing Paks.

She went in through the kitchen. The cook looked up. "You're later than I thought you'd be. Them villagers keep a-wrangling till dark?"

"No," Dorrin said. "They had a surprise for me."

"A wet one, I see," the cook said, glaring at Dorrin's boots and the floor.

"That's why I came in this way," Dorrin said. "Where are our guests?"

"Front hall. What happened? They throw you in the river?"

"No, there was a problem with the well." Dorrin squelched on through. "I need a bath; I'll go straight up." At least she could now bathe in more privacy than the servants' bathhouse without fear of being killed by some clever trap.

She came down, wearing the soft slippers she favored in the house. Paks and the royal courier were seated around a small table someone had moved from the kitchen, and one of the kitchen maids was dishing out something that smelled almost as good as the fire-roasted lamb. The maid glanced up and saw her.

"My lord Duke—shall I set a place in the dining room?"

"No—I'll sit here. Just bring a plate and things."

The courier had jumped up, almost knocking his chair over. "My lord Duke—"

"Sit down, both of you." Dorrin dragged a chair to the table. "I'm sorry I was later than I said I'd be. The visit did not go quite as planned."

"A judgment?" Paks asked.

"I thought it was to be a judgment, but as it turned out, it was several other things as well. But let us talk of lighter things as you eat. You were at Kieri's coronation, Paks, were you not?"

"Indeed." Paks swallowed hastily. "The Lady was there—it must be strange to have your grandmother as co-ruler."

"And you had good weather on your journey here?" She had no idea where Paks had been in the meantime, but that could wait.

"It rained one day," Paks said. "But the road was sound. And you?" she said, turning to the courier.

"Two days," he said. "How long is the ride to Chaya? I have a message for the king."

"And I a message for your prince from the king," Paks said. "He regrets he will be unable to attend the coronation, for concerns of state in his own realm. He will send an envoy."

After he finished, the royal courier excused himself to use the bath Dorrin had offered.

"I just found out today is my birth-day," Dorrin said when they were alone.

"You didn't know?"

"No. The name-day, not the birth-day, mattered to my family, and my name-day was Midsummer Eve. My villagers knew, though, and lured me out to celebrate it their way. If I had not been able to tell them of the prince's messenger, I'd be there yet." Dorrin looked at Paks; it was still hard to believe this young woman—so young—had been through so much. She still had the same open, engaging grin that had made her such an attractive recruit, but the gray eyes had wisdom beyond her years. "So—you are on your way to the coronation in Vérella, I suppose? I'm glad you came this way."

"No," Paks said, picking up another stuffed pastry. "One coronation a year is enough. I came here because I felt it."

"Felt—"

"I can't explain. I had to come, as I had to leave Chaya and wander the woods in Lyonya awhile. This is delicious—do you eat like this every night?"

"Not quite," Dorrin said. "The cook made something special for the prince's courier and, I suppose, you."

"This place is huge," Paks said. "The entrance hall's as big as some granges." She eyed the dish of plums and then looked straight at Dorrin. "Are you happy, Captain—Duke, I mean?"

"Happy?" Dorrin bit back the comment she'd almost made—happiness was a child's wish, not an adult's duty—but Paks was clearly happy, and she was no naive child. Paks's easy patience pulled answers out of her. "Sometimes. I had forgotten how beautiful it could be. Not the house; the house is . . ." She shook her head and left it there. "But the land. The land and the people. It's softer land than Kieri's—the king's—was. Settled longer, cared for longer. The kitchen orchard's thick with fruit this year. But as I said in Chaya, I never meant to come back. They didn't want me back. It was . . ." Again she stopped, feeling tears burning her eyes.

"Their evil is not your fault, Captain," Paks said.

"I know, but—" In halting phrases, at first, Dorrin told Paks what had happened, the discovery of Verrakai's use of others, even their own children, to transfer personalities from one to another, the traps and poisons she'd had to disarm before she dared sleep in any of the beds. The deaths.

"I had to do it," she said. "And I know that's what my family would say about what they did. They had to, it was . . . expedient. If I had not, they would have killed others—and how many there are loose in the land I do not know, since I don't know if all the transfers are recorded in the family book."

Paks reached out and touched her hand; Dorrin felt a rush of goodwill and strength. "You have a hard task," Paks said. "But you are faithful; that much is clear. Your people love you already, or they would not have celebrated your birthday."

"I am better than my uncle, under whom they suffered," Dorrin said. "Their gratitude is too great for the little I have done so far. It is all undoing—undoing curses, unsetting traps—before I can do anything real," Dorrin said. "Though today—" She paused.

"Tell me," Paks said, taking a plum from the bowl.

"The villagers had a well; my uncle cursed it." Dorrin told the rest of it, hurrying through the details and staring at her hands clasped on the table, for she felt tears rise again and did not want to cry in front of Paks.

"Undoing such evil is no small thing," Paks said, when Dorrin paused for breath. Dorrin looked up to see that Paks's eyes glittered with unshed tears in the lamplight.

"It is so . . . so sad," Dorrin said, past the lump in her own throat. "And it makes me so angry. All that waste, all that unnecessary pain and struggle . . . the years they had to send someone all the way to the stream for water, and why? Because my uncle chose it." She stopped again; Paks said nothing. "And then, at the end, where I expected water fouled past cleansing . . . the well was dry."

"Completely?"

"Yes. I felt the rock. Dry as Andressat in late summer; dry as if it had never been a well. I sat there, with the bones wrapped in my shirt, those pitiful bones—" Tears came despite her intent; she felt them on her face, but went on. "And when I asked the gods, no words came to me, nothing, and so I cried, as—as I am now." She choked, then found her voice again. "My family—does not—cry. All I could think—was the waste—the misery—the pain—we have caused. Year after year, and for what? And then the water came."

"Came how?" Paks asked, leaning forward. "And where?"

"Out of a cleft of the rock. It is—scarcely believable. I cried like a child, tears dripping right onto the rock, and then . . . the water came creeping out of that cleft."

"Did it frighten you?" Paks asked. "You down a well and the water rising? But wait—you had a rope, you could get out safely."

"Not quite," Dorrin said. "It came slowly at first and then suddenly, a gush that lifted me up like a branch in a torrent." An echo of the joy she'd felt at the water dried the tears on her face as she grinned. "What I'm sure will be told behind my back for the rest of my life, one peasant to another, is how I looked, rising up on that gush of water half naked, with my burden of bones wrapped in my shirt."

Paks stared. "No shirt? But—oh, but you had to carry the bones—but—" She shook her head, chuckling.

"It was not," Dorrin said, laughter replacing tears, "*not* the dignity of a duke. I did think of that, on the way up, but too late."

"In terms of undoing your family's pride—" Paks began, but was laughing too hard to continue.

"My uncle would be mortified," Dorrin said. Laughter and tears together had left her now, and she felt more relaxed than she had since—since she could not remember. "My mother—well, she disowned me, years ago, but this would leave even her speechless."

"It was a very good thing," Paks said. "That is how magery should be used."

"I hope the Council will see it that way," Dorrin said. "It is still against Tsaian law, since Gird's time."

"I came for more than a visit," Paks said. "You should go to the Tsaian prince's coronation . . . you have had the invitation—?"

Dorrin looked up, startled. "That must be what the courier brought. I had no time; I had to go to what I thought was a judgment, and then I forgot." She looked around, and saw the courier's velvet pouch, embroidered with the royal arms of Tsaia lying on a side table. Inside was a scroll tied with rose and silver ribbons. Dorrin unrolled the stiff parchment. In formal flowery language it requested the honor of her presence as a peer of the realm at the coronation of Mikeli Vostan Keriel, rightful heir to the throne of Tsaia, unto whom she, as peer, would pledge fealty. It carried the seals of Tsaia, the signatures of Dukes Marrakai and Mahieran, members of the Regency Council, and the crown prince.

A smaller, thinner paper, rolled into the scroll, bore a personal, less formal message from the prince himself.

If it be that your domain is still too unsettled to permit your attendance, I will forgive your absence and send instead a Marshal to take your vows. Others may interpret your absence differently; for your own sake it would be wise to come if you can.

No word of her family members sent to Vérella, no comment on her rule so far. She pushed both across the table to Paks. "You were right; it is the invitation to the coronation. But I cannot go. I've still not found the young men and older boys who were here before I came—evidence of their sudden departure, yes, but by the time I had dealt with those left behind, they were beyond tracing. I expected them to come back, to attack—I still do—but so far, nothing. I have no one here I can trust, yet, to guard it while I'm gone, no one who knows it well enough."

Paks read intently, her finger moving down the lines. "Why do the peers—that's lords I suppose—have to swear fealty again? If they aren't loyal already, why are they on the Council?"

"Didn't Kieri—the king—have them do that in Lyonya?"

"He was new to them," Paks said. "That made sense, but this— they've known the prince for years—"

"As prince, not as king," Dorrin said. "Now it will be personal, as yours was to Kieri in the Company."

"If all are swearing fealty again, you should go," Paks said. "They must all—all the lords, and the prince—see that you have a personal oath to him. And you should know them, as you are one of them now."

Dorrin traced the seal of Tsaia lightly with her forefinger. "And leave behind those the prince and Council told me to protect and rule?"

"Others do."

"Others do not have a domain infested with Verrakai malice to deal with," Dorrin said. "Come—I will show you." Taking a lamp, she led the way to her uncle's office. Along the way, she warned Paks of the many traps and spells. "I disarmed as many as I could. Some are magical, some not—but all are subtle and dangerous. Every piece of furniture, so far, has had its way of killing the unwary, many that I did not know of, since children were brought here only rarely."

The study was emptier now; Dorrin had removed one item after another, to be dismantled and its traps destroyed outside. "Here's the record of transfers—the words are hidden unless I unlock them with magery." She glanced at Paks; Paks nodded. At Dorrin's command, the hidden pages came into view. "Most give the new host only a single name, no location or occupation. Those within the family have this symbol—" She pointed.

"You use the lamp," Paks commented, "instead of your own light."

"I use magery as little as may be," Dorrin said. "Aside from practice and at need."

"Does it want to be used?"

Dorrin turned to her. "Every moment. It is like the pressure of a stream; once the Knight-Commander and you released it, it has been harder to contain than to use. When I arrived here, and my relatives used theirs against me, it swelled into a river. You and the Knight-

Commander had said you thought I had great power. So it proved, enough power to hold them all motionless, silent, under my will."

"Was that frightening at first?" Paks asked.

"Yes." Dorrin shivered at the memory. "Most frightening was how I enjoyed it. I can understand—do not wish to understand but cannot help it—how my ancestors fell into evil, from the sheer joy of having such mastery. So I use lamps, and climb the stairs, and reach for things I might command with a word. Today, with the well, is the first time I have used magery so openly among my people. Those here saw me control my family, of course."

"That is wise," Paks said.

"But this is not all I wanted to show you," Dorrin said. "Not only are there Verrakai abroad in others' bodies, enemies of the realm, of the prince and king-to-be, but here is something I have not dared explore, when I was the only one here with power I could trust."

She led Paks to the far end of the study, where the vault door still gaped open a little on the bare patch of wall and the remains of the picture and its frame lay on the floor in front of it. Paks came alight.

"That is blood magery—evil—!"

"Yes. It was a portrait of one of our ancestors. It was there in my childhood; it had been there, I was told, for long ages, since the Verrakaien came north. When I first came into this room, it radiated evil; it called my magery; it threatened me." She stared at the remnants on the floor. "It bled when I pierced it—bled like a man, Paksenarrion. It was not painted on wood or fabric, like most paintings, but on skin— I believe human skin. And the frame, which looked—you can see the upper part—like carved and painted wood, is actually made of bones, plastered over."

"That power is not all gone."

"No. I can feel that. The blood dried and vanished in a mist, and most of the power here went—somewhere. I prayed, Paksenarrion, that it might never return."

"What's behind the door?"

"I saw an urn filled with blood; the blood dried and vanished in mist like the rest. A casket of carved wood inlaid with colored patterns. There might be more. I have left it as I found it, the door slightly open so I could watch for new blood."

"Take it out," Paks said. Dorrin glanced at her. Her clear paladin's light filled the room, leaving no shadows. "Whatever it is, I know we must discover it."

Whatever it was, if a paladin told her to stick her hand in a hole and bring something out—she would. Dorrin opened the vault door wider and light filled the chamber. Paks's light, like her own magery, revealed the traps she had not seen before. Paks came nearer.

"Your ancestors trusted no one, did they?"

"I can't speak for all," Dorrin said, "but no one so steeped in evil as my uncle and his followers trusts."

"Let me see if I can—" Paks pointed at the traps revealed, and one by one they withered. She turned to grin at Dorrin. "You're right. It is fun to play with power—not something the gods grant often to paladins."

Inside the vault, the box gleamed in that light, its designs twisting, interlacing . . . moving? Behind it, Dorrin could just see something else, something wrapped in what looked like old gray leather. "I don't remember that," she said. "It may've been there, but hidden in the dark."

"First the urn," Paks said. "Filled with magical blood, you said?"

"Real blood, preserved by magery. I don't know whose." Dorrin touched it and felt a tingle up her arm. She jerked it back.

"Magery?" Paks said.

"Something."

Paks reached past her and took out the urn. Once clear of the vault, it changed in her hands to a goblet, jewel-encrusted.

"Holy Falk," Dorrin said. "Ward this house."

"Gird's grace," Paks said. "It has writing on it, but I can't read it—"

Around the rim, a script Dorrin had never seen before squirmed and reformed into something she could read. *Who drinks from me without a right shall live for aye in endless night; the true king's draught shall hold him hale until the day his magery fail.* Dorrin recited this aloud to Paks.

"What is it?" Paks asked. "What does that mean?"

Dorrin felt cold all over. "It is—it must be—a coronation goblet for some king. From very long ago, and from whence I have no idea. Why it was a blood-filled urn I do not know either. Unless drinking blood was part of the coronation rite."

"Here," Paks said. "You hold it."

"Just put it down on the table," Dorrin said.

"But if it made you feel something, maybe it has more to teach. Tammarion's sword, that was the king's—"

"I can hold it later." Dorrin fought her magery, that wanted to hold it *now*, fill it with wine *now*, drink from it *now*. "There's more—we should get it all out, and somewhere safe."

Paks set the goblet on the table. "Do you want me to take the things out?"

She did, but it was her own heritage. "I will," Dorrin said. The box, when she touched it, sent the same thrill up her arm, but this time she did not flinch and the box did not change shape when she took it from the vault. It was heavier than it looked; she carried it to the table and set it down. She and Paks stared down at the designs on the upper surface.

"It reminds me of the designs in Luap's Stronghold, in Kolobia," Paks said after a long moment. "Not just beautiful, but powerful."

"Yes," Dorrin said. Her finger wanted to follow the lines, her thumb wanted to press *there*. She did not realize she had done so until the box opened, not like an ordinary box but like an intricately folded paper, flowerlike.

Glittering in the clear light Paks gave were jewels—sapphires and diamonds—fashioned into pieces Dorrin instantly recognized as someone's crown jewels . . . a ring like a ducal ring, only larger, a pair of earrings, broad bracelets large enough for a man's wrists, a pin such as might hold a cloak to a shoulder, a belt clasp as large as her hand.

Yours. The voice in her mind was clear as her own. *At last.* A tendril of light rose from the goblet, arced over, and touched a sapphire on the ring, big as a grape.

"I didn't do that," Paks said mildly. "Did you?"

"Not intentionally," Dorrin said. "What—what have we found?"

"What have your family kept hidden is the better question. A coronation goblet, jewels like these, whatever else is in there—have they been thieves or—or what?"

"The stories—family stories—say we were once kings. I never believed them."

"When, in Gird's day?"

"I don't know. I didn't want to know, Paks. I wanted to get away and never come back."

"The box opened to your touch. The urn changed—"

"In *your* hands, not mine." But it would have, she knew. "If it is true—if these are crown jewels from Old Aare—that doesn't mean Verrakaien are royal. We might be thieves only. That would explain hiding them, wouldn't it?" Dorrin looked at Paks, then at the open vault. "I begin to think I was foolish to start this in darkness, without a troop of Marshals, Captains, and another paladin or two."

Paks shook her head. "The gods sent me; they must think we can do it. Whatever it is."

Dorrin touched her ruby for luck and reached into the vault once more. The bundle that had been hidden behind the box felt stiff to the touch like old dried leather. She shuddered at the thought that it was also human skin, but as she drew it out, it changed into a cloth embroidered in brilliant blue, gold, and silver, soft and unworn, wrapped around something heavy—she knew without unwrapping what it must be.

On the table, she unfolded the cloth. Centered on the cloth's design, a many-pointed star, alternating gold and silver points against the blue, was an obvious crown, itself glittering with sapphires and diamonds but for one blank spot.

Joy burst over Dorrin like a wave; the light in the room shimmered, and without her intent, the crown rose off the table and hung in the air before her.

You are the one. At last I am free.

"Not now," Dorrin said aloud. Magery ran like fire through her veins; she could scarcely see Paks, though the silver circle on her brow burned brightly. Dorrin reached out, nonetheless, and took the crown in her hands, setting it back in its wrappings.

"Was that what I—what *was* that?" Paks said. She did not sound alarmed, just interested. Her calmness steadied Dorrin.

"It talked to me," Dorrin said. "Did you hear it?"

"No. What was it saying?"

"From the first—the goblet—" Dorrin nodded at the goblet. "It said it was mine. And so did the crown." She drew a long breath. "If—if my family heard such voices, and believed them, it would explain—"

Nothing. The voice was implacable. *They bound us with blood we did not want. You are different. We are yours.* Dorrin shivered.

"It said something else?" Paks said.

"Yes. It said they—my family—bound these things with blood— blood it did not want. That I am different, and these things belong to me."

"There was more," Paks said, looking at the jewels in the unfolded box. "See this space here?" She pointed to an empty space with the slight impression of something in the velvet lining. She looked at Dorrin, brow wrinkled around the circle. "I've seen something— somewhere—that's like these. A necklace. I know—" She looked excited now. "Brewersbridge, when I was there before I went to Fin Panir. Arvid—that thief—gave it to me. I gave it to the Girdish treasury when they chose me for paladin's training."

Dorrin smoothed the cloth that had been around the crown. Not a worn stitch, not a frayed edge. "I wish I knew what this meant." She touched the star-figure inside the arc of the crown. "It must be symbolic, but—"

"I saw it in Luap's Stronghold," Paks said. "A cloth something like this, but I don't know what it means. It was in a small chamber, empty but for the cloth laid on the sleeping shelf. I wasn't thinking about that, then. I was already falling into Achrya's spell."

"Do you think these things are evil?" Dorrin's own magery insisted NO but she did not trust it. "The voices from an evil spirit, tempting me?"

Paks touched them one by one. "No. Whatever evil has been here has not corrupted them, not that I can tell. I felt evil in the room—the remnants of that picture and its frame among them—but not these things. Yet they have a power—"

"That I do not understand," Dorrin said. "Falk and the High Lord give us wisdom to understand what this means."

"And what we should *do*," Paks said. She touched the jewels again. "I wonder why such jewels would be in Gird's colors."

"I hadn't thought of that." Dorrin looked. The goblet alone bore jewels in other colors, not many; the crown and those in the unfolded box were all blue and white.

"Could it mean Gird was crowned king at some point?" Paks asked. "There's nothing about that at all in the legends."

"But in his colors. Would he have taken blue as his color because at the time it was a royal color?"

"That's not mentioned either. I admit, I was not that interested in the history they taught us in Fin Panir. Maybe the Marshal-General would know. She might be at the coronation: there's another reason you must go. And take these with you."

"Take them—" Dorrin felt a weight land on her shoulders. "I can't go; I told you. There's no one—"

"I'll stay here," Paks said.

"You—is this your call?"

"Yes," Paks said, with utter certainty. "I understand it now. You must go, for all the reasons the prince gave and because of these—" She tipped her head to the goblet, crown, and jewels. "They've been at the heart of treachery for generations, though they themselves were not at fault. You must find out what they are, all that they are, and to whom they really belong."

Me. They belong to me. The thoughts came unbidden to Dorrin's mind; her magery surged, wanting free, wanting to show Paks, everyone, what it could do. She fought that down, fought the desire to claim that regalia, and with it, whatever realm it offered.

"But if there's trouble here—I should be here."

"Leave me Phelan's cohort. If anything goes amiss, I'll send word. Selfer and the cohort will keep me out of trouble."

That was almost saucy; Dorrin found herself grinning. "Do paladins get into trouble?"

"I imagine we can. I certainly ate too much at King Kieri's coronation feast—they had mushrooms I'd never tasted before."

Dorrin shook her head. "I know you're a paladin, Paks, but sometimes you are so like the girl you were."

"And still am, inside," Paks said. "I know—it's very strange. To me you're still Captain Dorrin, who once terrified me—all you captains did. You knew everything I thought."

"You know our warts now—"

"No, it's not that. I know you're now Duke Verrakai, someone more important—as far as rank goes—than a captain in the Duke's Company. But the person I see is the same person, not the rank." Her brow wrinkled again. "I don't know why. I see people now a little differently than before, when I was with the Company those first three years. Gird, maybe, or maybe one of the gods, has let me see a little way inside."

"Or experience," Dorrin said. "You are older; you have been through many things—"

"Yes," Paks said. "But more than that—the light we paladins are given to help us discern truth lets us see a little into the hearts of everyone we meet."

Dorrin had a moment of stark panic. What was deep in her Verrakai heart? But Paks was still talking.

"I remember you as much like a fine blade—trustworthy, keen-edged, someone any of us soldiers could trust when our own captain was away, someone who never delighted in causing pain. Your own cohort respected you absolutely. When I met you again, last fall, you were the same, but now I could see the flame of life the Marshal-General told us all have. Yours burns clear and clean—it did then, and it does now."

"I—I am—I don't know—I make mistakes—"

Paks shook her head. "It doesn't matter. Remember when you told the Knight-Commander you had once dreamed of being a paladin?"

"Yes." Dorrin felt the heat rise in her cheeks. "It was a foolish child's dream—"

"Was mine?" Paks asked. "Mine was much the same, barring the part about not wanting to spend my time weaving and shoveling dung. It is not foolish to want to be better, to spend a life helping others."

"But I was a Verrakai. To think I might be acceptable to Falk, to the gods—of course it could not be." But even as she spoke, her magery surged again, yearning toward the crown she had put down.

Paks snorted. "If the gods could accept a sheepfarmer's daughter from the edge of nowhere why would they care about your family? They do not select paladins in family groups, but individually."

"And I was not fit."

"Captain—Lord Duke—"

"Oh, just call me Dorrin," Dorrin said. "We are past rank here."

"Dorrin, then. What you said that night of the torment you endured as a child—it was as bad for you as the torment the Liartians put me through in Vérella. Worse, for you had no experience of good, had you? And you but a child. I at least knew I'd been chosen. I had seen Gird and the others, when I was fully healed. When you came to the Company of Falk, you were still unhealed, is that not so?"

"Yes, but . . . what are you saying?" The old dream rose in her mind; her magery took it and held it fast.

"I say to you what Master Oakhallow said to me, in different words: You are what you are, and the gods may have plans for you now that you were not able to fulfill then."

"It is too late to become a paladin," Dorrin said, surprising herself as the words came out of her mouth.

"I don't know if that's what the gods intend for you," Paks said. "But consider what you did today. Removing the curse from a well is much like healing it, I would say. And you cannot have that—" She pointed at the table. "—for no reason. If they want you for a paladin, you will become one—after all, they made one of me, after so many thought me a useless coward."

"You were never that," Dorrin said.

"You were never a villainous Verrakai."

"Some were," Dorrin said, looking at the crown again. "Paks, supposing I do go—why should I risk these treasures on the road? What of thieves and—for that matter—attack by my own kin? I should keep them safe, where they cannot be stolen—"

Paks shook her head. "Think again. What are your relatives likely to tell the prince about you?"

"That I'm vindictive and not wholly sane, not to be believed. They are innocent and loyal; I'm the family traitor and having broken troth with them am inherently unfaithful."

"They will expect you to have the jewels, and they will expect you to keep them. That is what they would do. If they reveal the jewels and you are found with a crown . . . what do you think the prince will think?"

Dorrin scowled, then nodded. "That I am false, and planning to seize the throne. But I swear, Paks, it is not this throne the crown speaks of."

"It matters not. Your relatives will insist it is."

"And some will believe them, even though they distrust my relatives," Dorrin said. "Just as some will always believe me false, because I am a Verrakai."

"Exactly," Paks said. "The king told me that most judge not by actual deeds, but by reputation. Remember, when you were there, how the master of horse in Chaya believed grays were dangerous because of their color?"

"Yes," Dorrin said. "But I thought, sending my family to Vérella, as ordered, would prove my loyalty. I see now that someone might argue I had a grudge against those I sent, and did not capture those I liked."

"Yes. If you are at the coronation, if you present the king with these things—especially the crown—and explain that you found them hidden—and give your oath in front of all, that will go some way toward gaining the trust of those who have long distrusted Verrakaien."

Dorrin saw the logic of that, and yet— "These things belong somewhere else," she said. "Not in Tsaia at all. I feel I must find out where, and—and take them there, maybe."

"Not stay in Tsaia?"

"Not forever, I think. Kieri said—the king said—he thought the Tsaian king did not intend me to hold Verrakai forever, but to name an heir, one of those Verrakai who is found innocent of taint."

"I met such a one," Paks said. "On my way from the Duke's Stronghold to Lyonya. Ganarrion, his name was; he's in the Royal Guard. You might seek him out."

"I am past bearing an heir of the body," Dorrin said, "even if I wished to do so. I thought of one of the children here, but they have spent their whole lives in the influence of my uncle and his kind."

"How are they now?"

"Better, I think, but who can tell, with children? Having none of my own, I never studied how best to train them; I must leave much of that to the nurserymaids, and trust I have weeded out the vicious from among those."

"Another reason to let me ward this place for you while you're in Vérella," Paks said, grinning. "I am closer to my own childhood, as you said, and I had younger sibs—I like children."

"But never wanted some of your own?" Dorrin asked.

"No. Wiped too many dirty bottoms, and saw my mother's birth pangs too many times. A soldier's life is thought hard, and it is, but that day-by-day watchfulness and worry—I was not meant for that."

"Indeed, you were not," Dorrin said. "Nor was I. Well. I don't want to go, but I see I must." Another thought struck her. "Oh gods above!"

"What?"

"I have no court clothes." Paks looked blank. "Tsaian court clothes. For the coronation and everything else; everyone else will have them. They'll expect—it will be an insult if I turn up like this—" Dorrin gestured at her plain shirt and trousers. "And it's too late to get anything made in Vérella; every tailor will be racing to finish things ordered at the Evener or before."

"Did your relatives take all their clothes with them?"

"No, but—" Dorrin shook her head. "It is a jest, but a bitter one. I was so disgusted with their finery . . . I threw them out, all those fancy things, or most of them. Told the house staff to cut them up and make clothes for themselves, or give them to their families. And besides, nothing would have fit me—the ladies of this house had magery, not muscles."

"Must you wear skirts at court? You were titled duke, not duchess."

"I suppose—" Dorrin thought about it. "If I'm going to be an outcast anyway, and the only female duke, I might as well be outrageous in my dress. That's good; I hate skirts. Men's dress at court is still court dress, but I might contrive something more easily. I wonder if Verrakai House in Vérella has been sold—"

"Your family has two houses?"

Dorrin nodded. "Verrakai had more than two houses, if any are left to us, if the Crown did not confiscate them for my uncle's treason. A house in Vérella, where family attending court lived. Houses here and there for family members who wanted to live apart for a while."

"Perhaps your uncle left court clothes there, and you could use them."

"I would not want to wear anything that had touched his body," Dorrin said. "The touch of his magery—"

"Falk will protect you," Paks said with such confidence that Dorrin felt her own doubts vanish.

CHAPTER THIRTY-EIGHT

Dorrin left the next morning, escorted not by her Phelani troops, but by five Verrakai militia chosen by Selfer for their progress toward soldierly qualities. They looked nothing like the ruffians she'd first encountered; now their badges and buckles gleamed, their boots shone, their hair was clean and trimmed. Their saddlecloths were authentic Verrakai—that much had been found in the stables—though the horses were Phelan's. Dorrin had signed another note to Selfer acknowledging the debt.

With them, on Farin the cook's advice, were two of her assistants. "Efla can cook, passably," the cook said. "Jaim's too young, but you'll need an errand boy to help fetch and carry from market and the like. None of those militia I'd trust to boil water and make sib, let alone cook for the lot of you, and you don't know if any of the servants are still in the city house." A single pack animal carried only a light load—the royal regalia, now wrapped piece by piece in clean linen and then packed into a padded sack—and what she'd found that might be turned into court clothes later. Another carried supplies they might need in Vérella "in case the house was robbed after the old duke . . ." The cook laid her finger on her throat. Dorrin had the prince's invitation in her own saddlebags, along with the pass to travel to and from Vérella.

They reached Harway just at dark after a long day's travel, and found rooms at the same inn where, at the end of winter, she had lodged. "How many nights?" the innkeeper asked.

"Two or three," Dorrin said. "I need to find a tailor here, or some-where on the road to Vérella. I'm summoned to the coronation and have no court attire." She laughed, making a joke of it. "I did not anticipate needing any—do you know someone who might—"

"A court dress for a lady of your rank?" he said. "Even the best I know of cannot do that in one day or two."

"Not a dress," Dorrin said. "I know that is impossible. But the prince named me duke, and I've worn soldier's clothing since I was a young girl. Something suitable for a duke—shirts with ruffles or lace or something. A doublet—"

"Oh, that." His face cleared. "You'll want Durgeon & Sons for that. Pili Durgeon's an excellent tailor, and I'm sure he'll be able to find something to suit. It's from him your men got that blue cloth when you were here before, and since then he's had a shipment from the south. 'Tis late tonight, but I can send a lad to let him know you'll visit in the morning, shall I?"

"Thank you," Dorrin said.

She spent the next morning with the tailor. "I've got work I can-not put aside, even for a duke," he said. "But that will be finished this afternoon, and I can take your measurements and requirements now. Court clothes—yes, of course I know what's needed. As for the materials—look here." He led her to the back of the shop, past men and women busily at work in the light of wide windows, to a locked chamber. Inside, rolls of cloth filled shelves, but for a small section holding bundles wrapped in muslin.

"This—" He lifted a muslin-wrapped bundle and began unwrap-ping it. "The previous duke ordered this two years ago, to make up a robe for the coronation this year. Drew the design for the brocade and all, and I sent to the south, to the weavers there, to have it woven just for him."

Dorrin's skin prickled. What kind of design would her uncle have chosen? Something evil no doubt. Durgeon unwrapped the last layer of muslin and lifted out a long roll of blue and silver brocade. "I washed it and stretched it square, then made it up, but when the Order of Attainder came, I was sure I'd lost by it—for he never paid me; said he would pay when he took it to court. Crowns a span, it was, all my cost, but he was not to argue with . . ."

The cloth shimmered. Against a background of blues shading from dark to pale, star shapes that Dorrin recognized from the cloth around the crown. Those were done all in pale gray and silver. She touched it lightly and felt nothing, no evil at all.

"It would suit you, as well," Durgeon said. "With your height, and your dark hair. He chose a dark blue lining, you see, but if you chose dark for your formal doublet, I could change that out to pale gray in no time."

"It's beautiful," Dorrin said. She touched it again, lightly. Durgeon began to unfold it on the table.

"You see the wide band of fur on the sleeves. Silver clasps in front. The Verrakai arms embroidered on the back—"

"Is that necessary?" Dorrin asked, stroking the fabric.

"Have you not seen formal court dress—?" he began.

"No, I was never at court," Dorrin said. "If the stories you heard about me include exile, being disowned by the family, that's the truth of it."

"Well, then, my lord—" Durgeon turned the robe, showing her the back. "Every peer displays the family crest on the most formal of court robes—for such ceremonies as this. Every rank has its own required style. Dukes, for instance, have a fur cuff twice as wide as counts, and barons have but a finger-width edge. Your shirts, as a duke, should have wider lace, with gold or silver ribbon threaded through; your doublet will be embroidered on the heart side with the crest, in silver, and the slashes bound in silver cord. Your capelet, for the formal dinners, will have full four fingers of silver braid. And your shoes—" He looked at her boots, the plain black leather she had considered her dress boots, and shook his head. "You were right to stop here, my lord. In Vérella you will not find tailors or cobblers able to fit your work in, but Liam the cobbler can make you court shoes and boots."

Two days later, Dorrin set off for Vérella with many fewer coins and many more clothes. Shirts, semi-dress trousers, the short trews she would need for the coronation itself, doublets, jackets, capelets, capes, and the formal court robe. Shoes, hose, boots. Her escort had new blue velvet caps with the Verrakai badge to wear when they accompanied her in the palace.

As she neared Vérella, traffic on the road thickened, with wagons and carts bringing in supplies, merchants, travelers. At the city gate, she presented her pass and invitation once more. "There's no more lodging in the palace," the officer said. "I'm not sure, my lord, where you'll stay—the inns are crowded."

"Do you know if the Crown took over the Verrakai residence?"

"No." His mouth twisted with distaste. "You can look, I suppose."

Verrakai House, when she came to it, had no guards out front and no sign of life. It was on a corner; a busy street in front, a narrow alley down one side. Dorrin tried the door; it didn't move. She knocked. No answer. She became aware that some in the busy street were slowing to watch. She laid one hand on the door itself and one on the latch, and spoke the command words that came to her.

The door swung open silently. "Well," she said. "It looks empty enough. There should be stabling for the horses somewhere near. Wait; I will find the entrance."

Inside, the house smelled a little musty but had also the feel of a place enchanted, watchful. Dorrin touched her ruby, then her ducal medallion. "Verrakai!" she said. She sensed a relaxation. Wary of traps, she went down the passage ahead of her; it opened at the far end to a walled yard with stalls across the way; a closed gate to the left led, she was sure, to the alley. She unbarred the gate and went back through the house.

"Go down that alley—I opened the gate to the mews, I'll take this—" The padded sack, on top of everything else. She had not risked having it out of her sight on the whole journey. It had made a most uncomfortable bed companion.

Two of her escort came inside with her. The house was oddly shaped, not the simple square or rectangle its front suggested. Four stories above ground . . . Dorrin eyed the iron-bound cellar door that stank of blood magery and decided not to open it, at least not yet. The ground floor had two kitchens, large and small reception rooms. Above that, a large study, lined with shelves, very like her uncle's study on Verrakai land. She suspected it had many of the same traps. Bedrooms, also furnished with traps for the unwary. Above that again, more bedrooms, and in the attic, what had clearly been servants' quarters.

Evidence of her uncle's connection to the Thieves' Guild and the Bloodlord were everywhere. The Horned Chain above the fireplace, barbed whips in a stand in the corner, bloodstains on the floor, smeared into words. She was sure she would find worse in the cellars.

"Let's get these windows open," she said to her escort. Both hangings and windows were trapped; she disarmed them. Afternoon light and air rolled into room after room as she threw the shutters wide. When she glanced down, she saw people in the street below, looking up gape-mouthed. One took off at a run.

Within a half-glass, someone pounded on the front door. Dorrin had left one of her people in the front hall to answer; now she came down the stairs to find a troop of Royal Guard in the street, and an officer standing on the doorstep.

"—By what right are you here?" the officer was saying.

"I'm Duke Verrakai," Dorrin said, coming forward. "And this is Verrakai's house in Vérella."

"I know whose house it is," he said. "But I do not know you, and I know that Verrakaien are under Order of Attainder. Come forth, and face the justice of the Court."

"I am not under that order," Dorrin said. "I was summoned here for the prince's coronation, and I have a pass from the prince himself."

"You can explain that to the Court," the officer said.

"I will show you the pass." Dorrin had tucked it into her doublet at the city gate; she took it out again. "Here."

He glanced at it, then looked again and read it. "You are not under Order of Attainder . . . how can that be? Is this genuine?"

Dorrin waited, saying nothing.

"Stay here," he said. "I will take this to the palace and see if it is truly what the prince meant to say."

Dorrin looked at the man who was obviously his second-in-command.

"I have been riding all morning," she said. "I would rest—have one of my people bring a chair. And you, too, if you will."

"I am not going in that cursed house," the man said. "We could not enter it when the prince told us to make sure it was empty—and now you enter it with a touch, the witnesses say. It is a trap."

"Gani, bring me a chair, please," Dorrin said. "Set it here, where this gentleman can see." When the chair arrived, she had it placed so the door would not close, and sat down, smiling up at the man outside the door. "I have no intent to harm you, or anyone who does not harm me first. The prince knows why he appointed me Duke; my family disowned me tens and tens of years ago and I have served Duke Phelan for most of the time since."

"The one who's king now?" the man asked. "Did you meet that paladin?"

"Paks? Yes. She was not in my cohort, but Captain Arcolin's. She is watching Verrakai Steading while I am here, in fact."

"Lord Sir Ammerlin, he said he saw her make light over the whole battle, over there east when he was taking Phelan to Lyonya to be king."

"She did indeed," Dorrin said. "I was there and saw it."

His brow furrowed. "You were there. But—how?"

Dorrin explained, as briefly as she could, and then saw the other captain riding back at a quick trot, as those on foot scattered. He looked both relieved and embarrassed as he dismounted.

"My lord Duke, I am sorry—we have had such trouble, I did not trust your pass—but the prince says you are welcome here, and not under Order of Attainder, not you nor anyone with you. Please—my apologies." He bowed.

"You were wise to be cautious," Dorrin said. "And fortunate in not being able to enter here, for my relatives who practiced evil left many dangers for the unwary. I know you have other duties, but could you tell me where the nearest grange of Gird is? Or a Falkian field?"

"There's a grange not far," he said. "Do you need a Marshal?"

"This house must be cleansed," Dorrin said. "That is why I'm opening the windows, when I've untrapped them . . ."

"*Windows* were trapped?"

"Evil delights in darkness and secrecy," Dorrin said. "Anyone who tried to let in light, without knowing the dangers, faced certain death. If you like, come inside and I will show you."

"No," he said, backing up a step. "If the prince says you are welcome, you are welcome and I will pass the word. We do believe passages underground lead into the cellars here, but we were not able to penetrate them." He mounted. "Do you wish me to send a Marshal?"

"I will go myself and speak to the nearest grange," Dorrin said. "Though if you wish to tell them I will be coming, they might like to know. But first, when I have cleared enough of the house for myself and these my escort, I must present myself at the palace."

"I will tell them," he said. "Lest they think you are the other Verrakaien come back."

"Thank you," Dorrin said.

It was evening, the long slow twilight of near Midsummer, before Dorrin had enough rooms cleared for the safety of her escort and her kitchen staff. The boy, Jaim, had been to a market twice. In the stable, oats, hay, and straw seemed untainted by magery, and the horses they'd ridden stood quietly in the stalls, munching as if back home.

She had to bathe. In the kitchen, Efla chopped vegetables; steam rose from a kettle on its hook over the fire. In the scullery, an array of tubs hung along one wall. Dorrin set the largest on the stone floor and poured in cold water from the water butt and a little hot from the kitchen. It was so like her first days in the country house that she found it funny.

She was in the tub when a thunderous banging on the front door echoed through the house. It was the Marshal from down the street, her escort informed her, demanding to see her.

"When I'm dressed," Dorrin said. Her uncle had left linens in the house at least; she had placed a stack ready and grabbed one when she heard the knocking. "Put him in the safe reception hall; warn him that the house is not yet safe and tell him I will be there shortly."

She might as well put on the informal court dress she had brought to the scullery with her, what the tailor had told her was appropriate for submitting her credentials. She put on the gray trousers, a half-dress shirt with a handspan of lace at the cuffs and neck, a doublet of light blue and silver-gray brocade, dress boots with fancy spurs ornamented with silver chains. Her ducal chain of office; her ducal ring; her sword belt—she slipped her dress dagger into its sheath, the sword into the hanger.

The Marshal waiting in the smaller reception room had his lips compressed and a look of suspicion on his face. Dorrin expected that. She did not expect his first words.

"You're the one who brought Phelan's troop through the city, aren't you? I'm Marshal Tamis."

"Yes," Dorrin said. "That was I. You might have heard me spoken of as Captain Dorrin; I commanded one of his cohorts these past tens of years."

"I saw you," he said. "'Twas after Gird's paladin was freed, and we at last began the cleansing of this city. I saw you ride by with his soldiers, wearing his colors then. I never forget a face," he added, a little smugly.

"I'm sorry," Dorrin said. "I did not notice you—I was thinking only of catching up with Kieri—"

"What is it you want from me?" he asked.

"The former Duke did evil magery in this house," Dorrin said. "I found it full of traps, both physical and magical. Only a few rooms are clear, and in some of them are things I do not know how to clear. He and the others followed Liart; Liart's symbols and evidence of blood magery are in room after room. I need your help, Marshal, to cleanse the place."

"How did you clear the rooms you've cleared so far?"

"The physical traps—the poisoned pins and darts, the contact poisons on window latches and the like—are all things I'd seen as a child, and have disarmed at Verrakai Steading in the days since I've been there. The magery—you might as well know, Marshal, that the prince granted me permission to use magery against magery. It was the only way to subdue those of my family I captured and sent here for judgment."

"Magery . . ." He looked at her sideways. "You have the real magery, like the old ones?"

"Yes," Dorrin said. "Though I did not know it until recently. It was freed with the aid of Paks and the Knight-Commander of Falk, and was—they thought—the only way for me to carry out the prince's command to subdue those under Attainder."

"Your ruby proclaims you a Knight of Falk." That in a challenging tone.

"Indeed," Dorrin said. "And I have prayed more to Falk and the High Lord since I came to Verrakai Steading than in years of combat in Aarenis. Prayed for wisdom, for the right use of my power . . . and only with it have I been able to save those who suffered so long."

He huffed out a breath, then said, "The evening turns—you have made your bow at the palace already?"

"No," Dorrin said. "I was bathing when you came; days on the road left me in no condition to pay courtesies."

"Then show me the worst you know of here, and I will do what I can. I understand you will not want to leave me here to explore on my own—"

"Indeed not, not until I've uncovered every trap I can find."

Dorrin led him upstairs to what had been the Duke's study. "This room still has physical traps," she said. "I have not had time to disarm them all. What I do not know how to disarm is that." She pointed to the blood smears on the floor, under the horned chain of Liart hung on the wall.

"Gird's grace," the Marshal said. He turned to Dorrin. "Were I you, I would seal this room until I can bring another Marshal. It will take more than one of us. Are there other such?"

"A symbol of Liart in the bedrooms where I believe my uncle the former Duke, my other uncle his brother, and the kirgan Verrakai slept. Blood marks on the threshold of the doors of those rooms. Symbols in blood on the floor beneath the beds—I do not know their meaning. I have sealed those rooms. I have not gone into the cellars at all; they are clearly tainted."

"Where then will you sleep?" the Marshal asked.

"In that room where you waited," Dorrin said. "There are more rooms upstairs—the servants' quarters up in the attics might be safe, but I haven't had time to check them." At his expression, she grinned. "Marshal, I've slept on the ground or on floors many a night on campaign. A soft bed is pleasant, but not necessary."

He shook his head. "When I think of you as Phelan's captain, riding past at the head of your troops, I can believe it. But in court clothes, as Duke Verrakai? The only Duke Verrakai I've seen was very different."

Dorrin rode the short distance to the palace with only one of her escort at her side, as requested. At the gates, the palace guard looked far more like guards and less ceremonial than she had seen on other trips through Vérella. As Dorrin rode up, an officer stepped forward, the knots of a Serrostin in the collateral line on his uniform shoulder. He clearly expected her.

"My lord," he said, with a slight bow. "If it please you, dismount and let a groom take your horse and show your escort to the servants' hall, he will be taken care of while you proceed—the prince will see you shortly."

Dorrin dismounted and handed her reins to a groom in livery.

"And I'm afraid I must ask you to disarm," the officer said. "Your arms will be borne for you by one of the guard, and returned when you leave, or if the prince grants permission to carry them yourself . . ."

"I understand," Dorrin said. She took off the belt, sword and dagger still attached, and handed it to the officer, who passed it to another guard. "I wore no hidden weapons today, sir, though if you find it necessary, you may ask to search. I do wear mail, as I am aware of the hostility directed to my family—understandable, but I do not wish to die of it before I can report to the prince."

He gave her a long look, as if making up his mind in lieu of specific orders, and then shook his head. "No need, my lord Duke. Duke Phelan trusted you; the prince trusts him. Redeem that trust, if you will, or my honor is forfeit."

Serrostins, she recalled, were as honor-minded as Marrakai, another ancient family whose roots were somewhere in the deep south. Her family had sneered at them as having no magery, losing it early to presumed intermarriage with ignorant peasants.

"My relatives chose one path, sir," she said, meeting his gaze. "I chose another. Indeed, your honor risks nothing in trusting me."

"I am glad to hear it, my lord," the man said. "I will now lead you to the prince." He turned away and Dorrin followed him across the great outer court to the palace entrance. Paks had described it; she recognized the stairs, the pillars, the carvings.

"I must beg your courtesy," Dorrin said, as they neared the steps. "I spent my life as a mercenary captain, as you know. I had no training, after early childhood, in the etiquette of nobles greeting one another, or indeed a ruler, and none at all here in this court. Foreign courts were likely very different, and besides, as a mere mercenary . . ." She stopped. "The truth is, I do not know whether to bow or bend the knee to the prince when I meet him. I do not wish to offend in my ignorance, either this evening or at any of the ceremonies to come. To whom may I look for guidance?"

He almost stumbled, coming to a stop four steps up. "You—don't know *any* court protocol?"

"Not at all," Dorrin said. "I never came to this court, even when I came to Vérella. I did not wish to see my uncle the Duke, nor he to see me—my name was blotted out of the family records. Kieri or Jandelir reported to the palace—I mean," she said, seeing his confusion, "Kieri Phelan and Jandelir Arcolin."

"You will need a guide," he said. "Unfortunately, I cannot serve as your guide, beyond this meeting; I have duties that fill my time. I can introduce you to the Master of Ceremonies, but he, too, is busy organizing the coronation."

"I told Paksenarrion about this," Dorrin said. "She suggested I find a boy she knew—Aris Marrakai—"

"Marrakai! She told a Verrakai to ask a Marrakai for help?" He rolled his eyes. "My lord Duke, that suggestion could have come only from a paladin! It is in defiance of all Tsaian history, ancient and modern."

"I gathered," Dorrin said. "But at the same time, it is a paladin's suggestion, and a Girdish paladin's at that. Have you another?"

"No." He turned, and continued up the stairs. "I do not, and if Marrakai assents, it will do much to maintain your skin entire. Kirgan Marrakai is one of the prince's closest companions, as is my cousin Kirgan Serrostin." He nodded to the guards at the palace doors, which stood open to catch the evening breeze and led her inside. "I can tell you, my lord, for this first meeting you would be wise to go to one knee, heart-hand to your breast, like this—" He demonstrated, half-turned to her. "It is more formal than normally required, but it will look well."

"Thank you," Dorrin said. "I will do so."

Her passage through the palace brought many long looks, some hostile; Dorrin ignored them. She had no idea which rooms were which. They went this way and that, up a set of stairs, down another passage. The officer spoke to a guard at one door, who knocked, and announced "Guard-Captain Serrostin and a visitor" then flung the door wide for them to enter.

In a room lit by oil lamps, a cluster of men stood at one side, near windows that let in a cool breeze. Most were young; the prince and his companions, Dorrin thought. The older man in rose and white would be one of the prince's uncles; the other older man wore Marshal's blue.

"My lord prince, Duke Dorrin Verrakai," the officer said. Dorrin went down on one knee. She could feel the tension in the room.

The prince moved from the others and came to her, his expression guarded. "Duke Verrakai, do you come to tell me all your renegade family are safely confined?"

"No, my lord prince. I come at your request to pledge fealty and see you crowned rightful king of Tsaia."

"I have heard, from sources I do not fully trust, of a secret crown and secret realm."

Dorrin said, "My lord prince, there are matters we must discuss, but by your leave I would rather bring proof than words."

"You name me rightful king. Do you mean that?"

"Yes," Dorrin said. "With all my heart."

He put out a hand. "Rise, then, lord Duke, and be welcome here until such time as you choose another allegiance or play me false."

Dorrin took his hand and stood. "I intend neither," she said.

"The gods do not always cooperate with human intentions," the prince said. "Come, I will introduce you."

"My lord prince," the guard-captain said. "The duke's arms?"

The prince looked at Dorrin. "You would have known the paladin Paksenarrion—"

"Yes, lord prince."

"Where is she now, do you know?"

"Watching over Verrakai lands, my lord. She came from Chaya and urged me to accept your invitation, which I had been loath to do because I had not yet captured all you commanded. She said she would watch it for me, and indeed there is none I trust more."

"Well then, I will trust you to bear arms in my presence the same as any other noble of your rank." He nodded at the guard captain. "Return the duke's arms, and inform the palace guard that the Duke is as privileged in that regard as any other peer."

"At once, my lord," the guard-captain said. He gestured to the soldier who carried Dorrin's belt and sword. "If the prince will excuse me now—"

"Of course," the prince said. He smiled at Dorrin. "And now, let me introduce you—"

Dorrin recognized the colors, and had seen some of the nobles on the streets of Vérella; she had never met them. The older man, Duke Sonder Mahieran, the prince's uncle. High Marshal Seklis. Kirgan Marrakai, Kirgan Valthan Serrostin and a younger brother Rolyan, Kirgan Konhalt. All young men of breeding, near or just over majority, heirs of noble fathers. Dorrin bowed to each, and each bowed in return, though without real warmth.

"You arrived today, I think," the prince said.

"Indeed, my lord. It will seem strange to all of you, but—having been estranged from my family for so long—I had never been to their residence here, and finding it—and making it safe to inhabit even in part—took up the rest of the day."

"But you have been in Vérella before," the prince said.

"Yes, with Kieri Phelan's company, as his captain, guiding troops through the city. My dealings were with merchants, on occasion, or on Duke Phelan's business with his banker. Not with my family, and not here, where I might have met them."

"Your family's property was forfeit to the Crown as a result of the bill of attainder," the prince said. "I exempted the Verrakai lands, for the time, but the house here—we would have seized it, but that we could not. I grant you the use of it while you are here on court business, but nothing more, for the time being. Is that clear?"

"Yes, my lord prince," Dorrin said.

"Funds in the bank your predecessor used have been confiscated— that banker, we found, was involved in the Thieves' Guild, to the great embarrassment of the Moneychangers' Guild where he held an office of distinction. The Crown will release such funds to you as you require for attending us at our command, but the rest will remain in our control until such time as we are satisfied."

"I understand, Lord Prince," Dorrin said. She understood, but she did not like the thought of applying to the prince's clerks for money to buy every butt of water, every stick of firewood.

"We do not enjoy being harsh, but events—events have forced us to more caution than we otherwise would choose."

"Of course," Dorrin said.

"Then sit down with us. This is not a Council meeting, you perceive, but I wanted these men to meet you, and you to meet them. Two others will join us later." The others took off their swords and put them in a rack to one side; Dorrin did the same. The prince waved to the table, and Dorrin sat where he bade her. Duke Mahieran went to the door and called for a servant to bring refreshments, then came and sat beside her.

CHAPTER THIRTY-NINE

"When did you join Phelan's Company?" asked Duke Mahieran. "Was he then a duke?"

"He is some years older than me," Dorrin said. "I had met him at the Falkian Hall, where we both took training—he being already a veteran, having fought with Halveric Company a season or two in Aarenis. I was one of the youngest accepted, as he was one of the oldest, so it was years before I saw him again. I needed work, and the Captain-General of Falk sent me to Aliam Halveric. He knew Phelan was looking for a junior captain, and recommended me. It was his first independent command."

"I know about that," Kirgan Marrakai said. "My grandfather gave him a horse."

"I didn't know a Verrakai was in his service until he told us, the day the sword proclaimed him," Duke Mahieran said. "And yet I've seen Phelan's troops coming through Vérella spring after spring, and you were sometimes with them. To my shame, I saw only the mercenary captain."

"It is no shame to you, my lord," Dorrin said. "That is what I was, most of my life, and you saw the truth of it. I never expected to use my family's name again or take any part in the life of nobles."

"It did not bother you to set that wealth and luxury aside?" High Marshal Seklis asked.

"Marshal, if you knew what it was that you call luxury—I was glad to escape, and that was not my only attempt. I wanted nothing they had to offer me." Dorrin clenched her fists in her lap to stop them trembling. "The current Knight-Commander of Falk knows some of it. I told him, and Paksenarrion. If I must—"

"Not if it pains you," the prince said, holding up a hand. The two older men looked as if they would hear more.

Dorrin shook her head. "It pains me, my lord prince, but it is what made me what I am. I would prefer not to have it become a . . . a tale of dinner gossip. It is not trivial to me."

High Marshal Seklis frowned at the younger men. "Can we trust you youngsters not to chatter?"

They nodded. Dorrin looked them each in the face. They had been someone's squires, or were now: they should know how to keep secrets. She repeated again what she had told Kieri Phelan and Paks; the telling was no easier for being repeated. From their faces, they were first disbelieving, then horrified, disgusted.

"That's horrible!" the younger Serrostin burst out. His brother put a hand on his shoulder. "How did you—how could a child— survive—?"

"I don't know. I can remember little—so if there was someone who helped me, taught me—I do not know who it was." She went on, as quickly as she could, ignoring their exclamations and finished with the story of her final, successful escape and the sanctuary Falk's Hall had given her.

"A remarkable story," Duke Mahieran said, with an undertone of *if true*.

The young men were looking at her as she had had young men look before: squires to captains who had just revealed something of their own youth. High Marshal Seklis shook his head. "*I* believe it is true, Sonder. And the paladin is her friend. Whatever the other Verrakaien believed or believe, this one is not like them."

"There's still that story of conspiracy," Duke Mahieran said. "Mikeli's my nephew, my prince, and soon to be my king. We must know what she knows about that."

"I do not know what you have heard," Dorrin said. "But in my uncle's study in the house in our domain, I found proof of . . . of something. I don't know exactly what; I brought . . . things . . . here, to give to the prince."

"Liart's foulness, I suppose."

"No, my lord. I would still rather show, than speak of them. They are at the house, under guard."

"Back east, or here in Vérella?"

"Here. Paksenarrion has seen them; she thinks something is missing, something she once found, but then forsook."

"Do not play with us, Duke Verrakai," Mahieran said, turning sharply to face her. "Do you so distrust the prince and his closest companions—?"

"I distrust the air itself," Dorrin said. "I believe this matter will and should be made public, but what I think of these things will be nothing to the experience."

"Then let us go to your house here in the city," said Duke Mahieran. "Or just me and High Marshal Seklis, if you will."

It was late now, long summer twilight shading at last to dusk, but Dorrin nodded. "As you wish, my lords. The prince should come, as the matter does touch on royalty."

"Royalty!" Mahieran's eyes widened. "Then we will come, at once, and with us what force we might need. Can I trust you to tell us truly?"

"Truly, I do not know. The house itself still holds traps and dangers, as I've told the Marshal who visited today and your guard-captain. But what I brought should be safe enough to open."

Dorrin set out three wrapped bundles on the table. "I found these in my uncle's study, in a vault in the wall, behind a . . . painting that had been there when I was a child. I must warn you—blood magery was used on at least one of these things. And they have their own magic."

She unwrapped the goblet; when she touched it, she felt the now-familiar tingle. "This looked like a small urn when I first saw it; it was full of blood that then vanished in a mist."

"Holy Gird's protection be on us," High Marshal Seklis muttered.

"The inscription on the rim of the cup changed from a script I could not read to one I could," Dorrin said. She handed it to the prince, who took it gingerly and peered at the script.

"*I* can't read this," he said.

Dorrin quoted it for him. "Do you feel anything as you hold it?"

"Other than astonishment, no," he said, handing it back. "Do you?"

"Yes," Dorrin said. She unwrapped the box.

High Marshal Seklis peered at the designs. "That pattern—it reminds me of a drawing the Marshal-General sent, of something found in Kolobia."

"Paksenarrion said the same," Dorrin said. She ran her finger along the pattern on the box, and once more it unfolded to reveal the treasure within. "Paks and I think this is royal regalia from somewhere, but where, neither of us knows. Paks thinks the necklace found in a robbers' den near Brewersbridge was in the same set—see this empty space?"

The prince looked eager and interested; Duke Mahieran reached toward the box, perhaps to touch the lining, and the box snapped closed so fast it bumped his finger.

"What was that! Did you think I was going to steal it?"

Dorrin shook her head. "It never did that before—though this is only the second time I've had it open. The other time, Paks was there. I don't know, my lord—"

"You claim it did that by itself?"

"As it opened. Try tracing the pattern on the top, with your heart-hand finger, and then touching that blue stone in the center." Dorrin stood back, giving him room.

Scowling, he traced the pattern as she directed; the box opened very slowly, but when he tried to touch the lining it snapped shut once more. "It doesn't like me," he said.

"Have you taken anything out of it?" High Marshal Seklis asked.

"No. I've touched the inside, though, and it never closed on me like that." Once more Dorrin opened the box and stroked the blue velvet lining. The box did not move, until she touched the two ends, when it folded again.

"And the third thing?" Seklis asked.

"Ah. That's two mysteries in one," Dorrin said. She unfolded the cloth and spread it flat. "Paksenarrion says this design resembles one found on a cloth in Luap's Stronghold, laid on a stone bench in a room otherwise empty." She paused. They were all staring. "And then there's the crown."

As she spoke, the crown rose in the air and moved toward her. *You are mine; I am yours.* The voice in her head was so clear she thought the others must have heard it.

"How are you doing that?" All three were gripping their Girdish medallions as if for protection.

"I'm not," Dorrin said. "*It* is. It is very old, and obviously magical—" *Put me on.* "—and you should also know that it speaks to me."

"Speaks to you?"

Dorrin took the crown in her hands; light flashed from the jewels. She set it gently back in the center of the cloth and covered it. "Yes. I do not know when it came into our family, but I know it has lived surrounded by blood magery for a very long time and perhaps it— whatever it is—is confused at being at last free."

"In the archives," Duke Mahieran said, "the oldest records we have speak of the rituals attending the coronation of the old kings, the kings before we came over the mountains. What just happened—" He nodded at the three objects. "What just happened," he repeated, "would fit those old rituals, or the stories told about them."

"I brought these things to give you," Dorrin said, turning to the prince. "You are the rightful heir of this kingdom; you will be our king; you should have them."

"Not if they're going to nip his fingers off," Duke Mahieran said.

Seklis came closer. "Let me see that cloth again . . . if you can keep the crown from leaping to someone's head."

"*Her* head," Duke Mahieran said. "That seems to be its chosen head. And the stones, you notice, are sapphire and diamond . . . Verrakai colors. Not ours."

Dorrin unfolded the cloth again, and lifted the crown in her hands. It sang along her arms, commanding, pleading, for her to put it on. She did not, but waited while Seklis peered at the cloth.

"Sunlord," Seklis said at last. "I think that's the Sunlord's symbol. Very old, that would make it. And it's all embroidery, the entire surface. The cloth under it is white."

"What does it mean?" Mahieran asked.

"Many questions to which we have no answers," Seklis said. "But the only one that concerns me now is your purpose, Duke Verrakai, in bringing this here, now. That crown wants your head, unless I'm mistaken."

"It has said so, but I am not royal-born, and the prince is. I thought here, perhaps, it would speak to him."

"No," Seklis said. "I think not. The old Tsaian crown was said to be of rubies, broken up during the sack of the palace in Gird's day. This is not Tsaia's crown." He turned to Mahieran. "Would you know what realm in the south once had a ruling family with these colors?"

"No," Duke Mahieran said, rubbing his nose. "And I advise against risking the prince's life by trying that crown on him, if it does not choose."

"You brought it as a gift?" Seklis asked.

"Yes," Dorrin said. "As well, if I were found to be hiding a crown in a closet, you might think I meant to use it at some time, perhaps to claim the throne the prince is about to take in full power . . . especially since you already know the Verrakai retained some magery, and that I, too, have it." She looked from face to face. "Indeed, from what was said earlier, it seems you have heard rumors of a crown, have you not?"

"Indeed we have," the prince said. "I—the Council—discounted what Verrakaien said at their trial, and those trials were held in secret, but later rumors began in the city that the Verrakaien not only believed they were descended from kings, but had the proof of it, and a crown hidden that their magery could wake to great power." He tipped his head toward the table. "Like that one."

"We could not trace the rumor to its source," Duke Mahieran said. "The market wardens heard it first, and assumed it came from some southern caravaner. Then a Girdsman told her Marshal, and the Marshal brought it to another, whose grange was just then buzzing with it. Marshals told High Marshals; in days it was all over the city. The Verrakaien would return, return with proof at last that they should rule Tsaia and have power to enforce their will."

"A Verrakai started that rumor," Dorrin said. "Have you found any that had changed bodies, as I wrote you?"

"Does the person whose body is taken know it?" the prince asked. "On the night of the attack, Haron Verrakai appeared like Duke

Marrakai—fooled many of us—for a time, but Duke Marrakai does not remember being taken."

Dorrin shook her head. "No, that is a different thing, a glamour cast to confuse the eyes."

"Can you do it?" the prince asked.

"I've never tried," Dorrin said. "I do not know how." She felt around inside her magery, but nothing happened that she could feel. Yet those facing her fell back a step. "What?"

"You—you look like Kieri Phelan," the prince said. "As like as his twin."

"I don't know what I did and I don't know how to undo it," Dorrin said. When she looked at her hand, it looked like hers, but with a faint outline of another overlaid on it. She concentrated and suddenly that outline disappeared. "Am I . . . back?"

They nodded. "I hope that doesn't happen by mistake," Dorrin said. "I still don't know how I did it. And I don't want to." She wrapped the crown again, then the other items, and placed them back in the padded sack. They called to her; she bespoke them in her mind, telling them they would be safe.

"You want us to take these things?" Duke Mahieran said.

"I do. I thought perhaps the prince could wear them, that they would recognize someone of true royal blood—I was willing to think our family had stolen them long ago, in Gird's time—but I see now that might be dangerous to him. Still, if they are in your treasury and you know it, you can be sure they are not in my possession. That I am not plotting to put that crown on my own head—even if it does talk to me."

The prince nodded, then looked at Duke Mahieran and High Marshal Seklis before turning again to Dorrin. "It is not yet the day of my coronation, and for matters of state I must still consult the Regency Council. But here are two members of that Council. I propose, for your own safety, to take your oath of fealty here and now, before them. You will give it again with the other peers, but your oath now will lend weight to your protestations that you intend no treason. Are you willing?"

"Of course, Lord Prince," Dorrin said.

"That is well said, my lord prince," Seklis said. "We three have reason to believe the Duke honest, but others will not."

And would an oath make her honest? Had not her uncle forsworn himself a dozen times over?

"Are these chairs safe?" the prince asked.

"Yes," Dorrin said. She pulled one around, sat in it, and stood again.

"I would have taken your word," the prince said. He sat; Duke Mahieran and High Marshal Seklis moved to either side of him. Dorrin knelt before the prince, and phrase by phrase repeated the oath of fealty.

"Rise," the prince said when it was done; he stood and once more they clasped hands.

"So how do we convey these things in a way that continues to show your loyalty?" the prince said. "I cannot think that sneaking them into the palace in a sack is the best way to do it."

"Perhaps not, but soonest is best," Duke Mahieran said. "Our visit here tonight will not have gone unremarked . . . and if we come away with a mysterious sack, that story will be all over the city by midmorning tomorrow." He turned to Dorrin. "Is there anything like a chest or casket here that you could put these in?"

"I haven't investigated all the rooms," Dorrin said. "Every one I found had multiple traps . . . there were chests in the bedrooms my uncle and his brother used."

"But those, you said, were guarded by blood magery," Seklis said. "My lords, it is very late, and Duke Verrakai knows of peril in this house. It is my recommendation that she wait until morning—full daylight—to transport those things to the palace, and do it herself, with her own escort. We are not taking them from her; she has offered them. And by then, perhaps, she will have found a suitable container, though the sack would do."

Duke Mahieran chewed his lip. "Gird knows I don't want to wake any evil here tonight, if a box that wants to bite my fingers is not already evil."

"I think it is not, my lord Duke," Dorrin said. "Opinionated, but not evil."

"And I agree," Seklis said. "I sensed no evil in those things. Though I am not a paladin, I am usually alert to evil."

They left, then, with cordial farewells spoken outside in the street, where a few people still strolled past. "Do not worry," the prince said, loud enough to be heard by anyone listening, "about the upkeep of the house while you are here. I will tell the Seneschal and he will speak to our banker. We will meet again tomorrow."

Dorrin bowed. "You honor me, Lord Prince, and tomorrow I will be at your gates before midday."

They rode off in a clatter of hooves. Dorrin dismissed her escort to the stable, all but Eddes, who came with her into the house and barred the door. With him, she checked the windows on the lower floors, the kitchen entrance, the gate to the stableyard. Then she gathered the rest of her escort together in the main hall. They yawned almost in chorus; her jaw ached with fighting back her own yawns.

"None of us will get much sleep tonight, but we can make it up tomorrow," she said. She wished for a reliable junior captain or sergeant to share watches with, but what she had was what she had. "Jori, you're the stableyard guard. That's post one. There's the gate, the windows in the stable itself, the stable roof. Here in the city, thieves might come any of those ways. Eddes, post two, front door. If someone sounding official demands entry, tell me, but do not open it. Inder, post three, scullery door, same rules." If anyone came to the scullery door, it would mean Jori had failed his duty or been killed. She didn't mention that. "Gani, post four, the cellar door. They should be spelled shut, but we take no chances. Perin, post five, upstairs between the main stairs down and the stairs to the third floor. Now: there's a great glass in this house; your watch will last as long as the sand runs one way. Post one—that's you, Eddes, this watch—will check the glass and turn it when it runs out and ring the bell. Every time the bell rings and the glass turns, you will move to the next numbered post, starting with Perin . . . Perin to post four, the cellar door, and when he comes, Gani, you to post three, and so on. Do not move until your replacement comes, and if he does not come, raise a shout. If there's an alarm, do not cluster together like frightened chicks to a hen . . . wait for my orders. Clear?"

They nodded and muttered their agreement, shuffling off to their posts. Dorrin followed, making sure each was in his place, then went to the great glass in the downstairs hall and turned it, ringing the bell to start the watch. She went into the room where the royal treasures were, carrying the old trousers and shirt she slept in, and looked at the sack a moment. "I wish," she said, "you could tell me your history and why you think you want me . . ." Then she changed, laid her court clothes on the table and stretched out on the floor, a candlestick and her sword to hand.

The house creaked, as old houses did. She heard no mice or rats—with no food in the house since before the Evener, they would have moved to better quarters. The room was stuffy with its shutters closed, but she'd slept in hotter, stuffier places. The smells were old and dry, whatever they were; she knew that here on the floor she would be smelling odors tracked in from the street, as well as those intrinsic to the house. She dozed off.

When the bell rang, she woke at once, lit the candle with her own magelight, and went to check on the rotation of the watch. Overhead, she heard Perin coming down . . . and then one by one they moved as she had directed. When they were all in place, she turned the glass again and went back to get what rest she could.

Dawn came early near midsummer; Dorrin woke Efla and Jaim, and sent three of her escort to sleep as soon as they'd had breakfast. The other two, she promised, would have their time later. Her own breakfast she scarcely tasted, thinking of all that must be done: find a suitable container for the treasure, cleanse the taint of blood magery, find the many traps . . . and the day-to-day running of the house, the market trips, the laundry, carting away the horses' dung, fetching straw and hay . . .

A knock on the door interrupted her search for a suitable container—she had found three, but all heavily spelled—and she hurried downstairs as Eddes called her.

When she opened the door, two Marshals wearing formal blue tabards and two yeomen with blue sashes were waiting.

"Be welcome," Dorrin said. "May I have your names?"

"Marshal Veksin," one said, "and my yeoman-marshal Gilles." The other, Marshal Tamis, introduced another yeoman-marshal, Berin.

"We should start with the worst contamination," Tamis said. "Will you take us there, please?"

"Yes," Dorrin said, "but I am required at the palace this morning and three of my men—who had watch the night through—are sleeping there—" She nodded to the smaller reception room, where the men snored away on the floor and her clothes were still laid out on the table.

"How many servants did you bring with you?" Marshal Tamis asked.

"Just a cook and a boy to help," Dorrin said. "And five men for an escort and to manage the animals. I am more used to traveling light, military style, and did not think what a house this size might need."

"I hear the prince visited yestereve," Marshal Veksin said. He sounded as if he disapproved.

"The prince, Duke Mahieran, and High Marshal Seklis," Dorrin said. "They did me the honor of coming here after I went to the palace; given the circumstances, I scarcely expected it and was not, alas, prepared to receive them as handsomely as they deserved."

"They parted friendly, I heard," Veksin said.

"Indeed so," Dorrin said. "I had never met the prince, in my years with Duke Phelan's Company, but the Duke had told me about him. It was both honor and delight to meet him and the others."

A grunt from behind indicated that Veksin was thinking about that. Now on the second floor, she led them to her uncle's study. "That," she said, nodding at Liart's symbol on the wall and the bloodstains on the floor. "I am not wise in such matters, but it seems to me this is the worst. Next would be the bedrooms, with blood on the thresholds and bloodmarks under the beds."

"Are there simple traps here?" Marshal Tamis asked.

"Undoubtedly," Dorrin said. "I have found two hands' worth at least, so far, and expect to find more. No chair here is completely safe, nor drawer nor cabinet door, and I would not handle those things that look most interesting or valuable. I will show you one trap I have not yet disarmed." With the butt of her dagger, Dorrin pressed on the back of one chair; a spike emerged from the upholstery, its tip clearly darker than the rest. "That is poison," Dorrin said. "Anyone who sits in this chair, without the trap being disarmed, looses a spring and that spike will pierce clothing, even leather."

"Can you disarm it?"

"Not without taking the chair apart, which is itself dangerous. On Verrakai's own domain, I burned such things, which also destroyed the poison. Here, in the city, fire is too dangerous. I planned to have them broken up in the stableyard, and burn the parts containing poison in the kitchen hearth."

"Will you wish to observe our work?" Veklis asked.

"No," Dorrin said. "As I am required at the palace, I have things to do before then. Call if you need me; I will tell you when I leave for the palace."

Downstairs, she gave up on the two difficult chests, and looked into the larder. There she found a plain wooden box, untrapped, and in the linen press off the large reception room, a small tablecloth, heavily embroidered, for a cover. She herself packed the treasure into it, covered it with the tablecloth, and tied the cloth on with blue velvet ropes from the drapes. A certain sullen resentment emanated from the box; Dorrin murmured to it as to a child.

"You will be safe; you will be honored; all will be well."

I am yours; you are mine; no other will suffice.

"If you are mine, then it is my will you abide here for the time being," Dorrin said.

No more blood!

"No more blood," Dorrin said. "A place of safety and honor."

How long?

How long indeed? She had intended to live and die as a faithful vassal of the king of Tsaia. Yet the oath she had sworn did not say "until death" as many such oaths did. "I do not know how long," she said to the treasure. "But for now, abide in peace."

Until you come again, but do not wait too long.

The sense of resentment vanished, replaced by watchful patience. Dorrin laid her hand on the box, and through all the wrappings felt a tingle as if she held one of those treasures in her hand.

The rest of the morning, as she woke the first three from sound sleep and chivvied them back to work, let the other two sleep, answered myriad questions from the cook, from the escort who were awake, from the Marshals, she felt like someone trying to push a handful of balls uphill—the moment she let go of one problem, two others would roll down on her. Finally she was ready to return to the palace: properly dressed in clean clothes, the box lashed to the packsaddle of one horse, mounted on a horse she'd had to remind her escort three times to groom. Even as she turned to ride away, Efla appeared, to report that she'd seen a mouse in the larder.

Dorrin spent the short ride from the house to the palace wondering if she could find any trustworthy house staff for hire at such a time.

At the gate, this time, she was recognized and waved through; stable help took the horses and palace servants ran out to help, putting the box in a sling between poles.

"It is a coronation gift," Dorrin said. "The prince knows of it." They nodded and followed her to the entrance.

"The Master of Ceremonies wishes to meet with you," said the guard at the door. "He has been summoned."

The Master of Ceremonies, wearing a short cape of brilliant red over Kostvan colors, an eye-startling combination, strode down the hall toward her.

"My lord Duke, welcome! I apologize for not being at hand yestereve when you arrived; the prince bids you to luncheon with him, if you will, and has given me explicit instructions about your generous gift. It is not, I understand, suitable for public display?"

"As the prince wishes," Dorrin said. "He knows what it is; it might provoke . . . comment."

"Then come with me to the treasury, and we will see it safe housed." He signaled to the servants and led them all deep into the palace, again confusing Dorrin's sense of direction. "This is not the old treasury. The old treasury was found to have a tunnel entrance, from the days when it was the cellar of the original tower. That tower fell in the Girdish war, its secrets lost until, after the attack on the prince, we looked more closely. The new treasury is above ground, in the interior."

Guards stood at the door; the Master of Ceremonies signed a book on a stand to one side, then unlocked the door and led Dorrin and the servants with the box inside. It looked much like the bank vaults Dorrin had seen in Aarenis—a windowless room with shelves, boxes, heavy leather sacks, ledger books.

"Does the prince know what this contains?" he asked.

"Yes," Dorrin said. "He, Duke Mahieran, and High Marshal Seklis."

"It must be inventoried," the Master of Ceremonies said. "That is the Seneschal's task." To one of the guards he said, "Fetch the Seneschal."

The Seneschal and the High Marshal arrived together, and shooed the Master of Ceremonies away. "You can instruct Duke Verrakai on

the ceremony when we've inventoried the gifts." Dorrin unwrapped
the box, opened it, and then unwrapped the gifts, opening the box to
show its jewels still intact. The Seneschal, with no change of expression, wrote down a description of each one. Then he and Dorrin
rewrapped, retied, and finally she was able to leave and attend the Master of Ceremonies, a few paces away from the door, waving his arms
and giving directions to the servants.

"There you are! I must conduct you to the prince's dining hall for
luncheon, and on the way, explain the details of tomorrow's ceremonies. You will need—" He looked at Dorrin. "—you will need a
ducal robe—do you have one?"

"Yes," Dorrin said, stretching her legs to keep up with him, and
trying at the same time to understand where in the massive pile she
was. "I do—you mean the long one with fur at the cuffs?"

"Yes. And shoes, not boots. Your sword will do, but it must
have a tassel, in silver, the length of your hand; if you do not
have that, you should seek out the royal outfitters in Bridge Street.
Short breeks, tied at the knee with ribbons of your family colors,
with a rosette. The shirt to be adorned with lace—wider than that
on your shirt today. A velvet cap, with a feather—silver pheasant
is best."

He kept on, all the way down a set of stairs Dorrin was sure she
had not seen before, then announced her at the door of a room
that overlooked the front courtyard. After a moment, she recognized it from the evening before, but now the long table was covered with a green cloth, centered with bouquets of roses, cream
and pink and red and yellow, their scent filling the room. Besides
the prince and Duke Mahieran, she saw other men and women in
the dress of nobles . . . by the colors and insignia, this was the
Regency Council.

"Be welcome, Duke Verrakai," the prince said. One by one he
called the others forward to introduce her. Dorrin knew Marrakai
had been Kieri Phelan's friend; the burly man wearing the ducal
chain gave her an appraising look and finally nodded.

"You look like one of Kieri's men—and it was you who rode
through here like the winter gale to come to his aid, was it not?"

"Yes," Dorrin said. If he would not give her an honorific, she
would not either.

"You're very different from the previous Duke Verrakai."

"I should hope so." Dorrin smiled at him. "Whatever I am, my lords and ladies, your prince, tomorrow our king, found me worthy. If you have a quarrel with his judgment, do not bring it to me."

"Well said, Duke Verrakai," Duke Serrostin said. "I have no quarrel with you, but with your family I had several."

CHAPTER FORTY

The next morning, Dorrin arrived at the palace to find that she had been assigned a dressing room and two tiring maids to help. The tiring maids, used to helping noble ladies into their dresses, stared at Dorrin in her trousers and boots with some dismay. "But—you're a lady . . ."

"I'm a duke," Dorrin said. "And I've spent my life as a soldier. I brought the clothes I was told to bring."

Giggling, the tiring maids helped her into them: the elaborately ruffled shirt with its lace collar and cuffs, the striped, bloused short trousers, the slashed doublet through which the shirt's sleeves had to be carefully tugged to make symmetrical puffs, the stockings, the ribbons tied at the knee, the formal high-heeled court shoes, silver buckles decorated with yet more jewels in the Verrakai colors. Everything had ruffles or lace or jewels or some combination of these.

It was ridiculous, Dorrin thought, and yet . . . she did feel different, inside that magnificence. She fastened Falk's ruby to the lace of the collar, one drop of red in all that blue and silver and gray.

A knock on the door. "A half-glass, my lord," came a voice through the door. Dorrin picked up the blue velvet cap with its silver-pheasant feather and put it on, then looked in the mirror as the tiring maids lifted the formal robe and held it for her. She slipped her arms into the sleeves. In the mirror, she saw the transformation completed. No more Dorrin the runaway. No more Dorrin the student at Falk's

Hall. No more Dorrin, cohort captain in Phelan's Company . . . but Dorrin, Duke Verrakai. This was what people would see, now and in the future . . . not her past, but her present.

She smiled at the tiring maids, and thanked them for their help. Another knock on the door. "Time, my lord." The door opened. The Master of Ceremonies looked her up and down. "Excellent," he said. Behind him, a servant with a flat box. He opened it. "Your court chain of office."

Unlike the ducal chain the prince had sent before, this was all gold, the links beaten into the shape of the Tsaian rose. She bent her head and he lifted it, then laid it on her shoulders. "Come along," he said, as if to a child, and she followed him.

In the corridor near the Grange Hall, Knights of the Bells stood on either side, their mail shining, their swords belted on. The other nobles were milling about, chatting. Dorrin looked around. Duke Marrakai caught her eye and waved her over.

"We need to stay at this end, we dukes," he said. "You've met everyone, I believe." By "everyone" he meant the other dukes, Dorrin understood. Behind them, clusters of counts, and beyond that, barons. The dukes were easily the most resplendent.

And the hottest. Barons, Dorrin had noticed, had sleeveless court gowns, showing the puffs of their shirts, and only a narrow edging of fur at the neck. Even counts had less fur than the dukes, who were all, by now, fanning themselves. She had not brought a fan. Duke Marrakai offered his, but she shook her head, and in a moment a palace servant came up and handed her one.

The Master of Ceremonies reappeared, having gathered up some laggard barons, and chivvied them all into the right order. Dorrin was appalled to find herself at the head of the line, beside Duke Mahieran and behind the Lord Herald with his beribboned staff. "Don't worry," Mahieran said. "Just do what I do, only on the other side of the hall and right after."

Then the Bells of Vérella rang out, chime after chime, followed by the blare of trumpets; servants pulled back the doors, and they went in. At the far end of the Hall, the crown prince, all in white, stood below the throne between—Dorrin blinked, not having expected this—the Marshal-General of Gird and the new Marshal-Judicar. Dorrin led her file of nobles to the right, around the roped-off area in the middle of the hall; when Duke Mahieran stopped, she turned to face him.

She had not imagined that a trial of arms would be part of the coronation ceremony, but the prince and Marshal-General exchanged blows that could be heard clearly throughout the Hall. The Marshal-General stepped back and saluted. "He is sound of body and skilled in arms," she said loudly. "The Company of Gird accepts his sword."

"Accepted," the nobles said.

Then the lowest-ranking baron spoke up. "Is he without blemish, as a king must be?"

"Let it be shown," Duke Mahieran said.

Servants stepped into the central area, folding the prince's clothes as he took them off. He stood before them, bare as at birth, and turned. Dorrin could not take her eyes off that fair young body.

"He is without blemish," the baron said. "The company of barons accepts him."

The prince had dressed again. The lowest-ranking count spoke up. "Does he know the rule of law, or the rule of passion?"

"Let it be shown," Duke Mahieran said again.

The Marshal-Judicar came forward. He asked questions, so many that Dorrin lost count.

"He is a man of law," the count said finally. "The company of counts accepts him."

Duke Mahieran turned to the dukes beside him, and then across from him. "What say you, Dukes of the realm: Do you accept this man, Mikeli Vostan Keriel, as your king?"

"We accept him!" they said, Dorrin as loud as the rest.

The prince walked back to the throne and turned; servants lifted the robe, deep red embroidered in silver, and he put his arms into it. Then he sat.

Mahieran stepped forward; the Marshal-General met him, and together they lifted the crown of Tsaia from its stand. Together they held it over his head.

"All here witness the High Lord's blessing, Gird's grace, and the consent of nobles of this realm, of the crowning of Mikeli, King of Tsaia." They lowered the crown to his head and stepped back.

The Marshal-General handed him a different sword, this one

obviously old, in a battered scabbard. "Gird's sword: may you wield it to defend your realm." He took it, kissed it, and handed it back to her.

Mahieran handed him a scepter. "The staff of law: may you wield it to defend the right." Again Mikeli took it, kissed it, and handed it back. The Bells pealed again, a great clamor, and trumpets blew a deafening fanfare.

When silence fell again, Mikeli, now king of Tsaia, waited while servants removed the pillars and ropes. Then the nobles closed in from side to side, the two lines slightly offset so that Duke Mahieran was a half stride in front of Dorrin. As each knelt and gave the oath of fealty, he clasped their hands, and bent to kiss their heads as they kissed his hand. Dorrin found it more moving than she had expected.

After returning the court chain of office to the Master of Ceremonies and putting off the great robe, she mingled with other nobles and their families in the airy second-floor reception room before the formal procession. She'd been allowed to invite her distant relative Ganarrion Verrakai, cleared of any suspicion of conspiracy and freed from prison only a few days before she arrived in Vérella. He wore his Royal Guard uniform. They'd never met; they fumbled some time for a common topic before she mentioned Paksenarrion, and he brightened. "I met her, on her way to Lyonya," he said. "Were you her commander, in Phelan's company?"

Dorrin explained, and from there they chatted easily about military matters, horses, and the strange ways of the gods. The king had suggested Ganarrion as a possible heir; the more she talked to him, the more she was inclined to agree. They did not mention the Order of Attainder or the continuing search for their fugitive relatives. "Come stay with me in Verrakai's city house," she said.

"My pardon, my lord Duke, but I cannot. I am on duty, as we all are—this leave of a few hours is all I can spend with you. Please understand, it is not lack of respect."

"Of course not," Dorrin said. "But we should know each other better. Perhaps you can visit in the east—for Midwinter Feast, if that's allowed. If not, I will understand."

"Thank you, my lord," he said. "When do you return to the east?"

"In a few days," Dorrin said. "I have much to do there. I will return for Autumn Court, of course. I will be presenting an old friend, Jandelir Arcolin, who was Phelan's senior captain and is now to gain a title and take over that domain."

"I will try to come, though if I'm assigned once more to the northeast, I doubt very much it will be possible," Ganarrion said. "I would like to meet—do you know his title?"

"No," Dorrin said. "You should meet him, however; we've been friends a long time, and fought many campaigns together."

A servant in the palace livery came up to them and handed Ganarrion a folded note. He read it and shook his head. "My lord, I'm sorry—I'm called for. I hope to see you again before you leave."

"Go safely—I need not tell you to be careful." She watched him go, and sent prayers after him.

Duke Mahieran bore down on her. "I didn't want to interrupt while you were talking to your relative, but we need your advice about something."

"Certainly," Dorrin said. "What is it?"

"Let us find a quieter place." He led her to a smaller room. A moment later, Duke Marrakai joined them; Dorrin felt a sudden tension.

"What is it?" she asked.

"You reported that some of your relatives could change from one body to another and thus go undetected—and that you had found a few such. How did you know?"

"I found the first evidence in the family rolls," Dorrin said. "But those do not give the names—never the full name, and often no name at all—of the person whose body is taken. Those who make the transfer are marked as deaths in the rolls, with a special symbol."

"But how did you find those who had transferred? You sent word you had killed some—killed them permanently?"

"Yes," Dorrin said, thinking of the children buried in the orchard. "Those are definitely dead. How I knew them—as you know, the prince—the king—gave me leave to use my magery as I needed. That let me see something wrong about their eyes and spirit."

"Is this something you can teach others—us, for instance?"

"I doubt it," Dorrin said. "But what is it? Do you suspect someone here?"

"Someone tried to kill Camwyn, the prince's younger brother, and my son Aris, by poisoning their horses right before they rode out.

Planted a wax capsule under the saddle; we think the poison leaked out and into the horses' backs—"

Dorrin felt almost faint. "It was not just poison," she said. "Though it would have been covered in wax, around the clay. The wax melts with the heat of the horse and the pressure of the rider eventually breaks the seal of the clay. Then it is only a matter of time—were the horses restive?"

"Yes. They would not stand still. Then suddenly—"

"They went crazy—bucking, bolting—is that what happened?"

"Yes—their instructor thought it might be some kind of insect sting, a wasp or something, but he found no evidence, though the capsule remained. Broken, of course." Marrakai looked angry. "Did you know about this? What it is?"

"When I was a child," Dorrin said, "I heard of such things. You know there are flies and other creatures that lay eggs on livestock, usually in a wound, and infest the wound with maggots. Some cause illness—staggers or flayleg. And some give such a painful bite the animal goes wild."

"Yes, but—"

"Some of my relatives used magery to enhance those attacks—"

"They attacked *animals*?"

"As a way to attack people, my lord. I overheard, once—and was punished for having passed by the door at the wrong time—one of them speak of you, Duke Marrakai. You know they hated you, and they hated also your reputation for breeding the best horses. They had devised, they thought, a way to ruin your reputation by destroying your horses, but the process was arduous and they were willing to wait years, they said."

"They nearly destroyed my son," Marrakai said. "Though I suppose that, too, would have pleased them."

"No doubt," Dorrin said. "Do you know who saddled the horses that day? If it is the same thing, it must be placed on the horse no more than a glass before it is ridden. A groom—"

"None of the grooms admit to saddling those two horses—or any of the horses the boys rode that day. Most often the boys tack up for themselves, but sometimes it is done for them, especially if there's word they will be late to the stable."

"Were any of the grooms sick, between the time you captured and imprisoned Verrakaien—including the ones I sent you—and the time of this attack on the horses?"

"Sick?" Mahieran frowned. "I don't know, to be sure. All the grooms had been with us a long time—"

"One was," Marrakai said. "Don't you remember, Sonder? That fellow—what was his name?—who usually did stalls in the new wing. We asked for him—Pedraig, that was his name—and they said he was sick with the wasting. Then in two tendays, that he was like to die, a terrible fever. But he recovered."

Dorrin's stomach clenched. "That's your man."

"Pedraig? He's been with us for years," Mahieran said. "He'd never do anything to hurt a horse or a child, I promise you."

"Pedraig wouldn't," Dorrin said. "But the man in his body now is not Pedraig. Did any Verrakai sicken and die—or die suddenly, aside from execution—while imprisoned?"

"Three," Mahieran said. Now he looked worried. "Do you think—"

"I think a Verrakai contrived Pedraig's illness, and took him over," Dorrin said. "Perhaps one in prison, perhaps one living concealed in the city, or elsewhere in the palace staff. Though how he could manage that from a distance I do not know. What I do know is that I must go now, immediately, and see this fellow—"

"Now?"

"He will know I have come to the coronation—if it's not gossip in the stable I'd be amazed—and if it is one I captured and sent here, he knows I have the full magery. He knows I can reveal him. At least the king is safe here, or so I hope—"

Mahieran started. "Gird's arm! He was about to make his progress—!"

"What?"

"Come," Mahieran said, and Dorrin followed as he hurried back to the reception. Over his shoulder, Mahieran said, "The new king greets all the palace servants—including in the stables—and then mounts his horse to ride in procession through the city and around the bounds—Midsummer, you know."

"Take me to Pedraig," Dorrin said, turning to Marrakai. "Find the king," she said to Mahieran. "Don't let him come near his horse." She was halfway to the palace doors before she realized she had just ordered two senior dukes around as if they were her soldiers. And they had not protested.

Across the wide stone-flagged courtyard, the royal procession was forming: grooms held the horses of those who would ride—Dorrin had declined the honor, having no proper mount for the occasion. The horses were decked out with manes and tails elaborately braided and dressed with flowers and ribbons, bridles and saddles festooned with bells and brightwork. The king's horse, a Tsaian gray stallion, stood at the head of the line, tossing its head now and then and pawing with one massive hoof. Already some nobles had changed their court shoes for boots and were standing in clumps, chatting as they waited for the king to arrive. From the king's horse to the gate, a line of grooms held baskets of rose petals, ready to strew them in front of the king as the procession began.

"Pedraig," Dorrin said to Marrakai. "Is he here?"

"I don't see—there!" Marrakai nodded at one of the grooms with baskets, a nondescript light-haired man.

As Dorrin's gaze met that of the man in groom's livery, she knew at once he was Verrakai . . . and then, that he was her father. Her father, *here*? He smiled, a smile widening into such vicious glee that she felt cold all over, immobilized with horror. Before she could raise a shield of magery, he struck, a bolt of pure enmity and malice aimed not at her but at Marrakai. She parried it, but not fast enough: Marrakai fell as if hit by a stone.

Dorrin stepped over Marrakai's body, shielding him from further attack, and loosed her own magery, first trying to hold him at bay. But he was stronger than any she had faced before. Again he struck, this time at a horse in the procession, a flick of fire that set its trappings ablaze; it screamed, jerked loose from its handlers and plunged away. The other horses reared, squealing and fighting their grooms; instant turmoil followed, with shod hooves ringing on the stones, shouts of command, screams of fear, the rasp of swords from the sheath.

She glanced around, and a flood of power broke through her shield; she staggered against force that sought to hold her as the king had been held. The sense of weight increased; she felt her knees buckling. With agonizing slowness, she forced her head around to see her father grinning at her, that same feral grin.

You cannot stand against me—daughter. The remembered voice mocked her. *No once-born could. Your power came from me; it is part of mine; I am its master.*

"Falk's Oath, you are not," Dorrin said aloud. Her voice sounded odd, but she was able to force herself upright. "You are evil, your strength comes only from blood magery." She struggled forward, fighting the pressure of it, drawing her sword, ignoring the plunging horses, the screams and yells. "Falk and the High Lord defend me; they have given me the true magery—"

You sent the mother who bore you to her death; would you kill your own father as well? And you call me evil?

Dorrin ignored that, took step after slow step, as if wading through thick mud. His power pressed on her; she could see no effect of hers on him; he stood there smiling.

Remember those nights in the cell? Remember how you begged for your puny suffering to end? What a coward you were . . . and are still. Now you are old, barren, weak. An empty husk, useless for anything but torment. I will take your body but keep you as a mind-slave, helpless but aware, and use your power as my own.

Memory flooded her mind: the pain, the smells, the tastes of it. Her father, worse than Carraig . . . nausea cramped her belly; the vile taste filled her mouth. Unshed tears burned her eyes. Again her knees sagged; her hand's grip on her sword loosened, and the sword tip fell to the stone, ringing a warning. Her hand clenched tighter. Not again, not again . . . She tried to say Falk's name, but her mouth was dry, dry as bone-dust and as bitter. Dry as a cursed well . . .

A well that now brimmed with clean water. From the depths of despair, from that recent memory, she reached for the source of her own power, the power Falk promised was hers, untainted. Falk's knight, not her father's daughter; Falk's knight, who had freed a woman and her unborn child from a curse that bound them in unending torment, whose tears had renewed the waters.

"Falk," she managed. At once that sweet, cold water filled her mouth, washing away the taste of evils she had endured, washing away fear and hatred. As she swallowed, the water seemed to renew her whole body; her strength surged back, as water had done in the well. She saw her father's expression change even as she felt her power mastering him. Could he feel her new determination? Now she held *him* motionless, and knew he could not flee. Should she bind him for others to capture, or would it be better to kill him herself? She raised her sword, saw his concentration change to fear, and then to glee again . . . the look she had seen on the child's face who had been about to force a transfer.

"Falk!" she cried, pleading, and for the first time in her life cast the death spell like a spear, not knowing if it would truly kill.

His face contorted for an instant, and then he fell and lay motionless. Dorrin ran to the fallen body—she felt nothing there—no taint of evil, dire mist as she'd seen after Carraig died, no hint of lingering malice. "I'm sorry," Dorrin said, to the body that had once been an honest groom's, as she sheathed her sword. "You were a good man once; you deserved better."

She looked around—the courtyard was still in chaos. With a touch of magery she calmed the horses, put out the smoldering fire that had started the panic. She hoped no one would notice that part. Duke Marrakai still lay where he had fallen; now his sons crouched beside him, staring at her wide-eyed.

She walked back to them.

"You killed him!" Kirgan Marrakai said, eyes blazing. "You killed them both! He should have known you lied! You're just like the rest! Traitor!" He drew his dagger and lunged at her. Dorrin barely evaded the thrust, and backed away.

"Kirgan Marrakai—I did not!"

"I saw—he was beside you, he fell, and you tried to make it look like it was that groom. We know *him*; we've known him for years!"

"It was not that—" Dorrin stepped back again as the young man still advanced, dagger now in his left hand, right hand reaching for his sword.

"I saw it too," said one of the counts. "Seize her—"

Glancing around, Dorrin saw only hostile faces, weapons drawn. Nobles and palace guards alike, they formed a ring around her, all clearly frightened but determined. Was this the gods' punishment for killing her parents, even though they were evil? Well, if so, at least she had saved her king. She folded her arms and stood still, waiting for the blow that would kill her.

"Hold!" That shout from the palace stopped Kirgan Marrakai's arm in midswing. "Stand away—let me see her."

The Marshal-General of Gird, with Duke Mahieran and the king, came down the palace steps and across the courtyard. Slowly, reluctantly, the nobles sheathed their weapons and bent a knee to the king. Dorrin, arms still folded, made her bow as well.

Into the moment of silence, Aris Marrakai spoke, a boy's voice shaky with fear and surprise. "He's—he's breathing."

"What?" Kirgan Marrakai turned.

"Wait," the Marshal-General said. Everyone stared at her as she went to Duke Marrakai, knelt beside him, and looked him over. "How did he fall?" she asked. A dozen voices answered, tumbling over one another.

"She did it—he fell backward—he just fell—I didn't see but I heard—"

"He's alive," the Marshal-General said, "but he hit his head on the paving stones."

"She made him fall," Kirgan Marrakai insisted, pointing at Dorrin. "He was beside her and there was a flicker of light and then he fell. She used magery—"

The Marshal-General turned to Dorrin. "Well? What say you?"

"I did use magery, Marshal-General. Duke Marrakai pointed out the man we were sure had poisoned the horses a tenday or so ago . . . not the real groom, but a Verrakai who had taken over his body during his illness. I thought he would attack me first, but he attacked Duke Marrakai, and my attempt to shield him from that attack was not enough. To my shame."

"Is this what you were telling me about on the way, Duke Mahieran?"

"Yes, Marshal-General. I went to warn the king before he came out here, and she and Marrakai went to find Pedraig—the groom."

"You are convinced she was telling the truth?" Before Mahieran could answer, she turned again to Dorrin. "How did you kill him? And do you know which Verrakai he was?"

"I killed him by magery, Marshal-General, because he was too far away to reach with the sword when he attempted another transfer, to another innocent man."

"Which Verrakai was he?"

"My father."

The Marshal-General chewed on her lip for a moment. "To kill with magery condemns you to death, under the Code of Gird—you know that."

"Yes, Marshal-General."

"Did you think of that at the time?"

"No. I thought how horrible it was that another man might die— and hated what I did, but—I did it."

"The Code of Gird offers no alternatives to death for your act," the Marshal-General said. "Do you feel that is just?"

Dorrin just stopped herself from shrugging, which would add rudeness to her crime. "Marshal-General, laws are written as they are for a reason. I swore fealty to the king, which included swearing to obey the Code of Gird as administered in Tsaia. I have no complaints."

"I do," the king said. He looked from Dorrin to the Marshal-General. "I believe she saved my life—and other lives—by acting as she did. This man nearly killed my brother and Aris Marrakai; we asked Duke Verrakai to help us find the one who did so, and she has done that. By all reports, she has carried out the commands we first gave her, when we asked her to take on the Verrakai domain. I am not moved to waste a valuable peer for a quibble of law."

"You must, my liege," Dorrin said. "For if a king does not obey the law, how can his subjects?"

"I do not want to see you die, Dorrin Verrakai."

"And I am not particularly eager to die," Dorrin said. "But the law is the law, and we are both sworn to it."

"*As administered in Tsaia*," Duke Mahieran put in, quoting the oath. "And in Tsaia there are other things to be considered, mitigating factors, and also the King's Mercy. That Dorrin Duke Verrakai killed with magery is not—since she freely admits it—in question. But the King and Council may, if they choose, consider her motives, what alternatives she might have had available, and then at the king's discretion, he may choose an alternative punishment."

A mutter from those watching.

"Let us consider," Mahieran went on. "First that this man, as Duke Marrakai and I were both convinced from Duke Verrakai's words, did poison the horses of Prince Camwyn and Aris Marrakai, and thereby imperil their lives. He was guilty of treason, and for that alone would have been condemned in a trial to shameful death. Second, that since he was not really Pedraig the groom, but a Verrakai in Pedraig's body, his life was already forfeit under the Order of Attainder. Third, that he was no doubt conspiring to assassinate our king on the very day of his coronation by poisoning *his* horse—and perhaps others—the very same way he had done with the prince and young Marrakai's horses."

Mahieran looked around; the peers and palace guards were nodding.

"So that Duke Verrakai having killed this traitor is no crime, but a service to the Crown. She used magery to kill him, that is true, and killing by magery is against our laws—but suppose she had pierced his body with a poisoned blade? Killing with poison is also a crime—but is there anyone here who thinks if she had done that she would deserve death for so dispatching an enemy of the Crown and people of Tsaia?" Heads shook, the murmur rose.

"So I say, it is unfortunate that circumstances forced her to use magery, but if she had not, we would face worse problems. If this Verrakai had taken another body—if she had not been able to shield—at least partially—Duke Marrakai—if she had not been so determined to find and dispatch this villain that she ordered me around like one of her soldiers—" His glance at Dorrin was almost mischievous. "Then our king might be dead, and the realm in chaos worse than frightened horses loose in the palace court." He turned to the king and bent his knee. "I ask the King's Mercy for Duke Verrakai, my liege."

"And I—And I as well—" Other dukes chimed in, all but Marrakai who lay still on the pavement. Mahieran turned to Kirgan Marrakai.

"Will you answer for your father, Kirgan?"

"I—" The young man looked at Dorrin. "My lord Duke, I mistook you, and what I saw. My pardon, my lord." And to the king he said, "My liege, I also ask the King's Mercy for Duke Verrakai."

"Kneel," the king said. Dorrin knelt on the rough stone; she felt one of her stockings rip. The king drew his sword and put the tip at her throat as she looked up at him. "For that you have done this thing, your life is forfeit." Then he laid the flat of it on her head. "But for that you have done this thing in our service, and by it have served the Crown and People of the realm well, I pardon you, Dorrin Duke Verrakai, and if the gods would punish you, let the punishment fall on me, as your lord and king. Now rise."

Dorrin rose; someone in the rear of the throng clapped, but it died away; the matter was too serious for applause.

"And we still," the king said, "have a procession to ride. But we will see each horse unsaddled and examined."

Under the king's saddlecloth, Dorrin saw a brown lump, thumb-sized, just where the king's weight would break it. With the king's permission, she lifted it away by magery, and then ran her hand over the stallion's satiny back. "It is unbroken; it can have done no harm, and there is no irritation to indicate he did anything else."

All the Marrakai mounts had the same, but only two other horses, both Marrakai-bred.

By then Duke Marrakai had awakened, complaining of nausea and a severe pain in his head; the palace physicians insisted he must be carried in and put to bed.

"You must ride with us, Dorrin," the king said.

"I have no proper mount—these horses are all—" *Fancy* and *useless* were the terms that came to mind, that she must not use.

"Take my father's," Kirgan Marrakai said. "He would offer it, if he were here."

"I need my boots," Dorrin said, as she looked down at her torn stocking. But someone had already run to the palace, and before she could get to the doors, the tiring maids were there with her boots, her silver spurs, and the proper cape.

She rode out the gate near the head of the procession, side by side with Duke Mahieran and behind the prince, through streets strewn with flowers and good-luck charms, to the cheers of the crowd.

Acknowledgments

Many people have contributed to the rebirth of the Paksenarrion universe, and this book in particular, and it's impossible to thank all of them separately, though they deserve it. David Watson and others in the fencing group helped especially by working through various fight scenes as well as with research. David Stevens, director of the St. David's Parish Choirs, has deepened my understanding of fiction through his comments on musical structure, besides saving my sanity after a bad day at the computer by insisting that I pay attention to a different form of creativity. George Cardozo solved a plot problem for me; Carol Cardozo contributed several good suggestions. Ellen McLean, my first outside reader for the original Paks books, continues to be a perceptive and supportive (but also critical) reader. Husband Richard and son Michael continue to tolerate (and even enjoy) the chaos that surrounds a writer in full spate, bringing me chocolate and learning to cook their own dinners.

Even with this help, however, this book and those to come would not exist without the support of the Paksenarrion fan base, who kept asking for more, my agent, Joshua Bilmes, and the support of my first editor, Betsy Mitchell, who bought and then edited *Sheepfarmer's Daughter* for Baen, and is now back with me in this storyuniverse.

Former Marine ELIZABETH MOON is the author of many novels, including *Victory Conditions, Command Decision, Engaging the Enemy, Marque and Reprisal, Trading in Danger,* the Nebula Award winner *The Speed of Dark,* and *Remnant Population,* a Hugo Award finalist. After earning a degree in history from Rice University, Moon went on to obtain a degree in biology from the University of Texas, Austin. She lives in Florence, Texas.

ABOUT THE TYPE

This book was set in Apollo, a typeface designed by
Adrian Frutiger in 1962 for the founders Deberny &
Peignot. Born in Interlaken, Switzerland in 1928,
Frutiger became one of the most important type de-
signers since World War II. He attended the School of
Fine Arts in Zurich between 1948 and 1951, where he
studied calligraphy. He received the Gutenberg Prize in
1986 for technical and aesthetic achievement in type.